the finder of forgotten things

Books by Sarah Loudin Thomas

The Finder of Forgotten Things

The Right Kind of Fool

When Silence Sings

The Sound of Rain

A Tapestry of Secrets

Until the Harvest

Miracle in a Dry Season

the finder of forgotten things

SARAH LOUDIN THOMAS

BETHANYHOUSE
a division of Baker Publishing Group
Minneapolis, Minnesota

Published by Bethany House Publishers
11400 Hampshire Avenue South
Minneapolis, Minnesota 55438
www.bethanyhouse.com

Bethany House Publishers is a division of
Baker Publishing Group, Grand Rapids, Michigan

Library of Congress Cataloging-in-Publication Data
Names: Thomas, Sarah Loudin, author.
Title: The finder of forgotten things / Sarah Loudin Thomas.
Description: Minneapolis, Minnesota : Bethany House Publishers, a division of Baker Publishing Group, 2021.
Identifiers: LCCN 2021028759 | ISBN 9780764238352 (paperback) | ISBN 9780764239434 (casebound) | ISBN 9780764238352 (ebook)
Classification: LCC PS3620.H64226 F56 2021 | DDC 813/.6—dc23
LC record available at https://lccn.loc.gov/2021028759

Unless otherwise indicated, Scripture quotations are from the King James Version of the Bible.

This is a work of fiction. Names, characters, incidents, and dialogues are products of the author's imagination and are not to be construed as real. Any resemblance to actual events or persons, living or dead, is entirely coincidental.

Cover design by Kathleen Lynch/Black Kat Design
Cover image of scenic path by Kim Fearheiley / Arcangel

Author is represented by Books & Such Literary Agency.

Baker Publishing Group publications use paper produced from sustainable forestry practices and post-consumer waste whenever possible.

21 22 23 24 25 26 27 7 6 5 4 3 2 1

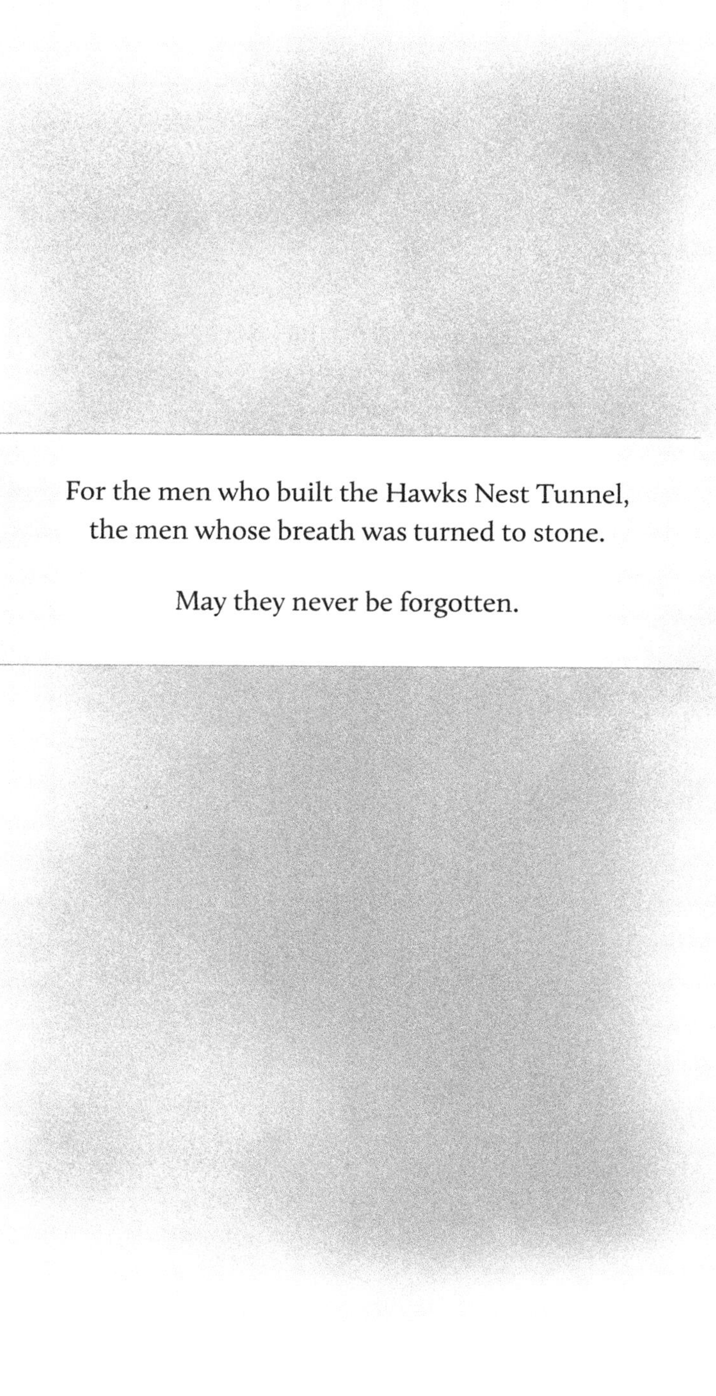

For the men who built the Hawks Nest Tunnel,
the men whose breath was turned to stone.

May they never be forgotten.

For the living know that they will die,
    but the dead know nothing;
they have no further reward,
    and even their name is forgotten.
Their love, their hate
    and their jealousy have long since vanished;
never again will they have a part
    in anything that happens under the sun.

Ecclesiastes 9:5–6 NIV

one

Kline, West Virginia
Late May 1932

Sulley tore a rag into strips and wrapped each coin before tucking it into the bib pocket of his overalls. Wouldn't do to jingle as he made his way out of Kline after the sun went down. Was it his fault this place hadn't had a good rain since Noah started rounding up all the animals two by two? It'd take a miracle to find water around here.

But he'd made the effort. Put on a good show. The second well they'd dug had even produced a little wet down in the bottom. But it was just a seep—not enough to matter. Still, his time and effort oughta be worth what he was tucking away with such care. Of course, not everyone would see it his way. Which was why he'd promised to give dowsing one more try in the morning.

Except he wouldn't be here come morning. He'd written out instructions for them to dig a well near a snowball bush heavy with powder puff blooms. It was a long shot, but who knew? Maybe they would hit water and he'd be a hero.

A long-gone hero. He tucked the last coin away and settled back to wait for the moonless night to hide his leaving.

Jeremiah Weber was pretty sure Sullivan Harris couldn't find his own belly button with both hands. But his neighbors had gone and hired the self-proclaimed water witcher, believing he was going to transform Kline by finding wells up on the hills and ridges. Currently, most everyone lived within water-toting distance of Mill Run, which was the only reliable source of water. Even Jeremiah's well—one of the best around—typically ran dry a couple of times each year. But he always managed—there were springs for drinking and cooking. As for bathing, well, that could wait when necessary.

As if finding a few wells would suddenly bring folks rushing in from the cities. For pity's sake, did they even *want* that? He'd read about Hoovervilles popping up around the country, and they sounded terrible. But the deacons at church had this wild notion they could attract businessmen who'd lost almost everything in that stock market mess two years ago. They argued Kline could capitalize on a return to the land and farming—especially with the drought out west—if they could ensure a steady water supply.

Jeremiah shook his head as he stepped up onto Meredith's front porch. Why they wanted strangers and hoboes moving here and causing trouble, Jeremiah did not know. But then he'd never been one to rock the boat. As a matter of fact, he'd long been the one they looked to when the boat needed hauling to shore, so the hole in the bottom could be patched.

"Meri? You ready?" he called through the screen door. Arnold and Wendy tumbled out, each one grabbing ahold of a leg. The boy was four and the girl almost three. They giggled and grinned up at him. "Alright then," he said. "Got a good grip?"

"Yes sir," Arnold crowed, latching on like a baby possum in a storm. Wendy just giggled some more and planted her little bare feet more firmly on top of his right boot. He began to walk around the porch, stepping wide and high as the children clung and laughed so hard tears ran down their cheeks.

"Jeremiah, you don't have to do that." Meredith appeared, wrapping a shawl around her shoulders and cinching it at her waist.

He shrugged. It wasn't any trouble, and young'uns in Kline had little enough to entertain them. Of course, lately, they'd had a water dowser putting on a show. And Jeremiah had a suspicion that's all it was. "Why they're giving that man another chance, I don't know," he said.

Meredith patted his arm. "Hope springs eternal," she said. "I think today's the day!"

"Hope so," he grunted. Meredith was forever an optimist, which was a wonder when she'd married young, had two babies lickety-split, and then lost her husband to typhus. "Now if I can pry this pair of possums off my legs, we'll go see if the third time really is the charm."

They started down the road toward the church, enjoying the warmth of a bright spring day. Jeremiah was well familiar with the church building since it served as their schoolhouse during the week and he served as the teacher. It wasn't something he'd set out to do, but while he looked like a lumberman, he'd actually gone to college and studied history. He'd meant to be a professor, until his widowed father took sick and he'd come home to look after him. It'd been twenty-five years now since Dad died and the locals asked him to teach their kids so they didn't have to go so far for schooling. He always had been a soft touch when someone needed help.

Which was why he'd tried to help by suggesting they run Sullivan Harris off. Advice that fell on deaf ears. Just the day before, Sulley said he thought there was a likely spot for water out back of the one-room church, much to the delight of the deacons. Having a good source of water there would be a boon.

The dowser had slept on the ground the night before, claiming it helped put him in "synchronicity" with the water. Jeremiah thought it was all blather and said so, but he'd been outvoted when he suggested they ask for their money back and run Sulley out of the country.

As they approached the church, Jeremiah could see a tight knot of people out front. When Joe Randolph—head deacon—looked up, he saw him blanch.

"Found water already?" he called as they drew closer.

Joe pulled away from the group, his eyes darting all around. "Well, no. It would seem Mr. Harris has left us instructions on where to dig."

"Instructions? What kind of nonsense is that? Where is he?"

Joe swallowed hard and stuttered, "I-it would s-seem he's not about."

Jeremiah knew his face had turned stormy. Joe held both hands up. "Now, the note said he'd stayed for as long as he could. Probably has family eager to see him."

"Then why in tarnation wouldn't he have mentioned that before?" Stomping around back, Jeremiah sized up the situation. There was no camp. No bedding laid out by a fire ring. No signs of someone spending the night. "Couldn't find water so he ran off with your money," he announced to the group trickling around the corner of the building. "Nothing but a swindler. I told you we needed to ask for that money back!"

Joe licked his lips and looked nervously around the group. "Let's not jump to conclusions. He left us information about where to dig." He held up a piece of paper. "It seems to me we shouldn't call the man a swindler until we're certain of the facts."

"Horsefeathers!" Jeremiah hollered. "When did you get to be so doggone trusting of strangers?"

"But what can we do?" This from another deacon who was wringing his hands. "We borrowed some of that money we gave him from the General Conference. We have to pay it back in a year. Getting a well was supposed to bring more folks in. Help fill the collection plate." His eyes were wide, and he looked like he might be sick.

"We've got our tools ready," Joe said, sounding like he was gaining confidence. "Best thing is to dig where he said, see if we hit water, and go from there."

"You're wasting your time," Jeremiah said. "Go after him is what I'd do. And quick, too, before he has a chance to get very far." As soon as he spoke, he realized his mistake. Hope dawned in several eyes, and Meredith stepped closer to curl a hand around his arm and bat her eyelashes at him. "You'd do that for us?"

"I wasn't . . . what I meant to say was . . ." He looked at the expectant faces around him. These folks scrimped and saved to be able to pay someone to find them water. Never mind that he thought they'd been taken for fools. He let his shoulders fall. "Alright then, dig your well. Here's hoping I'm wrong."

By dinnertime, Jeremiah felt pretty sure he hadn't been wrong. And by suppertime everyone else was in agreement.

The well started dry and stayed that way, hope fading with the day's light. Jeremiah might have enjoyed feeling vindicated if it weren't for the hopeful looks everyone kept throwing his way. Last thing he wanted to do was light out after some charlatan with a good head start.

Joe, who had stripped to his undershirt and was now covered in grime, hoisted another bucket of dirt from the well and added it to the mound. Jeremiah had taken his turn down in the hole and was now leaning against the side of the church, watching. Joe sighed and ambled over.

"I'm afraid you might have been right about Sullivan Harris." He wiped his face with a dirty handkerchief. "Thing is, we're stuck between the devil and the deep blue sea here. Did you mean it when you said you'd go after him?"

Jeremiah felt a knot forming in the pit of his stomach. "I was just saying what I'd do if it were my money. Wasn't exactly offering."

"Even so." Several other folks gathered around, hope shining through the dirt and weariness of the day. Meri and the kids had gone home, but he could still see their woeful faces in his mind's eye.

"We'll look after your place for ye." This from Able Stevens, his eighty-two-year-old neighbor who could outwork most men half his age. "School's about done, and we'll help out with gasoline."

Jeremiah closed his eyes and inhaled deeply, then let the air out like he was rationing it. *"Thou shalt love thy neighbor as thyself."* He'd often thought that verse was extra hard. "Alright then." He let his shoulders drop low. "Too late to start today. I'll head out come morning." He was pretty sure he was going to regret this.

two

Mount Lookout, West Virginia
June 1932

Sulley squinted into the sun as he ambled down what passed for Main Street. Hands shoved deep in the pockets of his new overalls, he whistled tunelessly as he took in every detail of the place from beneath the brim of his straw fedora. He flicked the brim, making sure it sat just right to shade the sun from his eyes. He had a good feeling about Mount Lookout. He'd surely find what he was looking for here. And at the moment what he was looking for was a few coins to rub together.

He'd had more than a few thanks to the good folks of Kline, but some good meals and a few needed items meant his funds had now run drier than those failed wells. He'd kept moving south and west ever since just in case those church folk were mad enough to come looking for him. He didn't think anyone would follow him this far, although he kept a sharp eye out just the same. Of course, keeping a sharp eye out was always a good idea.

"Howdy." He smiled and let his blue eyes spark at the farmer's wife stepping out of the general store. She flushed and smiled back before ducking her head and hurrying on. He smirked. He could charm a snake out of its skin if he needed to.

He swung through the door of the Mount Lookout General Store, willing his eyes to adjust faster. First impressions were important—the ones you made as well as the ones you took in. He blinked and was glad to find the space mostly empty of people. There were shelves of dry goods, a long wooden counter with items on display alongside a gleaming cash register, and glass cases with gewgaws to tempt the ladies of the town. A colored girl, maybe thirteen or so, gave him a shy smile as she ran a dustcloth over the shelves. In the back, he saw a postal counter. A petite woman with dark hair in those short waves all the women seemed to wear these days stepped into view and narrowed her eyes at him. Sulley ducked his head and headed for the tobacco display as though considering exactly which one of the three kinds on offer he'd most like to smoke.

"Has anyone seen my granddaddy's watch?" A voice roared out from the back of the room as a stout man with a balding head and bushy eyebrows stomped into view.

The woman behind the postal counter leaned forward. "George, there is no need to yell like that. We can hear you perfectly well."

The man began rummaging around the cash register, moving things and muttering under his breath. "Had it this morning . . . can't trust . . . things going missing." He glared at the colored girl, who stood there frozen, a look of fear painted across her face.

"George." The woman darted a look at Sulley as she hissed the man's name. "You have a customer."

Sulley quickly looked away and lifted the lid of a wooden cigarette display box. He picked up a pack of Lucky Strikes, planning to look thoughtful before putting them back—as though he were indecisive instead of broke. Something glinted as he lifted the pack. "Hey." He spoke loudly enough to attract attention. The woman frowned at him, and the man came closer, clearly trying to compose himself.

"May I help you?"

"Might be I can help you," Sulley said and held up the gold pocket watch he'd found inside the cigarette box.

"That's it!" George almost lunged for the watch, and Sulley dropped it into his hand. "How'd you find it?"

Sulley shrugged. "Always have had a knack for finding things."

"Well, you've saved me a whole heck of a lot of aggravation."

Sulley could see how the girl who'd been holding her dustrag like a shield relaxed her grip and began dusting again. Although she didn't take her eyes off the two men.

George stuck his hand out. "Name's George Legg. I own this place, and if there's anything I can do for you, just let me know."

Sulley gripped the man's hand and let a smile spread slow and easy. "Sullivan Harris. And as it happens, I'm passing through and sure could use a spot to rest up a bit before I hit the road again." He let the smile fall. "I'd be proud to pay my way, but doggone if somebody didn't steal my purse out there on the road."

George slapped him on the back. "Don't think a thing about it." He shook his head with a frown. "Country's overrun with hoboes and bums these days. All sorts passing through. Especially with that tunnel job down at Gauley Bridge." He drew back and gave Sulley a hard look. "That where you're headed?"

"Nope. I've got an aunt over in Charleston." He winked and lowered his voice. "I'm her only kin, and she's rich as Croesus. Seemed like a good time to visit."

George guffawed and elbowed Sulley. "Right you are. Come on to the house with me and the wife'll give you a hot meal and a soft bed." He turned to the woman who was sorting mail as though she weren't tuning her ears to pick up every word they said.

"Keep an eye on Arbutus. You know she'll lay off if you don't keep after her."

The woman drew herself up, and even though she was shorter and smaller than either of them, Sulley had the distinct impression that she was looking down on them. "I have every confidence in Arbutus's work ethic, but I will indeed keep an eye out if only so I might praise her when she does well."

Sulley saw the girl stand a bit straighter, even as George rolled his eyes. "Come on," he said, motioning for Sulley to follow. "Getting close to dinnertime." The words were music to Sulley's ears. He nodded to the woman behind her postal counter as they left the store. She nodded back without the least change in expression, but the look in her eyes made Sulley feel as though she'd seen through every lie he'd just spouted.

Gainey watched the stranger leave with George. While she loved his wife, Susan, like a sister, George grated on her nerves. And she'd be willing to bet—if she ever bet—that the handsome man with the piercing blue eyes and shock of sandy hair beneath his too-new hat was one of those very hoboes George complained about. He'd been sniffing around for a handout and had been wise enough to press his advantage when he happened to find the lost watch.

"Arbutus, didn't I see Myrtle's grandson handling that cigarette box this morning?"

"Yes'm. I think them other boys dared him to filch a cigarette, but he done lost his nerve when he saw you lookin' at him."

Gainey tapped a finger against her upper lip. That boy went from one scrape to the next. She wondered if he'd been stealing a cigarette or something more valuable. Regardless, what were the odds a stranger would walk in and find George's watch just as he was looking for it? She glanced at Arbutus, worry creasing her forehead. And if she wasn't mistaken, George had been on the verge of accusing his young employee of theft.

"Arbutus, be careful . . ."

The girl gave her a puzzled look. "What you want me to be careful about?"

Gainey shook her head. "Never mind. You're one of the most careful people I know. I'm probably borrowing worry."

"They's sure enough of that to go around without needing to borrow any."

Gainey smiled. "There certainly is. Thank you for the reminder." But even as she resumed her duties, she thought this Sullivan Harris would bear watching if he didn't move along in short order. Aunt in Charleston indeed.

Jeremiah flipped up the hood of the Model T and waved away the steam rolling out. Heaving a sigh, he fetched out a can of water and topped off the radiator. He'd been spending far too much time rambling around the country trying to track down Sullivan Harris. He was about ready to give up. Every time he thought he was on the right track, the trail ran cold. You'd think a rapscallion like Sulley would leave a trail of grief in his wake, but he was apparently lying low.

He'd gone out every other day in the beginning, counting

on Meredith to help as school wrapped up. But now, a good month later, he only ventured out if he thought he had a likely lead. Which is why he was broken down outside Summersville, miles from home, using up precious gasoline he didn't have to spare. Meri's cousin's neighbor here in town said someone had passed through offering to dowse for wells just a few days ago. She told Meri he was a real charmer with the prettiest blue eyes that made her almost wish she needed a well. If that wasn't Sulley Harris, he'd be a donkey's hind end. Which was what he felt like anyway.

Closing the hood, he pulled the choke and turned the hand crank. He was lucky that the nearly ten-year-old automobile wasn't too finicky about starting. Just a few miles farther along, he pulled in at a feed store and parked. He'd go around town on foot to save gas. If he didn't, he'd have to find a horse or a mule and turn his car into a Hoover wagon in order to get back home.

"Howdy," he called out to a man tossing sacks of feed over the wooden slats on the sides of a beat-up truck. The man nodded without pausing in his work. "Use a hand?"

"Always." The man didn't slow.

Jeremiah hopped up onto the loading dock and helped load the last few sacks. The man nodded, handed a ticket to the driver, and headed for the store.

"Got a minute?" Jeremiah asked.

"Nope, but if you're bound and determined to take one, I'll let you have it anyway."

"I'm looking for a fellow says he can find water."

"Can he?"

"If he can, he decided not to. Took some money from good folks and disappeared. I aim to get it back. One way or another. Heard he'd passed through here a few days ago."

"Whole country's passing through from one place to another these days, and none the better for it." He shoved his hat back and scratched his head. "Although come to think about it, there was a fella come through here who acted kind of slick." He snorted. "The kind that'd do well with the ladies whether he had two nickels to rub together or not."

"Blue eyes and curly hair?"

"Not that I paid much attention, but that sounds right." He leaned in through the door and hollered, "Say, Jenny, you remember that good-lookin' fella stopped off here the other day? Wanted to trade some roots or something for a handout?"

A stout woman with work-roughened hands and a square jaw walked over. She laughed from deep in her belly. "Boy, do I ever! Charm a bird off its nest." Her already-ruddy cheeks flushed a shade darker. "Talked foolishness, but I'll confess it was a pleasure to listen to him. Said he was good at finding things—water, missing trinkets, that sort of thing." She slapped her hands together. "Told him all I was missing was my youth and good looks." She shook with laughter. "And durn if he didn't make me think I'd found 'em for a while."

Jeremiah stepped closer. "When did he leave? And did he say where he was headed from here?"

"Headed out first of the week. Didn't say where to, but he walked off to the south, whistling as he went." She got a distant look in her eyes. "Gave him food and a place to sleep for a couple of nights and wished he would've stuck around longer, even though he weren't no more use to me than teats on a boar hog." She flashed Jeremiah a grin. "You find him, tell him he's welcome to eat at Jenny's table anytime."

Jeremiah figured this was the closest he'd gotten to finding Sulley. And with him on foot and Jeremiah in a car, he just might have a chance to catch up. He tugged at his ear, trying to think what to do next.

"You going after him?" The man he'd helped load feed was watching him closely. "He steal your woman, too?"

Jeremiah huffed a laugh. Sulley hadn't shown a minute's interest in Meredith once he saw her kids. "No, just the town's money."

"Shoot, these days, that might be worse, scarce as cash money is."

"I ought to go after him, but I won't have gas enough to get home if I do."

The man eyed him up and down. "You're a stout feller. I need a new outhouse hole dug and the old one covered over. It's raw work, but I'll trade you a can of gasoline for it."

Jeremiah knew that as desperate as men were for work these days, the offer was a generous one. "Appreciate it. I'm Jeremiah Weber by the way."

The man stuck his hand out. "John Fagan. I own this place, such as it is."

Jeremiah nodded and followed John out back to start digging. But he promised himself that if he hadn't found Sullivan Harris inside of two days, he was going back home and staying there.

three

Gainey sorted through the packet of stamps from the Post Office Department and was relieved to find they had finally sent the three-cent Washington Bicentennials with the Athenaeum portrait. Originally a two-cent stamp, when the first-class letter rate increased to three cents, the Post Office Department scrambled to rework the stamp. It was bad enough stamps were more expensive now, the least she could do was offer her customers the Washington Bicentennial rather than the Lincoln regular issue. Such details mattered even when times were hard. Perhaps particularly so when times were hard.

She was so focused on admiring the vivid lilac likeness of the first president that she didn't hear footsteps approaching. She sucked in a breath when she realized the man who'd taken up with George Legg was standing in front of her.

"Can I help you?" Her words were sharper than she intended.

"It's entirely possible you can." He gave her a winsome smile, although she steeled herself against it. She'd seen how charming he could be the last few days and she was all too familiar with the dangers of a charming man. "It just so happens I'm in a position to offer my services to the good people of Mount Lookout.

George says as postmistress you'd be just the person to know who might want to avail themselves of my unique abilities."

She pinched her lips and narrowed her eyes, hoping he could read her displeasure. Of course he was selling something. Wasn't everyone? "Indeed." She crossed her arms across her bosom and waited.

Her reaction must have been unexpected. Sullivan Harris licked his lips and cast about with his eyes as though looking for someone else to ply with his offer. Arbutus had stopped cleaning to stare at them. He latched on to her. "Miss, uh, is it Arbutus?"

Her eyes widened, and she looked like a fawn that suddenly realized it could be seen. "Yes sir," she whispered.

"Yes, just like the flower. Arbutus, you suppose there's anyone around these parts who might need a well dug?"

She ducked her head and began sweeping like the dirt had offended her. "I wouldn't be knowing 'bout nothing like that."

"Mr. Harris." Gainey used her coolest, loftiest tone to draw the man's attention back to her.

He dug up another one of those lazy grins. "My friends call me Sulley, and I'd be glad if you did, too."

"Mr. Harris," she repeated. "If there's something specific you'll be needing, you may direct your inquiries to me."

This time the smile climbed all the way to his eyes until they sparked and promised something good. Even at her age she felt a tug of attraction. He was handsome. No doubt about it. And while she was likely old enough to be his mother, she found she was not as well inoculated against his appeal as she would have expected.

"Well now, that would be a pleasure indeed." He moved closer and leaned one elbow on her counter. She took half a step back as the dimple in his left cheek deepened. "And your name would be?"

She exhaled sharply through her nose. "You may address me as Miss Floyd."

He winked at her, and she stiffened. She suspected he was just goading her now—could see that he had her off-balance. "I'll be aiming to know your first name before we're done, but Miss Floyd will do for now." As he straightened away from the counter, she made an effort to appear relaxed. "As to my business—I'm a finder of wells. A dowser. A water witcher if you're so inclined." He swept his arm out to indicate everything that lay beyond the walls of the store and post office. "And I'm curious to know if there's anyone 'round these parts who might require my services."

"We shore need water," Arbutus piped up.

Gainey cast a baleful eye toward the girl, who was now openly staring at them. "Arbutus, please mind your tasks. You have yet to stack those cans this morning."

"Yes, ma'am." The girl disappeared and quickly returned with a box that she tried to empty without taking her eyes off Sulley.

"Do you have references?" She saw the man swallow what might have been a laugh. He smirked instead.

"Sounds like there is, indeed, a need for water hereabouts," he said. He spotted the rocking chair next to the cold stove and settled into it. Gainey frowned more deeply. She was not impressed by his flippant attitude. "I'm a dab-hand with a dowsing rod."

"Don't the Johnsons . . . ?" Arbutus's words withered under Gainey's steely gaze.

"Speaking of water, you can fetch some and do the windows next." Arbutus's shoulders sagged, and she dragged her feet as she headed for the door. Gainey shifted her focus back to the interloper. "I don't have much use for drifters or ne'er-do-wells."

She sniffed. "And I have a feeling you may be both." Sulley gave her another lazy grin, although she thought she saw a crack in his veneer. "That said, it is true that Arbutus's family is in need of a well. The old one went dry recently, and they've been carrying water from a creek. With her brother gone off to work at the tunnel, it's a hardship for her parents." Sulley raised one eyebrow. Gainey rolled her eyes ever so slightly. This went against her better judgment. "So, in light of your lack of references"—she enunciated the word with great care—"I propose that you find a well for the Fridleys. If you do, I will pay you a token amount and put you in touch with a family in better circumstances who I happen to know could also use your services."

Sulley looked like the cat that got the cream. He grinned even bigger and winked at her again. "If we can pin down what that 'token' looks like, I think we'll have us a deal."

She blushed at the wink, which made her angry. She ought to have better control over herself than that. As a result, she stated a sum that was even less than what she'd had in mind. Even so, he nodded, stood, and stuck his hand out. She uncrossed her arms and slid her hand into his for the briefest of shakes. His palm was rough but warm and his touch gentle. She made sure her own grip was firm so he would know she meant business. And if she was not mistaken, she saw a glimmer of respect reflected in those morning-glory-blue eyes.

"Arbutus," she called to the girl. "Tell Mr. Harris how to reach your father's farm. He plans to find a new well for your family."

Arbutus lit up, her dark eyes dancing. "For true? Oh, I'm so glad." She ran a few steps toward Gainey. "Can I show him the way? Ain't been many folks in today, and Mrs. Legg said she'd be back after she gave Mr. Legg his dinner." She bit her lip, her eyes pleading.

Gainey sighed. She hated to manage the post office and store on her own, but the child had so few joys in life. "Go on then. You can come back this afternoon to do the windows." She let a smile quirk her lips and quoted from a favorite poem by Robert Frost: "'You have promises to keep. And miles to go before you sleep.'"

Arbutus clapped her hands and danced to the door. Mr. Harris looked at her with narrowed eyes, then tipped his straw fedora and grinned so big she found herself smiling in return before she caught herself. She pinched her lips and turned away. He was trouble, all right. She just prayed she wasn't going to regret hatching this scheme.

Sulley whistled all the way to the Fridley farm, Arbutus skipping along beside him. She chattered on about the town and her family. Sulley only half listened until she mentioned Miss Floyd. She'd risen in his estimation when she quoted Frost at the girl.

"I know she seems all high-and-mighty, but she's the best, kindest person I know. Mama says she's the way she is because of her disappointment, but I don't know what that mean."

Sulley plunged his hands deeper in his pockets. Sounded to him like Miss Floyd might've had a beau once upon a time. In his experience, that was what ladies meant when they talked about older single women being disappointed. "She never married?"

"Oh, law no." Arbutus stuck her chin in the air. "Ain't no man good enough for her around these parts." She wrinkled her brow. "Nor smart enough, neither. She's the thinkingest person I ever met."

Before Sulley could ask any more, Arbutus turned down a rutted lane ending at a foursquare house. A striking woman with high cheekbones sat on the porch, plucking a chicken. "Mama, this here is Mr. Harris. He's gonna find us a new well."

Sulley nodded and offered up his gentle smile—not too bright but winning. The woman paused and looked him up and down. "Is he now. Run 'round back and fetch your daddy. He's hoeing the garden." As soon as Arbutus disappeared, the woman went back to pulling feathers. "We ain't got no money for you to find us a well. Best you git before the girl comes back and gets disappointed."

"No charge," Sulley said.

"Hunh." Pinfeathers drifted in the air. "What else you selling then?"

Sulley moved closer and braced one booted foot on the bottom porch step. "I'm a dowser. But it seems I have to prove myself before anyone will hire me. You're my test."

The woman's shoulders shook as she laughed softly and nodded her head. "Oh, that Gainey. She done this. Just like her, too. Forever acting the mother hen to all us chicks." She laid the cleaned bird on some cotton sacking and wiped her hands on her apron. "My man Reggie will have the final say, but if Miss Gainey sent you, then it's alright with me. And I won't even ask what she promised you, 'cause it'd hurt her heart to think I knew."

Arbutus came tearing back around the house with a tall, broad-chested man trailing behind her—Reggie. His eyes were cautious as he nodded to Sulley. "What's this about a well? We cain't afford to hire nobody to find us a well."

"As I was explaining to your wife, my plan is to find a well on your property so other folks 'round these parts will know I can do what I say. You're my touchstone."

A slow smile split Reggie's face. "That sounds fancy. You a water witcher, then?"

"I am."

"We got a willow tree over yonder near the pig barn. I'll cut you some likely switches."

Sulley held up a hand. "I prefer peach if you've got a tree."

Reggie cut his eyes toward his wife. "Verna's mighty particular about her fruit trees."

The woman laughed. "Guess I can spare a branch or two if it means water." She motioned toward the far side of the house. "Tree's 'round there. Just finished blooming not long ago. See can't you find a branch without too many itty-bitty peaches on it."

Sulley chuckled. *Waste not, want not.* Looks like these folks planned to let him get down to business right away. He found the tree and took his time finding just the right forked stick. In his experience the most important part of dowsing for water was putting on a good show about it. Seeing a likely Y-shaped branch, he pulled out his knife and cut it off sharp against his thumb. Arbutus watched his every move as though memorizing him. He gave her a wink and tried the branch in his hands. Yup. This one would do.

"What's that stick for?" Arbutus asked.

"This here is a dowsing rod." He tapped her on the nose with the cut end. "I hold it like this." He demonstrated by turning his palms up and cradling the branch so that the bottom of the Y pointed forward. He closed his eyes and tightened, then loosened his grip. "Next, I walk round and round until that end there twitches. The stronger it twitches, the stronger the pull of the water below."

Arbutus ducked her head and looked at him sideways. "For true," he said. "You just watch and see if it don't." He knew Reggie and Verna were standing at the side of the house, watching him with only a little less intensity than Arbutus. Well, he'd give 'em a show no problem. Although he could see by the lay of the land that this wasn't the likeliest spot to find water. "Where's the old well?" he asked.

Arbutus thumbed over her shoulder. "Down past the barn. It wasn't close, but better'n going all the way to the creek."

Sulley puffed his cheeks and gave Arbutus a confident smile. "We'll just have to find you a closer one, then." He had his doubts this was going to work and began to formulate his escape plan even as he settled on a spot just past the peach tree, hoping its flourishing branches were a sign of water nearby. Some folks thought you had to have a special gift or ability to dowse water. In his experience, all you needed was a steady hand, a bit of showmanship, and a general knowledge of where water was likely to sit. Not to mention a quick tongue and quicker feet if you were wrong.

Sulley stepped past the peach tree and knelt down with his head bowed. These folks looked like the sort who would appreciate a show of prayerfulness. "Amen," he said and climbed back to his feet. He heard Verna echo the word softly. Tilting his head toward the sky, he began slowly walking the area in a sort of crosshatch pattern. He hummed as he went, although Arbutus was likely the only one close enough to hear him.

When he felt the stick twitch, he slowed even more, bowing his head over the limber branch in his hands. He'd felt a dowsing rod twitch seemingly on its own more than once. But mostly he knew how to make one appear to dip and sway. He was getting ready to do just that when the stick jerked in his hands.

Arbutus gasped. "You made that stick move," she accused.

"Something sure enough did," Sulley agreed, hiding his own

surprise. He must've gotten ahead of himself. "There's water here, and it's pulling hard."

"Just like that?" Arbutus asked. "I thought it'd be harder and take days and days to do."

Sulley chuckled. Sometimes it was worth dragging a job out. But when he was doing it for close to free with even odds he'd need to skedaddle with nothing for his trouble, it made sense to get it done quick. Back there in Kline, he'd been making the stick move. And then he had to scramble to make sure his feet got to moving before they finished digging that dry well. Here, though, the way the stick tugged made him think it just might be the real thing.

Moving the stick in circles, Sulley settled on the spot with the strongest pull. "Dig here and you'll have you a new well in no time."

Reggie disappeared around the house and then reappeared with a shovel in his hands. Sulley sagged a little. Of course, with only a woman and a child to help, he was going to have to offer his assistance. Normally he managed to avoid the digging, but this was a unique situation. "You get 'er started and I'll pitch in," he said.

Reggie stabbed the shovel into the soil with a heavy *chunk*. "Much obliged," he said with a grin and began digging in earnest.

four

Gainey fretted over sending that drifter out to the Fridley place. She didn't know a thing about him other than what he'd told her, and it could have been all lies. The fact that George and Susan had taking a liking to him wasn't recommendation enough. And while Reggie could hold his own and Verna was plenty wise, being colored put them at an automatic disadvantage. And that was the plain truth.

"That's the third time you've sighed like your favorite dog died." Susan's friendly look invited Gainey to share what was troubling her. But she wasn't one to bandy her worries about.

"Is it?" she asked. "Guess I was woolgathering." She glanced out the window. "Arbutus should've been back by now."

"Is that what's troubling you? Fretting over sending Sulley out to the Fridley place?" Susan was laying out lace-edged handkerchiefs in a glass-fronted case. She pursed her lips as she lined them up just so. "I doubt it'll cause any trouble and sounds like it might do plenty of good. He seems like a good fellow and just needs enough to get him on down to Charleston to that rich cousin of his."

"Cousin?" Gainey pounced. "I thought it was his aunt."

Susan shrugged. "Maybe so, I wasn't paying all that much attention." She raised up and smiled at Gainey—the woman always did have an easy smile and a knack for letting worries slide off her back. "Anyhow, I'd say it was awfully good of you to think of that poor family the way you did."

Gainey pinched her lips and tidied already-neat stacks of papers and stamps. "Yes, well, it's no excuse for Arbutus to shirk her duties here."

Even as the last word faded away, Arbutus came trotting through the door. "I come back quick as I could, but it sure was something watching that man and Daddy go to digging. I wanted to stay longer, but Mama said I'd better hightail it back here afore I lost my job." She blinked solemnly at Gainey. "I ain't lost it, have I?"

Gainey sighed. Again. "No, child, and I do wish you'd stop saying 'ain't.' Now fill a bucket and get after those windows. They aren't going to wash themselves." Gainey was itching to ask if Mr. Harris had indeed found water but couldn't bear to ask the question in front of Susan.

Fortunately, Susan had no such qualms. "Did Sulley find you a well?"

Arbutus stopped, empty bucket dangling from her hand. "Well, they're shore enough digging one. Don't guess they'd hit water, though, afore Mama made me come away."

Susan nodded. "I trust they will yet. Digging a well is hard work."

"Was Mr. Harris helping with the digging?" Gainey posed the question without considering whether or not it made her appear overcurious.

"He shore was. Getting just as dirty and wore out as Daddy."

Arbutus straightened her shoulders. "Although I think my daddy's stronger."

Susan patted her on the arm. "Most likely he is. Your daddy's a good man." Arbutus glowed under the praise as she scurried off to her task. "There now. You see? It's all working out just fine."

Gainey sniffed. "It remains to be seen if they hit water." She picked up her handbag. "I'm stepping out for my afternoon constitutional," she said. Susan smiled and waved her on as though finding water didn't matter one way or the other. Gainey left wishing she had Susan's ability to trust in the ways of the world.

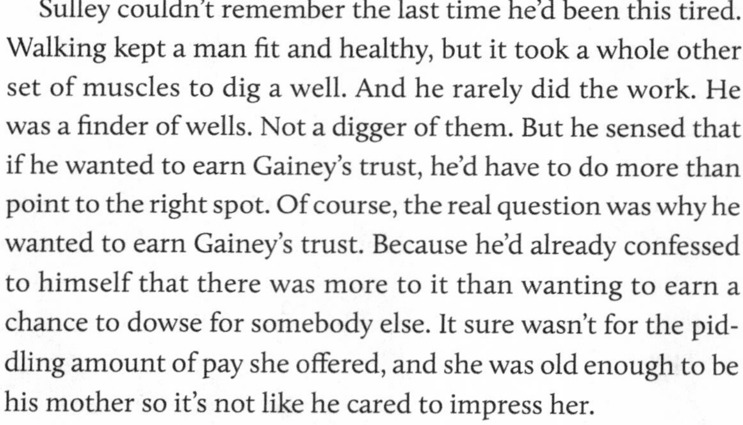

Sulley couldn't remember the last time he'd been this tired. Walking kept a man fit and healthy, but it took a whole other set of muscles to dig a well. And he rarely did the work. He was a finder of wells. Not a digger of them. But he sensed that if he wanted to earn Gainey's trust, he'd have to do more than point to the right spot. Of course, the real question was why he wanted to earn Gainey's trust. Because he'd already confessed to himself that there was more to it than wanting to earn a chance to dowse for somebody else. It sure wasn't for the piddling amount of pay she offered, and she was old enough to be his mother so it's not like he cared to impress her.

He groaned as he adjusted his body on the rough pallet Verna had fixed for him on the back porch. It had gotten too dark to dig—especially once they got more than twenty feet down with water starting to seep in—so they'd eaten a supper of corn bread and beans with a ham hock, then turned in. Arbutus had wanted to go down in the well to see the water, but they didn't let her. Wells were plenty dangerous for grown men, much less a slip of a girl with more curiosity than sense.

The girl mentioned that Gainey wanted to know who was doing the digging. He grinned. If she'd been hoping to learn he was a layabout, she'd been disappointed. He let the smile slip away. He wanted Gainey to think well of him—but why? Maybe because she hadn't been taken in by him the way most folks were. He had the notion she saw past his quick tongue and quicker smile. Not many folks did—or even bothered to try. Most folks were happy enough to be taken in by his big talk, and he always figured if nothing else whatever he took them for was pay for the entertainment he provided. Maybe that was it. He wanted to prove he could win Gainey over—charm her into believing whatever packet of lies he chose to offer. She was a challenge.

He shifted, trying to ease the kink in his back. Tired and sore as he was, he also felt an unexpected measure of satisfaction. He hadn't really thought to find water close to the house with the first try. And he sure as heck hadn't expected to feel this good about doing it. They weren't deep enough to call it a done deal, but he was sure it would be a good well. Reggie and Verna were so grateful, and Arbutus was like a new pup making them all smile and laugh.

For once, he hadn't needed to sell a bill of goods. And he might've even enjoyed helping out folks in need. Good folks who in turn gave him a meal and a place to lay his head. It almost made him want to walk the straight and narrow. He chuckled. Well, maybe he wouldn't go that far. But shoot, what better way to win over somebody like Gainey—pure as the driven snow like he suspected she was—than to actually do an honest day's work? Then, once he'd proved he could charm even her—and added a few coins to his purse—he'd mosey on.

He was too old and too set in his ways to change now. Yes

indeedy, he'd settle for just enough to let him live free, so he'd didn't need to care about what people thought of him—not even people like Gainey Floyd.

A rooster crowed, and Sulley tried to sit up. He moaned and stretched his stiff limbs before trying again, going about it with more care this time. A hound dog was sleeping beside him, his soft red fur and body heat welcome on the cool morning. Sulley chuckled thinking about the Bible verse some do-gooder had drilled into him along the way: "Give not that which is holy unto the dogs, neither cast ye your pearls before swine, lest they trample them under their feet, and turn again and rend you." He tugged a sock from beneath the dog's body. Thank goodness he'd never had any illusions about his own holiness.

The rich smells of coffee and ham frying reached his nose and he followed them into the small, neat house. Arbutus sat at the table, her bare feet swinging.

"Stop kicking your chair," Verna said. "We got company."

Arbutus stilled and watched Sulley wide-eyed as he slid into a chair. "Most white folks won't sit down to eat with us," she said.

"Arbutus Josephine Fridley." Verna pointed a two-pronged fork at the girl. "You hold your tongue."

Arbutus ducked her head. "What'd I say?"

Verna poked at the ham in her cast-iron skillet. "She don't mean no offense."

"I've been called worse in my day," Sulley said with a chuckle. He grinned at Arbutus. "And I'm right proud to put my feet under your table. Considering what I see coming off that stove, a man would be a fool to turn down an invitation here."

Verna's shoulders relaxed, and Arbutus giggled. Reggie swung in the back door with two buckets of water he must have hauled all the way from the creek. He nodded at Sulley. "You sleep alright out there with Red?"

Sulley laughed and rubbed his shoulder. "I think Red snores, but I was too tired to care."

Reggie hefted the buckets up onto the dry sink and sat as Verna began spooning eggs, ham, and grits onto everyone's plates. Sulley saw a look pass between the two adults. "Thought I'd better feed you men good if you're going to finish that digging today." Reggie nodded and squeezed her hand. Sulley had the notion this wasn't how they ate most mornings. He reached for his fork feeling an unaccustomed stab of guilt. It wasn't like he'd asked them to feed him.

"Lord, thank you for this food and the hands that prepared it." Sulley slammed his eyes shut. Of course they'd pray over every meal. "And thank you for sending Mr. Sulley here to get us water. We're grateful for your bountiful goodness. Amen."

Sulley waited a beat longer before opening his eyes. He knew God hadn't sent him, but for half a moment the notion that God might use someone like him struck him with a feeling of . . . lightness. He shook it off and ate what was on his plate. He figured the only thing worse than taking food from these good folks' mouths was not taking it.

"Ready to finish that well?" Reggie wiped his mouth with his sleeve and stood from the table.

"Can I stay home and watch?" Arbutus leapt to her feet and tugged at her father's arm.

"No, ma'am. You got responsibilities. Mrs. Susan and Miss Gainey expect you every day."

Arbutus wilted before their eyes.

"Say, whyn't you come get us started before you go?" Sulley asked.

She brightened. "How do I do that?"

"I'm gonna climb down in that hole. You drop me the bucket, I'll fill it, and you can pull out the first load."

Arbutus was out the door like a shot.

"Thank you." The soft words came from Verna. "I wish she didn't have to work for nobody, but way things are . . ." She pushed her lips into a smile. "Well, she can use a little dose of fun, and you're just the thing for it."

Sulley chafed under the compliment. It felt like shoes too big for him to fill. He nodded once, slapped his hat on his head, and went outside to do some more digging.

Gainey stewed. Arbutus had been less than specific about whether the well was any good. She said there had been mud, but did that mean the well was full? And the water was good? Gainey tamped the thought down for the hundredth time since Arbutus arrived and informed them that Mr. Harris had spent the night so he and Reggie could keep digging the well. Susan was unperturbed. She commented that sometimes you had to dig deep to find what you were looking for. Gainey hadn't cared for her friend's meaningful look when she said it.

"Arbutus, is your mother still taking in sewing?"

"Yes, ma'am."

"Well then, I'm going to walk out to your place this afternoon to talk to her about a project I have in mind." It was almost a lie, but Gainey had been thinking about making up a new Sunday suit out of some tweed she'd been saving for far too long.

"Can I come?" Arbutus bounced on her toes.

Susan walked out from the storeroom in back. "Yes, you may." She gave Gainey the same look she had earlier.

Gainey frowned. She suspected Susan just wanted a spy. Even so, she didn't protest. Arbutus was actually charming company. Most of the time.

five

Jeremiah dragged into Mount Lookout and pulled in at a dusty general store. He'd made up his mind to go as far as Gauley Bridge and then by golly he'd give up. Everyone he met was full of talk about jobs digging a tunnel down there on the river, and while he felt certain Sulley wouldn't be job hunting, he might smell opportunity in a place like that.

First, though, he'd stop off for a tin of sardines, crackers, and hopefully some information. Bone-tired and sick of his own company, he had half a mind to hunt up one of those jobs himself and stay put. He was at the point with Meredith where he needed to fish or cut bait and he wasn't altogether sure which he wanted to do. Was he really going to take on raising two young'uns at his age just so he'd have someone to do the cooking and keep his bed warm at night?

He climbed from the car, tried to smooth his wrinkled shirt, and stepped inside the store. The scents of tobacco, oil, and soap offered a comforting mix. Smelled like home, come to think of it.

A woman with wheat-colored hair was wrapping purchases for a customer, so Jeremiah located his can of sardines, found a packet of crackers, and waited his turn.

"Can I ring those up for you?" she asked with a smile.

"Yes, ma'am. And I'll take a hunk of that hoop cheese you've got there." She poised her knife over the cheese, and he nodded to let her know that looked about right.

"You headed for Gauley Bridge?" she asked. "Seems like just about everybody coming through here is headed that way."

"I am as a matter of fact. Trying to find a friend of mine."

"Oh?" She raised her eyebrows. "He hunting work? That tunnel job seems to be drawing 'em in like bees to honey." She handed him his change. "'Course, nobody else is hiring these days, so there's that."

Jeremiah pocketed the coins with a chuckle. "This fella isn't real big on the kind of work I'm betting they offer on that job. He fancies himself a dowser. Gets people to give him money or whatever else they've got and claims he'll find 'em water."

The woman tilted her head to one side like a bird considering a bug. "For a friend, you don't sound overly fond of him."

"Guess he's more of an acquaintance. Don't suppose you've seen him? About my height, light, wavy hair and blue eyes. He was wearing a worn-out pair of overalls last I saw him."

She narrowed her eyes. "Well now, that does sound familiar. Dowser, you say?"

Jeremiah felt hope surge. "That's right."

"Hmmm, seems like there was a fella like that. I think he mentioned heading for Fayetteville." She brightened. "Yes, that's right. Now that I think about it, I'm sure that was him."

Jeremiah frowned. Fayetteville was almost due south, while Gauley Bridge was more to the west. "When did you see him?"

"Oh," she said, waving a hand in the air, "guess it was a week or more ago."

Jeremiah furrowed his brow. A week would be too long for it to have been Sulley.

"Or maybe it was just a few days." She laughed in a way that sounded nervous. "I lose track of time easy."

Jeremiah gathered up his purchases and nodded. "Could be him. I'd have to change my plans a mite, though."

"Suit yourself," she said, then turned to greet another customer.

He might've been imagining it, but it seemed like she was glad to end the conversation. He shook his head and went back out to the Model T. He'd find a creek where he could eat his simple meal and ponder what it was he intended to do next.

The walk to the Fridley place wasn't more than a few miles, but Gainey still changed into her stout walking shoes, packed her fabric in a basket, and took up a walking stick. She didn't really need it but felt it wise to take precautions for safety. Plus it would come in handy if she needed to fend off a mean dog.

Arbutus nattered on as they walked briskly along the dusty road. Gainey marveled at the child's bare feet skipping over hard-packed ground, rocks, and grass alike. It reminded her of her own girlhood, when her feet had been like leather and shoes were saved for special occasions. She remembered how she'd carried her shoes to school even in her teens, putting them on before the one-room building came into sight so she could save them and keep them clean. And who had she wanted to impress? Why, Archie of course. Mr. Archibald Peterson. The memory of him had long ago faded to a dull ache. But even now the memory of what almost was—

"Miss Gainey! There they be, sitting under that tree resting. They must be done." Arbutus broke into a run and crashed into her father's arms. The sight brought a lump to Gainey's throat before she could catch it. A father and his beloved child. What could be purer or truer? And yet it was a breakable bond.

"Gainey? That you?" Verna stood on the porch, shading her eyes.

"She's come to see the well!" Arbutus shouted.

Closer now, Gainey could see the laughter in Verna's eyes. "I have come to talk to you about a sewing project," she said, indicating the basket.

"Either way, you're welcome." Verna waved her onto the porch.

Gainey tried not to gawk at the two men, eager to see if they were wet, if the dirt piled next to the large hole in the ground was damp or just dark. She thought Mr. Harris had a mocking look in his eyes, which helped her turn her attention elsewhere.

Verna touched her arm lightly. "I know it ain't why you come, but I sure would like to show you the well those two men dug." She smiled. "'Specially since it was you what sent the water witcher."

Gainey flinched. So much for not letting her right hand know what her left was doing. "Is there . . . did they find . . . water?"

"Come see." Verna led the way over to the gaping hole, and Gainey saw that the soil was indeed wet. "We just been letting the dirt settle afore pulling up a bucket to see is it good to drink."

Mr. Harris got to his feet like he had all the time in the world to do it. "Good timing there, Miss Floyd. I do believe it's about time to test the waters."

She blushed under his scrutiny and was ashamed to do so. He'd caught her being curious. Maybe even nosy. Well. At least he'd done what he said he could do.

"You should've seen him, Miss Gainey. He had a stick he held like this." Arbutus demonstrated with a twig she'd snatched up from the ground. "And he walked around and around until it just went to dancing in his hands."

"I have seen people dowse for water," Gainey said. "Although I have my doubts about its efficacy."

"Sure enough worked this time," Verna said softly with a nod. "Just hope it's good water, and plenty of it. Toting from the creek's hard on Reggie all day long."

Gainey huffed out a breath. Of course. That was why she'd risked sending this ne'er-do-well out here in the first place. "Let's see then, shall we?"

Mr. Harris grinned and lowered a bucket down the hole, which was lined with wooden planks. She heard it splash and smiled in spite of herself. He slowly drew it back up—as though dragging out the suspense. Gainey bit the inside of her cheek to control herself, but Arbutus had no such compunction.

"Haul it on up here, Mr. Sulley. I want me a taste," she crowed.

"Hold on there, girlie, and let your daddy test it first." He plunked the bucket down in front of Reggie, and they all leaned forward to peer inside. It was still a little muddy but otherwise looked fine. Reggie squatted down and waited a moment for any sediment to settle. Then he dipped his hands in, cupping the water in his pink palms. He sniffed it, smiled, and took a sip. Then he grinned and drank more deeply.

"Almost as sweet as my Verna," he said.

Gainey furrowed her brow. "Are you quite sure it's safe to drink?"

"Safe as most anything else in this world," Mr. Harris said with a wink. Verna produced a gourd dipper and scooped water for Arbutus, who drank it down and smacked her lips. Mr. Harris pulled a metal disk from his pocket and, snapping his wrist, opened it into a small cup—much to Arbutus's delight. He scooped some water and offered it to Gainey.

"It may not be the fountain of youth, but it'll do you good," he said. She hesitated. "If you plan to recommend me, seems like you'd best be sure I find good water." The gleam in his eye was too much.

Gainey frowned, took the cup, and swallowed the water down.

Arbutus cackled. "Good, ain't it, Miss Gainey?"

"It certainly seems adequate," she said, then peered over the rough edge of the hole. "Will it produce enough water for the whole family?"

Reggie indicated his still-damp britches leg. "Once it got going, water come up to here afore we could climb out. Gonna be a real good well." He slapped Mr. Harris on the back. "You sent us a good 'un."

"I wish James was here to see this," Arbutus said.

Verna's face clouded. "He's doing good work where he is. Lucky to get it, too." She smiled at Gainey. "That's another service you done us, helping him get that job down there at Gauley Bridge. Hard to get work these days." Her smile was back. "I reckon we owe you an apple pie soon as the fruit comes on."

Gainey felt heat rise to her cheeks. Why was Mr. Harris watching her so intently? "You don't owe me a thing. Reggie and Mr. Harris are the ones doing the real work."

That infernal man with his scheming look stretched his arms high over his head. "And it was work, too." He narrowed his eyes at her. "'Course, we're not done. Got to put a wellhead on it. Maybe a windlass for the bucket."

"Now, you done enough," Reggie protested. "I can handle the rest."

Mr. Harris slapped him on the back. "Probably handle it better than most. Still . . ." Gainey saw him toss her a glance, and did he flick his eyebrows? "A man worth hiring doesn't leave a job half done." He turned to the women. "Ladies," he said, then doffed his crisp hat and bent at the waist. "If you'll pardon us men, we'll get this well finished off."

Gainey bit the inside of her cheek again. Was he dismissing her? Them? And so what if he was? She had no desire to watch them build a windlass on top of the well.

"Verna, perhaps we could look at that fabric I brought."

"Yes, ma'am. I can make you up something right smart out of that good cloth." Verna frowned. "'Course, it'll be more for fall or winter."

"No matter," Gainey said, flushing again. "I'll be well prepared when the time comes."

She thought she heard Mr. Harris laughing as they walked inside the house, but she couldn't think why.

What was he doing? Sulley finished winding the rope around the windlass just as the last of the daylight faded. It wasn't like him to stick around and see a job through to the end. Of course, he liked this family. And Verna surely could cook, even if it was simple fare.

Reggie stood back and slapped his hands together. "The Lord was looking out for us when He sent you 'round."

Sulley pasted his easy smile on his face. Nobody sent him

anywhere. Least of all a God he'd given up on a long time ago. But if Reggie wanted to think so . . . "Glad to be of service," he said. "Now, who you reckon Miss Gainey Floyd plans to send me to next? Seems like your girl said something about a family named Johnson."

Reggie nodded. "Probably so. They's good friends of hers, and I heard they planted more orchard this year. But that'll take water to get it going." He patted the windlass and picked up the bucket brimming with cool, clear water at his feet. "Good folks, the Johnsons, and they can put you up a sight better than we can." He stretched his back, sloshing some water as he did so. "Speaking of which, Verna oughta have your pallet ready. If you're half as tired as I am, you'll sleep good tonight."

Sulley trailed after his new friend to the porch. "About that. If it's all the same to you, I'm gonna sleep out tonight." He looked at the dimming sky and the stars just beginning to show. "Only time I like a roof over my head is when it's raining."

Reggie nodded and held out a big, rough hand. Sulley took it and found his throat thickening as the other man squeezed and then let go. "You've done something real good for us," he said. "You'll be in our prayers from here on out."

Sulley swallowed past the lump and slapped his hat against his thigh. "Appreciate it," he said, then turned and walked down the dirt road.

He skirted town and made his way to the camp he'd set up before ever stepping foot in Mount Lookout. Everything was just as he'd left it. Not that there was much. He had a few clothes, some cooking gear, and a tattered copy of *New Hampshire* by Robert Frost. It was the only thing he had from his childhood. Allegedly, it had been in his meager sack of belongings when he was dropped off at the orphanage. There were a few notes and underlined phrases in it. When he was feeling optimistic, he sometimes imagined it would lead him to his family. He had an urge to dip into the book, but night was coming on and he decided a dip in the creek was more important.

The water burbled nearby, rushing over roots and rocks. There was a wide spot where the water pooled maybe two feet deep. He stripped, shaking his grubby clothes out as he went. Then he waded into the cold water and took a deep breath before dropping down to submerge as much of himself as he could. He snorted and blew, then rubbed himself all over, working the grime and sweat of digging out of his pores. Finally, he slipped from the water and stood on the bank where he shook like a dog. He dried himself with a mostly clean cotton shirt and then slipped clothes on that were only a little fresher than the ones he'd shed. He'd need to wash them too before long, but this was good enough for the time being.

He unrolled a blanket and settled himself, enjoying the sensation of tired muscles slowly warming. Turning his attention to the night around him, he heard the creek, the rustle of a mouse in last year's leaves, and the distant hoot of an owl. All too often he'd lain down in the woods at night tense and afraid of discovery. But on this night, he felt . . . contented. He'd helped a good family find good water. He'd been well fed and well appreciated. He might've even won Gainey Floyd over—something he suspected was hard to do. He smiled as sleep overtook him. And tomorrow he'd go see Miss Floyd. She owed him some pay, not to mention a glowing reference.

six

The mail was late. Again. Gainey drummed her fingers against the counter. A terrible habit she was trying to break. That Donnie Allman was the slowest mailman in West Virginia. She would give him a piece of her mind when he—

"Howdy do, Miss Floyd. Fine morning."

She jumped. How had she missed hearing someone come in? She turned to the visitor and stiffened when she saw Sullivan Harris standing there looking almighty pleased with himself.

"Good morning," she said, smoothing the fabric of her dress. Sulley grinned and rocked back on his heels. "Is there something I can do for you?"

"Seems like you owe me a reference." He rocked forward and back again. His britches—muddied from digging last time she saw him—were mostly clean once again. How had he managed that? "Not to mention the matter of remuneration."

She blinked. Apparently the man was educated. In some ways at least. "Indeed." She checked the watch pinned to her bosom. "If you will give me one hour, I would be happy to show you the way to the Johnson farm to introduce and recommend you as likely to be a satisfactory finder of wells." She made sure the watch was still pinned straight. "As for . . . remuneration, I have that prepared for you." She picked up her handbag and pulled out a small envelope, its thin paper crinkling between her fingers. She had tucked the cash inside just this morning, planning to take it to Sulley at the Fridley place. Clearly that was no longer where she would find him. She felt a pang at how insultingly small it likely was—she was unfamiliar with the going rate for finding wells—but it was the best she could do regardless.

Sulley took the envelope, folded it once, and tucked it deep in an overall pocket. She tried not to register surprise at his not opening it. "I'll just poke around some while I wait," he said. She nodded and, turning, was relieved to see Donnie saunter in with the day's post. She glared at him and practically snatched the mailbag from his hands. Sulley tipped his hat with a twitch of his lips and disappeared outside.

An hour later—to the minute—Gainey stepped out the door herself and found Sulley leaning against a post, hat pulled low over his eyes. He tilted it back with one finger when she appeared. "Ready?"

"I'm glad to see you're prompt to keep your appointments," she said and struck out for the Johnson farm.

Sulley strode along beside her. "When it suits me."

She tightened her lips. As she suspected. He was likely fickle and unreliable. "If I'm to recommend you to Mr. and Mrs. Johnson, it had better suit you."

"Don't you worry. My bread needs some butter right now." He produced a bit of straw from somewhere and stuck it in his teeth so that it bobbled as he spoke. "I'm unreliable over the long term, but when I take a short-term job you can count on me." He glanced at her. "I'm solid enough, just never felt the need to stick around long."

Gainey was surprised to find her curiosity piqued. "Why is that? Do you not get lonely traveling from place to place, never taking root?"

"Roots. Guess if you never had 'em, you don't much miss 'em." He lifted his arms. "I get my nourishment from the air and the dew. Most days, the song of the birds and the wind in the trees are all the conversation I need, and the dance of a stream headed my way the only company."

Gainey, much to her horror, snorted. She had not meant to make such an unladylike sound. Sulley grinned and cocked an eyebrow at her. "Do you doubt me?"

"I trust you believe your own hogwash," she said.

Sulley's laugh lifted to the sky. "Durn if I don't like you," he said. "Even if you don't much like me."

She pursed her lips and let the matter drop. She had no desire to talk more nonsense with this man—whom she did *not* like. Well, perhaps a little. Or maybe she just felt sorry for him. After all, she knew perfectly well what it was like to pretend not to be lonely.

Sulley resisted whistling as they walked along. He had the feeling Miss Gainey Floyd would not appreciate or approve it. He chewed on the bit of straw, finding it helped him think. Maybe he'd stay a little longer here in Mount Lookout than he usually did. Might be nice to stick around through the summer. He had a nice camp, a little cash money, and if he found some wells for the Johnsons, he'd be sitting pretty for a while.

He frowned and tossed the straw aside. Of course, there was always the risk of failure. Not to mention the risk that his most recent failure would catch up to him. But never mind—he'd just move on the way he'd originally planned. He glanced at Gainey, who set a stout pace for a woman of her age and slight figure. For a small woman, she appeared remarkably solid—neat and compact with a foundation of iron. Which, he supposed, was part of the fun in trying to rile her enough to shake that firm foundation.

He was trying to think how to poke at her when a farm hove into view. It was picture-perfect with a two-story farmhouse tucked back between pastures that swept up to rolling hills all around. Smoke curled from the chimney, and cattle grazed off to the right. The sun warmed their backs as birdsong tangled in the breeze. For once, Sulley could see why a body might want to settle in one place.

"I trust you will allow me to make the introductions."

"By all means," Sulley said with a sweep of his arm to indicate that she should go first. "I'm delighted to bring up the rear." She looked confused and frowned at him before striding on down the driveway. He didn't really mean anything by it, but watching her try to figure him out tickled his funny bone.

Gainey climbed the board steps and lifted her hand to rap on the door, but it flung open before her knuckles struck wood. "Gainey Floyd, it is high time you came to see us." A sprite of a woman with a slight accent—German maybe—and silvery braids coiled around her head peered over Gainey's shoulder. "And who might this handsome fellow be?"

Gainey cleared her throat and smoothed her dress. Sulley had the notion she was trying to find her place in the script. "Luisa, I'd like to introduce Mr. Sullivan Harris. He is a water dowser, and I know you and Freeman need more water for your orchard." She turned to Sulley. "Mr. Harris, this is my dear friend Luisa Johnson."

Sulley swept off his hat and bowed low. "It's a pleasure to meet you, ma'am. Do I detect a hint of a far-off land in your voice?"

"Mercy, handsome and charming, too. As it happens, I was born in Switzerland, but I consider this my home now. But where are my manners? Come in, come in!" She motioned them inside, holding the door wide. "I'll fetch Freeman, and we'll have some *kaffee* and *lebkuchen*." He wasn't sure what that was, but figured he'd give it a go.

Luisa scurried around the kitchen as a tall, lean fellow—all string and sinew—ambled in. Apparently the woman could fetch her husband simply by putting a pot of coffee on the stove. She set thick mugs on the small kitchen table and whisked a cloth off a plate of soft-looking brown cookies, releasing the aroma of cinnamon and spice into the air. Sulley's mouth watered.

"Howdy, Gainey, good of you to come see us."

"I've brought a water dowser, Freeman. This is Sullivan Harris. He found water for the Fridleys, and I thought he might be able to help you as well."

Freeman, whose drawl clearly marked him as a native of the mountains, rubbed his chin and folded his lanky body into a chair. "That right? Sit, sit. Luisa won't let you leave without you eat a bite."

Sulley slid into a chair, resting his muscles still tired from all that digging. He breathed in the smell of coffee as Luisa poured some in his mug. He sipped the hot liquid, feeling it brighten his senses. He bit into one of the cookies and thought it was just about the best thing he'd ever eaten. He almost thought he could tolerate being tamed if it was like this every day. Of course, he knew it wasn't. He was only a guest here in this comfortable kitchen. So he'd just enjoy it while he could.

"Good, ain't they?" Freeman asked with a smile. "I wasn't so sure about Luisa's foreign ways of cooking when we first got hitched, but now I know better." He winked and ate a cookie in two bites, washing it down with a slurp of coffee. "So, you're a water witcher?"

"Sure enough," Sulley agreed. "I can give you my pitch if you want it."

Freeman laughed. "Nope, save it for the next feller. If Gainey says you find water, that's good enough for me."

Gainey pinked. "All I can attest to is the well he found for the Fridleys." Luisa squeezed her hand and finally lit in a chair like a chickadee poised to take flight again.

Freeman leaned back and laced his hands where his belly would be if he had one. "We've put in a whole orchard out back. Cut back on cattle and planted mostly apple trees along with a few pears."

Luisa thrust a finger in the air. "And one peach. Do not forget my peach tree."

Freeman chuckled. "Yes, ma'am. I cain't never forget your peach tree."

"I will make a . . . how do you say, cobbler, with the fruit?" she said, patting her husband's hand.

He nodded. "As I was saying, we put in a whole orchard, but it's too dry. Trees aren't growing the way I'd like. We've been hauling water, but it takes so durn much . . . well, if we could find water nearer the trees, sure would be a help."

Sulley swallowed some more coffee. Normally he didn't pay too much mind to whether or not he thought he could actually find water. Most times he traded a measure of hope for a few dollars. If that hope panned out—all the better. But with the flavor of Luisa's lebkuchen still on his tongue and Gainey's eyes still on his face, he found he *wanted* to give these people water. What was it about this woman that made him care?

"Can't promise you anything, but I'll be glad to take a look and see if I think I can help," he said at last. Gainey looked thoughtful, which he took as a positive sign. He swallowed the last of his coffee, grabbed another cookie, and stood from the table. "Want to show me what you've got?"

Gainey and Luisa tidied the kitchen, then went out to sit on the back porch where they could see the men walking through the mature orchard to where the saplings stood. They couldn't hear their voices but could see their arms waving about. Gainey hoped she'd done the right thing.

"Your Mr. Harris is a handsome one," Luisa commented.

"I'd trust him more if he were less so," Gainey said in an unguarded moment. She shook her head. "That's unkind of me. Thus far he's proved to be what he says—nothing more and nothing less."

"A witcher of water?" Gainey nodded. "How does this thing work?" Luisa asked.

"I don't know if it's science, superstition, or something else altogether, but my uncle could do it. And I've seen or heard of others who could." Gainey squinted at the men in the sun. "Some say if you use a fresh branch from a tree that's drawn to water, even in a man's hands it will be pulled toward the water."

"Can anyone do this?" Luisa asked. "Perhaps I could try it."

Gainey nearly shrugged, but hated when others did, so resisted. "I suppose anyone could try. I even tried when I was a girl." She smiled at the memory. "It didn't work for me."

"Perhaps it requires a measure of faith," Luisa said. "I will watch how this Mr. Harris does it and see if I can believe also."

Gainey lifted her face to the soft spring breeze. Faith. Perhaps Luisa had the right of that.

Jeremiah struggled from the back seat of the Model T and tried to get the feeling back in his right foot. There was way too much of him to sleep comfortably in the automobile. But it was some better than sleeping on the ground, and no way was he spending money for a bed to lay his head on at night.

The trip to Fayetteville had been a bust. No sign of Sulley. No one had heard of or seen anyone looking even remotely like him. Well, that was it. He was done. He was heading back to Kline this very day. If anyone else wanted to try to track Sulley down, more power to 'em. He was finished. Plus he'd decided he was going to ask Meredith to tie the knot before the summer was out. If nothing else, this business had taught him it was foolish to waste time.

He started the Model T on the third try and pointed her nose for home.

seven

Sulley stood back and admired the stone wellhead and windlass Freeman and his hired men had just finished. He hadn't helped dig the two wells on the Johnson farm, but he sure enough found them. He'd felt a moment's worry when they didn't hit water right away. But then it was like striking oil the way the water rushed in and filled the stone-lined wells. Freeman whooped and threw his hat in the air like a kid.

It had been four days since Sulley ate lebkuchen at the Johnsons' table, and in that time he'd debated taking the down payment Freeman gave him and getting while the getting was good. But Gainey had gotten his back up. The way she still acted skeptical of him made him *want* to show her he could do what he claimed. Of course, he was never all that sure of his own abilities. Well, maybe of his ability to get people to hire him on and give him money. But producing water every time? That he knew, for a fact, he could not do. Which made him downright grateful he'd done it this time.

Freeman walked over and clapped him on the shoulder. "Fine week's work. I'd say you've earned your pay and then some." Sulley wilted a bit under the praise. Had he? All he'd done was point out a likely spot by making a stick jump in his hands. "Luisa is putting on a feast to celebrate. And she'll string me up if I don't make sure you're there."

"Suits me."

"Come on back to the house about six this evening. She's making *rösti*, and I promise you'll be glad you came."

Sulley didn't know what rösti was, but based on everything else Luisa had fed him, he felt pretty sure he'd like it. He headed for his camp and changed into the shirt and canvas trousers he'd gotten Verna to wash for him. He preferred his overalls, but he figured he ought to dress up as best he could.

When he arrived back at the Johnson farm, he followed his nose to the kitchen. Luisa shooed him onto the back porch, where Freeman sat with Gainey. He hadn't realized she'd be joining them and was glad he'd made an effort with his appearance. "Evening, folks," he said. "Sure does smell good in the kitchen." He felt awkward—which was unusual for him.

"Luisa already fed the hired men, but she made me wait." Freeman patted his stomach. "Had to come out here so's I could stand it." He smiled at Gainey. "Fortunately, Gainey come along to keep me company."

"It would appear you've been successful three out of three times, Mr. Harris," Gainey said. "Too bad I don't have anyone else to recommend you to."

Sulley leaned against a porch post. "Word has a way of getting around."

"Moves faster when it's the sort you'd rather didn't get around," Freeman said, laughing. Gainey's face pinched, and Sulley had the notion she didn't like that comment. Had she been the butt of gossip somewhere along the line? Well, an unmarried woman of a certain age—folks probably would talk.

"Gainey," he said. "That's not a name you hear every day."

She wet her lips. "As it happens, my name is Eugenia. My father was Eugene and was disappointed when Mother failed to produce a son. I resisted the nickname but had a younger sister who used it with such frequency, my efforts were for naught."

Sulley chuckled. "And I, on the other hand, insisted folks use my nickname. Sullivan is too fancy a name for me."

Gainey tilted her head to one side and sized him up. "You are certainly not fancy, but Sullivan carries a certain dignity to it that I believe you could support if you tried."

Sulley threw his head back and chortled. "You hear that, Freeman? Dignity." He shook his head. "No one's accused me of being dignified before."

"I did not say you were," Gainey corrected him. "I only said you could be."

Sulley's laughter faded. He wasn't sure he liked that assessment but was saved from thinking about it further when a bell rang.

Freeman clapped his hands. "Let's eat!"

Gainey watched Sulley closely as they moved inside. She could see she'd given him something to think about. The notion made her smile. She'd been trying to understand him since he first set foot inside the store and at last she thought she was getting somewhere. The man's charm and blather were a false front hiding . . . well, that she had yet to pin down. But she'd found a chink in his armor. Hopefully having done so would keep him from looking too closely at her own.

They sat, and Freeman blessed the food. Gainey loved eating with the Johnsons. Luisa was a marvelous cook and treated her guests to Swiss dishes that seemed almost exotic here in southern West Virginia. Even if they were little more than fancy potatoes, like the rösti she loved so much.

As they dug in, she saw that Sulley enjoyed the food with good appetite and no reluctance to try things unfamiliar to him, such as *Bolleflade* and *Schwartenmagen*. Although the second dish was very like the local souse boiled up at hog-butchering time, so maybe not so unfamiliar.

Once several moments had been given to savoring the food, Freeman spoke. "Where you headed from here, Sulley? Got any more wells to find?"

"Oh, I don't know. Always happy to hunt up a well, but for now I have all I need. Might even stick around awhile and just take things easy."

Gainey set her fork down. "Have you worked so hard you need a vacation, Mr. Harris?"

Sulley cackled. "My whole purpose in life is to never work so hard that I need a vacation."

Freeman laughed heartily while Luisa smiled politely, but Gainey could not abide such an attitude. "Don't you want to make your contribution? To have an impact on the world around you?"

Sulley took another helping of sauerkraut. "I'm hoping to get through this life without leaving much of a trail, so the answer to that question would be *no*."

"Not everyone is as civic-minded as you, Gainey," Freeman added. "While I can't say as I'd want to be a wanderer, there is a certain appeal to being free—not tied down."

"Oho, old man. So, what is it that ties you down?" Luisa poked her husband in the ribs.

Freeman laughed. "I'm no more tied down than I want to

be. I said there's a certain appeal, but so there is with a farm, a family"—he squeezed Luisa's hand—"and a good wife who makes the best rösti in all of West Virginia!"

Luisa's smile bloomed, then faded. "Yes, family. But our Noah—he has gone away from us, and now we do not know where he might be."

Gainey tensed. She hadn't expected the subject of the couple's only son to come up. He'd left the previous fall after exchanging hard words with his parents. They assumed he would take over the family farm, but he'd had other ideas that he'd made known. And as gentle and kind as Luisa was, she also had a fiery streak. Freeman had tried to make peace between mother and son, but Noah informed them he couldn't live with a woman who had so little respect for his "natural abilities." And he'd left with no indication of where he was headed.

Freeman laid a comforting hand over his wife's, but the sorrow and regret dampened the mood. Sulley, to his credit, didn't press for details. Or perhaps he simply wasn't interested.

After they finished their meal, Luisa made coffee and they returned to the porch to enjoy some of her *springerle* cookies. The change in scene brightened the mood again, although, as they sat making small talk, Gainey thought Luisa seemed uneasy. She kept stirring her coffee, even though she hadn't added anything to it.

"Mr. Harris," she said, suddenly setting her cup down with a *thunk*. "You are a finder of water, yes?"

"Sure enough," Sulley said. "Hope you don't doubt me now."

"I have heard that men who are finders of one thing sometimes are finders of another."

Sulley frowned. "I've heard that, too. Folks think dowsers can find gold or silver. I've found the odd lost gewgaw now and again, but if I could find more than that, do you think I'd be looking for water?"

"No, but perhaps you can find something more . . . meaningful. Such as a lost son?" Gainey saw such hope bloom on the woman's face that it tore at her own heart. She knew what it was like to pine for a child, although she'd put that particular pain behind her a long time ago.

Sulley set his mug down and clasped his hands between his knees. "Ma'am, I'm sure sorry you're missing your boy, but I wouldn't know the first thing about finding someone who's gone missing." He tried a crooked smile. "Don't reckon a forked stick would work anyhow."

Luisa's smile slipped sideways—like she'd barely caught it before it fell. "Ah well, as they say, it does not hurt to ask." Freeman took her hand in his, eyes watery and his own smile crooked. "The good Lord will bring him home when the time's right. Keep the faith, Lou." She nodded, and they all sat in awkward silence.

"But where are my manners?" Luisa said at last. "There are more cookies to enjoy." She offered the plate to Sulley, who held up his hands.

"Thanks, but I reckon I've had enough to hold me." He set his mug down and stood. "Time I'd best be getting on. Don't want to overstay my welcome."

No one, least of all Gainey, tried to stop him as he made his way through the yard. They sat in a thick silence, watching as Sulley suddenly stopped, crouched, and scrabbled at the ground. He meandered back to them, rubbing dirt off something in his palm.

"This belong to you?" he asked Luisa. She held her hand out, and he placed a dirt-crusted wooden button in it.

Her eyes lit up. "I had forgotten this. It has been gone for—"

she bit her lip and looked up—"two springs. It is two springs since my Noah lost this from his coat. But how did you find it? It is the color of the soil." She sprang forward and grasped Sulley's arm with such force he flinched. "You see. You are a finder of forgotten things, and this was Noah's. If you can find his button without even trying, then perhaps you can find him. It is a gift, and you will use it to help us. Yes? We will pay you well."

Sulley was already shaking his head and trying to back away. "No. That was pure chance. Just caught the shape out of the corner of my eye. Don't mean a thing."

"But surely—" Luisa began.

Sulley jerked his arm free. "I said no. Thank you for the fine meal." Then he turned and sped away until they lost sight of him around a bend in the road.

eight

The ground had never felt this hard before. Sulley was accustomed to sleeping on little more than a pallet—sometimes not even that. So why couldn't he get comfortable tonight? He tried to pin it on Gainey's comment about his dignity, and while that niggled at him, he knew it wasn't what made the earth feel like stone beneath him.

It wasn't the first time someone had asked him to find more than water. He wished he'd left that doggone button where it lay.

He'd known a fella once who claimed he could find gold or silver with a divining rod. Of course, he also claimed the process required him to slit the end of the rod and insert a piece of the desired metal. The silver dollar, say, would then be attracted to larger amounts of silver buried underground. Sulley figured it was a pretty good racket but not one he'd ever cared to attempt. At least with water, he found some more often than not.

But finding people? That was another thing altogether. He shivered and adjusted his rough blanket. Grave dowsing. He'd never tried it and never planned to. Of course, Luisa was hoping her Noah was still alive, which meant map dowsing. All of it gave him the willies. He wasn't a religious man, but he'd been introduced to God when he was shuffled off to an orphanage as a babe after his mother set him aside.

As a matter of fact, it was Franklin—the handyman at the orphanage—who had taught him to dowse. But the one time he innocently asked if they could dowse for his mother, Franklin warned him against ever hunting anything more than water. That old man had been just about the only consolation he'd had in those hard days. He'd once hung his head and cried over his mother. Franklin patted him on the back. *"Mebbe she didn't mean to leave ya,"* he'd said. *"Mebbe she jest forgot, and by the time she remembered, it was too late."*

That had been a consolation for a long time. He'd imagined his distraught mother out there somewhere looking for him. Until the day he'd let the idea slip, and an older boy had scoffed. *"Forgot? That'd be a poor excuse for a ma, wouldn't it, now? One that'd forget her own child."* That was when Sulley realized the only thing worse than being abandoned was being forgotten.

Which was exactly what God had done, over and over again. Sulley had never warmed up to the notion of an all-powerful somebody telling him what to do, but he'd developed a healthy respect nonetheless. And all this divining mumbo jumbo felt like something the Big Guy wouldn't appreciate. Using a peach branch to pick a likely spot for a well was a far cry from swinging a pendulum over a map in hopes it would point him toward a missing soul. No sir. Not for him. No one could ever pay him that well.

He rolled to his back and stared at the stars among the trees. A slight breeze stirred, and the gentle movement of branches began to lull him at last. But it was a lesser peace. He just wasn't comfortable here anymore.

Gainey was on her way to tell Myrtle Hampstead that she had a most interesting package when she saw Sulley headed for the store. "Good morning, Mr. Harris."

"I guess it'd be too much to ever expect you to call me Sulley," he said, but his tone wasn't as light as usual.

"If I were to get to know you well enough, I suppose I might."

"Well then, Mr. Harris it'll stay. I'm headed on soon as I pick up a few necessities at the store yonder."

The sense of disappointment took Gainey by surprise. Now, why would she care if Sulley moved on? "Oh, no more business for you around these parts?" She kept her voice light.

"None worth sticking around for."

Now he sounded downright sullen. Had Luisa offended him when she asked him to find Noah? Gainey felt indignation on behalf of her friend. What mother wouldn't do anything to find her son? The unbidden question pricked her sharply. So much so that Sulley apparently noticed.

"You ain't fixin' to miss me, are you?" he asked, a glint of humor returning.

"You aren't the one I was thinking of missing," Gainey snapped, regretting it immediately. She hadn't meant to even hint . . .

Sulley sobered. "Seems like everybody's missing somebody. Verna's missing her James, while Luisa is missing her Noah. Sounds like you got somebody you ain't seen in too long too." He shook his head. "Seems to me it's a far sight easier to turn loose of people as quick as they turn loose of you."

Gainey blinked and considered the man standing before her. It seemed he had a story, but then who didn't? She certainly did.

One no one here knew, and she'd just as soon keep it that way. Even so, she couldn't resist a final word. "Sometimes people don't let go. Sometimes their very reason for living is pried from their hands one finger at a time."

It was foolish to say even that much, yet seeing the look on Sulley's face gave her a moment's satisfaction. "Goodbye, Mr. Harris. I'm glad I was wrong about you." She felt his eyes on her back as she walked on to Myrtle's house, but she did not turn to see him go. Or to let him see the shimmer in her eyes.

When Jeremiah saw the turnoff for Mount Lookout, he took it. Wouldn't hurt to check in at that general store one more time. And the notion of it being a familiar place drew him. Inside, a colored girl was packing items for a customer at the counter. Jeremiah nodded at the man and the girl, then ambled back to the post office window looking for that woman he'd talked to last time. He peered inside but didn't see anyone. Turning back, he saw that the girl, finished with her customer, had come closer. "Miss Gainey be right back if you're hunting her."

"Is she the one with light hair who waits on customers?"

"That'd be Mrs. Susan. She ain't—isn't—here today. Miss Gainey's the postmistress." The girl puffed her chest out a notch as though proud of the fact. "She can help you with most anything."

"Well then, I'll bide a moment." The girl picked up a broom and began dabbing at the floor with it, but she was obviously watching him more than sweeping.

"What you want anyhow? Got a letter to post?"

The child was bold. Jeremiah leaned against the edge of the

window and crossed his arms over his broad chest. "No letter. I'm looking for someone."

"And you reckon he might've gotten some mail here?"

Jeremiah felt his lips twitch beneath his shaggy beard. "Something like that."

The girl poked at the floor some more. "I 'spect I know just about everyone 'round here. Who you huntin'?"

Bold and persistent. "I'm looking for a man who claims he can find water with a stick."

"Oh, you mean Mr. Sulley. He's done gone already."

Jeremiah frowned. "Right. Heard he left some days ago."

Now it was the girl's turn to frown. "No sir. He left just this morning, I'm pretty sure. Spoke with Miss Gainey before he lit out."

Jeremiah realized he'd let his mouth drop open. Had the man been here in Mount Lookout the whole time? Had he been sent on a snipe hunt? Surely that woman hadn't lied—although Sulley did seem to inspire foolish allegiances wherever he went.

"You needing water? He sure enough got a well for us. Saves Mama ever so much running back and forth." The girl stood a notch taller. "'Specially since I got to work and can't tote for her all the time."

Now Jeremiah was bewildered. She did use the name Sulley, didn't she? Surely it wasn't the same man—not if he'd found water for these folks. "He found you a well? How much did he charge your family for performing that service?"

"Not a thing." The girl was clearly warming to her subject. "He come out to the house, cut him a peach branch off'n Mama's tree, and walked 'round like this." She demonstrated, hands out in front of her. "Until that stick went to bending and bobbing, and by golly when Daddy and him dug right there, they hit water in no time at all."

"He helped your father dig the well?"

"Sure enough. Now we just draw up howsomever much we need and don't have to go but forty feet from the house." She sighed and leaned on her broom. "I thought he might stick around, but after he got two wells for the Johnsons, he lit out."

Jeremiah heard a sound behind him and turned to see a regal-looking woman with piercing eyes and rich brown hair curling around her face in short waves. "Arbutus, shouldn't you be working?"

"Yes, ma'am." The girl ducked her head and scampered to find her feather duster.

"May I help you?"

Jeremiah had the notion this woman—who must be the girl's Miss Gainey—had just invited him to take a test. "I'm looking for Sullivan Harris. I understand he's been finding wells 'round these parts."

"May I ask who is inquiring after Mr. Harris?" She was cool, hands with blunt nails folded on the edge of the window between them.

"Name's Jeremiah Weber. From up near Kline."

"I'm not familiar with Kline," she said.

"But you are familiar with Sullivan Harris? I'd sure be grateful to have a word with him."

"I'm afraid we can't be of any help on that count. He's moved on."

Jeremiah blew out a mouthful of air. "You know where he was headed next?"

"Even if I knew, I'm not certain I would say. He struck me as a very private man."

Jeremiah laughed, which seemed to take the woman by surprise. "Sounds about right. Say now, I gave you my name, might I know yours?"

She flushed and held out her hand. "Eugenia Floyd. I'm the postmistress here in Mount Lookout."

He took her hand—which was just as strong as it looked—and gave it a warm squeeze. "Well, Mrs. Floyd, if I can't have a word with ol' Sulley, maybe you can point me toward a hot meal and a place to bed down for the night?"

"Miss," she said and flushed more deeply.

"What?"

"I'm a miss, not a missus. As for room and board, Myrtle Hampstead can likely host you. She takes in boarders from time to time." She folded her hands again—more tightly this time. "Of course, Arbutus's family also hosts travelers, but some folks prefer more . . . customary accommodations."

Jeremiah read her intent and thought he was being tested again. "Miss Arbutus," he called out to the girl who was obviously eavesdropping. She sprang forward. "You reckon your ma and pa could feed me and put me up for the night?"

"Yes sir! Mama's the best cook around, even if all we're having is beans and corn bread."

"You just hit on my favorite dish," he said with a wink. "Reckon you can tell me how to get to your place?"

"Oh, I'm 'bout done here. I can walk you." She looked toward the window. "That alright with you, Miss Gainey?"

Eugenia—Gainey—looked Jeremiah over from the top of his head to the tips of his dusty boots. "We look out for our own here in Mount Lookout," she said. "Are you a trustworthy man, Mr. Weber?"

Jeremiah was surprised by how much he wanted this woman

to think well of him. He stood straighter, tempted to salute. "People who know me best think so. I own a home and some land back in Kline. I'm a teacher, and my neighbors entrusted me with the task of seeking out Sullivan Harris." He looked her right in the eye. "I go to church on Sundays, and I'm a God-fearing man. I hope that upon further acquaintance you will, indeed, find me trustworthy."

Miss Floyd's posture relaxed just enough for him to notice. "That was an excellent speech, Mr. Weber. You are, if nothing else, well-spoken." She looked him up and down again, taking in his travel-worn clothes and shaggy beard. "A teacher, you say?" She turned to Arbutus. "Go on then, child. Take Mr. Weber to the house and try not to talk his ear off along the way."

Arbutus did indeed bend Jeremiah's ear more than a little. By the time they reached the small house with its neat yard, he felt like he knew most of the whos, whats, and wherefores of Mount Lookout. As they neared the front porch, a lovely woman with high cheekbones and a glow of health stepped outside.

"Who have you brought us this time, Arbutus?"

"Mr. Weber here is a-huntin' Mr. Sulley and needs a place to stay the night."

Jeremiah swept his hat from his head and gave a small bow. "I understand you sometimes provide overnight accommodations and a meal or two. If it wouldn't put you out, I'd be glad to pay what you think is fair."

"We'd be proud to have you. I'm Verna, and my man Reggie will be along shortly." She pursed her lips. "We host folks here when we can, but other than Mr. Sulley . . . well, we don't get many folks of your—" she frowned and twisted the string of her apron around her hand—"complexion."

Jeremiah understood her but acted like he didn't. "Guess I am a touch swarthy from being out in the sun and likely none too clean at the moment. Give me ten minutes and a pan of water and I'm sure I can make an improvement."

Verna snorted. "Alright then. If'n you don't mind, neither do I. Arbutus, fetch the man a bucket of water."

The girl's eyes lit like she'd been offered a lollipop and a new kitten. She scampered around the side of the house, and Jeremiah could hear the creak of a windlass followed by a distant splash.

Verna shook her head. "She'd draw ten buckets up in a row if I let her, she's that proud of our new well."

Jeremiah sat down on the edge of the porch, wishing he could take off his boots without being impolite. "Heard tell Sullivan Harris found that well for you."

"That he did. And quick too. You looking for him to find you a well?"

"You could say that." Arbutus reappeared with a bucket sloshing with water and thumped it down beside him. He scooped some and drank it from his hands. It was good water. "If you don't mind me asking, what did he charge you to find this good water?"

"I done told you he didn't charge a thing," crowed Arbutus.

Skeptical, Jeremiah looked to Verna. "It's true, although I have my suspicions about Gainey getting involved. That woman can't help but take care of people."

"And he helped dig?" None of this made sense to Jeremiah. He was hunting a scoundrel and ne'er-do-well.

"Worked like he was digging it for his ownself," Verna said.

"Would have took Reggie way longer without him. All he'd take was a few meals and a place to bed down. And if Gainey did pay him, I don't want to know and spoil the fun for her."

"Sounds like a good man," Jeremiah said.

"Yes sir. The best. We was sorry to see him move on to Gauley Bridge." Jeremiah perked his ears as Verna turned back to the door. "Once you're cleaned up, come on in and I'll show you where you can bed down on the back porch. It's got a screen around it." She said this like she was offering him a four-poster bed with a canopy. He smiled. Come to think of it, a screened-in porch on a warm night sounded even better than a fancy bed. He was looking forward to supper and a night's rest—goodness knows he had some pondering to do when it came to Sulley Harris. And whether or not he was going to pursue him on to the town he'd been aiming at before he'd been . . . misdirected.

nine

"You lookin' for work?" The man who'd given Sulley a ride as far as Ansted leaned out his car window.

"Not if I can help it," Sulley answered with a grin.

"Well, Union Carbide's putting in a tunnel down there at the river between Hawks Nest and Gauley Bridge. Hydroelectric power or some such. Hiring men as fast as they can." He slapped the side of the car. "If you take a notion to do some work, I expect you can get on easy."

"I'll keep that in mind," Sulley said. He ambled on through the small town, nodding and smiling at folks. His plan was to head on down the mountain and work his way along the New River—aim for Charleston and see what might crop up along the way. Mostly he just wanted to be shut of people for a while.

As he considered the pleasures of the solitary life, he came up on a general store and decided to treat himself to a chocolate bar before his jaunt along the river. He slipped inside and skirted the room, taking stock of the clientele. A stove in the rear seemed to be the spot for the old-timers to drink coffee and spin their yarns. He wandered over and looked a question at the coffeepot.

"It ain't fresh, but it's hot," said a grizzled fellow with tobacco stains in his beard. "Extry cup's right there."

Sulley sloshed some of the hot liquid into the cup and swallowed a mouthful. The old-timer was right. It was bad coffee.

"You lookin' for work or huntin' gold?" the man asked.

Curious, Sulley settled into a caned chair and tilted it back on two legs. "Neither one, but if I had to choose, sounds like hunting gold's the way to go."

The man cackled. "You'd think so. Ain't nobody never found it, though. If'n I thought it was out there, I shore wouldn't be telling you about it." He spit a stream of tobacco juice into a spittoon that had been missed as often as hit. "The Phillips gold. Buried at the foot of the cross, they say. Pure hogwash."

"You ever look for it?" Sulley asked.

"When I was young and foolish. You'd be better off getting on with that Union Carbide job down at Hawks Nest or Gauley Bridge." The man frowned. "Although I heard some folks been gettin' sick." He shook his head, making his long beard wag. "Probably them colored boys comin' from too far south. Cain't handle the mountain weather." He thumped his chest. "Best if you're born to it."

Sulley downed the last of the bitter coffee. Didn't Verna say something about her boy, James, working a job at Gauley Bridge? "Thanks for the cup of joe. Guess I'll be getting my candy and heading on."

The man nodded. "If'n you find that gold, don't forget to come back by here and give me some." He cackled again. "Finder's fee."

Sulley grinned. "I'll do it."

He made his purchase and tucked the chocolate in his rucksack, then headed on down the mountain. He could smell the loamy dampness of the woods, and it filled him with a sense of excitement. Soon it would be just him and nature—maybe an occasional train going by. Who needed a job? Who needed an empty promise of gold? He chuckled. Of course, he might keep his eye out for that cross all the same. He knew he couldn't really divine for gold, but it's not like trying would hurt anything.

"Miss Gainey, Mama done heard from James." Arbutus stood breathless in front of the postal window, her eyes wide and excited. "He's sick, though, and she don't know what to do."

Gainey longed to correct the girl's grammar but supposed now was not the time to fuss about it. "Is he still building that tunnel on the New River?" she asked.

"Yes, ma'am. Guess there's been a whole lot of pneumonia in the camps over the winter and into the spring, and it's not getting any better even now that summer's on." She bit her lip. "Mama seems real worried about it."

Gainey found this news troubling. She'd been responsible for James seeking out that job. When she'd heard the project was hiring on large numbers of colored men coming from as far away as South Carolina and Georgia, she'd encouraged James to look into it. He was a good boy and bright. She'd hoped he could work his way up—maybe even become a supervisor or manager of some sort. Of course, they'd never let him supervise white men, but with so many Negroes from out of state, she'd felt certain his chances for advancement were good.

"Do they have good doctors? Is he being treated?"

"Mama read the letter out and sounds like the doctor don't much look after the coloreds," Arbutus said. "James wants to come home more'n anything, but he's got no way to get here."

She sighed and slumped against the counter. “And we don’t got no way to fetch him.”

“Don’t have any,” Gainey snapped.

“Yes, ma’am. I’m sorry.”

Gainey sighed. “Oh, child, I’m the one who’s sorry. It’s my fault James went to Gauley Bridge, and proper speech is the least of your concerns right now. Let me think if there’s anything we can do. You go on home today and be a comfort to your mother.”

Arbutus perked up at that, although not as much as Gainey would have liked. Worry about her brother was clearly weighing the girl down. Gainey paused to lift up a prayer that the Lord would either heal James or help her find a way to bring him home again.

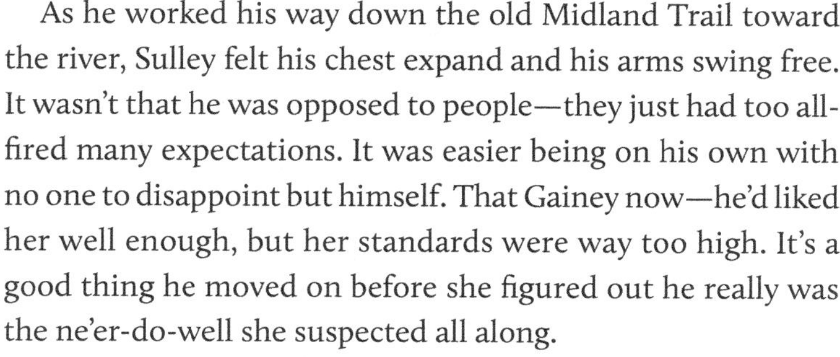

As he worked his way down the old Midland Trail toward the river, Sulley felt his chest expand and his arms swing free. It wasn’t that he was opposed to people—they just had too all-fired many expectations. It was easier being on his own with no one to disappoint but himself. That Gainey now—he’d liked her well enough, but her standards were way too high. It’s a good thing he moved on before she figured out he really was the ne’er-do-well she suspected all along.

The country was steep and folded in on itself with water running down everywhere through the rhododendron and mountain laurel. Full summer now, the trees were lush and green, and wildflowers dotted the open places. Sulley stopped at a cascade tumbling over rocks to scoop up a drink and fill his canteen. The cold water made his teeth ache and tasted like the sky on a winter morning. He grinned. Now this was living life on his own terms.

He pushed on until he sensed the trees opening up somewhere ahead. There was a feeling of wide-open space—unusual in the mountains. Exploring farther, he came to the edge of a gorge with the New River flowing far below. He stepped onto a massive rock jutting out into nothingness. He picked up a stone and tossed it over the edge. Watching it fall made his stomach drop almost as fast as the rock. He crept closer to the precipice and felt the air from the gorge rising up on currents. He guessed maybe he knew how the birds Hawks Nest was named after felt when they took to the air. He dropped his pack and spread his arms to the breeze, closing his eyes.

It was as if he could feel the pure nothing waiting at his feet. It reminded him of how he'd felt when he finally realized he didn't belong anywhere or to anyone. He'd been left at an orphanage when he was just a tyke. He could almost remember his mother—or maybe he only thought he did. It was when he was five or six that the truth hit him. He was playing with some kids from town and got in a tussle with one of them—a big boy who was older than him. The other boy lit into him, and Sulley held his own, maybe even blacked the boy's eye. He'd been feeling right proud of himself, until the other boy's mother appeared. She gathered her son up, hugging him and fussing over his injuries.

The boy acted like he didn't want to be made over, but all Sulley could see was the pleasure in having someone who cared. No one came for him, and when he dragged himself back to the orphanage, the matron made him tend to his own cuts and scrapes while the other boys ate their pitiful supper. He lay in bed that night, sore and sad, finally understanding that he was a void—brought into the world by accident. And he knew there was no sense in trying to belong, and so from then on he didn't.

Without opening his eyes, he inched forward on the rock. He could feel it beginning to slope forward. He might even come to a rough spot, a jag that would make him stumble. He ought to open his eyes . . .

"Lover's Leap. Ain't it purty?"

Sulley froze, then took a step back, opened his eyes and sat down with a thump. He looked around and saw a man sitting on a rock, his shirt stained with sweat and open to the sun. He looked right puny. "Hey, howdy," the man said.

Sulley nodded, noticing his breath was coming hard. "Howdy yourself."

"Name's Lewis Street. Who might you be?" He coughed hard.

Sulley stood on legs that were oddly shaky and stepped closer. "Sullivan Harris, but folks call me Sulley."

"You come around looking for work? Might do better to go ahead and jump."

Sulley shook his head and managed a weak smile. "Folks keep asking me that. Guess I don't look near as lazy as I am."

Lewis laughed, then coughed again, deep and long. "Whew," he said when he got his breath. "That was a good 'un."

Sulley took a step back. "You sick?"

"When a man tries to bring up his lungs day in and day out, he gets the idea that he might be. Even if that doctor says I'm just trying to get outta work." He coughed and wheezed some more.

Sulley was debating just turning around and walking away before he caught whatever this fella had, but the man held up a hand in a *wait* gesture. Sulley shifted uneasily.

"Tunnelitis," he said at last. "That's what the men call it. Reason I asked about work is to warn you against hiring on with that tunnel job." He breathed in like he had to chew off bites of air and work them down. "I wasn't half joking about jumping being a better choice. Too many of the workers sound just like me." He shook his head. "Pay was good to start, but it's gone down with all the workers pouring in and ain't no amount of money worth this." He gulped a wheezing breath.

"How long you been working there?" Sulley asked.

"Six months."

"Were you sickly to start?"

"Nope." He got a cagey look. "How old do you think I am?"

Sulley shrugged. Fella looked to be in his sixties maybe. Too old to be digging out a tunnel. Skinny with sunken cheeks and too-bright eyes. "Reckon you're getting along to be old enough to think more about putting your feet up than working a shovel all day long."

He expected a laugh, but instead Lewis just nodded. "I'm forty-four but feel like I'm eighty. Look it too." He took a stuttering breath and coughed it back out. "My wife, Ruby, says the pay ain't worth it, but we can't get far enough ahead to even think about moving back to Ohio. I want to see her took care of. So I keep going back." He gazed out at the view. "Cain't hardly make it up here to sit on this rock anymore, but the way the air washes over me makes me feel like I can breathe easier."

Sulley, rarely at a loss for words, didn't know what to say to that.

"Anyhow, I wouldn't sign on if I was you." A grim smile turned up the corners of his mouth. "Unless you can hold your breath an extra-long time."

ten

Gainey drove the borrowed mule and cart out to the Fridley place as the sun rose over the mountains. She felt awkward doing it, not having driven a wagon for quite some time. The mule kept casting her glances that felt judgmental—as though he were critiquing her ability. Well. Mules and men were much the same. Just needed a firm hand. She sat up straighter, determined to give him exactly that.

As she approached the house, Arbutus stood on the porch bouncing on her toes, clearly excited to know what Gainey was up to. "Miss Gainey, where you going with that trap?" she called out. "I ain't—haven't—ever seen you drive."

Gainey pulled to a stop as Verna and Reggie joined Arbutus on the porch. "I hope I haven't disturbed your breakfast," she said.

"We's just finished," Reggie said. He swung down from the porch and took the mule by its bridle. "Fine animal you got here. Sturdy." He felt along the animal's neck and down its foreleg. "Take you a long way if you've a mind to go."

"I'm glad you approve. As it happens, I intend to take him

to Gauley Bridge and bring James home." Her announcement was met with stunned silence.

"No, now, Miss Gainey"—Reggie shook his head and patted the mule's nose—"don't talk foolishness. You cain't be doing any such thing."

Gainey glanced at Verna and saw that she had a fist pressed against her lips. Gainey smiled and spoke brightly. "It isn't foolish at all. Why, I'm looking forward to the outing. If you'll give me James's direction, I'll start immediately."

Blank stares.

"Reggie, you go," Verna finally said. "I can manage here for a day or two. Arbutus will help me. You run Miss Gainey on back to the store and then go fetch our boy home."

Gainey felt her cheeks heat. She'd hoped to avoid this. "Verna, I'm afraid that's not possible. I have . . . well, I've taken responsibility for Tobias here—the mule's name is Tobias—and I really must be the one who sees to his care . . ." She let her dithering fade away. She'd handled that explanation poorly.

The mule nuzzled Reggie's pocket as though hoping there might be something good inside. "This here's George Legg's mule, ain't it?" he asked. Gainey nodded mutely. "He know you're planning to haul a colored boy in his wagon with his mule?"

Gainey wanted to toss her head and tell a lie, but she couldn't do that to Reggie. "No, he does not. And there's no need for him to know. When I asked him for the use of his mule and cart to transport a friend from Gauley Bridge, he was wise enough not to press me." She did toss her head just the slightest bit then. "He's grateful to have me on hand to manage the post office and values my willingness to help out in the store."

Reggie chuckled. "Verna, if I was to be seen driving Mr. Legg's mule and cart and it got back to him . . . well, I doubt I'd be long for this world after that."

Gainey felt some of the starch go out of her spine at his words. They were all too true. Black men had been killed for less. Much less.

Verna was biting her knuckle now. "What about if I go with you? Cain't let you go on your own."

"I'll go, Mama." Even as she spoke, Arbutus was clambering up into the small wagon. "Miss Gainey likes having me around, and Daddy needs you to feed him and look out for him." Gainey saw that Reggie was fighting a smile. Verna, on the other hand, looked like a mama hen trying to round up her chicks.

"Child, you ain't been any farther from home than your grandma's house. And you've got a job at the store to mind."

Gainey didn't want to distress the family any more than she already had, yet the thought of having a companion on her trip—especially one who knew James well—was comforting. "Susan is aware of my errand," Gainey said. "She and her husband don't always see eye to eye on every little thing. She's minding the post office, and her eldest daughter is watching over the store. I imagine if you went by and did Arbutus's chores, all would be well." She cast her young friend a sharp look. "And I expect you can do them in half the time."

Arbutus laughed, clearly delighted with the notion of going on a trip. "I expect she can. I'm terrible slow when I get interested in things."

Reggie stepped up beside his wife and spoke low in her ear. She nodded. "Alright then. Let me pack a few things in a sack for you." She turned dark, anxious eyes on Gainey. "Can you wait just a few minutes longer?"

"Of course," Gainey said. Arbutus squealed and made herself

comfortable in the back of the cart while Verna disappeared inside.

Reggie ducked his head, then lifted it and looked Gainey in the eye. Something he rarely did. "You a good woman, Miss Floyd. Better'n we deserve. I'll be prayin' the Lord smiles on your journey."

Gainey swallowed past a sudden thickness in her throat. "As will I, Reggie. As will I."

Sulley had no interest in signing on to work with this Hawks Nest Tunnel business, but running into Lewis stirred his curiosity. He could at least see what was going on to attract every able-bodied man looking for a job from as far as three states away. And anytime there was a big job like this, there were sure to be bigwigs who might need a dowser—or some other similar service. Finding water wasn't the only way to convince people to part with their money.

Yes siree, wouldn't hurt to look into the situation and explore his options. Never knew what a man with charm and quick wits might stumble into. He and Lewis walked down to the workers' camp near the river. According to his new friend, they were drilling out the tunnel from both ends, with camps here and over at Gauley Bridge. They were supposed to go a good mile and a half from each end and meet up in the middle. If nothing else, Sulley thought he'd like to see a hole through the mountain like that.

Lewis didn't talk much along the way—he obviously needed what breath he had just to keep moving, even downhill. As they entered the outskirts of the camp, Sulley could see it wasn't the sort of place he'd want to stay for very long. The men were living in little more than shacks, maybe twelve feet by twenty feet. He peered through an open door and saw two bunks making up four beds with a little stove—dormant with the warmth of summer—in between them. There was little else.

Closer to the work site, Lewis drew up at a similar shack with just one bunk. He thumped down on the steps leading to the crooked door. "Whew. One of these days it's going to be too much for me to go up there and back."

"This where you live?" Sulley asked.

Lewis coughed so hard Sulley wasn't sure he was going to stop. Tears ran down his cheeks, and his face turned scarlet. Finally he got calmed down enough to answer. "If you want to call this living," he croaked at last. Clearing his throat and spitting, he pointed back at the first shacks. "Colored men live up there. Them having it worse is about the only thing that makes this place bearable."

"Where is everybody?"

"Shift change. We're supposed to work ten-hour shifts with two hours in between for the dust to settle." He half laughed, half coughed. "First off, the dust don't never settle. Second, you start working when the boss man says start. Dust or no dust." He rubbed those too-bright eyes. "Guess I'd best be getting down there. I'm late, but it's getting harder and harder to care." He stood again and began making his way along a dusty road that led toward the river. "Comes a day when the notion of dying seems like a blessing."

Sulley opened his mouth to ask what Lewis meant when he saw others headed his way. He stepped to the corner of the shack and watched them come.

They were dusty, sure enough, looking almost uniformly pale with the coating of rock or whatever it was they were carting out of that hole in the mountain. There was an unearthly hush as the men approached alone or in twos and threes. They mostly ignored him as they ghosted by, and Sulley—the sort of man who always had something to say—felt like he'd been struck mute.

Finally, a man approached Lewis's shack. He took off his hat and slapped it against his thigh, raising a choking cloud. Sulley waved a hand in front of his face. "Who might you be?" the man asked.

"Friend of Lewis," Sulley answered. "Just curious to see this hole in the mountain. I'm not looking for work."

The man smiled, the wetness of his mouth sharp against his powdery skin. "Then you're smarter than the rest of us." He pulled out a handkerchief and blew his nose noisily. He examined the results. "Like toothpaste," he said.

"What?" Sulley was confused.

"One of the other fellers said when he blows his nose, it looks like toothpaste." He wadded the handkerchief up and shoved it back in his pocket. "He weren't lying." He flung some gear into the shack.

Sulley was beginning to think he might be better off turning around and going back the way he came. But he'd always been overly curious. "Think I can get away with taking a closer look?"

The man shrugged. "Probably. They's a lot of men milling around down there. Usually a handful hoping somebody won't show for work so's they can step in. Just steer clear of anybody carrying a pistol."

Sulley darted a look all around—he hadn't noticed any guns. All he saw was tired men trying to wipe dust from their faces and bodies.

"Don't worry. They ain't but a few of 'em and they mostly

come around when it's time to run the sick ones out of their beds."

"Sick like Lewis?"

The man hacked, coughed, and spit. "Or sicker sometimes. 'Course, lots of 'em don't last that long. They give up and go on home. Or die." He laughed without mirth. "Ain't hardly anybody makes it more than six months here." He nodded up the hill. "Not even the coloreds."

Sulley furrowed his brow. "But I didn't see any colored men. Do they work a different shift?"

The man smiled grimly and shook his head. "Most of the men what just passed by you was colored." He barked a laugh. "That's how bad the dust is. We go in two colors and come out one."

Gainey and Arbutus passed back through town on their way to the old turnpike road. Gainey saw a man with his head under the bonnet of an automobile that had seen better days. He straightened as they approached, and she recognized Jeremiah. She slowed her mule and he turned, a smile lighting his bearded face. Gainey felt her own smile in response, not to mention a bit of a, what, lightness of heart?

"Good day, Miss Floyd. Arbutus," he said with a nod to each. "You look to be setting out on a journey."

"We are," Arbutus cried. "We're off to fetch my brother home. He went to get him a job building a tunnel down on the river. But he's bad sick, so Miss Gainey said she'd fetch him. And I get to go, too." The words came out in a rush before Gainey could stanch the flow. She felt heat rise from her chest to her neck.

Jeremiah turned keen brown eyes on her. "That's good of Miss Gainey."

Now the heat suffused her face. She knew it would do nothing for her looks. A change of topic was in order. "And what are you up to, Mr. Weber?"

"Trying to head for Gauley Bridge. I understand Mr. Harris was traveling that direction, and I still hope to have a word with him. But my mode of transportation isn't cooperating this morning."

Gainey felt suspicion rise. She'd looked up the location of Kline on a map and it was well to the north. Why would a man from that far away be so determined to track down Sullivan Harris? It was true that upon first meeting him, she'd wondered if he might be a jackanapes, but he'd proven himself—hadn't he? And yet she hesitated to ask this man what he wanted with Sulley.

"That's where we're going," Arbutus offered. She gave Gainey a pleading look. The child would be delighted if they picked up every stray they found along the road. But then Jeremiah was hardly a stray. And it might be wise to have a man with them—safer with all the hard-luck travelers on the roads these days.

Gainey wet her lips. "Perhaps you would like to travel with us?"

"I'd be grateful, if it's truly no bother," he said.

"We'd be delighted to have you." Even as she spoke, Gainey realized the seat she sat upon was only just wide enough for two. Of course, Arbutus would stay in the back, but should she also ride back there? Was it improper for her to sit so close to a man she'd only recently met? Before she could think any further, Jeremiah was climbing up and settling beside her. His presence filled her senses. She could feel heat from his body, could smell sweat and something piney, could see the green flecks in his brown eyes and the curve of his mouth beneath a soft beard. She quickly averted her eyes.

He smiled and nodded toward the reins. "I'd be happy to drive if you like." She handed the leather straps over without comment, feeling oddly tongue-tied.

Arbutus held on to the seat behind them, almost bouncing with her excitement. Jeremiah glanced at her over his shoulder, winked, and slapped the reins.

eleven

Jeremiah took the arrival of Gainey and Arbutus as a sign that he had made the right decision in pursuing Sulley a bit farther. As they bounced along the road, he could feel Gainey holding herself stiffly, trying not to jounce against him. He smiled to himself. He couldn't remember the last time he'd had much of an effect on a woman. He had no illusions about Meredith's interest in marrying him. She simply needed a man to take care of her and her children. He thought she liked him well enough, but it was little more than that.

He was truly unsettling Miss Gainey Floyd. And he found himself enjoying it.

After an unexpected jolt that forced her shoulder into his side, she righted herself, resettled her hat—an atrocious thing in mustard yellow that hid the gleam of her mahogany hair—and apparently decided that some conversation was in order. She looked back at Arbutus first. The girl had managed to make herself a nest in the wagon and was now sleeping. The line of Gainey's mouth firmed. "I don't mean to pry, but I must admit to some curiosity about your business with Mr. Harris."

Jeremiah considered what to share. "He had dealings with

some friends of mine, and it wasn't altogether satisfactory. I'd like to discuss the matter with him."

"Is he a confidence man?"

Jeremiah glanced at her, surprised by the directness of the question. "I thought he was a huckster sure enough, but what I've been hearing from Arbutus and her family, not to mention you, has aroused my curiosity."

Gainey nodded. "I, too, found his actions at odds with what I instinctively expected from him. I hoped that I had simply been wrong in my estimation."

Jeremiah worried his lower lip. What was the harm in telling Gainey the truth? He wasn't sure, but something held him back. Finally, he said, "Guess we can still hope for that."

"You don't mean him harm, then?"

Jeremiah huffed a laugh. "I don't mean anyone harm. Guess it's not so much that I hope to harm Sulley as I hope to help my friends."

She smiled, and he heard how it warmed her voice. "A noble intention. I'll be hoping along with you."

Jeremiah basked in her smile and the warmth of her eyes—like a cup of good, strong tea. He liked this woman. And just then he might have guided their mule to hit another rut so she'd have no choice but to bounce against him one more time.

Sulley approached the gaping hole in the mountain where the river would soon run with force enough to supply electricity to thousands of people thanks to hydroelectric power. Electric lights and cookstoves were fine things, but he had to wonder if they were worth all this bother. Lewis and the man at the shack hadn't begun to prepare him for what he saw.

The tunnel opening was situated in a wasteland of raw, exposed earth and rock. The site was a beehive of activity, allowing Sulley to mix in with the workers. He saw a rail line disappearing inside, along with a long tube near the top of the tunnel that he guessed was some kind of vent or air shaft. Men walked inside, quickly fading into the cloud of haze that hung there like fog on a cool morning. Sulley moved closer to the rough stone opening that had to be more than thirty feet high. Even out in the open he felt as though his breath were catching on something heavy in the air. The ground shook with the rumble of machinery. He could smell the stink of the gasoline-powered engine as it thrummed toward him from deep inside the tunnel, bringing out rock and debris.

A sharp-eyed fellow with two gleaming pistols and a blackjack at his belt hollered at him. "You there, get to work!"

Sulley ducked his head and scurried after several men, then fell back as they moved deeper into the tunnel. He could hear the rock drills running somewhere inside, like angry hornets looking for someone to sting. The air was so heavy he thought he could reach out and grab ahold of it. He watched a man stoop to a bucket of water and try to clear the thick film of dust on top before lifting a dipper to his mouth. The wetness of his lips stood in stark contrast to the gray sameness of his hair and skin.

Moving a little farther along, Sulley noted that the tube hanging high in the ceiling had been torn—likely by falling rocks—and whatever air it was meant to carry in or out escaped like a sigh on a hot day. Muckers loaded debris into the railcars mechanically. No one smiled or joked—not that they could hear themselves above the roar of machinery.

Suddenly a surge of men came pouring toward him, grim-faced and intent on reaching the opening. Joining the exodus,

Sulley tried to make eye contact with someone so he could ask what was happening, but no one would look at him. Then he heard a thudding boom, and a wall of dust so thick it looked like it would knock him down came roiling along the tunnel. The men reached the open air just ahead of the cloud. They stood, many of them gasping and looking utterly defeated. Sulley tried to beat the dust from his clothes. "Don't bother," said a fellow standing nearby. "There's plenty more where that come from."

After about ten minutes, the man with the pistols reappeared and began pushing workers back toward the opening. "Quit your goldbricking. Company ain't paying you to stand around. Get back in there."

The man who had just spoken to Sulley mumbled, "Don't much pay us anyhow," as he trudged back toward the tunnel that swallowed men up behind its curtain of dust.

"You're supposed to let the dust settle before sendin' us back in." The voice rang clear above the knot of men. Sulley stood on tiptoes to see who had spoken. A man—colored, he thought—stood with defiant fists braced on his hips and his feet spread wide. "I ain't going back until it settles some more."

A few other men nodded in agreement. Someone hollered, "That's right."

Sulley had trouble trying to piece together what happened next. He never would have guessed the paunchy man with the pistols could move that fast. But suddenly he was standing over the colored man, whose blood left streaks in the dust on his face. A hulking black man, who Sulley now realized had always been just a step or two behind the man with the pistols, stood with his fists clenched. He'd struck the rabble-rouser. Felled him with a single bloody blow.

"I said get back in there! You're lucky you got a job, and I'll be happy to give it to somebody else if you've got no use for it."

"I ain't going till the dust settles," the man grunted from where he lay, hand to his nose. "You're goin' to kill us all."

The superintendent, or whatever he was, pulled the blackjack from his belt, and Sulley had to look away. But he could hear the thuds, the kicks, the grunts, and other sounds that made his stomach curdle. He waited for someone to step in, but no one did. When he could stand it no longer, he ran from that hellish place.

He found a creek well above the camps and washed what he could of the dust and grime from his skin, shook it from his clothes, and rinsed his mouth over and over, spitting the water on the ground. He felt contaminated—soiled—party to something horribly wrong. He'd bamboozled folks over and over again, but when he did it, well, sometimes they didn't even know it. What he'd witnessed this day felt like pure evil.

After an hour or so of thinking, Sulley roused himself. He decided to go back and wait for that Lewis fellow to get off work. See if he couldn't talk him into leaving this place. He knew it wasn't any of his business—shoot, he specialized in keeping his nose out of other people's business—but he had to do something. He couldn't just walk away from here like these people didn't matter.

He slipped back down the mountain, skirting the camp for the Negroes. Even here, the trees were coated in a fine film of dust, the leaves dull and the bark gray. Sulley felt oddly superstitious about it, like the dust might follow him even when he left here. He saw a man up behind the shacks just sitting, leaning against a rock outcropping. As he drew closer, he saw the bruised and battered face. Was this the man he'd seen beaten earlier? "Hey, buddy, you alright?" he called. The man didn't move. Sulley figured it probably hurt too much. "Need some help?"

Sulley stepped closer, his breath catching on what felt an awful lot like fear. But shame for how he'd run before urged him on. He crouched down and watched the injured man intently. He could not see the rise or fall of his chest. Could not detect air moving from between his lips. He reached out a tentative hand and confirmed what he feared.

The man was dead.

Grief unlike anything he'd ever felt before pierced his soul, nearly felling him. He wrapped his arms around himself, gripping his shirtsleeves in clenched fists. He'd been standing right there. Might have stopped this. Might have done something . . . anything . . .

Sulley leapt to his feet and whirled all around, looking for someone to tell. He saw a white man with a slouch hat walking into the camp—maybe a foreman? "Hey there. I think this man is . . . I mean, he isn't . . ." Sulley couldn't find the words.

The other man walked over. "Is he dead?"

"I think so. Can't see that he's breathing." Sulley felt anger rise where the fear had taken root. "He took a heck of a beating down there at the tunnel today."

The new fellow nudged the leg of the man on the ground with his foot. "Sometimes a beating is what it takes to keep 'em in line. And this one had been sounding pretty sick lately—tunnel pneumonia's what done it, I'd say. I'll get a crew." He moved back among the shacks and returned with four black men, none of whom spoke or even glanced at Sulley. They didn't look all that healthy themselves. "We've got this, unless you aim to help dig the grave," the man in the hat said.

"What about his family?" Sulley said. "What about a funeral?" This time one of the black men cast him a sideways look.

The man in the hat grunted. "Doubt he has any, and funerals are expensive." He nodded at the men. "You know what to do, fellers." Then he pierced Sulley with a look. "And I'd recommend you move along now. The company don't take kindly to meddlers."

Sulley watched them carry the body away. And then he walked as deep into the woods as he could go before falling to his knees.

Now he sat alone, high on a mountain, gazing out over the river. *Tunnelitis. Tunnel pneumonia.* The men digging that infernal tunnel were dying of something. Sulley couldn't get the image of the dead man out of his mind. He couldn't have been dead long. And they just hauled him off to bury like a dog. Would he have a marker? Surely someone would miss him and would wonder what had become of him.

For the first time in his life, Sulley wondered if he would have a marker when he died. If anyone would miss him when he was gone. Probably not. He didn't spend much time anywhere. Didn't have anyone he'd call a friend. And if he had family out there somewhere, they didn't want him when he was alive, so he doubted they'd care when he was dead.

Sulley had never been one for self-pity, but on this day he felt as though the mountains could easily swallow him as if he'd never existed. He wished he'd followed the men and helped them dig that grave. Found out the name of the dead man. Then at least one more person would be able to stand witness to the fact that he had ever existed at all.

Gainey was deeply grateful to have Jeremiah along once they reached the camps around the tunnel project. There were shacks built up around each of the headings where men were burrowing into Gauley Mountain. And while there were women and even a few children around, none of them made Gainey feel overly confident about receiving assistance should she require it.

Jeremiah handily took the lead in asking after James, which was also just as well since Gainey and Arbutus got suspicious looks from almost everyone, and Gainey's sense was that the men didn't much want to talk to her. Especially not in the colored camps, which they soon discovered were separate. It was in the second camp that they found Martha, a woman who had set up a sort of makeshift laundry for the men. When Jeremiah spoke to her, she looked around him to Arbutus.

"Child, does James belong to you?" She eyed Jeremiah and Gainey. "'Cause I know he ain't got nothing to do with these two."

Arbutus, who had been wilting like her namesake in the glare of too much light, squared her shoulders and stepped up. "Yes'm. He's my brother and we got word he's bad sick."

"Hunh. He ain't the only one. What do these ones want with him?" Martha asked, rolling her eyes at the pair of them.

"Miss Gainey is our friend. She's come to fetch him home. We have a wagon." Arbutus puffed her chest out a notch.

"Hunh. If you say so. James is workin' right now." She squinted at the sun. "He oughta be draggin' in any minute now."

"Working?" The word burst from Gainey before she could catch it. "But he's sick."

Martha shook her head, and Gainey noticed the threads of silver in her dark hair. "Rouster don't care who's sick. Only way to get out of work is to hide, and James is too proud for that." Her expression softened. "He's a good boy. Hard worker. Cain't help it if that tunnel's poisoned him." She sighed. "Poisons everybody. Black or white, the tunnel don't care." She nodded behind them. "Here they come now."

Gainey turned to see white men straggling up the hill. She assumed the black men would be following, but as they drew closer, she realized dark skin showed through where they were trying to brush off a thick layer of dust. One man took off his shirt, exposing dark flesh beneath. He gave the shirt a shake, a cloud of dust billowing around him. He headed toward Martha, then stopped abruptly when he saw she wasn't alone.

"Come on up here and give me that shirt, Calvin. I still got a good rinse or two in this wash water." She nodded at her company. "These folks is huntin' James. You seen him?"

Calvin slid his shirt back on. "I'll bring this 'un back when I get another 'un to put on," he said. "James give out a little bit ago. Some of the fellas are carrying him up now."

Arbutus cried out and rushed toward a group of men carrying what looked like a sack of flour. "James!" she wailed. "Is he alive?"

The next moments were a blur for Gainey as she tried to calm Arbutus and ascertain James's condition. Finally, they settled him on a pallet near Martha's shack, and Arbutus was given a bucket of water and a sponge to clean her brother's skin. The boy appeared to be unconscious, although great racking coughs shook his body. Gainey realized she was wringing her hands and forced them to be still. Jeremiah stood with his hat in his hand, looking like a man who wanted to be anywhere else.

She needed some steel for her spine. She whispered, "Lord help me." Not a prayer exactly—more like a plea. But she felt stronger. "Can he travel?" she asked.

"Mebbe," one of the men answered. "But if he don't stay, he won't get his day's pay. That's three dollars gone."

Gainey started to suggest his life was worth a great deal more than three dollars, but the look on Arbutus's face told her that was a significant amount of money. "Where are his things?" she snapped. The man looked confused. "His belongings," she said. "We need to gather his belongings. If he's able to collect his day's pay, we will leave immediately after."

"Belongings." The man pointed. "He stays in that shack over there. If he's got anything, guess that's where it'd be."

"Arbutus, would you go see if there's anything to pack? I'll see to James's pay so we can begin the return journey home."

She saw Martha exchange a look with the men who'd brought James. She would have called it skeptical if she were describing it to someone. "Will one of you direct me to whomever disburses the pay?"

"You might oughta go over to the contractor's shack and talk to Cap," the man said, pointing again.

Gainey squared her shoulders and walked with firm intent. It was her fault James and his family were in this predicament. She would do what she could to see that he received any money due him.

Reaching the door, she rapped on the frame and peered inside. A white man sat with his feet on a table and his slouch hat pulled low over his eyes. He sighed and poked the hat up with one finger. Seeing Gainey, he slowly sat up, dropping his feet to the floor with a thud. "Well now," he said.

It was not the greeting Gainey had expected, yet she did her best to take it in stride as she stepped through the door. "Perhaps you can help me."

"Doubt it," the man said.

She sucked in a sharp breath. "I am Eugenia Floyd and I've come from Mount Lookout to collect James Fridley. He is ill and needs to be nursed properly by a physician as well as his family."

"Company doctor looks after him."

This sounded like good news. "Indeed? I'm glad to hear it. Nonetheless, we are removing him from here and restoring him to his mother."

The man sniggered. "Mama's boy, is he? Guess he is pretty young at that." He waved dismissively. "Go on then, take him. Cain't hardly work anymore anyhow."

Gainey did not care for this fellow. "We will. But first there is the matter of his pay."

"Ha! I knew you was after something. Heard he had to be toted out today. Guess maybe he wasn't worth his pay."

Gainey wet her lips, noticing there was a film of fine grit on them. The man might very well be right. As she hesitated, she felt the boards beneath her feet shift and creak. "We'll be needing his pay," Jeremiah said, his voice deep and oddly thrilling to her ears.

The man flinched and sized Jeremiah up. Apparently he was sufficiently impressed with what he saw. "Alright then." He pulled a box over and lifted out a slip of paper and a pen. "Of course, his shack rent is due, that's seventy-five cents. Then there's the doctor bill, the hospital bill, and the electricity at twenty-five cents each." He scribbled notations, biting his tongue as he did so. "That means he's due a dollar fifty." He wrote something with a flourish and held it out.

Gainey approached, trying to appear confident. "That all seems rather steep."

He snatched the paper back toward him. "I can keep it all if you'd rather."

Suddenly Jeremiah was beside her, leaning on the table. He moved surprisingly fast for a man of his bulk. "Hand the lady that pay right now," he growled.

The man sat motionless for a moment, then slapped the paper down on the table between them. "Go on then. You'll need to go by the commissary to cash it."

Gainey took the paper, lifted her chin, and spun toward the door. She could feel Jeremiah coming close behind her. "I'm sorry," he said. "You didn't ask me to butt in. It's just I've dealt with men like him before and I hated to see him being disrespectful toward you."

A frisson of pleasure took Gainey by surprise. "I'm grateful for your assistance," she said. "Now, I'm off to the commissary." She said the words brightly to hide the fact that she was terrified. Would they give her trouble there as well?

"I'll come along if it's alright. I've never seen a commissary." Jeremiah's eyes twinkled.

Gainey laughed with relief. "That makes two of us."

twelve

Jeremiah's blood had settled to a simmer by the time they walked up to the long commissary building. It was obvious to him that this place was not treating its workers well. And he wasn't at all certain that James was going to live to see his mother. He felt a wave of protectiveness for the woman preceding him through the door into a sort of dining hall as well as a general store. He guessed maybe it was because he felt a generous dose of respect and admiration mixed in as well. This woman had courage.

He followed Gainey closely, glowering at any man who looked her way. It was a rough place, and he was glad he'd come along.

Gainey approached a man behind a tall counter. "I'd like to cash this," she said, pushing the slip of paper toward him. He took it without comment, eyed her up and down, flicked a glance at Jeremiah, sighed, and began counting out cash. He handed over a dollar bill and then some change. Gainey watched. "That's just thirty-five cents," she said. "The check is for a dollar and fifty cents."

The man released a world-weary sigh. "Ten percent fee to cash the check." He squinted at her. "I haven't seen you around."

Gainey's shoulders drew back. "No. You have not. I'll take the check back and cash it at a bank. Thank you."

The man shook his head. "No good at a bank. Company checks can only be cashed at the company commissary." He recited the words like he'd said them a hundred times.

Jeremiah felt his simmer roll back up to a boil. He pushed forward, hands fisted at his sides. But before he could unleash the words ready to spill from his tongue, Gainey had turned and placed a hand in the middle of his chest. It was a firm hand, and he could feel the outline of each finger.

"Some battles cannot be fought in the moment," she said, her voice low and resonant. "I can see the righteous anger ready to be spilled, but I think now is not the time." She glanced back at the man behind the counter, who looked nervous. "I do not suppose this fellow has any real power here. He's only following orders."

"That's right," the man said quickly. Then his face darkened. "What I mean is, I'm the one to enforce the rules around here, and the rules say ten percent for cashing a check."

Gainey narrowed her eyes. "'But woe unto you, Pharisees! for ye tithe mint and rue and all manner of herbs, and pass over judgment and the love of God: these ought ye to have done, and not to leave the other undone.'"

Then she gathered the money and marched out the door. Jeremiah followed her but not before taking a moment to enjoy the flummoxed look on the man's face.

The pair walked in silence for a moment. "That was some pretty fancy Scripture slinging you did back there," Jeremiah said.

Gainey frowned. "I probably should not have done it. It was as though the words welled up in me and I couldn't help but speak them. I've memorized a great many verses over the years, and sometimes it's as if the world calls them out of me." She flushed and glanced sideways at him. "I suppose that sounds odd."

"Maybe," he said. "But I like the way it sounds."

James's eyes were open when they returned with his paltry earnings. Arbutus's face was streaked with tears. It was obvious even to her he wasn't long for the world. The boy's breathing was ragged and rough. Air wheezed in and out over lips tinged a purplish-blue. When Gainey leaned closer, she could hear a crackling sound deep in his chest, like flames consuming fat-wood.

Arbutus had finished cleaning her brother's face and hands and was now trying to brush dust from his clothing. "Stop that," James whispered. Even those two words sent him into a coughing fit. Arbutus held his hand, and Gainey could see that he was squeezing hard, but the girl didn't complain. When he finally got his breath again, he spoke slowly, like he needed to sneak the words out lest he awaken his cough again. "Don't stir that stuff. Bad enough I've breathed it in."

"We've come to take you home," Arbutus said, voice thick as she fought back her tears.

"Be good to see Mama," James rasped.

"Miss Gainey brung me in a cart, and we're gonna load you up and run you on home."

James tried to sit up, which started another coughing fit. Even in his weakened condition he kicked and clutched at his throat as if fighting to get more air inside.

Gainey shifted her alarmed gaze to Martha. "Have you seen this before?"

Martha bit her lip and nodded her head. "Git him home quick as you can."

Gainey felt like she was choking herself. What had she done suggesting this boy come here to find work? She'd condemned him to this unspeakable suffering. And for what? She still held his pay in her hand. She curled her fist around the money, wishing she could fling it away.

"Arbutus," she said, her voice husky. "Here's his pay. Tuck it away somewhere safe."

The girl took the money without really looking at it and shoved it into a pouch she often wore at her waist. She turned her wet face to Gainey. "Can we take him home now?"

Without waiting for an answer, Jeremiah scooped the boy into his arms. Gainey could see now that he had wasted until he was positively skeletal. Each breath was a gasp and seemed to take all his focus and attention. Arbutus scurried ahead of Jeremiah to arrange blankets in the back of the wagon. The big man settled the boy there as though he were a babe.

Gainey swallowed past an impossible lump in her throat. She wanted to cry, to rail at the injustice, but first she needed to get James to his mother.

Jeremiah stepped up beside her. "The ride's going to be rough on him. We'll need to go real slow. Might not make it back before dark."

"You're coming back with us?" Gainey had never considered that Jeremiah might help them. She'd only been offering him a ride.

He gave her a crooked smile. "Seems like the right thing to do."

She choked on a sob. "People so rarely do the right thing. I'm not sure what to say."

"How about say you'll share whatever dinner you packed with me. I could eat a bite as we go."

Gainey realized that she too was hungry. Only eating while James suffered seemed the wrong thing to do. "Let's get a little way away from here and then we can eat," she offered. "Arbutus, are you ready to go?"

"Yes, ma'am." Perched in the back of the wagon beside her brother, the girl looked like a bird ready to take flight.

"Well then." She turned to Martha. "Thank you for your help. I wish there was some way I could be of help to you . . ."

Martha waved an unexpectedly elegant hand in the air. "No trouble. Just glad the boy ain't gonna die alone."

"Oh, but we'll nurse him . . ." The words fell away from Gainey's lips. Martha's expression told her there was no hope. She supposed she'd better get used to thinking that way.

Once they cleared the camp, they pulled over along a little stream, and she retrieved a basket with the last of the previous fall's apples, some cold potatoes in their jackets, and a wedge of corn bread—all provided by Verna.

They didn't even get out of the wagon. Just handed the food around and fell to, trying to eat quickly so they could move on. In spite of the circumstances, Gainey thought it would have been an enchanting spot for a picnic if it hadn't been for the sound of James's breath rasping in and out and in and out and—

Without warning James began to thrash, kicking desperately at the wooden side of the cart and knocking a board loose. He clutched at his throat, almost clawing. Gainey could see his eyes—the whites seemed unnaturally large—and the desperation in them almost stopped her heart. Then he fell back and was still.

Arbutus sobbed and cried for them to help him. Jeremiah took the boy by the shoulders, his hands huge against the boy's frail frame. He gave him a shake and thumped him on the back, but James's head lolled and there was no response. He gently laid the boy back down, bowing his head. He turned wet eyes to Gainey. "His suffering has ended."

Sulley hurried along the road as dusk drew closer. He couldn't wait to get shut of this place. *Curiosity killed the cat,* he thought. And so would working in that tunnel.

His intent was to avoid people as much as possible, so when he heard the sound of voices and saw an olive-green van with a cross on the side, he moved off the road into the brush where he could watch and listen. He guessed the vehicle was some sort of ambulance. Two black men stood nearby, rolling cigarettes. They lit them in the slanted afternoon light.

"I still say we shoulda waited for his widder woman," a man with a thick beard said.

"Cap said to get it done and get back to the tunnel," answered the other man with a drawl. "I ain't talking back to him lest I end up in a box with them other fellers."

"Ain't right," the bearded man continued. "His woman wanted to wash him and dress him in his good clothes."

"Waste of good clothes. Cap's doing her a favor, even if she don't know it."

Sulley shifted his position until he could see through the rear window. There were two wooden boxes just the size of a man. Sulley felt a cold finger trace his spine. How many dead were there?

The second man was speaking again. "Just glad to be out in

the air for once. I'm tired of eatin' that dust all the time." He hacked and spit. "I'm movin' on afore some fool's gotta dig my grave."

"How you gonna make money?"

"Dunno. But I'd rather starve than get buried in this godforsaken place. Might should head back to Georgia."

They continued smoking. Sulley shifted his pack. He wanted to know where they were going. He wanted to know if the man he'd seen beaten and killed was inside one of those boxes. He wanted to . . . help. It was a new feeling for Sulley, and he tried to tamp it down. It was one thing to feel sorrow about a situation and a whole other thing to get mixed up in it.

He told himself he was a fool even as he walked out into the road like he just happened along. The two men looked at him, wide-eyed. Sulley nodded and kept walking past them, but then he stopped and turned back. "Say, you wouldn't be able to give a feller a ride?"

They glanced at each other, their eyes carrying on a conversation Sulley couldn't hear. But if he had to guess, he'd suppose it went something like them wondering if turning down a white man would get them into more trouble than giving a stranger a ride wherever they were headed.

Sulley fished in his pocket and pulled out two nickels. "Got a coin for each of you for your time."

This apparently clinched the deal. The bearded man nodded. "Alright then. We's headed up toward Summersville. Cain't take you no more than that."

Sulley almost changed his mind. That was back the way he'd just come. Then again, maybe he'd start over and head southeast this time. Aim for Lewisburg. He didn't suppose anyone was following him, but if they were, doubling back would be smart. "Right where I'd like to end up," he said and handed over the coins.

The second man went around back and climbed inside with the boxes while the bearded man slid behind the wheel. Sulley climbed in beside him, and they headed out. They drove in silence for a few minutes.

"What's your name?" Sulley asked.

"Calvin. That's Luther in the back."

"Folks call me Sulley." Calvin nodded but didn't take his eyes off the road. "You takin' those . . . crates all the way to Summersville?"

Calvin gave his head a little shake. "Look, friend, you're welcome to ride along, but all them questions make a man nervous."

Sulley understood that. He didn't much like being asked questions, either. "Only reason I ask is . . . well, I walked up on a fellow that was . . . he was just sitting there in the woods and he was—"

"Dead?" Calvin filled in.

"Yeah."

"Might've been Dewey. We lost him today." The man flicked a look toward the back of the van. Sulley guessed Dewey was in one of those boxes.

"What's this tunnelitis folks keep talking about?"

Calvin shrugged. "Not sure. Workers think it's from breathing all that dust the drilling kicks up, but the bosses say it's 'cause we don't eat right or drink too much corn liquor." He rested one elbow in the open window. "Me, I don't touch the stuff."

"You sick with it?" Sulley asked.

"Hope not. They say it steals your wind and makes you cough like you've got the TB." He looked thoughtful. "Guess I can't walk the hills like I used to. Maybe I'm just getting old." He grinned, but it was weak.

"Guess at least Dewey will get a proper burial." Sulley cut his eyes at Calvin. He was fishing to know if this was a funeral procession.

Calvin unleashed an expletive and slapped the steering wheel. "Ain't nobody dies on that job gets buried proper. Not even the white folk." Whatever reticence he'd been feeling gave way with his indignation. "And the black folk—shoot, stack 'em up like cordwood and pile 'em two and three at a time in one grave. I reckon there's a reason we haul them poor souls twenty-five miles up to the undertaker's mama's farm to bury in a cornfield."

This was more information than Sulley figured on getting, and he didn't quite know what to do with it. "So," he said at last, "you want help burying those boxes in the back?"

Calvin shook his head and sighed. "I hope you ain't meaning to get us in trouble, but since you offered, well, I ain't gonna turn down the help."

thirteen

They covered James with a blanket, and Arbutus lay down beside him in the wagon, alone in her sorrow.

"Evening's coming on," Jeremiah said. "I hate to disturb her, but we'd best get going."

Gainey nodded, unable to speak through her own sorrow. They traveled in silence for a long time, passing the occasional automobile or local astride a horse. Gainey did her best to sift through her feelings. Guilt for having suggested James leave home to work. Anger at the conditions she'd seen at the camp at Gauley Bridge. Frustration that she could not help. And threading them all together was sorrow. A son dead, a child lost, a brother taken too soon. How was she going to face Verna with this? Especially knowing firsthand the agony of having a child torn from her.

As they wound up the mountain toward Ansted—the midpoint on their way home—Gainey felt an overwhelming need to take action. When others had insisted she give up the child she'd brought into the world, she'd given in. She'd looked into that sweet, perfect face and allowed the fear and the shame to pry him from her arms. It had taken many years, but she had finally found the grace to accept that God could forgive even such a sin as that. Although it was a few years more before she'd been able to forgive herself. Realizing that it was foolish to withhold what God himself so freely gave finally convinced her. But now—could she forgive herself now if she turned a blind eye to the suffering of so many other mothers' sons?

Gainey grasped Jeremiah's arm so that he looked down at her. "I want you to go with Arbutus to take James to the family." Gainey had a plan and she anticipated resistance. "I'd also appreciate it if you would deliver a letter to Susan at the store. She'll need to continue minding the post office for a time, which I'm confident she can do once Arbutus has returned to help with customers."

Jeremiah furrowed his brow. "What in tarnation are you talking about?"

"I intend to stay and provide nursing for the men who are sick. It seems the company doctor isn't doing very much for them." Gainey tried to speak the way she would if she were talking about plans to attend a quilting party or a corn shucking. There really wasn't anything out of the ordinary about a good Christian lady stepping in to offer help where it was needed.

"What kind of foolish—" Jeremiah caught himself. "I know it's not my place to say, but it seems like those camps aren't the safest spot for a gentlewoman like yourself."

Gainey was momentarily distracted by the pleasure of being referred to as a "gentlewoman" by this bear of a man. Still, she would not be dissuaded from her plan. "I understand I may find appropriate lodgings at the Tyree Tavern in Ansted, and it is but two and a half miles from there to the camps at Hawks Nest." She clasped her hands more tightly. "We'll pass it shortly. When I'm unable to find transportation to the camps, the walk will do me good."

Jeremiah opened his mouth and then clamped it shut again. "While I haven't known you long, I get the sense you're a woman who isn't easily swayed by the opinions of others."

Gainey swallowed hard. "I was once." She used the flat of her hand to smooth back some wayward strands of hair she could feel tickling her forehead. "I have since learned that God's opinion is the only one that matters, and He is clear on the point of caring for our fellow sufferers in this world." She looked back toward the river, picturing the place where men disappeared into the bowels of the mountain. "'Freely ye have received. Freely give.'" She wasn't sure Jeremiah heard those last words, but she didn't need him to. She'd been speaking to shore up her own resolve.

Jeremiah narrowed his eyes and tugged at his ear. "I . . ." He shook his head. "Never mind. Takes courage to do what you're doing. I admire that."

"Thank you," Gainey said, though she longed for the words to say so much more.

They soon arrived at Tyree Tavern, also known as the Half-way House since it was located almost exactly halfway between Charleston and Lewisburg. Arbutus seemed to have gone to sleep—or perhaps she simply didn't have the strength to look upon her brother. Gainey climbed down and reached over the side of the wagon to squeeze the girl's shoulder. "Your mother will need you now more than ever," she said in case Arbutus was listening. "You are a blessing to her." She paused, not sure what else to say. "Remember the good days and trust they will come again." She saw that tears were dripping from the girl's nose and turned quickly before she lost her own composure. That was something she could do later—when she was alone.

"I don't much like leaving you here," Jeremiah said.

She pulled an envelope from her satchel and scribbled a note to Susan on it. "And I regret interrupting your business," Gainey answered, handing him the slip of paper. "But if I leave this place, I'm afraid I will lose my resolve to return."

"That sounds like a good reason to haul you on back to your postal counter."

Gainey allowed herself a thin smile. "I don't believe anyone has ever successfully hauled me anywhere."

Jeremiah laughed, a deep resonant sound that soothed Gainey. "Well then, I'll pretend I'm leaving you here by choice." He winked. "To save my masculine pride." Gainey thought she might be blushing but knew she was too old for such nonsense. "You be careful now," he said in a more serious tone. Then he nodded and drove the cart away. Gainey watched it go, trying not to feel as if she'd been left on an island and was watching the last boat disappear toward the horizon.

Smoothing her hair and straightening her shoulders, she turned and stepped up onto the porch. There was an exterior staircase leading to the second floor and two front doors. She chose to enter through the one on the right. Emblazoned on the lintel were the words *1862 Head Quarters of the Chicago Gray Dragoons*. She assumed it had something to do with the Civil War. She'd been born just fifteen years after those words were carved. Her father had even shared memories of seeing the soldiers when he was a boy. Of course, that was when her father still claimed her. She hadn't spoken to him in decades and hadn't heard anything about him since her mother died five years earlier. Even when Mother was alive, letters had been few and far between.

Gainey broke her reverie and pulled the door open. Inside, she arranged for a room and then went back outside to climb the stairs to her lodgings. The room wasn't large, but it was tidy and provided what she needed for comfort. She set her bag on the candlewick bedspread, then sat down and had a good, long cry.

Darkness was upon them by the time the truck with its strange cargo pulled up at a field outside of Summersville. Calvin shut off the engine and they sat for a moment. The days had been plenty warm as the calendar moved into July, but once the sun disappeared, the nights cooled off.

"We gonna camp out and bury 'em in the morning?" Sulley asked.

Calvin snorted. "Man, the whole reason we're here right now is we bury 'em at night." He gave Sulley a hard look. "You sure you want to help with this? Might be some folks wouldn't appreciate it."

Sulley wasn't at all sure he wanted to help. He'd made a lifelong habit of never forming attachments, but seeing what happened to Dewey, how he stood up for what was right and then died because of it . . . An old wound had broken open inside. Back at the orphanage, Franklin, the black handyman, had been his only friend. He'd plowed the garden, milked the skinny cow, and fixed anything that broke. If Franklin couldn't fix it, it couldn't be fixed. He'd let the kids tag along behind him as long as the matrons weren't around. He didn't exactly welcome them, but he didn't shoo them away either, especially not Sulley.

And he'd even taught Sulley a few things. Like dowsing. One day a matron accused Sulley of stealing some buns from the kitchen. He hadn't done it. At least not that time. And Franklin stood up for him, said Sulley had been with him all morning and couldn't have taken the food. The man in charge of the orphanage had them both whipped. Sulley for stealing and Franklin for lying. Sulley had raged and railed, screamed, kicked, and bit so that the man tasked with whipping him finally gave up after a couple of licks. Franklin, though, he just took it. Bared his back and flinched each time the slender branch the man used bit into his skin. Sulley had run away the next morning and decided from then on no one would have the upper hand against him again.

What happened to Dewey made him wish he could go back and stand up for Franklin. Sulley pushed the memories aside and reached for the door handle. "Don't know why I'd start caring what folks think at this late date," he said. Then they all climbed out of the van and took up their shovels.

It was serious work. Sulley had been party to digging many a hole, whether he was holding a shovel or just watching in case he needed to make a quick getaway. Men would sweat and curse, but they would also laugh and tell stories. There was a camaraderie among men working together that often made the job lighter. Not so this night.

The only sounds were the *chunk* and *thud* of shovels slicing into soil and piling up dirt, along with the occasional call of a night bird. Calvin lit a lantern as the night drew close around them. The air cooled, making the work a little easier. And the fact that they were digging in the middle of an old cornfield meant there weren't too many roots, although rocks were plentiful.

Sulley stopped a moment to lean on his shovel and catch his breath. Calvin did the same while Luther went to the truck to fetch a jug of water. He'd uncapped it and started to take a drink when Calvin gave him a sharp look and nodded to Sulley.

Luther wiped the mouth of the jug with his sleeve and handed it over. Shame washed over Sulley, but he figured the only way to make it worse would be to refuse the first drink. He took the jug and swallowed a great mouthful of the cool water, then handed it back.

As the men drank in the dim light of the lantern, a whippoorwill began calling. They all stood and listened for a moment. "Bad to hear a whippoorwill call near the house," Luther said. "Sign somebody's gonna die."

"We ain't near a house, and a whole lot of somebodies are already dead," Calvin answered. "I hear Indians say if you answer the call and the bird calls back, it means you'll have a long life."

Luther tilted his head back and whistled a perfect *whip-poor-will.* He was met with silence. "What's it mean if they don't answer?" he asked.

"Don't matter," Calvin said. "Pure nonsense."

"What's it mean?" Luther demanded.

"Aw, the way it goes is if they don't call back, you're gonna die, but it's just a foolish superstition. Probably only applies if you're an Indian."

Sulley could see that Luther's eyes had widened, and he jerked out a handkerchief to wipe his neck. Just then, the bird called again. Luther released a burst of air that was almost a laugh. He coughed—a harsh, hacking sound, then cleared his throat. "Guess we all gonna die sometime."

"Sure enough," Calvin said. "Now let's get this job done so's we can get on with living before we gotta die."

Once they'd covered their cargo over with dirt, the three men settled in to get some sleep. Calvin stretched out on the front seat of the van while Luther lay down in the back now that it was empty. Sulley found a likely spot on the ground—his preferred location for sleeping.

His rest was fitful at best. That doggone whippoorwill called throughout the night, his whistle growing sharper and faster as morning crept toward them. Finally, Sulley must have slept because he suddenly sat up as if someone had just walked across his own grave. He looked around, thinking something must have awakened him.

The sun was just sending its first trial rays over the horizon, and while the whippoorwill had stopped, other birds were tuning up their morning chorus. Sulley squinted and rubbed his eyes. What had startled him?

All was quiet at the truck. Or rather, he could hear Luther sawing logs but nothing else. He stood and stretched the kinks out of his back and took in his surroundings now that he could see them more clearly. The field they'd been digging in was pocked with what Sulley could only assume were graves. Too many graves. The chill he felt was more than the cool morning air could account for.

And then he saw it. In the far edge of the field, there was a massive tree, one of the chestnuts that had yet to succumb to blight. It must've stood nearly a hundred feet tall with a trunk bigger than some houses he'd seen. And from this angle he could see something odd—like somebody had climbed up there and took a chisel to the bark. He remembered the story the old-timer told him about the Phillips gold being buried at the foot of the cross. He walked toward the truck and examined the tree from another angle. Nothing. He walked back to where he'd started. There it was again—lines carved into the trunk in the undeniable shape of a cross.

Sulley chewed his lip. Probably nothing. Pure coincidence. But since he was here . . . might be worth checking out. "You need a ride anywhere else?" Calvin dropped from the truck and went to the edge of the field to relieve himself.

"Naw." Sulley walked over to the truck. "Guess I'll walk from here."

"We can at least drop you nearer civilization," Luther said, emerging from the back.

"Never had much use for civilization," Sulley said. "Say, could you leave me one of them shovels?"

Calvin frowned. "Cap keeps up with his tools pretty good."

"You could tell him you left it here for next time," Sulley suggested. "I'll leave it over there along the fence when I'm done."

Calvin shook his head. "Man, I don't want to know what you want it for, but I reckon it's the least we can do for the way you helped."

"Appreciate it," Sulley said as the men got into the truck and began their journey back to Hawks Nest.

fourteen

Jeremiah wasn't sure how he'd gotten so far off track. Maybe he'd just been on this wild goose chase so long he didn't care anymore. Or maybe he'd found something more important to care about.

It was well past dark by the time he passed his own broken-down car on the side of the road. Arbutus stood in the bed of the wagon behind him, holding on to the back of the seat. She'd been all light and laughter on the way to Gauley Bridge, but now she was pure solemn. Jeremiah dreaded the moment they would arrive at the Fridley farm.

"Do you think James is in heaven?"

Jeremiah wasn't prepared for the question whispering over his shoulder in the moonlight. "I expect so," he said.

"I hope I get to go to heaven, too."

"Can't see why you wouldn't," Jeremiah offered, trying to sound cheerful.

"I'm not always good."

Jeremiah slowed the mule to a stop and turned to look into the girl's big sad eyes. "No one is. That's not how you get to heaven."

She ducked her head and sighed. "I know. Jesus takes you there. Cain't get there any other way." She looked up again. "It's just, I worry I might do something so bad He won't take me after all."

Jeremiah pondered that. While he taught Scripture lessons at school, this conversation was deeper than he was used to. "Did you ever make your daddy mad?" he asked. "I mean really mad?"

She almost smiled. "Yes sir. Real mad. Maybe more than once."

"Did he stop loving you?"

She shrugged. "He whipped me that once, but I guess he still loved me."

"Right. And God loves you more than your daddy does. No matter how mad you make Him, He'll still love you." Jeremiah looked at the draped figure at Arbutus's feet and felt a lump rise in his throat. The mule shifted, likely eager to get on home now that they were close. "Not all daddies are as good as yours, but God, He's good all the time."

Arbutus nodded and smiled like she was testing her lips to see if they could still do it. "Guess me and James will see each other again, then." She glanced at the body. "One day."

"I'm sure of it," Jeremiah said past a sudden hoarseness. He turned and clucked to the mule.

It wasn't but ten minutes more before the Fridley farm came into view, shadowy and silent in the darkness. Arbutus's hand tucked around his upper arm. He thought she might not even realize she'd done it. And he was surprised at how much he liked the feel of her fingers pressed against his rough shirt. There was something trusting about it that gave him strength. And when he saw Verna step out onto the porch, face bright with hope even in the dim light, he knew strength was what he was going to need.

Verna rushed down the steps and then stopped like she'd come to an invisible fence. She strained on tiptoes, the look of hope shifting to worry. Jeremiah stopped the cart, and she walked toward them, slow and careful, as though the ground might turn to quicksand beneath her feet. Arbutus's grip tightened, and he could feel her nails digging in even through the cloth of his shirt.

"Did you find . . . ?" Verna's voice trailed off as if she'd forgotten what she meant to say. "Arbutus, is your brother . . . ?"

Those small, strong fingers let go, and the girl jumped down to meet her mother. "We found him, Mama. I got to talk to him some before he . . . before he . . ." Her face crumpled, and Verna rushed to the cart. She grabbed the side and sagged against it as though it were a boat and she was drowning at sea.

Jeremiah couldn't think what to do. He wished Reggie were there.

"Will you . . . Mr. Jeremiah, will you . . . ?"

He realized Verna was talking to him, although her eyes were fixed desperately on the figure under the cloth. He reached back and gently pulled the fabric aside. The sound that came from Verna was like a rabbit caught in a trap. Arbutus rushed to her mother, pushing up under her arm close to her side. Jeremiah couldn't tell if it was for comfort or to keep her mother from falling to the ground.

"We'll see him again in heaven, Mama, I know we will," Arbutus kept saying over and over. "We'll see him again."

Reggie appeared then and lifted his son's body from the cart. He turned bottomless-well eyes on Jeremiah and nodded once before carrying the body into the house while Arbutus helped her mother to follow.

Jeremiah thought he might should go inside and offer to

help, but no one turned to look at him and he figured they didn't much need him right then. He cleared his throat. "Get on, mule," he said in a voice he barely recognized. The mule twitched its ears and plodded on from that place of tears.

Gainey was in over her head, yet she would never admit it in a hundred years. At least not out loud. Though in her heart she was crying out, no one needed to know that.

The worst of the cases were in the camps for black men, but there were plenty of white men with the hacking cough, the loss of strength, and the wasting frame. And, alarmingly, many more who still looked robust enough but were clearly in the early stages of what they called "tunnelitis."

Just in her first day she had seen the dust billowing from the tunnel, had seen their clothing covered in what looked like flour, had seen them ingesting the dust on their food and even in a layer on the surface of water in buckets. It was everywhere. And she felt certain it was responsible for the horrors these men were suffering.

"Got another 'un for ya to look at, Miss Gainey." Martha shuffled toward her as soon as Gainey drew near. The washerwoman had become Gainey's unsolicited assistant. She knew who was sick, how bad off they were, and if they'd let someone help. "He done hid from the rouster this mornin' so he wouldn't have to go into that tunnel. He's up there in his cot now." She pointed toward a tar-paper shack with its door standing open.

The July morning was humid, and Gainey knew it would get worse. She'd already sweated through her shirtwaist. She wished she'd asked Susan to send her a few items of clothing when she sent her note. Of course, seeing how the men lived—some with wives and children—in the tiny shacks with hardly any belongings . . . well, she knew she was blessed to have a clean shirt back at the tavern to change into. Not to mention clean water to rinse this one out.

Thankfully, she'd been given a ride in a truck by a farmer that morning. A garrulous fellow who had much to say about how the tunnel work was spoiling the natural beauty of the area and bringing in "all kinds of riffraff" to overcrowd their towns. Gainey did not tell him that she was nursing the riffraff; she was simply grateful that the man was polite. She'd been subjected to quite a few crude comments and even intimidating looks, although once Martha dressed the men down and they realized she was there to help, they gentled.

All in all, Jeremiah had been right. This wasn't a safe place. There were tales of men beaten to death while drinking or gambling. Of others hearing there was work and, flat broke, hopping trains to West Virginia and being thrown from moving cars by bulls. Of women waylaid when traveling alone. But Martha was spreading word that she was to be treated kindly. And while not everyone welcomed her, enough did that she felt, if not safe, at least appreciated.

Steeling herself for what she would find, she trudged up to the shack. She carried what food and clean water she had been able to scrounge and wished she had enough medical knowledge to do something more than meet the basic needs of the men who were suffering. As she neared the open door, she recognized the smell of too many bodies living in close proximity. Some of the shacks, though meant for only four men, housed ten or more. Even when empty, the walls and sparse furnishings reeked with what was surely the scent of desperation.

She poked her head inside and saw a man flat on his back on

one of the filthy bunks. He lifted his head at the scuff of her boot and sat bolt upright as he was convulsed in violent coughing. He placed both hands on his chest as though he could physically push his lungs open to accept more air. When he stopped, he managed a feeble grin. "You the one comin' round to doctor us sick ones?"

"I wouldn't call it doctoring," Gainey said, holding her breath as she stepped inside. "But I hope I might offer you some comfort."

"I could use a whole bushel of that."

She reached into her basket and pulled out a jar of chicken broth and a baked sweet potato. "Good food is a start. Do you feel like eating?"

"Naw, but if'n you think it'll help, I'll get it down." He took the potato and peeled the loose skin back. "I sure enough like a sweet tater." He took a breath, his whole body rising and falling with the effort it required to breathe in and out. He nibbled at the potato. "That's good," he said, but Gainey suspected he was only humoring her.

"Can you get out in the fresh air somewhere?" she asked. "Away from the camp?"

A smile quirked his mouth. "Far enough, I reckon. That's where I gotta go to hide from the rouster. If I had a way, I'd leave from here." He took another bite. "I'm sure as shootin' not going back in that hole."

Gainey bit the inside of her cheek, trying to think how she could help him escape this place. "I don't suppose you have any money?"

"Naw. Store takes back every penny a man earns." He shook his head, slow and mournful. "Come here to get ahead, and now look at me."

Gainey felt frustration rise but was determined not to let it show. "I shall ponder how we might get you away from here. Where are you from?"

"Virginny. Down Roanoke way. Some feller come 'round with chits to ride the train up here and go to work." He wrapped the potato in a handkerchief and lay back down. "And here I lay, weak as a new foal. Shoulda known when it sounded too good to be true."

"Do you have family there?"

"Not to speak of." He laughed and coughed but the fit was short this time. "Guess I should say not that'll speak to me." His laugh was a heavy *hunh hunh*, each sound accompanied by a short puff of air.

Gainey sighed. There was little else she could do for this man. She reached into the deep pocket of her skirt and extracted a bottle. She was opposed to strong drink, but Martha had recommended this blend of corn liquor and honey as a remedy for coughing. She'd persuaded Ruth, the proprietress of the Tyree Tavern, to let her have some old bottles that had accumulated in the pantry. She was afraid they'd held hair tonic but wasn't in a position to be particular. Then she'd used some of the money she'd brought—which was little enough—to buy a bottle of moonshine and a jar of honey, again with Martha's help. They'd filled seven bottles after she arrived and had already handed out five, counting this one.

"Take a tablespoon of this to help the coughing," she said. "Probably best to take it when you're ready to sleep."

The man held the bottle up to the light coming from the door. It cast a swath of amber across his face, making his dusky skin glow. "Pretty as it is, it's bound to help." He swallowed and hung his head. "I'm ashamed I can't pay you for all this."

"I am only glad I am able to do something." Gainey took up her basket and turned, then stopped, staring out the door. "I had a son once."

"He a good boy?"

"I don't know. I gave him away." She was appalled at her lack of control, blurting such a thing out to a stranger. And a colored man at that. But she couldn't seem to stop. "I hope that if he were ill, someone would look after him."

"I'll be praying for him."

Gainey fought the tears rising in her throat. "Then you will have paid me well."

fifteen

Sulley waited until dusk was falling before finding the perfect dowsing rod. There weren't any peach trees, but he found a hazel and that was almost as good. He'd only seen one car go by all day and no one on foot, so he guessed there weren't many folks coming around, but if there was one thing he'd learned in his twenty-eight years it was that a man could never be too careful.

As the moon rose, he made his way to the tree where he'd seen the rough cross. Sure enough, the lines seemed plainer and plainer each time he looked at them. He closed his eyes and held the forked hazel stick loosely in his hands, palms up. He let it balance there, easy and gentle. Then he opened his eyes and began walking back and forth, slow and steady. He knew it was supposed to work better with a gold coin or piece of gold jewelry, but if he had such as that he wouldn't be out chasing after tall tales. Not to mention the fact that he was skeptical about anyone's ability to dowse for gold regardless.

On the third pass he thought he felt something. A twitch of the fresh wood against his palm. He backed up and moved forward again. There, a distinct quiver. Maybe even a tug. He'd felt a pull like that dozens of times before. Had even faked it many a time. But tonight the movement of the inanimate stick in his hand made a chill crawl up between his shoulders and spread across his chest.

Then the end of the stick dipped downward dramatically—a definite motion that made him breathe in sharp and freeze. He'd never felt anything like that before. He realized he was panting as though he'd been running. He paused to let his breathing even out and kicked at the sticks and leaf litter thick on the ground beneath his feet. He knelt and cleared a patch of dirt. Now that was odd . . .

The sound of a truck motor laboring along the road made him drop the stick and duck down. Headlights flashed over his head and came to rest along the fence on the far side of the field. The engine sputtered and died. Doors creaked open and slammed shut as voices spoke softly. Too softly for him to make out. He figured it might be Calvin and Luther come back. But then again, it might not. He jammed his dowsing rod in the ground and sifted leaves back over the patch he'd cleared. Then he half crawled over to and through the fence. Unmown hay had grown up tall on the other side, and he crept closer to the newcomers, careful not to make too much of a rustle or disturbance. He crouched behind a tangle of multiflora rose and listened to voices that did not belong to the men he'd worked with the night before.

". . . up here tonight. I say one big hole's enough." Another man grunted in response, and the first spoke again. "It's not like anybody's gonna come put flowers on the grave." They sniggered, then came the clanking of tools. "Say, there's a shovel over there at the fence. Them good-for-nothin' coloreds must've left it. Cain't trust 'em to take care of anything."

Someone came closer to get the shovel Calvin had left behind. Sulley ducked and tried to shrink in on himself. He nearly stopped breathing, until the figure moved away again.

The second man spoke. "Best get to digging. Even if it's just one hole, it'll have to be big."

Sulley didn't care for the sound of that. He eased on down the fence line until he came to the road well behind the truck. He slipped into the ditch and made his way to the tree line, then quickly lost himself in the forest. He'd come back in the morning.

But when the sun rose and Sulley ambled back along the road, whistling with his hands in his pockets, he saw that the truck was still parked in the field. The two men—both white—were sprawled on bedrolls, sound asleep. They began to rouse as a rooster crowed nearby.

A third man walked around the truck and spotted Sulley. "Hey there. What are you doing here?" He sounded angry. "This is private property. Get on now!"

Sulley had thought to try to see what he could learn from the men, but when he saw the pistol on the third man's hip, he held up both hands, ducked his head and hurried on his way.

"And keep outta here!" the man yelled after him.

He was just going to have to come back after they were good and gone.

Sulley jiggled some coins in his pocket—part of what Freeman had paid him. Summersville wasn't far, and he wouldn't mind spending a little on a restaurant meal. He hadn't eaten proper since leaving Mount Lookout. He'd just go treat himself to a real breakfast and return here later. He glanced over his shoulder and saw all three men were staring after him now. Much later.

Jeremiah couldn't stand it. He'd thought to resume his search for Sullivan Harris, but he was losing his taste for the hunt. And there was a good family hurting nearby. Not to mention a fine woman trying to be a help back at the tunnel. Seemed like there were more important things he could be doing than going on a wild goose chase.

And if he was being honest with himself, he simply couldn't get Gainey Floyd out of his mind.

He stepped inside the Mount Lookout General Store not quite sure what he was after. As if he could buy something that would put his mind at ease. He stuck a hand in his pocket and laughed. As if he could buy anything.

Susan Legg stood behind the postal counter pulling mail out of a sack. When she saw him, she waved him over. "Any chance you'd go fetch Gainey back home?" She looked frazzled. Tired.

"Be glad to, if she'll come," he replied.

The storekeeper blew a strand of hair from in front of her eyes. "You might be able to persuade her if you'd but try." She looked at him over glasses perched on her nose. "You're a good-looking fellow. She might act like an old maid, but she's not immune."

Jeremiah felt his face heat and hoped his beard hid the worst of it. "I don't know what you mean."

Susan shook her head. "Don't pull that act with me. I saw you looking at her. She's a fine woman—a good woman. I'm betting you're the sort to see more than skin-deep."

"What if I were? What difference would that make? I live up in Kline. Got a house and some land. Got a life far from here."

And, he failed to add, a woman most of the town expected him to marry.

Susan pulled out more envelopes and began sorting through them. "Well, if you can't see the potential, then I wish you'd just go get her and haul her home for my sake. Arbutus tries hard, but she's like a bird with a broken wing right now." She began sliding mail into slots. "And I'm plumb tired of running the store and the post office."

Jeremiah drifted over to the case with handkerchiefs in it, and Susan let him go—apparently deciding she'd given him enough to chew on. And she had. He did admire Gainey. When he set her up in his mind next to Meredith, it was like comparing a fully grown oak tree to a spring redbud. The redbud might be pretty, but it wasn't much for providing shade or fruit or anything else. And he'd always liked the look of an oak.

"Reckon I can use your cart again?" he asked Susan.

"I wish you would," she said.

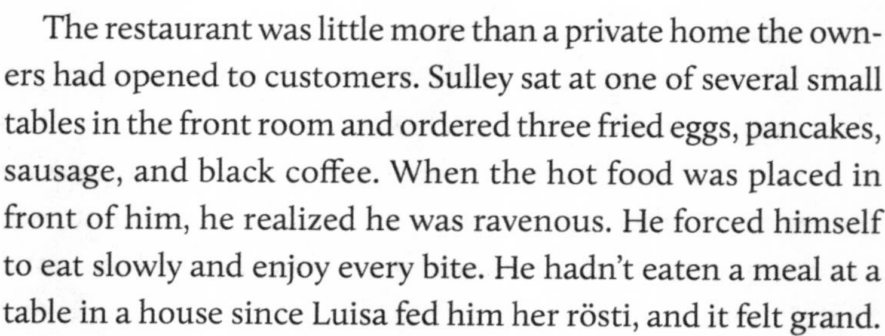

The restaurant was little more than a private home the owners had opened to customers. Sulley sat at one of several small tables in the front room and ordered three fried eggs, pancakes, sausage, and black coffee. When the hot food was placed in front of him, he realized he was ravenous. He forced himself to eat slowly and enjoy every bite. He hadn't eaten a meal at a table in a house since Luisa fed him her rösti, and it felt grand.

Customers sat at two other tables. As Sulley savored his meal, he tuned his ears to pick out anything interesting. Most of the talk was of farming and family, but when the colored girl waiting on them came in the room with more coffee, the conversation changed.

"Junie, what's this I hear about the Fridley boy over in Mount Lookout?" a man asked.

Sulley inclined an ear, although he supposed there were plenty of Fridleys around. Not likely the ones he knew.

"Oh, Mr. Spangler, he come home dead from working in that tunnel down to Gauley Bridge. His mama cain't hardly stand it, I hear. They had him laid out two days now and they've gotta bury him tomorrow."

"I guess so," the man answered. "Good folks. Reggie's helped with my tobacco a time or two." He shook his head. "Shame. I hear they're dropping like flies down there around the tunnel."

The girl came to fill Sulley's cup next. "Is that Reggie and Verna's boy you were talking about?" he asked.

"Yes sir. You know them?"

"I . . . Yes, I do."

"They'll do the buryin' tomorrow. Guess lots of folks will go to help lay poor James to rest." Sulley nodded and pushed his plate away with a few bites still on it. "You done?" the girl asked.

"Yeah. Guess my appetite wasn't quite as big as I thought."

She sloshed more coffee into his cup, then took his plate to the kitchen. Sulley sat and stared out the window. He'd never in his life gone back to a place where he'd found a well. Water or no water, he always took his money and moved on. But the thought of Reggie, Verna, and Arbutus mourning the loss of their son and brother made his eyes prickle and his throat tighten. Maybe it was the thought of a mother losing a child she actually wanted—loved and cared for. Maybe it was the thought of poor Dewey back there in the field without anyone to cry over him.

He laid some money on the table and retrieved his pack from the front porch. He guessed the Phillips gold had waited this long for somebody to find it. It could wait a little while longer.

sixteen

Jeremiah couldn't stop thinking about Gainey alone down there in those camps around Hawks Nest and Gauley Bridge. Susan had given him some of her things to take to her—clothes mostly—but also her Bible and a book of Wordsworth's poetry. She'd also given him strict instructions to try to talk her into coming home before he let on that he'd brought all that plunder. "This is just in case," Susan said as she hid the parcel under the seat.

As he started out of town, Jeremiah realized he'd go right by the Fridleys. They were burying James today. Maybe he could give them his condolences and still make it to Hawks Nest before suppertime.

When Jeremiah pulled up in the yard, Arbutus was sitting on the edge of the porch, drawing circles in the dirt with her big toe. He climbed down and sat beside her.

"Where're your ma and pa?" he asked.

"Daddy's talking to the preacher. Mama ain't left James since you brung him home."

"Is she inside?" The girl nodded. "Think it'd be alright for me to go in and speak to her?" Arbutus shrugged.

Jeremiah made his way in, trying to step lightly. Verna and two other women sat in the front room, where James was laid out on a wide board balanced across two kitchen chairs. He was dressed in a shirt and tie with a quilt tucked over him. A kerchief had been tied under his chin to keep his mouth closed. Jeremiah had seen many a body dressed for the wake, but it never got easier.

As he drew closer, he saw that James had been covered with a graveyard quilt in somber grays, browns, and blacks. The coffin-shaped piece of fabric with the boy's name on it had been moved to the center square and stitched neatly in place. Jeremiah saw other names there—those who had gone on before. His own mother kept a graveyard quilt. He was the only one of his siblings to have lived past the age of twenty. Illness, accidents, old age—too many names had been moved from the edge of the quilt to the center. Once his mother died, he wondered who would move his own block and stitch it down when the time came?

Verna's eyes were red-rimmed, and her face looked dull, as though grief had stolen something from her flesh. Jeremiah shifted from foot to foot, his hat in his hand. "I've come to pay my respects," he said. "Then I'm headed on to see about Gainey."

Verna's eyes lifted at the mention of Gainey. "You gonna bring her back home?"

"Sure hope so." He tried a smile. "Although I get the feeling she does what she wants most of the time."

"Does what she knows is right," Verna said. She reached a tremulous hand toward her son. "Like fetching my boy."

Jeremiah twisted his hat. "I could stay to help with the burying. An extra hand rarely goes amiss. Then I'll head on down to Ansted after—"

"You go on now," Verna cut him off, her face livening for the first time since he came in. "We got plenty of help for James's homegoing, and Gainey needs someone like you to look after her." A tear slid from her eye down her cheek. Jeremiah had the notion she didn't even know it. "You will look after her—won't you?"

Jeremiah cleared his throat. "If she'll let me, it'd be my pleasure."

Verna nodded and turned to the woman on her left. "Fetch Mr. Weber here some of that food in the kitchen for his trip." She took a deep breath and sat up a little straighter. "Folks brought enough to feed the whole county. You take some for you and Miss Gainey."

As he climbed back in the wagon, a poke of food stowed with Gainey's things, he marveled that he'd come here to try to be a help and had been helped instead. The Lord surely did work in mysterious ways.

As Sulley approached the Fridleys' house, he saw a cart headed toward the turnpike as well as some men working on a knoll. He veered toward the men. If he wasn't mistaken, they were digging the grave, and that was something he knew a thing or two about.

The men worked steadily, shirts stained with sweat and faces glistening. There were several grave markers that looked homemade. Must be a family burying ground. Sulley walked up to Reggie, touched him on the shoulder, and reached for his shovel. Reggie handed it over and stepped aside, wiping his face and neck with a bandanna.

"That boy was supposed to dig my grave, not the other way around," he said.

"Too many things in this world don't go the way they're supposed to," Sulley said, dropping into the growing hole with another fellow and sinking the shovel with a solid *chunk*. He heaved some dirt onto the pile, where a third white-haired man sat, a jar of water sweating at his feet.

"The Lord uses the sinful things of this world to show us how good He is." The man picked up a handful of soil in his huge, callused hand and let it fall through his fingers. "'The world passeth away, but he that doeth the will of God abideth forever.'"

He looked hard at each of the men, and Sulley was surprised to see that he had eyes like the flash of a bluebird's wing in contrast to his mahogany skin. "James was a good man. Honored his father and mother. Worked hard. Loved the Lord. God will find a way to use his dying for good."

Sulley glanced at Reggie and saw that tears washed his face as he spoke. "Thank you, Reverend. I know you're speaking true, but it's real hard to remember it when it seems like you're laying hope in the ground and covering it over."

The man stood slowly, like it took some effort to straighten his limbs. He limped over to Reggie and laid one of those big hands on his shoulder. "You tell your doubts and fears to God. You tell Him all about your hurt and sadness. You tell Him how mad at Him you are." He smiled and those blue eyes lit. "He's big enough to take it."

Reggie smiled through his tears, and Sulley was struck by what a handsome fellow he was. There was something . . . beautiful about the man. Sulley felt a stab of lonesomeness just then. At least James had a father and a mother to weep over his grave. Sulley didn't have anyone. He put his head down and went back to digging. But even as he tried to make himself tired enough to forget, he thought he could feel lake-blue eyes boring into his soul.

The funeral service was a lengthy affair with much singing and even some wailing, but once it was done and the handful of white folks had gone home—except for Sulley—the Fridleys' friends and family began the procession to the gravesite.

The dark-skinned, blue-eyed preacher led the way. Once they were all in motion, he began to sing: "'There's a better day a-comin', fare ye well, fare ye well.'"

Everyone joined in on *fare ye well*, their voices swelling into the sky. The man repeated the first line and then moved on to: "'When I see King Jesus, fare ye well, fare ye well.'"

The words of the chorus were "'In that great gittin' up mornin', fare ye well, fare ye well,'" and even Sulley found himself joining in. The way the rhythm and cadence of the lyrics matched the sound of tromping feet as friends and family carried the pine box uphill to that empty hole in the ground drew him on. He felt as though he had no choice but to lift his voice and move his feet in time to the syncopated beat.

Finally, they reached the top of the knoll and stopped. The sudden cessation of sound left even the birds speechless. Sulley froze, uncertain of what came next. Then a woman stepped forward and began to sing in a rich voice, like pouring molasses over pancakes:

> "There is a balm in Gilead
> To make the wounded whole,
> There is a balm in Gilead,
> To heal the sin-sick soul . . ."

Verna and Reggie held each other, tears wetting their cheeks. Arbutus wedged herself in between them, and the three stood there as if they were a single being pouring out sorrow over this unfathomable loss. Sulley focused on the treetops. He couldn't bear looking at them even one moment longer.

It was a relief when Sulley could finally take up a shovel and help to cover the simple coffin. Everyone stayed until the last cut of sod was laid back in place. Then the women stepped forward with flowers and began laying them over the scar in the earth. There were daisies and wild roses and branches of rhododendron. At last, Reggie pounded a homemade cross with JAMES carved in it at the head of the grave.

And then, after all the singing and crying and preaching, everyone drifted silently back down to the house where Sulley knew there was almost enough food to see the family through the winter. He stood there considering the day's work. Considering his part in it.

They didn't call it a funeral. They called it a "homegoing." Sulley didn't guess he'd ever felt like he had a home to go to. There'd been a place or two he thought he might could make a home, but something always came up and he moved on. Before that, there'd been the orphanage and that had surely never felt like home.

Except . . . He remembered Franklin letting him sit by his fire of an evening. Or on a bench down by the creek in the summer. Franklin never sought Sulley out, and they rarely had much to say to each other. Sulley guessed it was just the way the old man had made him feel . . . easy. From the moment he arrived at the orphanage, he knew he had to be on the lookout. For other kids, for grown-ups who were cruel or demanding. For the situations he didn't see coming as well as the ones he did. But when he was with Franklin he'd relaxed. Felt safe. Like he could let his guard down if only for an hour.

Strange that he felt that way now. Standing alone beside the grave of a young man he'd never met, peace washed over him. And the fact that he'd done nothing to earn it filled him with wonder.

He heard a sound, turned, and was surprised to find Arbutus there, looking at him. "Mr. Sulley, Mama says come on down and get you a bite to eat."

"Not sure I belong down there," he said. He glanced back at the mound of flowers. "I didn't even know your brother."

"Is it because you're white?" Arbutus asked. "That you don't belong?"

He laughed, short and sharp. "I doubt it."

"Between you and Mr. Jeremiah, we're gettin' downright used to havin' white folks around."

Sulley jerked his head up. "Mr. Jeremiah?"

"Didn't nobody tell you? Guess they're all too caught up with losing James." She shifted some flowers around in a way that seemed to please her eye. "Mr. Jeremiah come through looking for you. He's the one what helped bring James home."

"Looking for me? What'd he say?"

Arbutus screwed up her face, thinking. "He wanted to know all about you digging our well. I figured he must need one himself. Probably hoping to hire you."

"You remember his last name?"

Arbutus shrugged. "He's a big fella. With a beard."

Sulley's blood ran cold. Sure enough sounded like Jeremiah Weber from back in Kline. Could he really still be hunting Sulley after all this time? "When'd you see him last?"

"This morning. He went off to fetch Miss Gainey home from

the tunnel camps. She stayed there after finding James for us. Wanted to see could she help the ones that're sick."

Sulley's first thought was that meant he had time to get away from here before Jeremiah and Gainey returned. His second thought was that Jeremiah Weber didn't have any right to come here and turn these people's good opinion against him. Especially not Gainey's, which he suspected was hard-won and easily lost. For once in his life, he'd been nothing but good to the folks in Mount Lookout. Shouldn't he have a chance to start over again?

Of course, the real question was, did he even want a chance to build something new? He hadn't planned on setting down roots, but this place and these people drew him. While he honestly didn't know what it meant to have a family, he thought it might be something like the way the Johnsons and the Fridleys longed for and mourned over their missing sons. What if he had a mother somewhere who longed for him like that? He hardly dared to let himself think that way. Hope wasn't something he'd ever had much use for, beyond hoping he found a place to rest his head each night and hoping he could find another mark willing to part with money in exchange for that very thing—hope.

Shoot. He'd given those folks up there in Kline all kind of hope. Was it his fault it hadn't panned out? No sir. Didn't mean it wasn't worth something. And Jeremiah Weber had no business acting any different.

The more he thought about it, the less inclined Sulley was to move on. Of course, if he did find the Phillips gold, he could just give the folks back in Kline some money. Maybe even more than they'd paid him. Then it would have been an investment. Jeremiah—who Sulley thought had been a little too ready to act superior—could just put that in his pipe and smoke it.

"Tell your mama I'll come around another time," Sulley said to Arbutus. She sighed and hung her head. He stuffed his hands in his overalls pockets and considered her. "Guess you're awful sad." She nodded. "'Weeping may endure for a night, but joy cometh in the morning.'"

She squinted at him. "Where'd you hear that?"

It was his turn to shrug. "Something somebody told me once. I've heard a lot of things over the years that were pure nonsense, but I like to think that one's right." He reached out and touched her shoulder, gave it a gentle squeeze. "'Course, I'm still waiting for the morning."

She smiled at him. "Thinking about getting joy again one day makes me feel kind of happy right now."

"There you go," he said, then raised a hand in parting and struck out north, considering how he'd get back to Summersville and that cornfield with the cross without running into Jeremiah. As he walked, he whistled realizing that he, too, felt kind of happy.

seventeen

Gainey collapsed into a rocking chair on the porch of the tavern. She'd gotten as clean as she could using a pitcher and bowl but still felt grimy and unkempt. She knew she should go up to her room to scrub her shirt, rinse it, and hang it to dry before supper, but her eyelids felt weighted with lead and her very bones were weary.

The evening breeze swept across the porch, promising rain. She imagined how good it would feel to stand in a downpour right now. Then she closed her eyes thinking she would just rest a minute before going in to eat.

When she opened her eyes, dusk had gathered, and an early moon was rising bright over the mountains. She stretched, hoping no one had seen her sleeping on the porch. But then she saw the plate with a slice of beef lying across a piece of light bread and supposed it was too late to worry about being embarrassed. She ate the food with gratitude and drank a dipper of cool water. The rain had fallen while she slept, freshening the air. She stood on the porch and marveled at her courage—or was it foolishness?—in continuing her work at the camps. The man they called Butch—the one who wore pistols on his hips—had made it clear she wasn't welcome. He'd called her names, the least offensive of which was "meddlesome harpy." But surely he wouldn't actually harm her . . .

The sound of wheels bouncing over the rough road caught her attention, and she watched as a mule-drawn cart approached the tavern. In the dim light it looked a great deal like the Leggs' cart, but she supposed they all looked alike. The shape of the man driving it, though, that seemed even more familiar. Gainey's breath caught as he pulled the cart to a stop, climbed down, and handed the reins to a boy who came from the stable. What a bear of a man. Just like Jeremiah Weber. It filled her heart with such hope and joy she wondered briefly if she was dreaming.

"Gainey, is that you?" The man moved toward her more gracefully than seemed right for someone his size.

"Jeremiah? Is anything wrong?" It occurred to her that something might have gone amiss on his trip back to Mount Lookout or with the Fridley family. He stepped up beside her on the porch, and Gainey, who hadn't felt feminine or girlish for decades, now suddenly felt petite and . . . womanly.

"Nothing's wrong. And I'm awful glad to see you. I was worried you might not be here."

"Where else would I be?"

He shuffled his feet, the side of his face catching a gleam of moonlight. "Down there at the camps. Waylaid somewhere in between. Seems like an awful lot of ways a woman could end up in trouble, and it didn't feel right just to leave you here." He took off his hat and slapped it against his leg. "Been regretting it ever since I left."

Gainey's emotions were at war. On the one hand, it was delightful to have a man considering her well-being. On the other hand, she could certainly take care of herself. Had been doing so for years. She attempted a lighthearted comment. "Well, as you can see, I'm perfectly well."

Jeremiah squinted at her, and it occurred to Gainey that she likely looked terrible. Her hair had wilted long ago, and she'd done little to set it to rights when she arrived back at the quiet tavern thinking it didn't matter. At least she'd washed any dirt from her face, but that was little enough to satisfy any woman's vanity. Even one who prided herself on a lack of vanity.

"You look tired," Jeremiah said.

She bristled. "Well, as it happens, I've had a very busy day. There is much that needs doing here, and few willing to do it. If you drove all this way to tell me that, I'll thank you to be on your way." She was turning to go inside when a hand on her arm stopped her.

"I . . ." Jeremiah cleared his throat. "Guess I said that wrong. I admire what you're trying to do here. But I . . . that is to say, Susan asked me to come carry you back to Mount Lookout. Said she sure needs you there."

Gainey stiffened and eased from his grip. "Susan is more than competent, and she would not ask me to leave if she had any notion how extreme the situation is at the tunnel. The need here is infinitely greater."

"Doggone it, woman!" The words burst from Jeremiah and seemed to take them both equally by surprise. He shook his head. "You seem determined to not like anything I have to say, and maybe I'm saying it all wrong, but there are people who care about you and want to make sure you're alright. Quit acting like a toddler determined to hold her own cup."

Gainey froze. Then she burst out laughing. "Why, Mr. Weber, that's a delightful metaphor for my ill behavior. I suppose my only excuse is that you have taken me quite by surprise." She picked up the plate that had held her supper. "Come inside, then, and we'll sit down like civilized people and have a conversation. While it is true that I am indeed tired, I think I can manage to stay awake a little longer."

Jeremiah chuckled as well. "Now that sounds like a mighty fine plan."

She smiled and considered the proverb, *"A merry heart doeth good like a medicine."* It was the first time she'd really understood what that meant. "Perhaps you will even allow me to persuade you not to take me home but to stay and lend a hand?"

Jeremiah shook his woolly head. "I don't know about that, but I'll be happy to listen to anything you have to say."

Her heart, so heavy after all she had seen the last few days, danced in her breast. And she allowed herself to believe that even the hard things of this world could step aside—if only for a moment—to let joy shine through.

Gainey persuaded Jeremiah to at least come see the camps with her before trying to convince her to leave this place of need. Turned out he was a fair hand at carpentry, so he traded work for a place to lay his head for the night. When she arose and gratefully dressed in the clean clothing he'd brought her, she went downstairs and found that he'd already built a new half door in the stable where an ornery mule had kicked the old one out.

"That should hold," he said, thumping it with his fist. He smiled at her, and while she'd always thought men should be clean-shaven, she found herself liking the bearded look of him with a hammer in his hand and an expression of self-satisfaction warming his eyes.

"Breakfast is ready if you'd like a bite, and then I was hoping . . ." She flushed. "Well, I've arranged a ride in a delivery truck to Gauley Bridge—to the other end of the tunnel. I spent yesterday in Hawks Nest and want to see to the other camps at the far end today. I was hoping you'd accompany me."

Jeremiah dusted his hands and wiped his hammer off before replacing it on a workbench. "I'd be delighted to serve as your escort," he said with a grin.

Gainey turned back to the tavern before he could see her flush deepen. She was unaccustomed to male conversation beyond crops, the weather, and the state of the mail. She hardly knew how to take anything this man said to her.

Once they'd eaten and Gainey had gathered what she could in the way of comforts for the sick men, they set off down a curving road that seemed determined to twist around and look at itself in places. Their taciturn driver did not speak, merely turned his head now and again to spit tobacco juice out the open window. Gainey sat in the middle of the wide seat with Jeremiah beside her. The trip was torture as she slid back and forth around each turn. The harder she tried not to bump her hip into their driver, the more she found herself pressed against Jeremiah. The two of them quickly gave up any attempts at conversation, using all their energy to watch the road ahead while trying to anticipate the next turn.

"There she be." These were the first words the driver had uttered since wishing them a good morning at the beginning of the trip. Gainey sighed in relief. The road had finally straightened out a bit, and they were approaching a bridge into a town that appeared to have sprouted—mushroom-like—in the juncture of the Gauley and the Kanawha Rivers. She was surprised to see what looked like household goods and debris scattered along the road. It certainly wasn't a tidy town.

"Where are the camps?" she asked.

"On up at the mouth of the tunnel. Ye'll need to walk a bit. Workers' office is along the way if your man wants to sign up." He shook his head. "They's always hiring, if you're fool enough to get took on."

Gainey and Jeremiah offered their thanks and made their way into town. More than one resident watched them with a suspicious eye. Jeremiah chuckled but it sounded nervous. "We must be a mighty unusual sight," he said. "You a proper lady and me a mountain man."

Gainey smiled. "Our traveling together might be scandalous if I weren't such an old maid."

Jeremiah stopped and turned to her, so she stopped as well. "Do you consider yourself an old maid?"

She forced a laugh. "Everyone else does."

"What does that make me?" he asked. "I expect I'm older than you and I've never married."

She began walking again, hoping he'd follow along. "I suppose that makes you a confirmed bachelor."

He fell into step beside her and touched her arm lightly. "Are you single because you want to be?"

"I . . . suppose I am." She stared straight ahead. "There was a man, once." She risked a glance at Jeremiah. He looked interested and nothing more. "He died."

"Well then, you're one up on me." He picked up his pace. "There's a woman I'm supposed to want to marry, but doggone if I do." He darted a look at her, then ahead again. "She's nice enough, but I guess I always thought I'd have stronger feelings about a woman I was meant to marry."

Gainey allowed him to get a few paces ahead. "You're engaged, then."

"No. Not really. It's just something folks in the community think ought to happen." He watched a flock of birds fly, moving in an undulating formation. "Sometimes it's hard to go against expectations."

Gainey bit her lip. Something she wouldn't have done if he were watching her. "Other people's expectations can make you do all sorts of things against your better judgment."

He glanced back at her, and she saw a flash of understanding that made something bloom inside her that she'd long thought dead. But now was not the time to dwell on it.

"There're folks gathered up ahead. Let's see if they can point us in the right direction."

Gainey agreed, feeling as though she was going in the right direction for the first time in a long time.

Jeremiah marveled at himself. He'd never been what you'd call spontaneous, but here he was escorting a lady into a strange town so they could offer comfort to men who'd traveled long distances to find work only to discover hardship instead. He felt downright noble—like he had a purpose that was a whole lot more important than running one scoundrel to ground in hopes of getting some money back.

He stuck his chest out a notch and approached the group of mostly colored men outside a dingy building. "Any of you know the way to the tunnel camps?" Heads went down and no one would meet his eye. Just then a man came out of the door with a piece of paper clutched in his hand and crossed the street to a door marked with a doctor's name. Jeremiah pushed his way inside.

Several men sat against the wall as if waiting their turn. A pasty fellow sat behind a desk, asking questions of a man in front of him. Apparently satisfied, he gave the man a piece of paper and he headed out the door.

"Who's next?" the man droned.

"Say, can I just ask a question?" Jeremiah stepped up to the desk.

The man frowned deeply. "If you want to work, you'll need to answer the same questions as everyone else. No exceptions."

"I'm not here for work. I have a lady outside who wants to help the workers who are sick."

The man jerked backward like Jeremiah had taken a swing at him. "Who the dickens are you?" he demanded. "And who said there are sick workers?"

Jeremiah had the notion he'd just made a mistake. "I'm, uh, that is to say, we're—"

"Meddlers and do-gooders," the man broke in with a sneer. "That's what you are. Like that woman from New York. Social worker, she says, like that's any kind of authority." He stood and leaned his fists on the desk. "My advice to you is to turn right around and go back to where you came from." A drop of spittle landed on Jeremiah's shirtfront. "We ain't got no use for organizers around here."

Jeremiah knew he should back down. Should go outside, collect Gainey, and do what the man said. But the thought of trying to turn that battleship of a woman gave him pause. She would not want to go. And durn if he wanted to, either. He leaned closer. "We'll take your suggestion under advisement." He spoke slowly, deepening his voice. He was gratified to see the man's eyes widen as he drew back.

"See that you do," he squeaked out. "Next!" The next man sitting in the row of chairs dragged to his feet and came forward.

He looked at Jeremiah like he couldn't believe he'd just spit in his soup. He tilted his head and shrugged his shoulder just a little. It was as close as he dared come to giving an apology.

When he went outside and explained the situation to Gainey, her eyes narrowed. "Surely the camps won't be that hard to find," she said. "All we have to do is follow the cloud of dust."

They set out again but hadn't gone a half mile when a flatbed truck ground to a halt beside them. "You'uns best get in," the driver said, glancing all around.

Gainey stood on tiptoes to see in his window. "Will you give us a ride to the nearest workers' camp? I have provisions here to help the sick men."

"Lady, yer playin' with fire. Git on up in here and I'll take the pair of ya back where you came from. And won't even ask ya to thank me fer savin' yer life."

Gainey frowned deeply, and Jeremiah could see she had no intention of cooperating. He, on the other hand, was beginning to think they might have stepped into more than they'd bargained for.

"Can you tell us what's going on around here?" he asked.

The man blew out a sigh of frustration. "Sure, sure. I'll tell ya what ya wanna know. Just git on up in here afore we're all in trouble."

"Gainey, I think it might be best to go with this man. Once you learn more about what's happening, you'll be in a better position to figure what help's needed." He herded her to the passenger door and opened it. "I'm not sure what I did, but that fella back in that office was almighty displeased with us for being here. Might be best to retreat and fight another day."

They looked back the way they'd come and saw two men on horses headed toward them. Jeremiah practically lifted Gainey into the truck, climbed in, and slammed the door. The driver released the clutch, and they were off the way they'd come not an hour before. And without knowing exactly why, Jeremiah was almighty glad of it.

There'd been people around when Sulley got back to the burial field and what he hoped was the cross marking the Phillips gold. He moseyed on by as though on his way to visit someone. But he felt eyes on him as he passed, so he went a good mile before ducking into the woods, circling through fields, creeping along hedgerows, and even passing a house or two to wind his way back to some trees behind the field. He settled himself where he couldn't be seen, got comfortable, and waited for night to fall once again.

eighteen

Gainey jammed her feet hard under the dashboard of the truck, wedging herself so that she didn't slide into either of the men in the cab with her. It was tiring, but she used her anger, fear, and frustration to give herself strength.

What did Jeremiah mean by hurrying her away from Gauley Bridge? She'd asked for his help but had not imagined he would impose his will over hers. Although . . . the driver, Harold Barker, certainly gave her the impression they had been in danger. Of what, she wasn't altogether certain.

"Not too smart," Harold said, keeping his eyes on the twisting road. "Other folks have come 'round trying to interfere with the workers. Some woman from up around New York's been poking around. Says she's a social worker, whatever that is. They think you're here to try to organize the men, and they'll shoot you as soon as look at you."

"Oh, now, really. I think you exaggerate—" Gainey felt Jeremiah's hand clamp down on her arm. Hard.

"We appreciate the help and the warning." Jeremiah relaxed his grip but didn't remove his hand. "Guess they must need a lot of workers, based on all the men we saw coming into town."

Harold grunted. "Wouldn't need so many if they didn't wear 'em out so quick."

"What do you mean?" Gainey wasn't going to be stilled this time.

"Shoot, most of 'em don't last more than a few months. They get sick so's they can't work, or they get smart and quit." He waved a hand at the clutter on the roadside. "See all that stuff? That's what's left when folks are run out of here without two nickels to rub together. Just abandon their goods when they can't carry 'em anymore." He glanced in the rearview mirror. "Then there are the ones leaving town feet-first."

Gainey felt tears prick her eyes at the thought of James dying. She hadn't even asked Jeremiah about Verna or Reggie. He must have seen her distress because he squeezed her arm again, only this time it was comforting rather than confining. "Do many die?" she asked, her voice small in the cab of the truck.

"Too many," Harold said. "Mostly the coloreds. And half of 'em don't have nobody to care one way or t'other. Load 'em up and haul 'em off to a burial field up in Summersville."

"There's a colored cemetery there?"

Harold snorted. "Not so's you'd notice. Don't guess they even mark the graves proper. Just get 'em in the ground and hire some more."

"That's terrible." Gainey couldn't hide the horror in her voice. "Who would do such a thing?"

"Lady, what rock you been hidin' under? The world's a mean place. Especially now that there's not much work to be had, and what work there is can kill ya."

Feeling chastised, Gainey remained silent the rest of the way to Ansted. Jeremiah's hand remained on her arm, but it was little comfort. When they arrived at the tavern, she couldn't get out of the truck quickly enough. Jeremiah helped her down and spoke to the driver as she hurried inside. She wanted a bath, a meal, and to go home. She'd done nothing to help and might very well have caused trouble for those who had welcomed her ministrations. Her earlier frustration with Jeremiah gave way to embarrassment. Yet she would have to endure it so that he could carry her home.

She waited on the porch, turned so that Jeremiah could only see the side of her face as he approached. "I suppose it's too late to start back today," she said. "Shall we start out early in the morning?"

"If you want to head on home, I'm game," he answered. "Might be getting on up in the day, but we can make it if you gather your things right quick while I hitch up Tobias."

"I won't be more than five minutes." She scurried up the stairs to pack her few belongings. When there was something unpleasant to be done, it was just as well to do it quickly.

Sulley jerked awake when he heard a truck door slam and an engine start up. He crawled around the tree and peered out across the burial field. The men were leaving. Several new scars marked the ground, though there was little else to hint at what lay beneath the fresh dirt. Sulley watched the truck drive away and waited until he was sure they weren't coming back. Dusk was falling and he wanted to find his dowsing rod before it got too dark.

He worked his way around to the chestnut and looked again to make sure he hadn't dreamed the cross carved there. Sure enough, it remained. And this time he noticed something scratched into the bark beneath it. The carved marks were smaller and not as deep, making them impossible to read in the gloom. He hoped it wasn't directions or something like *The Phillips gold buried here*. He grinned. It was good to make a joke. Things had been too serious for his liking of late.

He began scanning the ground where he thought he remembered jabbing the dowsing rod in the dirt. There—still sticking up as though a heavy wind had thrust it there. He knelt down and began scraping away leaves and debris.

Jeremiah wished he could put an arm around Gainey. She was acting hangdog and clearly feeling discouraged. There were few things worse than setting out to do a good deed and having your best intentions thrown back in your face. She remained quiet as they made the trip back to Mount Lookout in good time.

"I'm sorry if I hindered you," Jeremiah said at last.

Gainey sighed and offered him a weak smile. "I suspect I was doing a fine job of hindering myself. It's not like me to be spontaneous—to go blindly into a situation without a great deal of thought and planning." She patted his arm. "I'm grateful you were there to, as Arbutus would say, 'pull my fat out of the fire.'"

Jeremiah felt a tightness in his chest that crawled up into his throat and kept him from saying anything. Probably just as well. Anything he said would likely be wrong.

"Tell me how Verna and Reggie are faring. I'm ashamed that we have yet to really talk about them."

"They were pretty tore up over James. Verna in particular, although I think Reggie just didn't show it as much." Jeremiah shifted on the seat. "I stopped off there on my way to look for you. I thought to stay for the funeral, but Verna said I'd best come on and fetch you home." He cleared his throat. "Said I oughta look out for you if you'd let me."

A gentle look of amusement brightened Gainey's face. "Verna thinks every woman needs a man to look out for her. But then she thinks all men are like Reggie."

"Maybe some are," he said, stealing a look at her out of the corner of his eye.

She bit back the smile, but he could see it sitting there just beneath the surface. "Maybe some are," she agreed. "What about the burial? I assume they buried James in the family plot."

Jeremiah let her change the subject without a fight. "I didn't stay for that, but yes, looked like that's what they were planning. Had a passel of folks there already and more coming if I had to guess."

"Yes, they're well respected and have many friends and family." Gainey fell silent as the earlier moment of levity disappeared beneath something heavy rolling off her like a fog. "I can't stop thinking about what Harold said about men dying at the tunnel and being buried in a cornfield." She turned plaintive brown eyes on him. "It seems so lonesome. A sadness on top of a sorrow."

"I suppose so. Seems like they oughta have somebody to speak over them—to leave a marker in case anyone wanted to find them." He stared ahead and saw that they were approaching the turnoff to Mount Lookout. "Maybe we could go there—see if there's something we could do for them."

"How would we ever find the place? Saying it's a field in Summersville does little to narrow it down."

"I asked Harold for directions."

Gainey's head whipped around, and she stared at him. "What in the world possessed you to do that?"

Jeremiah wanted to smile but didn't think it was the right time. "Had a notion you might want to visit. Asked just in case."

"Why, Jeremiah Weber, that is . . ." She seemed to be struggling to find the right words. When she finally spoke, her voice was low and rough. "That's incredibly thoughtful and kind. I can't remember the last time someone took such pains to think . . . well, it was generous of you." She cleared her throat. "And, indeed, I would like to visit. Perhaps if I could go and see the place, then return home to gather whatever is needed—perhaps take a minister to hallow the ground." She rattled on, thinking through how they might mark an anonymous burial ground. "But really," she finally said, "I must see it first and then we can decide."

"No time like the present." Jeremiah urged the mule on past the turnoff to Mount Lookout.

nineteen

Once Sulley had cleared a good-sized space at the foot of the tree, he cut a fresh branch and dowsed one more time. Again the hazel rod tugged at him like a child wanting a treat. The sensation made his mouth go dry, which was odd since he'd felt it dozens of times before, although perhaps not so strongly.

Dropping the dowsing rod, Sulley fetched a likely looking stick he'd spotted earlier. He needed a digging tool now that the shovel was gone. The stick was good and stout, with a point he sharpened with his pocketknife. He began thrusting it in the cleared ground to work the soil loose. The earth had some clay in it but wasn't too hard or too wet, and while this was sure slower than using a shovel, he'd do all right. He'd also rounded up a flat rock he could use to scrape and scoop the loose dirt to the side.

As he worked steadily on, the moon rose bright and luminous behind the trees. He could sure enough see the man in the moon tonight, and it gave him a twitchy feeling of being watched. He put his head down and worked that much harder, trying to be grateful for the light of the moon limning everything in silver. Shoot, maybe it was a good omen, this silver cast predicting that he sure enough would find some precious metal before the night was out.

Gainey watched the moon rise, wondering how it was she was suddenly making a habit of spontaneity. She'd rarely done anything on a whim and now she knew why. The fact that she was riding along a country road in a mule cart with a man she barely knew, looking for a hidden graveyard, spoke of a silly campfire story—not her staid and steady life.

But what could she say at this point? She'd come along readily enough, and it would hardly do to chastise Jeremiah for her own foolishness.

"Perhaps we should turn back," she said.

"You know, I think you might be right. Guess I got ahead of myself thinking this was a good idea." Jeremiah chuckled. "I don't have near enough practice doing things on the spur of the moment to try to start now."

Laughter burst from Gainey. "That is almost exactly what I was thinking. I haven't done anything without thoroughly considering the consequences since . . . well, it's been a very long time, and I had imagined I was a great deal wiser."

Jeremiah's shoulders shook. "Never did think I was what you'd call wise, but I did think I had the sense God gave a goose." He drew the mule to a halt. "Although doggone if I don't feel more alive and full of you-know-what and vinegar than I have since I was a young buck." He slapped his thigh. "By golly, this is an adventure!"

Gainey got so tickled she had to hold her sides as she laughed. "Somehow I thought an adventure would be more glamorous."

She composed herself. "Do you propose, then, that we venture on?"

"No way," Jeremiah said. "I say we get on back to Mount Lookout and hope no one's watching the road. I don't think I can stand to feel too much livelier than I do right now."

Gainey snickered at him. "Coward. However, I'm willing to go along." She lifted her chin and tossed her head as though she were making a great concession.

"I'll just bet you are," Jeremiah said and leaned in so close she could see his eyes twinkle.

The sudden proximity seemed to take them both by surprise and they froze. Gainey felt her eyes go wide and drew in a sharp breath—actions that happened entirely without her permission. Jeremiah cleared his throat and leaned back, allowing Gainey to breathe normally again. Although she was surprised to find that she wished . . .

"I'll just turn this cart around, and we'll get on back where we belong," he said.

"Yes, that would be wise." Wise and yet . . . Gainey almost wished that for once she could be unwise, reckless even.

Tobias seemed reluctant to cooperate with Jeremiah. He kept trying to turn the mule in bits and pieces, but the animal simply would not do as requested. Then the back corner of the cart dropped precipitously, and Gainey cried out. She clapped a hand over her mouth.

Jeremiah uttered a word under his breath that wasn't very gentlemanly. "We're in the ditch," he said.

Gainey bit her lip. A habit she'd worked years to halt. "Can we get out?"

Jeremiah climbed down and examined the wheel. "Probably, but I'm not sure this wheel will keep turning if we do." He started to repeat the earlier word but cut it off before it got all the way out. He heaved a sigh. "Do you mind climbing down while I try to get this cart back on the road?"

Gainey carefully made her way to the ground. "Is there anything I can do to help?"

"Maybe walk on up to the top of the rise there and see if you can spot any lights. Might need to ask somebody for help if they're close by."

"Certainly." Gainey struck out at a brisk pace, glad for a task she was competent to do. Yet the thought of trying to explain what she was doing riding around in the night with a man wasn't very appealing. Then again, she didn't suppose she'd need to explain to a stranger. Encouraged, she topped the rise and looked around her, grateful for the brightness of the moon giving everything an otherworldly glow.

"See anything?" Jeremiah called.

She bit her lip. Hard. She did see something. And it just might be the very thing they'd been seeking. She moved on into a pockmarked field as though drawn by an unseen hand.

Sulley froze when the edge of the rock he was using to scrape dirt out of the hole hit something that felt different. The moonlight cast odd shadows and made everything look strange. He held his breath as he reached down to check for what he'd hit.

A firm, flat surface.

He worked his fingers across it until he found an edge. Seemed like it might be oilcloth. Wrapped around something square. His breathing came in ragged spurts now. Had he found it? Had he really found the Phillips gold?

From out of nowhere a woman shrieked, and Sulley did too,

stumbling, tripping, and falling on his backside. He jerked around to see what in the world . . . "Gainey?"

"Who is that?" She clutched at the neck of her blouse. "Mr. Harris?" Gainey stood gaping at him.

"Fancy meeting you here," he managed at last.

"This is a burial ground," she blurted. "What are you doing?"

He looked at the hole he was practically sitting in. "What? This? Oh, no. Burial ground's that way." He jerked his chin back toward the field. "This . . . well, I dowsed to find this."

"A well?" Her brow furrowed. "Why are you digging a well here?"

Sulley was flummoxed. How to steer this woman away from his find? And what in tarnation was she doing here in the first place? He clambered to his feet. The best offense was a good defense. "Woman, what are you doing out here poking around in the middle of the night?"

It wasn't quite the middle of the night, but his comment had the desired effect. Even in the moonlight he could see her flush. She lifted her chin. "I'm here to try to give some dignity to the poor men who've been buried without the benefit of a preacher, or markers to help their loved ones seek them out."

"In the dark?"

She chewed at her lower lip. "It was later than I realized. Perhaps waiting until morning would have been the better plan." She looked thoughtful, then speared him with a look. "Now, what about you?"

Sulley gave it up. Anyway, he liked Gainey. And the fact that she cared about the men buried here made him like her even more. "Aw, the heck with it. I'm huntin' buried treasure."

She laughed. "You're what? As if there really were any such thing."

"Maybe. Maybe not. Fact is, I just found something when you purt near scared me into tomorrow."

Now her eyebrows shot up. "What did you find?"

"Come see," Sulley said, turning back to the mysterious wrapped object still stuck in the dirt.

Jeremiah called out to Gainey twice more without getting an answer. He kicked at a rock. This night was getting worse and worse. He felt like a foolish boy who'd been shown up when he tried to impress a girl. Everything about this was foolishness. He'd just have to own up to the fact that he liked Gainey Floyd more than a little, and he wasn't doing himself any favors trying to show off for her.

"Gainey?" No answer.

He'd managed to turn the mule and thought the wheel would hold. Now, where had that woman gotten off to? He tied the mule's reins to a fence post and headed off the way Gainey had disappeared. When he topped the rise, he thought he'd been poleaxed. They'd found the cemetery. If you'd call it that. It was a field rolling away across a knoll with far too many scars in the earth. Some grown over and weedy, some so fresh he could still smell disturbed soil.

But where was Gainey? He scanned wider and saw her on the far side of the field, intently focused on something at the base of a massive chestnut tree. He opened his mouth to call to her, then stopped. Hollering across the field felt irreverent. He began walking around the edge, headed for her.

As he drew near, her focus continued to be on something—or was it someone?—scrabbling in the dirt. He frowned. Was someone burying one of those poor souls even now? She finally glanced toward him and beckoned him closer. As he drew even with her, the man in the dirt stood holding something aloft triumphantly. "Got it!" he exclaimed.

"What is it?" Gainey asked. But before the man could answer, his eyes locked with Jeremiah's, and both men froze. Jeremiah had finally found his man.

twenty

With a rush, Gainey remembered that Jeremiah had come to Mount Lookout seeking Sullivan Harris. And she had been suspicious of his intentions. How had something so basic slipped her mind?

"Jeremiah, I believe you already know Sullivan Harris," she said.

"And so I do. Hadn't expected to find you here," he said to Sulley.

"Didn't expect to be found." Sulley shook his head. "By anybody, much less the pair of you."

"Well . . ." Gainey was determined to take control. "You gentlemen can sort out whatever business you have later. Right now, I want to know what Sulley is holding in his hand."

Sulley chuckled. "It ain't what I hoped." He folded the oilcloth back, exposing a leather-bound book. Gainey gasped. "Appears to be a Bible." Sulley handed it over.

Gainey accepted the book with reverence—and not only because it was God's Word. "I've seen this before." Her voice was so soft she barely heard it herself.

"Yeah, well, maybe there's something else here." Sulley grinned at Jeremiah in a way that was clearly a challenge. "You want to help?"

Jeremiah grunted. "What are we digging for?"

"Gold." Sulley pointed up to a mark on the tree Gainey had not noticed before. "Supposed to be buried at the foot of the cross."

"Why in tarnation not?" Jeremiah took up the flat stone Sulley had been using and began scooping dirt as Sulley loosened it. Gainey watched them, too stunned by what she held in her hands to say more.

"Whoa now." Sulley laid a hand on Jeremiah's arm. "Let's take a step back here."

"What'd you find?" Jeremiah asked.

They both moved back, and Gainey peered in the hole. It was hard to tell what she was looking at in the silvery light. Sulley pulled a hand torch out of the shadows and clicked it on. He shined the light into the hole, and Gainey thought she might swoon.

The men had exposed a withered hand laid across a shirt-front.

This night wasn't at all going as planned. Sulley wasn't sure whether to laugh or cuss. Both seemed to fit the current situation. He'd failed to find gold and had dug up some poor soul instead. He'd been run to ground by Jeremiah Weber, who was likely to want cash money or a pound of flesh, and Sulley didn't have enough of either to spare. Plus, all his troubles were unfolding in front of the first person whose opinion he'd given a tinker's cuss for since he couldn't remember when.

"Unless this feller's name is Phillips, I don't think we're in the right place."

Jeremiah swore under his breath. "What have you gotten us into now? Is this one of those poor colored workers?"

"First off, I didn't invite you here. Second off, that hand looks white to me, and it's lying across a real nice shirt and tie for some traveling laborer."

Gainey made a sound, half cough, half squeak. Sulley went to her. Of course she was upset. Everything about this was unsettling. "What say we cover this poor feller back up and get out of here?"

"I think I might . . . have an idea . . ."

"Wait. You hear that?" Jeremiah twisted toward the road. "Sounds like a truck grinding gears. What say we finish this conversation somewhere else?"

Sulley was already pushing dirt back into the hole, and Jeremiah bent to help him. "Gainey, get on back to the wagon. We'll be along in a minute." She mutely clutched the Bible to her chest and did as Jeremiah said.

They kicked leaves back over the grave. "Not the best job, but I don't guess those men burying workers up here care anyhow," Sulley said. "I don't suppose this is the place where you'd be wanting to part ways?"

Jeremiah put one of his big paws on Sulley's shoulder. Felt like it weighed ten pounds. "Thought we might have a chat first. Back in Mount Lookout once we get Gainey safely home."

"Never have been one for talking," Sulley said and felt Jeremiah's grip tighten. "But seeing how you came all this way, I guess it's the least I can do."

"The very least."

They topped the rise and jogged down to the wagon, where

Gainey stood, head down, as though in a trance. "Good thing I got this cart turned around. Jump in," Jeremiah said, finding he had to prod Gainey more than a little.

They arrived in Mount Lookout in the fullness of night. It was the time when night sounds have stilled and the dawn birds have yet to waken. It felt sacred to Sulley. Which was a joke since hardly anything was sacred to him.

"Where you been bunking?" he asked Jeremiah.

"Now that you mention it, I stayed with the Fridleys. Hardly seems like the right time to show back up at their place, though."

Sulley was about to suggest they head for his old camp, which he figured meant he'd have half a chance to get shut of Jeremiah before dawn. "You can make up pallets on the floor in the sitting room," Gainey said. They were the first words she'd uttered since . . . well, since he'd handed her that Bible. "It wouldn't be proper if it were just one of you, but two? I don't see why not."

Jeremiah had driven to her little cottage on the outskirts of town. She climbed down without waiting for either of them to help her and disappeared inside. The two men watched her go, then exchanged looks.

"She alright?" Sulley asked.

"Can't tell," Jeremiah answered. "And to say I'm a poor judge of what women are thinking or feeling is the plain truth."

Sulley chuckled. "That makes two of us." The men traded smiles, which seemed to take them both by surprise.

"Let's get this mule taken care of," Jeremiah said. "I don't fancy letting you much out of my sight." With that, the moment of camaraderie passed, and they set about their chores.

Jeremiah was pretty sure he hadn't slept more than ten minutes during what was left of the night. What with keeping an eye and an ear out for Sulley to try to slip away and worrying about Gainey, he found the rising of the sun a welcome relief.

He'd done little more than stretch and ponder where he might find the outhouse or if Gainey had inside plumbing when she appeared. She was neatly dressed, and her hair was mostly hidden by a scarf. She looked . . . fine-boned in a way he surely had not noticed before. No one would ever suggest that she was a delicate woman, but this morning there was a fragility about her that made him want to jump up and take her arm.

"Good morning, gentlemen. I hope you rested well." She eyed them and seemed to come to a decision. "I'll put the coffee on and then I'd like to have a word with you both." She moved to the kitchen, then stopped and, without turning around, said, "There are, uh, facilities out back should you require them."

Jeremiah looked at Sulley, whose hair stuck up in back, giving him a boyish look. "Hope it's a two-seater, 'cause I'm not letting you out of my sight." Sulley barked a laugh, and they headed out back together.

When they returned to the back door, Gainey had placed a basin of water, a bar of soap, and some toweling on a table there. They washed in turns and stepped back inside to the welcome aroma of coffee brewing. Gainey waved them toward a kitchen table and poured steaming mugs of strong coffee. Jeremiah lifted his mug, blew on it, and took a slurp. Oh now, that made a man think life might be worth living again.

Gainey sat at the table across from him, dashing his hopes of breakfast. He drank some more coffee and guessed he ought to count his blessings ahead of such a small disappointment. She laid the Bible Sulley unearthed on the table between them and rested her hand on the cover. "This was mine once."

Jeremiah choked on his coffee. "That's your Bible?"

"It was. I . . . passed it on." She cleared her throat and took a sip of her own coffee. "That's what I'd like to tell you about." She set the cup down and traced the gilt letters pressed into the leather cover. "I gave this Bible to my son."

Jeremiah risked a look at Sulley. His hands were wrapped around his own cup, and his attention appeared to be riveted on Gainey. Jeremiah thought there was something different about him. He looked closer and realized the curl of Sulley's lip that made him look perpetually amused was missing.

"When I finished my schooling, my teacher, Mr. Peterson"—her face softened—"Archie, encouraged me to apply to college. I was accepted." She flicked a look at each of them. "But the thought of leaving made me realize how much I cared for Archie." She smiled. "Fortunately, he loved me as well. He proposed marriage, and we made plans. I was nineteen years old." A shadow settled over her face. "Then the influenza struck. He died." She stood abruptly and turned her back to them, fussing with the coffeepot. "I was with child. The shame . . ." She choked and paused, then went on in a rush. "I went away and stayed with an aunt until my son was born. She knew someone who placed the boy with a family." She shook her head. "I never knew the details. It was better that way."

She turned back to the table, her face flushed and tears glinting in her eyes. Resuming her seat, she pulled the Bible toward her and opened the cover. The inside leaf had writing on it. She turned it so the two men could read it.

E. K. F.—Christmas, 1895

"My only condition was that this Bible go with my son. My aunt assured me that request would be honored." She fanned the pages with her thumb and spoke softly. "He underlined passages. Made notes." Tears rose again. "Gentlemen"—she lifted her chin and looked directly at them—"I need your help in determining if the body in that grave is my son."

twenty-one

Jeremiah was in a quandary. He figured his first job at this point was to hog-tie Sulley and haul him back to Kline, where folks could hold him accountable for skinning out with their money. But what he *wanted* to do was stay right here and help Gainey find out the truth about her son.

Gainey had gone on to her postal counter, saying that she'd leave the two men to decide if they might be in a position to help her. She said she'd understand if they couldn't, but the sorrow in her eyes said otherwise. Now they were sitting on her back porch staring at nothing in particular.

"I expect I could outrun you," Sulley said at last.

Jeremiah snorted. "I expect you could, but if I got close enough I could sure enough whip you. And quick too."

"I won't dispute that."

They sat in silence a bit longer. Jeremiah kept rolling his responsibilities around in his head, wondering how it was he'd collected so many of them when he was just a lonely old bachelor.

"You got any of that money left that the folks back in Kline gave you?"

Sulley tilted his chair on two legs. Jeremiah frowned. He was pretty sure Gainey would not approve of what Sulley was doing to her furniture. "I've got three dollars and forty-eight cents to my name."

"I thought you dug some wells for the Johnsons. Didn't they pay you?"

"Some. Spent most of that. Took the rest of my pay in trade." Sulley squinted up at the clouds like he didn't have a care in the world.

"Trade for what?"

"None of your business."

Jeremiah blew out a gust of air. This wasn't getting him anywhere. "Doggone it! I oughta knock you in the head and drag you back to Kline for the folks there to decide what to do, but I'd way rather stay here and lend Gainey a hand." He stood and paced to the edge of the porch. "You're nothing but a thorn in my side."

"Taken a shine to her, haven't ya?"

Jeremiah whirled on Sulley. "What's that you say?"

Sulley held up both hands. "She's a handsome woman. Old enough to be my mother, but fine-looking, smart, and more kindhearted than she lets on. Can't say as I blame you."

"Quit talking nonsense."

Sulley let his chair thump down on all four legs. "Alright then, I have a proposal for you."

Jeremiah narrowed his eyes. He didn't trust this man any more than he'd trust Lucifer himself, but at this moment he was ready to grasp at any straw. "Go on."

"I'll give you my three dollars. Call it a retainer. And we'll both pitch in to see if we can't find out if that's Gainey's boy back there under the chestnut tree."

Jeremiah crossed his arms and leaned against a porch post. "Now why would you do that?"

Sulley shrugged and looked away. "I like her, too." He chuckled. "Not like you do, but let's say she's made an impression on me."

"I don't trust you," Jeremiah said.

Sulley laughed long and loud. "You'd be smart not to."

Jeremiah grunted and stuck out his hand. Sulley fished out some coins and two bills and slapped them in his palm with a defiant look. "Alright then. Guess we're partners."

"Partners," Sulley agreed, a devilish grin spread across his handsome face.

Gainey was so distracted at her postal counter that she nearly misdelivered some mail. If Arbutus hadn't bounced over to ask a question, she would have tucked the Johnsons' letter in the slot marked for the Jones family. She thought about Luisa and how she longed to know what had happened to her son. Gainey sympathized. She'd buried that longing herself once upon a time, but all it took to bring it back was holding that Bible in her hands. And now the notion that her son was dead and buried caused a stone to lodge in her breast.

Had it been foolish to ask Jeremiah and Sulley to help her? There was something hard between the two men. She felt certain Jeremiah hadn't come this far seeking Sulley out of friendship. And yet both men had acted in ways that predisposed her toward thinking well of them. She smiled. Although they were as different as night and day.

Jeremiah was a wise old owl, solemn and regal in his way, taking everything in before deciding what to do. And Sulley was more of a jaybird, flitting from place to place yet never alighting for long. She had the feeling he'd seen some hard times in his past and as a result didn't trust easily. Well. Neither did she. Although you wouldn't know it by how quickly she'd trusted two near strangers with the truth of her youthful indiscretion. Perhaps it was the fact that they didn't know her well and would, presumably, move on from here that made the telling easier.

Lost in thought, Gainey reached for a pencil and knocked the glass chimney from a hurricane lamp just as Susan approached her counter. The thin glass shattered like a sheet of ice. Gainey cried out and felt embarrassment wash her face in a rosy glow.

"Well, that's something I won't have to clean tomorrow," Susan said with a laugh. Gainey felt the burn of humiliation deepen. "You seem . . . uneasy, Gainey. Is everything alright?"

"Of course." Gainey spoke so quickly she gave lie to her words. She waved Arbutus over with her broom and took it from her to sweep up the mess. "I suppose I'm upset by how terribly workers are being treated at that tunnel project. I feel I should have done more. Should perhaps still do something more."

"I'll be praying for them and for you," Susan said.

Gainey thanked her and finished sweeping up the broken glass. Praying—that was what she should have been doing all along. In the early days she'd prayed for her son every morning and every evening. But the frequency had dwindled as the pain became not less, but such a part of her that she hardly noticed it anymore. Perhaps she should be asking for help from someone with more wisdom and strength than Jeremiah or Sulley.

"We thought we'd head back up to Summersville to see if we can find out anything about the fellow Sulley uncovered,"

Jeremiah said. He'd taken the lead on this project, and Sulley seemed content to let him.

"I'll come as well," Gainey said as she ladled potato soup into their bowls.

"We might do better on our own," Jeremiah said. "If there's trouble, I'd hate for you to get mixed up in it."

Gainey scoffed. "What do I care for trouble?" She looked down her nose at him. "If there's any shooting, I'll be sure to duck."

"Well now, I wasn't thinking there'd be anything like that." Jeremiah could see Sulley sniggering in his sleeve. "Although back there in the camps seemed like that wasn't a farfetched idea." Why did he always feel he was losing ground to this woman?

"I would like to revisit the grave in the daylight," Gainey said. "And if there happen to be workers burying men from the tunnels, it might serve you well to have a woman along. I'll claim that I suspect someone dear to me is buried there and I'll carry flowers as though I've brought them to lay on the grave."

Jeremiah had to admit she made a good argument. "Alright then. I've let that old Model T of mine sit long enough. We'll head out first thing in the morning."

Sulley flopped into the back seat of the dusty automobile and pulled his hat low over his eyes. Jeremiah opened the passenger door and handed Gainey in. She thanked him and clasped her hands in her lap, still feeling the strength of his fingers wrapped around hers. The two of them attempted conversation, but it soon petered out and they rode the last few miles to the burial field in silence.

Gainey reached for the bunch of black-eyed Susans she'd gathered and wrapped in newspaper. While she'd spoken boldly to Jeremiah, her prayer now was to find the field empty of anyone living on this hot July day. She didn't think she had it in her to put on a show.

Her prayer was answered. As they approached the spot, the phrase *silent as a tomb* came to mind. Even the birds and insects seemed to have hushed in honor of the unknown dead. As they got out of the automobile, her two companions lagged behind a few paces as though she really were visiting the grave of her son and they wanted to give her space for her grief. Well. She wasn't quite ready to grieve yet.

"Are you tired?" she asked, glancing back at them. They exchanged surprised looks and hurried to catch up with her. All three approached the tree, unmistakable in its girth.

"What made you look here?" Gainey asked.

"Some old-timer told me a tale about the Phillips gold buried at the foot of the cross." Sulley pointed up. "When I saw a cross carved on this tree, I figured it was worth a try."

She furrowed her brow. "But how did you know where to dig?"

"Dowsed for it."

"For a body?"

Sulley heaved a breath. "For gold, I thought. Never did have much use for folks trying to dowse for the dearly departed."

Gainey shuddered. Nor did she. Squinting up at the cross, carved a good twenty feet high, she thought there might be something more there. "My eyesight isn't so good anymore. Are there words carved up there?"

Sulley peered up. "Luke twelve, six through seven. Guess that's a Bible verse."

Jeremiah spoke the words in his deep, resonant voice: "'Are not five sparrows sold for two pennies? Yet not one of them is forgotten by God. Indeed, the very hairs of your head are all numbered. Don't be afraid; you are worth more than many sparrows.'"

Gainey was impressed. She admired a man who carried Scripture in his heart. "Hardly seems a clue to buried treasure," she said.

Sulley shrugged. "Didn't say it was. All I saw was the cross, and this"—he pointed down—"is the foot of it."

"Maybe if we head into town and ask around, we'll find someone who knows about this place," Jeremiah suggested.

"Perhaps." Gainey wasn't sure what she'd hoped to find here, but she was disappointed. The cross, the verse, the grave—how was she to know what any of it meant? "Then again, what does it matter?" She laid her flowers at the base of the tree. "If this is my son, he's beyond my reach. If it's not, it would be foolhardy for me to attempt to seek him out." She dusted off her hands. "I don't know what I was thinking." She looked at her two escorts. "Thank you, gentlemen, but I believe it would be best to put all of this behind me." She began walking back to the road with purpose.

"Now hang on there one doggone minute." She felt a rough hand grasp her arm. She turned to find Sulley, his easygoing smile absent. "What mother wouldn't want to find her son? You went and spilled your guts to two near strangers. Makes me think you were pretty serious about wanting to figure out who's in the ground back there." He jerked a thumb over his shoulder.

"I changed my mind." She turned back to the road and began marching in the direction of home. Jeremiah caught up to her but didn't speak. Sulley stomped along behind, muttering under his breath.

She spun to face him. "What son would want the mother who abandoned him to suddenly reenter his life?" She felt hot—hotter than the day could account for. "It was a moment of weakness, my confession. I released my child and I have no right to attempt to re-claim him. I only pray that he doesn't know—" she paused, considering the grave—"or never knew, if he's no longer in this world, that I abandoned him."

She longed to fall to her knees and sob out her deeply buried, nearly forgotten sorrow over the loss of her child, but she would not—could not—allow herself that luxury. Instead, she swallowed her pain and marched blindly toward the auto. Her only consolation was that she had not confessed her shame to someone who would still be part of her life a month from now. Or—she glanced at the two men trailing meekly behind her—a week from now, if she did not miss her guess.

twenty-two

When they arrived back at her house in Mount Lookout, Gainey simply thanked Jeremiah and Sulley for accompanying her on their "outing," then disappeared inside.

The two men stood looking at each other. Finally, Jeremiah spoke. "I'm betting Verna would let us both sleep on the back porch. Might feed us, too."

"You sure there's room for the both of us and that hound?"

Jeremiah chuckled. "We'll let the hound decide."

As they drove out of town, Jeremiah thought Sulley seemed a hundred miles away. "I can hear the cogs turning in that brain of yours. You trying to figure out how to get shut of me?"

Sulley looked up in surprise. "What's that you say?"

"I said what's got you thinking so hard?"

Sulley shook his head. "You think she meant it?"

"Meant what?"

"That she doesn't want to know what happened to her boy?"

Jeremiah ran his fingers through his beard. "Can't say as I've ever been real good at understanding women, but I'd have to guess she didn't mean it." He watched two jays chase a hawk. "Probably she's just afraid of what she might find."

Sulley nodded and punched his fist into his palm. "I think we oughta keep on looking."

"For her son?"

"Yeah. That might not be him in that grave. If we learn something that's real bad, we don't have to tell her. I grew up in an orphanage. I'd give my eyeteeth to know what happened to my mother." He slapped his palms against his thighs. "And if we find him—alive, that is—we can ask him if he wants to see her. If he doesn't, we'll just leave it alone. That way she won't get her feelings hurt."

"This sounds an awful lot like meddling," Jeremiah said, covering his surprise at Sulley's offering a glimpse into his past.

"Yeah, well, most people make a sport of meddling. Guess we can handle it."

"But what about the folks back in Kline?" Was he actually entertaining this notion? "The whole reason I cornered you was so they could get some good out of your hide."

Sulley grunted. "Who you want to please more—them folks back in Kline, who didn't hesitate to get you to do their dirty work, or a real lady who's been nothing but good to you?"

Jeremiah felt a headache starting behind his eyes. He had a home and friends back in Kline. Common sense said he should find a way to get himself and Sulley back there and be done with this nonsense. Get back to living his life. Maybe settle down with . . .

"Alright. I'll give it a week. Been gone this long, what's a little longer?"

Sulley slapped him on the back. "You're doing the right thing, brother." He began whistling as the Fridley place came into view.

Jeremiah drove on with a warm feeling in the middle of his

chest. He decided to focus on that instead of the little voice in the back of his mind whispering he'd just made a deal with the devil.

The two men set out early the next morning, their bellies filled by Verna's generosity. Arbutus had begged to come with them, and Sulley halfway wished she could. He'd been hungry for adventure himself when he was that age.

"You keep an eye on Miss Gainey for us," he told the girl. "She's sad right now—kind of like your mama is. But if she asks about us, you just tell her we went on back to Kline." Arbutus nodded, a knowing shining in her eyes that was much too deep for someone so young.

"Where you figure on starting this grand adventure of yours?" Jeremiah asked.

Sulley looked at him sideways. Was he making fun? But the big man didn't seem to mean anything by it. Sulley guessed if he had to be cornered by someone, he was glad it was someone as easygoing as Jeremiah Weber.

"The old men are the ones sitting around in one spot long enough to gather up the news of a place." He motioned down the road where they could see the sun making long morning shadows as it cleared the mountains. "If we hurry, there might still be some coffee when we get there. You can use that money I gave you to put gas in your automobile."

He figured the old-timer who told him about the Phillips gold might know another thing or two. And he was willing to bet the man would be sitting in his chair next to a cold stove in the back of that store in Ansted.

He tried not to think too hard about what he was doing as

they made their way down the mountain in the cool of the morning. Birds were flitting around like they knew something he didn't, and the breeze felt good flowing over him. He could almost be content right now. So why wasn't he?

He pictured the look on Gainey's face when she decided to give up on looking for her boy. Had his own mother worn that expression at some point in her life? Did she wonder what happened to him, and had she resigned herself to never knowing? Was there any chance Gainey might be . . . That thought wasn't worth finishing. Of course she wasn't. And yet . . .

"That the place?" Jeremiah asked, pointing to the ramshackle store up ahead.

"Sure is," Sulley answered. "And if I'd bet you that old-timer would be sitting beside the stove, I'd have lost the bet."

"How do you know that?"

"'Cause that's him setting in a rocker out front under a shady tree."

Jeremiah chuckled. "Let's go see what he knows."

The man perked up when he saw them draw near. Most likely he'd worn out the ears of his friends and neighbors, and seeing two new pairs of them coming was an unexpected boon. "Morning, fellers. You lookin' for work?"

"You asked me that last time I came by here," Sulley answered. He squatted down and settled himself for a visit. Jeremiah leaned against the tree.

"Thought you looked familiar. You find that gold I told you about and come back to give me some?"

Sulley grinned. "Naw, I'm hunting something else this time around."

The old man waggled his brows. "If you're lookin' for a woman to wed, we've got some what don't hurt to look at around here."

"You ever run across a fella wearing a real nice shirt and a blue plaid tie?"

The man narrowed his eyes. "I don't believe we've been rightly introduced."

"Sullivan Harris is my name." He jerked a thumb over his shoulder. "That there's Jeremiah Weber."

"That man with the shirt and tie—he in some kind of trouble?"

Sulley chewed on that question a minute. "No, I guess not. Just trying to find out who he is." He almost said *who he was* but caught himself.

"Don't guess it matters," the man said, setting his chair to rocking. "Ain't seen him in months. Coulda been that preacher what tried to spread Jesus to the coloreds in the camps." He shook his head. "Harold, Harper—something like that. Made the bosses mad. We all figured they'd run him off." He squinted at Sulley. "That sound like the feller you're hunting?"

"Could be." Sulley considered that it would explain his having a Bible, although not why it was one that had belonged to Gainey. "Anybody else around here who could tell us about him?"

"Doubt it." He chuckled. "Not many folks as forthcoming as me. You'uns being strangers and all." He spit tobacco juice. "Although he did spend a fair amount of time down at Turkey Creek Church. Guess they might remember something."

"We'll give it a try," Sulley said, rising to his feet. "If I find that gold, I'll be seeing you again."

The old man grunted. "I'll try and hold off on planning my funeral until then."

"You do that," Sulley said with a grin. "Might mean you'll live a good long time."

"Blue plaid tie?" Jeremiah said as they walked off in the direction of the church.

"Best I could make out with all the dirt that's what the fella in the grave was wearing."

"Not many men wearing ties around these parts."

Sulley nodded. "So I noticed. Seemed like a good place to start."

Jeremiah smiled. "You might be smarter than you look."

"Considering how handsome I am, that must be right smart."

"Of course, it's the middle of the week and we're headed for a church. That might not be so smart."

Sulley picked up his pace. "Middle of the week's right. I'd expect a good churchgoing feller like yourself to know lots of folks have Wednesday night meetings after supper."

Jeremiah thought to mention that he was a Methodist but didn't suppose it mattered. "Are you sayin' we're going to church?"

"That we are." He chuckled. "So long as lightning doesn't strike me before I make it through the door."

"You're not a regular churchgoer, then?"

"I'm what you'd call an irregular churchgoer. Never noticed that God had much use for me, and the feeling's mutual." He rolled his shirtsleeves down and fastened the buttons. "But that doesn't mean the *folks* who go to church aren't useful." He finger-combed his hair. "Plus, church folks are prone to feeding people."

Jeremiah considered whether or not he ought to somehow preach to Sulley—tell him about God's love and Jesus' sacrifice—but what would be the point? He was clearly too hard-boiled to listen. And Jeremiah had never been altogether comfortable talking about such things anyway. No—if God wanted to redeem Sullivan Harris, He'd use someone holier, more patient, and better with words. He brightened. Maybe He'd use the pastor at Turkey Creek Church. Now, wouldn't that be something?

As they neared the church with its white clapboards and steeple pointed heavenward, they could indeed hear folks singing inside.

> "There's a land that is fairer than day,
> And by faith we can see it afar,
> For the Father waits over the way
> To prepare us a dwelling place there.
>
> In the sweet by and by,
> We shall meet on that beautiful shore . . ."

For a moment, Jeremiah was transported back to his childhood. He'd listened to those words and pictured an old man standing on a far hilltop above a lake, with a stout cabin behind him sending up a curl of smoke. There'd been a feeling of welcome and belonging that washed through him, and he guessed if that were heaven, he could get used to it.

Goodness, the things a body could forget over the years.

They slipped inside and found a spot in the back pew. They'd missed the sermon if there'd been one, but the congregation seemed fond of singing as they ran through two more hymns before the pastor went to the front to pray. And did he pray! Jeremiah bowed his head and tried to be properly somber, but the prayer went on and on. He guessed the preacher was lifting the whole county up, one at a time. Seated with his eyes closed, he might have dozed the least little bit. At least that's what he guessed when Sulley jammed a sharp elbow in his ribs, and he realized everyone was stirring, getting ready to leave.

He blinked rapidly and gave Sulley a sheepish smile. "Coulda got shut of you if I'd wanted," Sulley said. "Guess that prayer was pretty dozy."

"I would have sensed you trying to sneak away." Jeremiah grinned. He guessed he liked trading jabs with Sulley better than he did trying to run him down. If he weren't such a scoundrel, he could get to like him.

They hung back until most of the congregation had left, then stepped up to shake the pastor's hand at the door. "You fellers from down to the tunnel?" he asked. "I'm Pastor John Trotter, and we're always glad to welcome working men who know they have need of a Savior."

"Not exactly," Jeremiah said. "But we're trying to track down a fella who spent some time at the camps."

"Oh? And you thought I'd be able to help? He must be a fine, upstanding churchgoing fellow, then!"

"He's a preacher, but we're not sure of his persuasion," Sulley said. "His name was maybe something like Harold, and he was preaching to the coloreds."

The pastor's smile slipped. "Well then, he wouldn't have been what you'd call popular around the camps."

"No, that's the story we got. Thinking is the company men ran him off. And now nobody knows where he's ended up."

"Fellas, I'm here to do the Lord's work, which means I try to keep my nose out of the world's business." Pastor Trotter didn't look all that pleased with them anymore. "I'd recommend you do the same."

Jeremiah didn't suppose they could have been shown the

door any plainer. He slapped his hat on his head. "Pastor," he said with a nod and spun on his heel.

"Well, that was a bust," Sulley said. "And the singing wasn't even all that good."

A figure stepped into the path ahead of them. Drawing closer, they could see that it was a half-grown boy with bare feet, wearing ragged but clean overalls. Jeremiah remembered seeing him at the church and guessed he must have lingered to listen in on their conversation. "Come with me if you want to know about Harmon," the boy said.

Sulley took the lead. "Is he the preacher from down to the camps? You know where he is?"

"That's him, and not exactly—but I know who can likely tell you." He motioned for them to follow. "He ain't well, though. Might not be long fer this world. I been tryin' to get that church preacher you were talking with to come say some words over him, but he said he won't do it." The boy hung his head. "I been let down afore, but I thought a preacher would be different."

Jeremiah saw something flash in Sulley's eyes. Was it pain? Anger? He laid a hand on the boy's shoulder. "If you find anybody who won't let you down, you hang with 'em from then on. They're rare as hen's teeth."

The boy smiled and started down a side trail at a trot. Sulley lit out after him. Jeremiah hung back half a minute, wondering if it was wise to follow a ragamuffin into who-knew-what kind of a situation. Then he shrugged and followed. In for a penny, in for a pound.

twenty-three

It was as she expected. Jeremiah and Sulley had moved on. Gainey still felt a niggling curiosity to know if Sulley would offer Jeremiah and his friends back home satisfaction, but she supposed she would never know.

There were so many things she would never know.

Nevertheless, this evening she would indulge herself in a favorite pastime. In the absence of any particular person to care for, she'd come to care deeply for the woodland garden behind her house. She'd cosseted the garden over the years, and it had become her soul's delight. Mid-July was not a time for abundant blooms, but it was a time to savor the cool peace of a shade-dappled glade. Donning her gloves and slipping an apron over her day dress, she laced on a pair of sturdy shoes, took up her trowel and clippers, and headed outside.

A creek burbled behind her small house, and she'd hired some local men to build a bridge across it. Nothing fancy, nothing that would take attention away from the beauty of nature. She trod the boards and stepped into a clearing that was clear only because she made the effort to keep it so.

Inhaling deeply, Gainey felt her recent stress and strain begin to slip away with her exhalation. She ought to be in church for Wednesday evening services, but some days she found God more present in her woodland garden than in the church filled with neighbors and noise.

While the day had been humid, the cool of evening was close at hand. She could smell soil and leaf litter, could feel a breeze as it stirred the deep green leaves of summer. And there—the first of the season's Turk's-cap lilies. She'd transplanted them two summers ago and they hadn't bloomed the previous year—likely in shock from the move. She'd been holding out hope that they would unfurl brilliant orange petals this time around. Seeing them filled her with joy and hope.

Smiling, she set to work harvesting bee balm. The bright red flowers invited a hummingbird to dart from stem to stem before eyeing Gainey and disappearing. She watched it streak out of sight, then began stripping petals and leaves. She would dry plenty of them to use for Oswego tea and even for sweet sachets she could tuck among her linens.

She hummed as she worked, her eyes constantly distracted by the woodland Eden she'd created. Turtlehead flowers flashed pink and white, while the cardinal flowers showed swelling red buds. She'd either transplanted or encouraged most of the flowers in her little corner of the forest. And she loved each bloom as though she'd been the one to design the petals.

Virgin's bower twined along the creek bank, and she imagined how pretty it would look once the delicate white flowers opened. There was so little she could control in this world, but her garden was her pride and joy. People often told her it was impossible to transplant the wildflowers of these mountains, yet she'd done just that. From spring's trout lilies and trillium to fall's bottle gentian, she'd babied every plant she could find.

Hearing a sound, Gainey stood from her work, placing a hand in the small of her back to help her straighten. Arbutus stood on the bridge, her bare toes curled against the planks. "Hey there, Miss Gainey. I hope I ain't botherin' you."

"Aren't bothering me, child, and no—you're not. But why aren't you at church with your family?"

"Why ain't—aren't—you?" The girl stuck her chin out, knowing she was being sassy.

"I don't have a family to go with." Gainey knew that wasn't what Arbutus was getting at but intentionally misunderstood her anyway.

"I thought the church was your family."

Gainey sighed and removed her gloves. Arbutus was too smart for her own good. "You're right, of course. It's just that sometimes family can seem too—" she paused as she searched for the right word—"close."

Arbutus exhaled a world-weary sigh. "You got that right. Onliest one I want to be around right now is James, and he's gone." Tears rose in her eyes.

Gainey moved to a bench crafted from a split log and patted the spot next to her. "Come, sit, and we'll have our church right here."

"Can we do that?" Arbutus asked, settling her slight body beside Gainey.

Gainey smiled and tilted her head to gaze at the canopy of leaves above them. "While there is an argument to be made for the importance of the community that meets within the walls of the church building, God certainly cannot be contained by wood and glass." She made a sweeping motion with her arm. "And this seems an apt cathedral where two or more may gather in His name."

Arbutus giggled. "I like it when you talk grand."

Gainey found herself laughing along with the child. "I did sound awfully grand, didn't I? Well, there's nothing wrong with grand, but today I thought I'd like to see God in a lily bobbing in the breeze and hear Him in the song of a wren. So I came here."

Arbutus looked around, her eyes taking in the beauty of the place. "I'd like that, too. I like all the singing and hollering 'amen' at church, but some days a body just wants peace and quiet."

Gainey sighed. "Yes indeed. Peace is all too often a difficult thing to find. And when you have lost your peace, sometimes you just have to whip up a new batch all on your own."

When Sulley saw the young man sitting up in a rocking chair with a patchwork quilt laid across his knees, he felt his hands tingle. He shook them out, then flexed his fingers. If he'd been holding a dowsing rod, he'd say water was close to hand.

The man—little more than a boy really—was all hide, bone, and leaders. His skin was taut across his skull, and the tendons in his neck stood out like he was straining to hold his head up. His eyes were unnaturally bright. Sulley guessed the boy who'd led them here was right about his not having long to live.

"Jackie, who have you brought?" he asked.

"These fellers want to know about Harmon. They was asking the preacher up at the church about him."

A woman stuck her head in the room and frowned. "I hope you'uns aren't come for supper."

Sulley had already taken in the fact that the house was little more than a shack, with newsprint tacked up on the walls to keep the draft out. He spoke up quick. "No, ma'am, but we do have some cornmeal we can spare if it'd be a help to you."

"Don't need charity," she said, eyes darting.

Jeremiah, who was carrying their belongings in his rucksack, pulled out a small parcel. "I've been toting this all over creation, and it's weighing me down. You'd be doing me a favor if you could put it to good use before the weevils get in it."

The woman narrowed her eyes. "Set it on the table there if you don't want it," she said at last. She cast a look at the boy. "Jackie, don't forget your chores." Then she disappeared back into what Sulley figured was the kitchen. Jeremiah set the sack down on a wooden table, looked thoughtful, and added some of Verna's molasses cookies.

The young man in the chair began coughing with such violence, Sulley jumped. The coughing came so hard and fast he couldn't get air back in his lungs except through great wheezes. Jackie sat on the foot of a nearby bed, seemingly unaffected by the fit. Sulley thought back to Lewis, sitting on a rock at Lover's Leap. He thought he could guess what was ailing this fellow.

"Whew. That was bad," he said. "Let's see if I can't get some talking done before it hits again." He managed a smile. "So, you want to know about Pastor Harmon Wilkins come to spread the good news. I didn't know him much, but the men down at the tunnel told stories about him trying to carry Jesus—or something—to the colored camps."

"You worked in the tunnel?" Sulley asked.

"I was a mucker till the tunnelitis got me." He shook his head. "Gets everybody sooner or later, best I can tell." His face softened. "I'd been trying to earn enough to wed Maryanne." He looked toward the door where the woman had stood. He grinned at the boy. "Had it in mind to be a husband to her and a daddy to this one. Then when I got sick, I told her there wasn't any need to take me on." He shook his head, and his voice roughened. "But she showed up with Harmon and he married us. Now she's taking care of me when it oughta be the other way around."

"Where is he now?" Sulley could see the veins in the man's neck throbbing with each beat of his heart. Just the effort of talking seemed to require all his energy.

"Don't know. Been six months since he married us. I kept working for a while after that. I'd tie a wet handkerchief over my face against the dust and that helped some, but then I got to where I was passing out down in the tunnel, and Maryanne finally made me give it up." He ran a hand over the quilt in his lap. "What do you want with Harmon anyhow?"

"We've got a friend who's looking for her boy. She thought your preacher might be him."

A shadow fell across the man's face. "A lost son? She's missing him, is she?" Sulley nodded. "Guess not every mama would want her boy back. Especially not if there were hard words before he ran off without a backward look."

Sulley started to say something sharp when he felt Jeremiah lay a hand on his arm. The big man spoke. "In my experience, mamas are usually willing to forgive an awful lot. Say, we have yet to introduce ourselves. This here's Sullivan Harris, and I'm Jeremiah Weber." He stuck out a hand and the man took it.

"Noah Johnson. Pleased to make your acquaintance."

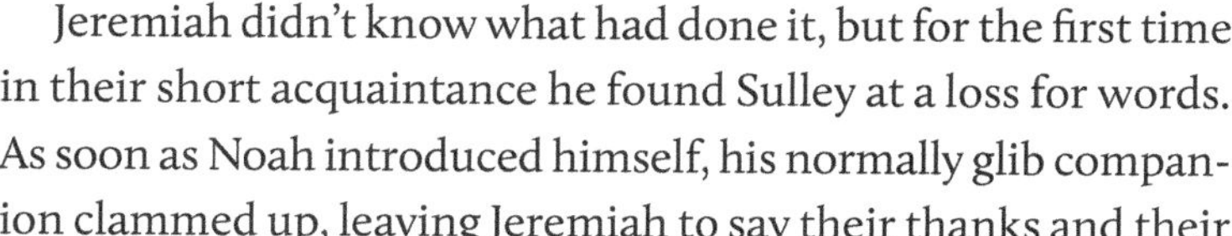

Jeremiah didn't know what had done it, but for the first time in their short acquaintance he found Sulley at a loss for words. As soon as Noah introduced himself, his normally glib companion clammed up, leaving Jeremiah to say their thanks and their farewells. He'd suggested they make their way to the nearest camp for black workers so they could ask around about Pastor Harmon Wilkins. Sulley nodded mutely, and now they were headed down the mountain toward the tunnel camps.

Jeremiah couldn't stand it any longer. "What's stuck in your craw?"

Sulley looked at him and blinked as if he'd just woken up. "Nothing."

"Then how come you haven't spoken since that feller back there told us his name?"

"I dowsed some wells for his ma and pa. They wanted me to dowse for him, too." Sulley crossed his arms over his chest and stared through the windscreen.

"Dowse for a person? Can you do that?"

Sulley shrugged. "Some folks claim they can, although it's mostly for dead people. I don't ever aim to try." He frowned deeply. "Unnatural."

"So why didn't you tell Noah his folks are looking for him?" Jeremiah was puzzled. Seemed like Noah would be glad to have word from home.

"Maybe he doesn't want to be found." Sulley's shoulders pulled in tight.

Jeremiah let silence reign for a few minutes while he pondered this. "You gonna tell his parents you found him?"

Sulley's head whipped around and he glared at Jeremiah. "I didn't find him. It was pure chance."

"Alright. You gonna tell them?"

Sulley shrugged again. "Don't know that I'll be seeing them again. Guess it's not any of my business anyhow."

Jeremiah decided he'd leave the conversation there. Although he still wondered what was eating at Sulley.

Each time he successfully dowsed for water, Sulley got a particular feeling. He'd never tried to pin it down, but if he had to, he guessed he'd call it a feeling of completeness. A finishing of a task he'd been set. He had that feeling now and he wished he didn't. He'd looked closely at the boy in that chair and saw something of Freeman's long face and Luisa's smile. He hadn't dowsed for their boy, but he'd sure enough found him.

And now Jeremiah was after him to do something about it. Well, he hadn't tried to find Noah. Hadn't asked to find him. Had no reason to stick his oar in. Finding—or not finding—water was one thing, but people were a whole other kettle of fish. Water didn't care one way or the other if it was found. People—now, they tended to have strong feelings.

For most of his life, he'd wanted to find his own mother. The little bit he knew about dowsing for graves came from that. If she were dead, it would explain why she never came for him. It was one thing to be abandoned by choice, but something else altogether if she'd been dying and gave him up because it was the best she could do.

But as he'd told Jeremiah, the process felt unnatural to him—unholy even. He'd never been able to bring himself to try it or to even let someone else try it on his behalf. And of course, she might not be dead, though that hadn't mattered with Noah.

He flexed his fingers, trying to shake that tingling feeling. What if he did have a knack for finding lost people? And if his mother was alive, what if he could find her? He balled his hands into fists.

What if he'd found her already?

twenty-four

The camp was quiet when they walked in around dusk. Women and a few men were sitting on the steps to the shacks while a handful of children played in the dirt. Jeremiah noticed they were awfully quiet for young'uns.

He spotted Martha and lifted a hand. She hurried toward them. "Where's Miss Gainey at?"

"She's back home," Jeremiah said.

The woman's shoulders relaxed and she nodded. "Good. Butch didn't much like her comin' round. I don't want to see her get into no kind of trouble." She squinted at Jeremiah. "How come you're back? And who's he?" She stared at Sulley

"This is my, uh, friend Sulley Harris. We wanted to ask after a preacher who was comin' around a while back. Harmon Wilkins is his name."

"Hunh." Martha wrinkled her nose like she'd caught a whiff of last week's unwashed socks. "Preacher is what he called hisself, but a meddler is what he was."

"What do you mean?"

"He acted like he was here to bring some Jesus to the . . . now, what did he call us?" She wrinkled her forehead. "'Downtrodden masses.' That's what he said. Told us we were being ill-used, and Jesus would save us." She snorted. "Like we didn't know. He was just tryin' to start something. Just about got it done, too."

"What stopped him?" Sulley leaned in, clearly eager to hear the story.

"Rouster and that big black fella what follows him around run him off. Least we're pretty sure that's what happened. Anyhow, he ain't been around since, oh, spring I guess."

"Do you think he was trying to help?" Jeremiah asked. "Maybe this Wilkins fellow saw how bad conditions were and thought to do something about it."

"If he was tryin' to help, it wasn't the kind of help we needed. All he did was get a few of our men to stand up for theirselves, and they paid the price in blood and bruises." She shook her head. "Same kind of trouble y'all could stir up." She darted her eyes all around. "If you stay too long and act too interested, they'll run you off, too."

"What about you?" Jeremiah was beginning to feel worried about Martha. Was she risking her own safety by talking to them?

"Aw, they might give me a hard time, but I'm too valuable around here. So long as I don't try to stir anybody up—just do the washing and keep watch over the women—they'll leave me be." A hand went to her throat where a scar disappeared under the neckline of her dress. "Mostly."

"What was Harmon wearing the last time you saw him?" Sulley asked.

"Funny you ask—he was a right snappy dresser." She closed her eyes and tilted her head to the sky. "He most always wore a tie—even when he first come around last August in the heat of the summer." She nodded and opened her eyes. "That's right. He had on a white shirt, worn at the cuffs, and that blue tie of his with the plaid pattern." She smiled. "Noticed there was a stain on it—probably coffee."

"Did he carry a Bible?" Jeremiah asked. He didn't think they needed much more confirmation, but every little bit helped.

Martha laughed. "Not much. Saw him with one a time or two, but I always got the feeling it was mostly for decoration." She glanced over their shoulders. "Time you two got on," she said and hurried back to her washpot, casting nervous glances toward two men headed up the path. Jeremiah could see it was a white man with pistols on his hips, followed closely by a giant of a black man.

"I'm inclined to agree," Sulley said in a low voice. Jeremiah turned to speak to him just in time to see him disappear into the trees. He kicked up his heels and followed.

The two men sat around a cook fire later that evening, eating the last of Verna's corn cakes and pondering what to do next. "Sure enough seems like the fella in that grave is this preacher man. And him having Gainey's Bible inclines me to believe he's her missing boy," Jeremiah said. "Guess we oughta go back and give her the news."

Sulley nodded mutely, and yet he wasn't so sure. It didn't feel right. If he were willing to admit it, he'd have to say the uneasy feeling he had now was a whole lot like the feeling he got before pointing someone toward digging a dry hole. It's how he'd felt when he set those folks back in Kline to digging that last well. Something in him knew there wasn't water, knew they were going to be disappointed. And so he'd gotten while the getting was good.

He'd always told himself dowsing was for chumps. The fact

that he found water more often than not was because he knew the likely spots. And so he let people pay him for putting on a show. But if he was honest, he *did* feel something when water was near. And he sure enough didn't get that feeling when there wasn't any water. It was only now that he was getting the same feeling with people that he was really paying attention—noticing it in a way that made it hard to pretend otherwise.

And it was making him almighty uncomfortable.

Gainey dabbed at her neck with a handkerchief as she paused in sorting the day's mail. July had turned even hotter with thunderstorms most afternoons. It was an aggravation when you were trying to hang out laundry or cut hay, but at least the storms meant they didn't have to carry water to gardens, and they usually broke the heat. She sighed. Wasn't that the way of life? Just about everything that was good for one thing was bad for another.

Hearing someone enter the store, Gainey glanced up and was surprised to see Jeremiah walking toward her. He'd obviously washed his face and wetted his hair moments before, probably down at the creek. His hair was slicked back, his beard glistening where he hadn't dried it completely. She almost smiled at the notion he'd taken pains to look presentable before coming to see her. But no. More likely he'd just been cooling off on a hot day. The bigger question was what he was still doing here in Mount Lookout.

"I thought you'd be back in Kline by now," she said, dabbing at her face with the lace-edged handkerchief. She must look a sight.

"Headed that way shortly, but first me and Sulley made a side trip." She noticed that he was fiddling with the strap on the bag he wore slung across his back. What was he nervous about? "You think we could talk somewhere private?" He glanced toward Susan, who stood behind the front counter watching them with unabashed interest.

"Surely." She managed a smile. "Fortunately, Arbutus is running an errand or I doubt we'd be able to find a quiet spot." She led him out back to the stream where Susan's husband had placed a crude bench so the ladies could take their lunches out there. They sat side by side, Gainey keenly aware of the masculine solidity mere inches from her—much as she'd been when they were in the wagon together. How was it that she'd gone for years without being aware of the physicality of any man, and now suddenly she couldn't escape the presence of this one? And—more shockingly—didn't want to?

"Gainey, me and Sulley did a little of what you might call investigating after we left you."

She stiffened, not liking the sound of two men prying into her business, even though she'd originally asked it of them. "And where is Sulley?" She attempted to divert Jeremiah.

"He's making us a camp over yon in a clearing. Can't keep taking advantage of Reggie and Verna."

"Oh, I doubt they'd see it that way." Gainey opened her mouth to prattle on when she saw the seriousness in Jeremiah's eyes and felt his stillness touch her spirit. She hushed.

"We went back and talked to Martha." Again she started to speak—to ask after the washerwoman—and again Jeremiah's expression silenced her. "She told us a preacher by the name of Harmon Wilkins had been coming around, stirring up trouble with the black men in the camps. He disappeared maybe four months back."

Gainey found herself hanging on his words, almost holding her breath. Had these two men gone off and found her son? Was it possible? Hope and fear warred inside her.

"Well, he was run off is what Martha said." Jeremiah took a deep breath and spoke more quickly. "He was wearing a white shirt and a blue plaid tie last Martha saw him. Carried a Bible, too." He shifted on the bench, making it creak beneath her. "Just like the man in that grave Sulley found."

Gainey felt the world tilt and swirl as colors danced before her eyes, then gave way to nothingness.

"I have never, in all my life, swooned before." As Jeremiah helped Gainey back to a sitting position, he thought she seemed more upset about fainting than about the identity of the man in the grave. "Mortifying. Absolutely mortifying!"

"I guess it was a pretty big shock."

Gainey sighed and fanned herself with a lacy handkerchief. "I did not ask you to look further," she said. "As a matter of fact, I requested that you *not* do so."

"Well. Now. I suppose that's true. Only Sulley thought—"

"So you lay the blame at Mr. Harris's feet? Now that you mention him, why in the world were you so determined to find him?" She waved toward the woods beyond the creek. "And why have you delayed returning home?"

Jeremiah blew out a long, slow breath. Was this another pickle Sulley had gotten him into? Anger and frustration flared. "As it happens, he fleeced some good folks back in Kline. Told them he could find a well and then disappeared with their money."

She lowered her hand and stared at him. "He stole from them?"

"Lied and stole, the way I see it. We dug three wells, each one drier than the last. Not much of that town left, and some of those folks put all they had toward the hope of water." He shook his head. "And Sulley up and left."

"And you have been pursuing him since," she said, the words in a low voice. "Why do you not set the authorities after him?"

"Once he disappeared, wasn't much for the sheriff to do. He put out word, but these are hard times and I guess there are harder things for the law to deal with."

"And so you set out in pursuit."

Jeremiah nodded. "Been hunting him for a couple of months now."

"And why do you suppose he won't flee again?" Gainey glanced toward the woods as though she might see Sulley looking back from behind a tree.

Jeremiah patted his pocket. "I've got his money. What little he had left."

Gainey tucked the handkerchief she was still clutching into her sleeve. "I was suspicious of him at first, but he won me over. He found several wells for us here. And he helped the Fridley family. Charmed the Johnsons. I just . . ." She swiped at her eyes with the back of her hand. "I'm so very disappointed in him."

"Even a blind hog finds an acorn now and again," Jeremiah said. His discomfort was growing. Now that she'd mentioned the Johnsons, he felt bound to tell her about Noah, yet he was no longer certain how she would take the news. Would she think it was simply more meddling? "About the Johnsons—"

"Don't tell me he cheated them in some way," she said sharply. "I saw the wells and tasted the water myself."

"No, it's not that. Seems like they were looking for their boy, too." She nodded, a mixture of suspicion and fear in her eyes. He hated that he'd put that expression there. "Thing is, we found Noah."

She gasped. "Where? Is he well? We must go tell Luisa immediately."

"He's not far from Ansted. I've got the way written down here." He produced a bit of paper with the directions scrawled on it. "He worked in the tunnel until he got so sick he couldn't do it anymore. Thing is—"

She was already on her feet, grabbing the paper from his hand. "I'll go. It will be better coming from me." She looked down at him—not something he was used to, big as he was. "I'm almost willing to forgive your meddling in my situation, thanks to this. At least one mother will have her child restored to her."

Jeremiah reached out and grasped her wrist. He tugged gently, and she silently resumed her seat. "Before you run off to the Johnsons, let me tell you the rest. Noah's married and there's a boy." Her eyes widened. "Not his, I don't guess. But the Johnsons will need to know that, too."

"They wanted him to marry Myrtle Hampstead's granddaughter. I think that was part of the reason he left." She looked into Jeremiah's eyes, and he felt suddenly light-headed. "This may be difficult for Luisa to accept." Jeremiah nodded, at a loss for words. "Thank you for slowing me down," she said and squeezed his hand. Then she hurried back toward the store and disappeared inside.

Jeremiah watched her go. When he said he didn't much understand women, he'd been speaking the truth. She was mad that he'd stuck his nose in her business but glad he'd done the same for the Johnson family. He guessed maybe it was just as well that he needed to haul Sulley's sorry carcass back to Kline. At least he knew exactly what Meredith wanted from him.

Still pondering the ways of women, he followed a narrow critter trail into the woods. Sulley said to go about a half mile until he came to a place where water spilled over a ledge of rock not much higher than a man. Sulley said there was a pool there where they could wash and rest before heading back to Kline. And Jeremiah was looking forward to it. Stripping down to his skivvies and getting clean was about the only thing that made sense to him just then.

As he moved through the rhododendron and tulip poplar, he heard the sound of falling water. Drawing near, he saw the prettiest little pool at the base of a small waterfall. There was a fire ring and a scuffed spot where someone had clearly lain down. Unfortunately, that was all he saw. Sulley was nowhere to be found.

twenty-five

Frustration and elation warred for top billing in Gainey's mind. She was tempted to break into a run in her eagerness to take her good news to Luisa. At the same time, she was angry that Jeremiah and Sulley had taken it upon themselves to find her son. And now she supposed it really was her son dead and buried in the edge of that field in Summersville. She supposed the sorrow of that would sink in at some point, but right now it felt distant. All she could manage in the moment was to take consolation in the fact that he had been a man of God. Surely such a man would have forgiven his mother long ago.

Luisa was in the garden gathering half runner beans. She wore a broad-brimmed hat and had one of Freeman's bandannas tied at her throat. When she saw Gainey, she stood and waved, then lifted her basket to her hip and made her way toward the house. Gainey met her halfway. "I have some news for you. Is Freeman about?"

"He's out fussing with his apple trees. He'll be along in time for supper if you want to join us. It's just cold leftovers, but you're welcome."

Gainey bit her lip, wanting to blurt out her news but wanting even more to tell them both at the same time—it felt like the right thing to do. "Only if you'll let me help," Gainey said.

"Of course I will. I'd be glad of your hands alongside mine." Luisa led the way to the kitchen.

Gainey managed to make stilted conversation as they set out a simple supper of bread, slices of cold roast beef, and a salad of tomatoes and cucumbers still warm from the garden. Luisa dressed the vegetables with her own sour cream and dill she'd snipped from a pot outside the kitchen door.

Gainey was hugely relieved to finally see Freeman's lanky form striding toward the house. He greeted her warmly, and she thought she saw a look pass between the couple before they sat, said grace, and began eating.

"I have significant news to share," Gainey said before they'd even filled their plates.

Luisa stopped and folded her hands in her lap. "It seemed to me that something is weighing you down."

Gainey looked back and forth between the couple. How had she come to this point without knowing precisely what she would say? "Jeremiah has brought me some news."

Luisa looked surprised, then got a sparkle in her eye. "Has he now. I had not suspected your news would have to do with him."

"Oh. No. I only mean that he's been looking into . . . well, he found . . ." Gainey flushed and felt twice as flustered. She laid her hands against the edge of the table to ground herself. "It seems he has discovered where Noah is living." Luisa paled, and Freeman clutched his wife's hand as though to keep her from falling. Or perhaps it was to keep himself steady. "He was working in the Hawks Nest Tunnel and is now living not far from Ansted." She felt it was important to let the couple know their son was sick, not to mention married and stepfather to a half-grown boy, yet she decided to let the initial news sink in before going on.

Freeman was the first to find his voice. "You say he was working in the tunnel? What's he doing now?"

"Never mind that." Luisa leaned toward Gainey. "Is he well? How did he look? Why has he not come home or written?"

Gainey wet her lips. Where to begin? "It seems he's contracted the tunnelitis so many of the men working there suffer." Luisa's hand flew to her mouth to stifle a gasp. "That's why he's no longer working in the tunnel. His . . . well, Jeremiah said he's married, and his wife convinced him to quit."

Luisa fell back against her chair and clutched the neck of her blouse. Freeman had relaxed his grip and was now patting her hand, although Gainey felt certain he didn't know he was doing it.

Freeman cleared his throat. "And did he say why he hasn't come home so we can take care of him?"

"I don't believe they discussed that. Jeremiah and Sulley went to him to ask—" she hesitated, as the Johnsons had no idea she'd ever had a son—"about something else."

Luisa's eyes widened, and she looked at Freeman in wonder. "Sulley has found our son—just as we asked him to do." Her hand went to her mouth again. Tears shone in her eyes.

"So it would seem," Freeman answered, voice husky. "I'll fetch him home tomorrow."

"But . . ." Gainey bit her lip. "What if he doesn't want to come home? What if he wants to stay with his wife?" Though the questions were not her business to ask, she couldn't contain them.

"We'll bring her, too," Freeman said.

"There's also a boy," Gainey blurted. "The woman must have had him already. Jeremiah thought he was nine or ten."

"*Das enkelkind*," Luisa breathed. "Oh, Freeman, a child!" The couple stood as one and clasped each other, tears flowing.

Gainey wasn't certain what she had expected, but this wasn't it. The pair laughed through their tears and finally sat to eat the meal, praising Gainey for bringing such good news and urging her to eat more—to feast with them. "I'll leave first thing in the morning," Freeman said to his wife. "Cook a fine supper tomorrow—that will be the real feast!"

"Gainey, will you come again to celebrate with us?" Luisa asked. "You are part of this joy now. Please come, and perhaps invite Jeremiah and Sulley, too. We will have *das fest*!"

Gainey couldn't imagine wanting anyone with her if she'd ever been reunited with her son. But that would never happen now. She felt a lump form in her throat. She'd told herself she didn't deserve to grieve that man in the unmarked grave, but seeing a mother's joy . . . She swallowed hard and stiffened her resolve. "Of course I'll come," she said.

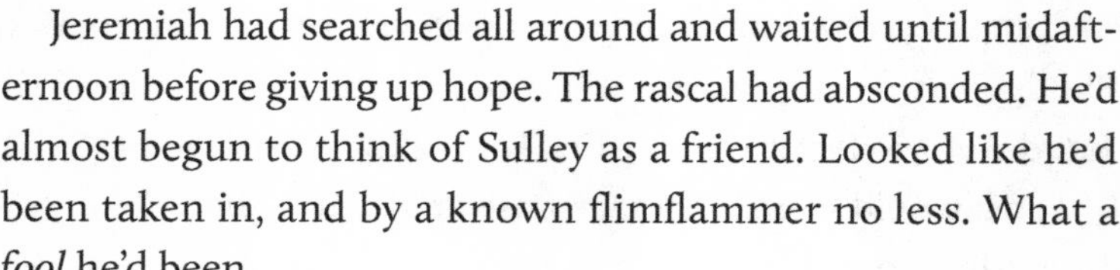

Jeremiah had searched all around and waited until midafternoon before giving up hope. The rascal had absconded. He'd almost begun to think of Sulley as a friend. Looked like he'd been taken in, and by a known flimflammer no less. What a *fool* he'd been.

He went ahead and had his bath and brushed his clothes as best he could before trudging back to town. He was through with this nonsense. Come morning he'd use some more of Sulley's money to gas up the Model T and head home. The good people of Kline might be disappointed in him, but then again, he'd done more than any of them had been willing to do. They could like it or lump it. And as soon as he got back, he'd propose to Meredith. Might as well.

He walked to the store. Maybe Gainey would be back from giving the Johnsons the news about Noah, as he wanted to say goodbye. At least finding Noah was one good thing that had come out of all this. He glanced at the sun. It was getting late. She might just go home, and he wasn't sure he had any right to follow her there.

Arbutus was sweeping the porch when he walked up. "Is Miss Gainey back from the Johnsons'?"

"No sir, and the store's closed now so I don't expect to see her until tomorrow. It ain't—isn't—like her to stay gone so much." The girl gave him an appraising look. "She's been acting funny ever since Sulley showed up. I can't figure her out anymore, and she's always been easy to figure out before."

Jeremiah chuckled. "That makes two of us. Glad I'm not on my own." He winked and headed along the road toward the Johnsons'. Maybe he'd meet Gainey on her way back. As he passed a pond, he thought he heard something out of place and paused to listen.

There. It sounded like crying. Noticing a trail around the water, he walked a short distance and came upon Gainey sitting on a rock, rigid back toward him. She did not move, but he had the notion she knew he was there.

"Am I bothering you?"

She cleared her throat. "Not at all. Just taking in the beauty of the evening."

"Mind if I join you?" She flipped a hand over her shoulder, and he took that to mean *do what you want*. He sat—not too close and a little behind her.

"How'd Luisa take the news?"

"Freeman is going after Noah first thing tomorrow. He intends to bring him—and his family, I assume—back here." She picked up a twig and twirled it between her fingers. "Do you suppose . . . well, certainly he'll come home. Won't he? Even if there were hard words before he left?"

Jeremiah felt like she was asking something else but didn't know what it could be. "I sure would if I were him."

"Is he as bad off as James was?"

This time, he thought he knew what she was asking. "Maybe not. He was pretty puny, but regular food and the love of family might be just the thing to make him well again."

"I pray that it is," she said, the words soft as a sigh.

She glanced back at him, and he could see that her eyes were red, as was her nose. He hated when women cried. He never knew what to do about it. "Where's Mr. Harris?" she asked.

Jeremiah grunted. "Rapscallion ran off."

This time she shifted so she could face him—not fully but more than she had been. "Ran off? But I thought he was making camp for the two of you."

Jeremiah's earlier anger rose again. "That's what he said, and fool that I am, I believed him." He picked up a rock and threw it as far as he could out into the pond where it disappeared with a satisfying *kerplunk*. "Guess he knew an easy mark when he saw one."

"What will you do?" Gainey was clear-eyed now, seemingly distracted from her sorrow by his difficulty.

"I'm going home. I've had enough of Sullivan Harris, and if anyone wants more than the little bit I got out of him, they'll have to go after it themselves."

Gainey's eyes had gone wide. "He really is a confidence

man, then?" She pulled out a handkerchief and dabbed at her eyes. Looked like she might be welling up again. "I know you told me that already, but I'd hoped . . ." She sighed. "I don't know why I even bother to hope anymore. It's so often a futile act."

Now Jeremiah felt bad. When he'd heard her crying, he thought to ease whatever was troubling her. And all he'd done was deepen her sorrow. "Well, he is a charmer, and I guess he didn't do any harm around here. Helped me find Noah, and sounds like that might work out alright."

"Why don't you come with me to the Johnsons' tomorrow?" She flushed and began to fuss with folding and refolding her handkerchief. "What I mean to say is, Luisa and Freeman would surely welcome you since you played a key role in finding Noah. It would be nice for you to be present for his homecoming." She laughed. "As a matter of fact, Luisa mentioned it, and she'll make enough food for the whole town. I have the feeling we could both stand to see a little joy right now." She lifted those liquid brown eyes to his. "What's one more day?"

Jeremiah nodded. He could use a dose of joy, and another day would hardly matter. "I'll walk out there with you. I'd like to see something good come out of all this running around."

"Well then." She stood and dusted her skirt. "It's decided. If you'll come to the store at five, we can walk over together."

Jeremiah got to his feet as well. "Sounds like a fine plan. And in the meantime, might I walk you home?"

She laughed. "I hardly need an escort."

"True, but I need some company, and yours is better than average." Jeremiah felt his neck heat. What was he doing? He was leaving here in short order. She smiled and fell into step beside him, and although they didn't say much more all the way back to the house, he found himself relaxing. She gave him the same feeling he had when snug by a crackling fire in the depths of winter. The world might be inhospitable, dangerous even, but right here, right now was good. He didn't dare stop to examine the feeling too closely.

twenty-six

Gainey was glad she'd invited Jeremiah along for Noah's homecoming. And even more grateful he'd agreed to stay. It had been such a spontaneous action—she was beginning to wonder if her personality was taking a turn. Perhaps it was the death of the hope of ever finding her son. Losing that had freed something inside her, loosened something she didn't know had been too tight. And today she realized she was angry that other women—her friends—could openly talk about and even mourn their sons, while she carried a secret that was now dead and buried in more ways than one.

Luisa had prepared a feast. Gainey offered to help, but it was obvious Luisa needed every single task to distract her from waiting. She welcomed Jeremiah with joy and immediately settled the two of them on the porch with glasses of lemonade. Gainey took a sip of the sweet, tart drink and felt the condensation on the outside of the glass drip onto her cotton skirt.

"Looks like rain," Jeremiah said, gazing at the sky. Indeed, dark clouds were unfurling from the peak of the nearest mountain, and Gainey hoped Freeman would return with Noah before the rain began. Then she considered that, in all honesty, she just hoped that Freeman returned with Noah.

"I think they will be here soon." Luisa bustled out on the porch with her pitcher of lemonade and seemed disappointed that they'd barely begun drinking what they had.

"Sit with us a moment," Gainey said, patting the glider beside her. "I know you have everything ready."

Luisa placed her pitcher on a small table and perched on the edge of the cushion, clearly ready to take flight at the least provocation. "I hope they are not delayed." She squinted at the darkening sky. "With Noah ill, it would not be good for him to get wet."

Gainey ached for her friend. She certainly knew the dangers of hoping for something that might not happen.

"Did I ever tell you the one about the fella interviewing for a job as stationmaster?" Jeremiah asked. Luisa's head swiveled like an owl's. Gainey suspected she'd forgotten about her second guest.

"You are a storyteller?" She smiled and slid back onto the glider. Gainey set it into motion, and Luisa relaxed another notch.

"This fella—George was his name—was trying out for the job of running the train station over in Thurmond. He thought he pretty well had it licked, but he had to go to one more meeting with the town council, and one councilman—I think he was the banker—decided to ask a real hard question. He said, 'Imagine you have a train coming northbound at forty miles per hour and then see you also have a train coming southbound on the same track at fifty miles per hour. What would you do?'" Gainey watched Jeremiah become more animated. He appeared to be a showman when he took a notion. And Luisa was now completely focused on him, the worry over her boy set aside, however briefly.

"Well, George knew he was in a pickle, so he said the only thing he could think of. 'Why, I'd call my cousin.' That banker sat back in his chair and asked, 'Now, why in the world would you call your cousin? Do you think he could help solve the problem?' George laughed. 'Naw,' he said. 'It's just my cousin ain't never seen a train wreck before.'"

Luisa blinked, then clapped her hands and burst into a peal of laughter. "Oho," she said, wagging a finger at Jeremiah. "This appears to be a funny story, but there is a lesson besides." She nodded her head and folded her hands in her lap, still chuckling. "There are some things we simply cannot do anything to change. And so we must sit back and see what will happen, then make the best of the situation."

Serene now, she stood and reached for the handle of the screen door. "And now I think I can wait more calmly. Thank you." Beaming a smile at Jeremiah, she breezed back inside the house.

Gainey stared at the big man, swigging his lemonade. "That was wonderful," she said. "It was the perfect thing to say."

Jeremiah shrugged. "I'll confess I just thought it was funny. Hoped it might distract her from worrying." He laughed. "I think she might have just taught me a real good lesson." Gainey laughed low and deep—the kind of laugh that made her feel clean from the inside out. She was trying to think how to tell him how much she was coming to value his friendship when he set his glass down and stood.

"Here they come," he said as thunder rolled down the mountain. "And just in the nick of time, too."

That night, Jeremiah settled his bulk into a bunk in the Johnsons' barn. Strictly speaking it should have been more comfortable than Verna and Reggie's back porch, but he missed the breeze blowing through the screen and he maybe even missed that old hound dog, too. There was something consoling about the whiffles and whimpers of a sleeping dog. Might have to get one once he was back in Kline.

Luisa said she wished she could give him the guest room, but it was happily full of family. And that was a true statement if ever he'd heard one. When they came up into the yard, they were riding double on Freeman's two mules, Noah and Maryanne together on one and Jackie holding on to Freeman on the other. Although he had to be nearly sixty, Freeman had hopped down like a man half his age and lifted the boy after him with a whoop and a shout of joy. "Luisa, come see your grandboy!" he hollered.

Luisa burst through the door laughing and crying, and Freeman lifted his grown son down from the mule with a tenderness that put a lump in Jeremiah's throat. He'd offered to put up the mules, and Freeman slapped him on the back and shook his hand, saying "Thank you" over and over again.

Once he returned from the barn, the family was gathered around a table set with a lace tablecloth and rose-strewn china. The room was filled with voices, laughter, and the smells of roast pork and fresh bread. Even Gainey looked young and free in a way he'd not noticed before. And boy did he notice it now, although since he was leaving he figured he'd better stop.

They ate and talked and told stories, and Luisa had him tell the stationmaster story all over again. Everyone laughed like it was the funniest thing they'd ever heard. And although Noah's cough was terrible, the pinched look he'd seen on Maryanne's face back in Ansted had eased. Jackie had the look of a boy who'd been given his first hunting rifle and horse all on the same day.

When it was time to go, Jeremiah and Gainey were barely out of the yard before Freeman called them back. "I've got a bunk out there in the barn—you're welcome to use it if you'll give me a hand in the orchard the next few days." He grinned. "Noah will help once he's healed up, but I sure could use your help until then." Jeremiah opened his mouth to say he was leaving in the morning, then glanced at Gainey and saw her expression tighten and her lips turn down. And just like that, his plans changed. "I'd be proud to help," he said, and they shook on it.

As he walked beside Gainey along the dirt road, he found himself still smiling. There'd been such joy all evening—a person couldn't help but smile.

"While I appreciate your behaving like a gentleman, I'm truly fine to walk home on my own." Gainey's voice pulled him from his reverie.

"I know," he said. "I've rarely met a more capable or competent woman. But it's a pleasant evening—cool after that spell of rain—and I think I mentioned once before that your company suits me."

She sighed. "That's kind of you to say."

"Nothing more than the truth." He felt expansive, like even things that appeared to be going all wrong might somehow be going right after all.

"Do you think he'll . . . ?" Gainey hesitated. "Tunnelitis caused James to die. Might it not do the same to Noah?"

Jeremiah had thought of this as well. "It might." He tried to formulate his thoughts. Gainey wasn't someone to ramble on with. "I guess we're all dying. Some of us faster than others. Some see it coming, some don't. But the way I look at it,

Freeman and Luisa are about as happy as two people can get right now. And even if that boy dies tomorrow, they will have had tonight."

Gainey had two fingers pressed tight to her lips like she was trying to hold something in. She lowered her hand. "Maybe, if I'd been a better mother, I would have had at least one night of joy with my son."

Jeremiah could have smacked himself. Of course she was thinking about her own boy. "I bet you would've been a real good mother if you'd had the chance," he said at last. "I see the way you are with Arbutus—gentle and loving but you hold her accountable. I'm thinking you would have been just the same with your own young'un."

She was quiet a long time, and Jeremiah figured he'd put his foot in it even worse. Then she whispered, "Thank you for that." He wanted to take her hand more than anything then, but he didn't dare.

Now night was falling, and Jeremiah lay alone staring at the rafters of the barn, wondering how he could ease Gainey's pain even though he knew it wasn't his place to do it.

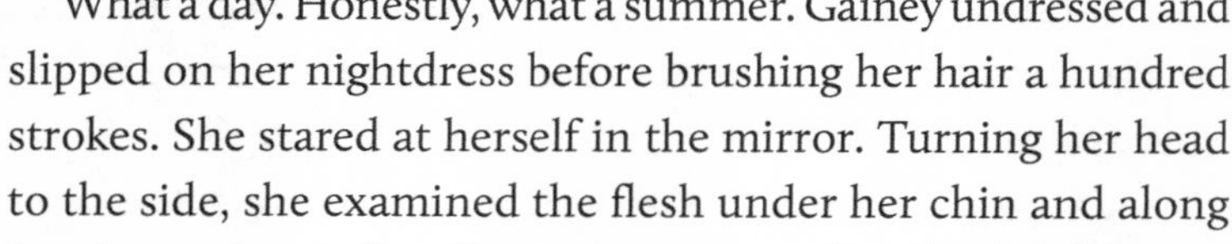

What a day. Honestly, what a summer. Gainey undressed and slipped on her nightdress before brushing her hair a hundred strokes. She stared at herself in the mirror. Turning her head to the side, she examined the flesh under her chin and along her throat. It wasn't as firm as it once was, but she didn't have a turkey's neck yet. And her hair was still more pepper than salt.

She flung the brush down on the vanity and strode across the hall to the washroom. She thought she'd felt something this evening—a kinship of spirit. She'd told Jeremiah her darkest secret and he did not scorn her. She'd even considered that he might admire her a little. But she supposed that was just wishful thinking, stirred by her joy over Noah's return and her sorrow over the final loss of her own son. She'd been grasping at straws.

Of course, she'd told Sulley her secret as well and that had been foolish indeed. She'd had high hopes for the man in spite of her initial caution. But he'd proven that her confidence was misplaced. She supposed she should have trusted her first instinct. Second-guessing oneself was rarely wise.

And while Jeremiah had agreed to help Freeman in the orchard, she knew that he, too, would soon be gone from her life. She felt tears threaten but refused to let them flow. She'd had a good cry beside the pond where Jeremiah found her. She smiled, grateful that the memory of his kindness helped keep the tears at bay.

She would just have to put this summer behind her and continue moving forward. Toward what, she was uncertain. She supposed she'd been harboring some notion that she might find her son and win his love one day. Now she knew it would never happen, and she must resign herself to the fact that some things could never be restored. She returned to her room, turned down the coverlet, and slid between the cool sheets. Perhaps one day she would purchase a marker and place it on her son's grave.

Harmon Wilkins. It was a good enough name, although somehow it did not fit the man she had long imagined her son would grow into.

twenty-seven

It was good to be on his own again. Sulley woke with the sun and stretched before climbing to his feet and starting a small fire to boil water. He needed a shave and a wash if he was going to do what he planned. And while he'd shaved with cold water many a time, today he had time for hot water, and by golly he'd take it.

Once he was presentable and as clean as he was likely to get, he walked on toward Chimney Corner on the other side of Hawks Nest. He'd heard there was a country store there—only just opened a few years earlier—and he hoped he might find someone who could point him toward the information he was hunting. Of course, Jeremiah might light out after him yet, but he trusted his head start plus the fact that Jeremiah wouldn't know which way he'd gone would give him the time he needed.

It was a fine day in July, the sort of day that hinted autumn wasn't as far away as you'd think. Sulley shivered. He'd spent more than one winter night in a cold barn, or worse, with no shelter, and didn't look forward to doing it again. But maybe if things worked out the way he hoped, he'd have a place to put his feet up this winter. If he thought God had a soft spot, he'd ask

Him for help right about now, but he knew God had forgotten about him long ago, so he kept his peace.

The store was set on the inside curve of a steep turn in the road. It had a fine front porch and a creek running in a gulley out back. The woods here were cool and deep. Sulley thought he might take up storekeeping himself if he could do it in a place as pretty as this.

He swung up on the porch and glanced in through the window. Folks moved around inside, doing their trading. The money he'd handed over to Jeremiah really and truly was all he'd had, so he didn't go in. There was a barrel on the porch with a checkers board on it and two rickety chairs beside it. He settled in one chair and methodically reset the board, whistling softly under his breath.

"Well, hey howdy, ain't seen you around afore." An old woman settled in the opposite chair and peered at the board. "You play?"

"It's just about my favorite thing."

"Well, you go first then," she said, adjusting her ample girth in the chair. She fished a corncob pipe out of her apron pocket and stuck it between her teeth. Sulley moved a disk and waited. "Let me guess—you're here for that dad-blasted tunnel project."

He'd trusted there would be someone like this—unable to resist a game of checkers and some conversation. "Actually, I'm hunting my cousin what said he was headed this way. His ma took sick, and she don't know where to write him."

"She bad sick?"

He could tell the woman was eager to taste someone else's sorrow so she could leave off chewing on her own. "Bad enough. Doctor thinks it's the cancer."

"My, my." She shook her head and *tsk*ed around the stem of her cold pipe. "That's a bad business. What's the name of your cousin?"

"Harmon Wilkins. He's a preacher."

She got a cagey look. "Preacher, is he? Guess there's preachers, and then there's preachers."

Sulley laughed, low and easy. "You got that right. Sounds like you know him."

She jumped one of his pieces and chortled. "Oh, I seen him around. He come in the store a time or two." She watched his next move like a hawk and then quickly shifted another of her discs. "Nice enough but seemed worldly for a reverend."

Sulley nodded. "That's him. Probably talked about his ma back home."

"Not his ma, but he did say something about being from down around Fayetteville." She squinted at him. "That where his ma is?"

"Sure is. Don't guess you know where he is now?"

She jumped two of his pieces and slapped her knee. "Sure don't. Ain't seen him in months now you mention it. He was mostly down around those tunnel camps." She leaned in close and looked all around. "Saw him talking to some of the bosses, too. I think he was up to something." She winked and sat back.

"Guess I'll go ask around there next," Sulley said.

"You be careful if you do. I hear they ain't the friendliest kind." She removed her pipe and pointed at him with the stem. "Say, you might go talk to that doctor over in Gauley Bridge. He and your cousin had a set-to out here on the porch one time. Something about those workers getting sick." She stroked her chin and tilted her head. "Seems like your cousin didn't think whatever they were sick with was all that bad, and the doctor was trying to get him to change his mind since he'd set out to make 'em his flock." She thumped the barrel with the flat of her hand, making their pieces jump. "Doc quoted Jesus at him about feeding His sheep." She smiled. "Always did like the sound of that."

"It does sound nice, doesn't it?" he said. Then he looked down at the board. "Well, would you look at that. I think you've about got me licked."

She smiled and crossed her hands across her belly. "I'm a dab-hand at checkers. You want to play again?"

Sulley held his hands up. "No, guess you've shown me what you can do. I'd better get after running Cousin Harmon down." He stood and tipped his hat toward her. "Appreciate your help, ma'am."

"'Tweren't nothing," she said, resetting the board. "You come on back next time you feel like getting whupped."

Sulley headed off along the road to Gauley Bridge. He was tempted to go ahead and start for Fayetteville in the opposite direction to see if he could find Harmon's family, but something told him it would be worth his time and trouble to talk to this doctor.

Sometimes physical labor was just the ticket for an overtaxed brain. Jeremiah stopped and stretched his back out. Freeman had tasked him with removing any suckers from the roots of his new trees. It was hard work, but it felt good. He'd been chasing Sulley for too long. Being in one place doing a solid day's labor filled him with a peace he'd been missing. That and the fact that he'd given up on Sulley made the knots in his shoulders untie for the first time in weeks. He walked over to a tree where he'd stowed a jar of cool water when he started that morning. It was tepid now but still tasted mighty fine.

"Wish I could help." Jeremiah turned to see Noah approaching. He used a cane to walk and came along slow, but already he looked better than the day he'd arrived. The gray pallor of his face had warmed, and he stood straighter. Jeremiah guessed not having to worry over how he'd feed his family helped as much as anything.

"I'm glad to have the work," Jeremiah said, "not to mention the chance to put my feet under your mother's table."

The young man shook his head. "Took that for granted for too many years. Guess that's not the only thing, either. Speaking of . . ." He extended a paper-wrapped bundle. "Ma sent me out here with some bread." He laughed. "Said a big man like you would need something to tide him over till dinner."

Jeremiah peeled the paper back to find two thick slices of bread smeared with butter and grape jelly. He grinned. "I could get used to this. Want to sit with me a minute while I do your mother's cooking justice?"

Noah eased down in the shade of an apple tree, and Jeremiah settled beside him, biting into his food immediately. While chasing Sulley there'd been more than a few times when pickings had been slim, and he meant to enjoy every minute of Luisa's spoiling.

"Good to be home?" he asked through a mouthful.

"You don't know the half of it," Noah said.

Jeremiah swallowed. "So why didn't you come home sooner?"

"Didn't know I could. It's not like I figured my parents wouldn't be glad to see me, it's more like I didn't think I'd be glad to see them." Jeremiah munched, letting the boy talk on. "I was full of big talk when I left. How I was going to do bigger and better things than grow apples and keep a garden." He flushed. "Or marry that girl in town."

"Like what?" Jeremiah asked.

"I was gonna work my way up at the tunnel, get to be one of the bosses. Then I'd get on with Union Carbide. Maybe move to the city and wear a suit every day." He laughed and poked at a clump of grass with his cane. "I'd have a big house and a fancy wife and eat in fine restaurants. That's when I figured I'd come home. Bring Ma a pretty necklace and Pa some cigars." He leaned his head back against the tree. "I was going to be so fine they'd hardly recognize me."

"What happened?"

"Turns out you need a whole lot of schooling to do all that. But I was going to get it—earn some money and do those write-in business courses." He sighed. "I was an idiot and coming home would have meant admitting that." His eyes went soft. "And then I met Maryanne. Well, I met Jackie first and guess I fell for that kid before I fell for his mama."

Jeremiah finished his bread and folded the paper in a neat square, handing it back to Noah. "He's a great kid."

"Yeah, but I figured I was really asking for trouble then. Working a nowhere job. Married without telling anybody. And too sick to take care of my own." His eyes grew wet. "You know what Pa said when he came to get me?" Jeremiah shook his head. "We thought you were dead and now you're alive again." A tear broke free and streaked his cheek. "That's from the Bible—the story of the prodigal son. That's when I knew I could come home." He hung his head. "That's when I knew love is stronger than any mistake."

Jeremiah couldn't think what to say to that. He'd thought

Noah something of a fool himself. But sounded like the boy had learned a powerful lesson.

"I'd better let you get back to work," Noah said, climbing to his feet. He coughed hard but recovered quickly and took a deep breath. "I think I might even be getting better." He grinned at Jeremiah. "Don't get too comfortable around here. I plan to take over your job as quick as I can."

Jeremiah smiled back and thumped the young man on the shoulder. "Don't you worry. I'm planning to head home myself before too long." He watched Noah make his slow way back to the house before he settled into the rhythm of pruning once again.

Home. How was it that he wasn't sure he knew what that word meant anymore?

twenty-eight

It didn't take Sulley long to find Dr. Leonidas Harless's office. He held the door open for a woman with a croupy child on her way out. She gave him a thin smile. He thought he knew how she felt.

Inside was a small waiting room, and through a doorway beyond he saw a little man with round glasses seated at a desk, making notes and muttering to himself. "Be with you in a moment," he called out without looking up.

Sulley took his hat off and tried to make his hair presentable. Finally, the man flung down his pen and approached Sulley, squinting slightly as though he might need stronger glasses. "If you're wanting a physical to work in the tunnel, I'm no longer employed by Union Carbide to do those."

"No, as a matter of fact, I was hoping you might be able to help me find my cousin—Harmon Wilkins." Sulley had the notion this fellow would appreciate it if he didn't mince words. Never mind if his words weren't strictly true.

"Him. You're related?" Sulley thought he saw suspicion in Dr. Harless's eyes and figured this nut would be a lot harder to crack than the old woman at the checkerboard.

"You've seen him, then?" Sometimes the best way to answer a question was with a question.

"Bah. He was a meddlesome fool, and I won't apologize for thinking so, even if you are family."

"Why do you say that?"

Dr. Harless put his hands on his hips. "The sicker the tunnel workers got, the more he told them they needed to pray. He claimed to be carrying God's Word to the men, but if you ask me he was carrying someone else's word, and that word was to keep working no matter what."

"Do you know where I can find him?"

"No idea. Haven't seen him since that day I dressed him down at the store over in Chimney Corner."

Sulley was beginning to wonder if Harmon had been mixed up in something that got him killed. So he pushed a little deeper. "And what was that about? The workers?"

"You might say. He was helping to promote those little black pills that were supposed to help with tunnelitis. Told those men God was looking out for them. Say a prayer, take two pills, and keep working." He flung his hands in the air. "Tunnelitis, my foot. Those men are dying of silicosis, and there's no pill that can fix that."

Sulley paused. He wanted information about Harmon, but if this man knew what was wrong with Noah—what had killed James . . . "What's silicosis?"

"Deadly is what it is. Those workers breathe in tiny particles of silica, which become embedded in their lungs. It essentially turns lung tissue to stone."

Sulley stepped back as though there might be silica in the air right here in the room. "Then what?"

"Then, my friend, their breathing becomes more and more labored until they suffocate."

Sulley thought about James laid out in his parents' front

room. That had to have been a terrible way to die. "And Harmon was encouraging men to work anyway?"

The bell on the door jingled, and Dr. Harless looked over Sulley's shoulder to see who it was. "Looked that way to me. If you find him, kick him in the seat of the pants for me. Now, if you'll excuse me."

The doctor ushered his next patient into an examining room and shut the door. Sulley drifted back outside. He'd come here hoping to track Harmon's movements—to learn his history. But now he thought he might've found the reason the man ended up in an unmarked grave in a cemetery full of unclaimed bodies.

It was time to go home. Jeremiah bundled his few belongings into the rucksack he'd carried all over half of West Virginia and tried to work up some excitement for getting back to his place and a new school year come September. He wondered if the folks in the community really would have done what they said and kept the place up while he'd been coming and going.

He looked up and saw Luisa standing in the door, watching him. "And so you will be leaving us?"

"Yeah, it's time I got on home."

"We will miss you. You have been a good helper." Luisa crossed her arms and cocked her head to one side. "I will confess I thought that perhaps there would be something here to keep you. Is this not so?"

Jeremiah scratched under his beard. "I'm not sure what you're getting at. If you mean Sulley, I've decided to let the Lord deal with him."

"No, God will surely deal with Sulley and maybe not in the

way you think." She laughed, light and soft. "It is only that I could see how Gainey became a new woman with you nearby."

Jeremiah coughed and shifted uneasily. "Mrs. Johnson, I guess I'm not used to such plain talk. Are you suggesting I should court Gainey?"

"Oh yes, I most certainly think so—don't you?"

Jeremiah couldn't remember the last time he'd felt this off-kilter. He was always glad to help someone out where he could, but this was a whole other kettle of fish. And the worst of it was, he wanted to meet Luisa's expectations—for purely selfish reasons. "Well. I suppose I wouldn't be opposed to it. Do you really think she'd like that?"

"Yes. Although maybe she does not know that she would like it." Luisa giggled, an unexpected sound. "But I do not think it would take much courting to convince her."

Jeremiah felt a foolish grin spread across his face and found he couldn't do a thing about it. "Well now. You've given me something to ponder." He smiled even more broadly, thinking out loud now. "And since she's already told me about her son, I feel like we've got a pretty good start on knowing each other already. Do you think—?" He stopped cold. The look on Luisa's face didn't make sense. She'd gone from pleased to pale in a heartbeat.

"Son? What is this about Gainey's son?"

"Well, I . . . the one she gave up for adoption. Turns out he's . . ." Jeremiah trailed off. "You didn't know about that?"

"But she is not married. She's a miss, not a widowed missus. How can this be?"

Jeremiah felt his face go hot and his head go light. Had he just given away a secret? But surely Gainey wouldn't tell him something like that when her friends didn't know, would she?

"This is most upsetting." Luisa was shaking her head and twisting her hands together. "I hold Miss Floyd in such high esteem. And to learn that she . . . Are you certain?"

Jeremiah leapt at the straw she offered—flimsy as it was. "No, ma'am, not at all certain. Maybe I misunderstood. Probably it was a nephew or something like that."

Luisa narrowed her eyes at him. "I will have to know more about this," she said. "Perhaps this is why you are determined to go." Jeremiah opened his mouth to protest, but she'd already turned and was hurrying back to the house.

He sank down on his bunk and dropped his head into his hands. What had he done?

The basket was heavy enough that she'd had to switch which arm she carried it on twice now. Arbutus, who begged to tag along, offered to carry it for her, but she wouldn't impose on the child, eager as she was to please. Gainey supposed food was the last thing the Johnson family would be lacking, but she was well known for her black walnut cake and thought the books she'd selected would help Noah pass the time as he healed. *If he healed.* Gainey pushed that thought aside. No need to weigh her basket down further with worry.

She tucked a stray wisp of hair behind her ear. What had possessed her to wear it in this fussy style today? Of course, she knew very well what it was—the notion that she might see Jeremiah one last time. Might have a chance to tell him goodbye. Nonsense, but then it had been years since she allowed herself to indulge in a little nonsense.

Striding up the walk to the back door with Arbutus skipping beside her, Gainey put on a smile. She'd lost a son, Verna had lost a son, but Luisa's son was found. They would rejoice in that and not borrow trouble from another day. She pecked on the wooden edge of the screen door, making it *tap tap tap* against the frame. "Luisa? Are you in there?" She saw movement and stepped back so Luisa could push the door open. But she didn't. She stood, looking solemn, her hands tucked beneath her apron.

"Oh, Luisa, is Noah alright?" Had trouble come already?

"He is better. I thank you for asking."

Gainey frowned and held the basket a little higher. "I brought a walnut cake and some books I thought he would like."

"That is very kind but not necessary." Luisa's face was still troubled.

"Luisa, are you alright?"

Luisa opened the door and eyed Arbutus. "I must ask you a difficult question. Perhaps one not for young ears."

Gainey was mystified. "Arbutus, will you take this basket inside for Mrs. Johnson?"

Wide-eyed, the girl took the basket and slipped past Luisa. Once the door slapped shut behind her, Luisa stepped closer and lowered her voice. "Is this true that you have a son and no husband?"

Gainey felt as if the top of her head were floating away. She wanted to reach up and clamp it back in place, but all the strength had gone from her body. She could not move. "What did you say?"

"Jeremiah, he tells me you had a son you gave away."

Gainey felt the earth beneath her feet roll and sway. But no, it wasn't the earth, it was her own foundation. The one she'd constructed so carefully, maintained with such care. Jeremiah had just knocked the cornerstone out. "I . . ." She couldn't remember ever being at such a loss for words.

"I see from your face that it is true." Luisa shook her head and took a step back. "I am sorry, Gainey. This is very shocking to me. Perhaps there is an explanation?"

"Oh, Luisa. I . . . was engaged. He . . . died before." She covered her mouth with both hands. "I'm so ashamed," she whispered, hot tears leaking between her fingers.

Luisa bit her lip. "I think maybe your grief is for more than the loss of your sweetheart."

A sob escaped before she could suppress it. "My son," she gasped. "I gave him away."

Luisa nodded. "Of course. It had to be so." She looked over her shoulder as though seeing her own son somewhere inside. "You have been punished, then. Maybe more than you deserved." She reached a tentative hand out and touched Gainey's shoulder. "It is not right to have a child and no husband. But once you have a child . . ." She shook her head and sighed. "It is too hard, what you have suffered."

Gainey bowed her head and let the slender woman wrap an arm around her shoulders. She had come to terms with this loss long ago and thought she had done so a second time, but today it felt fresh and raw in a way she'd meant to forget. Arbutus reappeared in the doorway, and Gainey made an effort to pull herself together. She wiped her eyes, sniffed, and forced a smile. "Thank you, Luisa, for not judging me."

"It is not for me to judge," she answered with a tight smile and a pat. "Now, I must return to my Noah."

Gainey nodded and motioned for Arbutus to join her. The girl peered up at her with tears in her own eyes. "Are you sad, Miss Gainey?"

She inhaled deeply and let the breath out slowly. "Yes, Arbutus, but it's an old sorrow and one I'm used to."

They started down the walk together when Gainey saw Jeremiah exit the barn. He froze. Their eyes met. She'd admired those eyes with their intelligence and kindness, but now all she saw was shame. As she turned and hurried Arbutus away, the question she pondered was whether it was his shame at telling her secret or her own shame at having it known.

Jeremiah lifted a hand and took a few hurried steps after Gainey. But what was the point? He'd seen the look on her face. Devastation. And it was his fault. He'd wounded her in the worst way possible. He doubted there was any chance of recovery. He cursed—something he'd given up years ago—and kicked at the stump Freeman used to split firewood.

Then he went back in the barn, fetched his rucksack, and flung it into the Model T. He'd failed as thoroughly as he knew how. First he'd found and lost Sullivan Harris. Then he ruined the reputation of one of the finest women he'd ever met. For someone bound and determined to be a help, he'd done more than enough damage. It was time to go home and lick his wounds.

twenty-nine

Sulley could have hitched a ride to Fayetteville, but he decided to keep to the woods instead. He followed the river as far as Chimney Corner, steering clear of people and even ducking low when trains whistled by staining the air with clouds of coal smoke. He had some thinking to do.

By the time he arrived in Fayetteville, he'd come to a decision. If Harmon Wilkins was Gainey's son, he would leave the matter alone and just keep moving south. Maybe end up in Virginia or North Carolina. Just keep living the life he knew best, tied to no one and nothing. But if he wasn't Gainey's son—if he was the grifter Sulley suspected—well, then he'd head back to Mount Lookout and set Gainey's mind at ease. And maybe, just maybe—even if he never knew for certain what became of that boy she gave up—he could live like he belonged somewhere and to someone.

Sulley spent the better part of his first full day in town asking folks if they knew Harmon Wilkins. Even making use of the full power of his charms, he got the cold shoulder more often than not. With times so hard and hoboes and panhandlers forever turning up, there was more than enough suspicion to go around. For once, Sulley wished he had some better clothes to put on.

Late in the day he saw a sign for a soup kitchen at a church, and while he was proud to rarely need a handout, his growling stomach told him swallowing his pride would make a mighty fine appetizer.

He accepted a thin slice of bread and a bowl of watery beans, then squatted in the side yard to eat quickly so he could move on. He told himself he didn't need to be ashamed since no one there knew him, but he felt the burn of it just the same. Soon finished, he carried his empty bowl to a woman rinsing dishes in a tub of water. Her sleeves were pushed above her elbows, and hair stuck to her sweaty forehead, but she managed to be pretty just the same.

"Sorry we don't have something better," she said as he handed his bowl over.

"Nothing to be sorry for. I appreciate you sharing what you've got." She smiled, and the light of it took some of the sting of the day away. "Say, you wouldn't know of a Harmon Wilkins, would you?"

She laughed. "Do you mean . . . ? No, but that's silly."

Sulley stepped closer. "What? You know him?"

"Well, I know a Henry Williams who used to say he was going to change his name to something better one day. And seems like Harmon Wilkins was what he came up with. But what a scallywag! I haven't seen him in, what, a good year or more?"

"Is he a preacher?"

She laughed harder. "No, but he did like to talk about how preachers could get away with anything. Why, you know someone going by that name?"

"Heard of him," Sulley hedged. "Is he from around here?"

"Sure, his brother lives over on the east side of town. Has a nice spread over there that belonged to his parents. Good thing, too, with four young'uns to raise and times gettin' harder every day."

"Brother. Hunh. What's his name?"

"Logan Williams—farm's out near Sugar Creek. If you've seen Henry, I imagine he'd be glad to hear about it."

Sulley thanked her and headed east, away from the setting sun. He might not get his answer before night, but at least he had a place to start come morning.

"Why you moping around?" Gainey jerked her head up when Arbutus spoke. She'd been staring at the same postal notice for a good ten minutes and still didn't know what it said.

"What do you mean?"

"You're all hangdog." Arbutus sighed deeply as if the weight of the world were on her shoulders. "Seems like everybody's sad. Mama, Daddy, you. Is it 'cause of what you and Mrs. Luisa talked about?"

"What do you know about that?" she asked more sharply than she intended. Had the child been eavesdropping? Arbutus shrugged one shoulder, and Gainey decided to let that sleeping dog lie. She knew she should make more of an effort. Arbutus was hurting over the loss of her brother. Surely that was worse than the loss of one's reputation. Even so, Gainey wasn't sure she had it in her to put on a cheerful face. She tried to work up a smile but was saved when the bell on the door jangled. A man entered and made a few selections. In Susan's absence, Gainey moved to the cash register to tally his goods.

"You'uns hear about the cave-in down to the tunnel in Hawks Nest?" he asked as he handed over his money.

Gainey felt Arbutus step up close behind her, all ears and eyes most likely. "We haven't. Was it bad?"

"Bad enough," the man said. "Six dead is what I heard." He looked around like he was making sure no one else was listening. "You ask me, they was the lucky ones going quick like that." He accepted the paper-wrapped package Gainey handed him. "I wouldn't wish that tunnelitis on my worst enemy." He tipped his hat. "Ma'am."

Gainey watched him go. Here she was fretting over the truth about her son getting out after more than thirty-five years while men were working, suffering, and dying just down the mountain. She gritted her teeth and nodded once, confirming something to herself. She wasn't going to sit around here, hoping her secret would go no further than Luisa. No. She was going to do something useful.

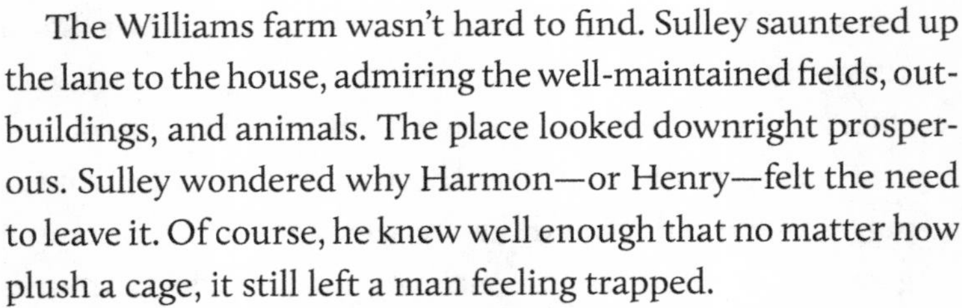

The Williams farm wasn't hard to find. Sulley sauntered up the lane to the house, admiring the well-maintained fields, outbuildings, and animals. The place looked downright prosperous. Sulley wondered why Harmon—or Henry—felt the need to leave it. Of course, he knew well enough that no matter how plush a cage, it still left a man feeling trapped.

A pretty girl of maybe sixteen and a boy who looked a year or two younger were in the garden picking green beans into bushel baskets. They both paused to look at him. The girl put a hand to her straw hat to hold it in place as she peered at him.

"Ma, somebody's coming!" This from a boy carrying a bucket of early apples around the side of the house. He looked like a twin to the boy in the garden. Sulley raised a hand in greeting and approached the house. A round-cheeked woman with curls escaping a kerchief greeted him at the door. He saw a circle with an X in it marked on a porch post. If he were a hobo, that would tell him this was a good place for a handout.

"Are you hungry or in need?" the woman asked with a smile.

Sulley debated posing as a hobo and then trying to get his information but decided to just come straight to the point. These seemed like good people, and he didn't want to bamboozle them. He smiled back. "I'm most always hungry, but what I'm really after is knowing if the name Harmon Wilkins rings a bell with you."

Her hand went to her throat. "Oh my. That would be Henry." She bit her lip. "My husband and eldest son will be in from the field shortly. Will you come around back and make yourself comfortable on the porch until they get in?"

Sulley nodded and followed the boy around to the rear of the house. He settled into a rocking chair and for once just took in the beauty of the day instead of trying to scheme and plan his next move. He was tired of trying to keep a step ahead of everybody else. This time he'd just wait and see if this Logan Williams fella could shed light on the mystery of Gainey's son.

His hostess brought out a glass of cold milk and a slice of apple pie with cream poured over it. "Even if you aren't hungry, I expect that'll go down alright," she said.

Sulley felt an inexplicable lump form in his throat. "Thank you," he said around it. Why was this woman's kindness getting to him?

By the time he finished the pie and wiped the milk from his upper lip, two men were approaching from the barn, laughing and talking. They looked alike, although one was clearly older. He guessed the son to be approaching twenty. Sulley had been on his own since he was thirteen—and wished he'd gotten away sooner. But if he'd had a family like this . . .

"Howdy, stranger, has my Annie been treating you good?"

"That she has. It's a wonder you aren't big as your barn with pie like hers."

Logan laughed and slapped his belly. "One of these days I'm going to turn this farm over to the young'uns and just sit around getting fat." He winked at his son. "Not today, though." He turned back to Sulley. "You lookin' for work or just passin' through?"

"He's here about Henry." Annie had stepped out on the porch with a pan of wash water for the men.

Logan's look got serious. He scooped water and sluiced it over his face, then shook his head like a dog. He patted his face and hands dry with a piece of toweling and sat in the rocker next to Sulley. "My brother's been gone from here too long. What word do you have of him?"

Sulley felt like the table had been turned on him. He hadn't considered that this family would be hungry for news of a missing brother. "I . . . well, it's complicated." He rolled lies around in his head. What could he say that would get him what he wanted without putting these good people out with him?

Logan leaned back and set his chair to rocking. Annie stood at the door with a dish towel flung over her shoulder, and the eldest son settled on the edge of the porch with one ear cocked toward their conversation. Sulley had always loved being center stage when he was selling his services, but just then he felt out of his depth.

"Henry always did make things more complicated than he needed to," Logan said at last. "If you're afraid to tell me that he's either in jail or on the run from the law, don't be. He's had more than one run-in before." He laughed without mirth. "A good part of why he liked calling himself Harmon. That name wasn't as well known to the authorities."

Sulley settled on a piece of the truth. "I haven't actually met him. Just . . . heard some things about him."

"What did you hear?" Annie asked.

"Well, seems he was a preacher." The son snorted, then glanced at his father and ducked his head. "He was hanging out around the camps up at the Hawks Nest Tunnel job."

Logan gave him a sharp look. "But he's not now."

"No, not now." Sulley decided to rush ahead. "Thing is, I was wondering if he was, well, blood kin to you, or if maybe—"

"He's my stepbrother," Logan said. "And I'm getting the feeling there's something big you're not telling me."

Sulley flushed. Which was unusual. He'd been able to keep his feelings from showing in much more challenging circumstances, but there was something about Logan Williams that was so . . . honest. It was throwing him off his game.

Logan sighed heavily. "He's dead, isn't he? Was he shot for cheating at cards? For messing with the wrong woman?" He darted a look at his wife. "Sorry about that, Annie."

Sulley felt sick to his stomach. Harmon—Henry—likely was Gainey's son. And now he'd brought news of his death to more good people. Why hadn't he left well enough alone? Just kept moving south until he was anonymous again.

"Don't guess I can say for sure and for certain, but there was a body . . ." He darted a look at Annie, whose face was tight and pale now. "Ma'am, I hate to talk about this with you here."

"I'm no stranger to death," she said. "I've walked that road with my mother and a child with scarlet fever. I suppose I can stand this, too." She stepped closer and laid a hand on Logan's shoulder. He grasped it, and they waited together. Sulley had a sudden picture of what it meant when the Bible said "the twain shall be one flesh."

"Fella we found was wearing a blue plaid tie." Logan lowered his head. "And he had a Bible." Logan's head jerked up. "Thing is . . ." Sulley took a breath—this would be the clincher. "Thing is, a woman I got to know said it had been hers once."

Logan's fingers were white where he grasped his wife's hand. "Was there an inscription inside?" Sulley nodded. "Did it say *E. K. F.—Christmas, 1895*?"

"It did." *That was that,* Sulley thought. The fellow in the grave had been Gainey's son. Which meant he was not. All he was, was a fool for allowing himself to even imagine such a farfetched idea.

Logan stood suddenly and paced to the edge of the porch, then back again. "And you say you know the person whose initials are E. K. F.?"

"I do. She has the Bible now, knows that's her boy who died. Guess I was hoping maybe it wasn't. Wanted to tell her the boy—the man's—still alive."

"He is," Logan said, stopping right in front of Sulley and looking at him with eyes full of wonder. Sulley felt a surge of hope before Logan's next words dashed it to pieces. "That's my Bible. My parents adopted me when I was a babe."

thirty

The folks back in Kline took Jeremiah's news better than he expected. Thanks to Freeman, he'd been able to buy gas and still have a few dollars of Sulley's cash to return to the church. It was only a fraction of what they borrowed, and they'd likely never see their own money again, but the Methodist Conference had agreed to accept payments along and along. While it was still terrible news, it let them make the first payment.

Of course, times were still hard. Didn't look like Kline was going to see sudden growth of any kind. With the last few months of goose chasing under his belt, Jeremiah felt more worldly-wise and doubted that easy water would have made much difference anyway.

Able had done better than his word, and it was all Jeremiah could do to keep up with the harvest from his little garden. While the families of his students would help keep him supplied over the winter—it was as close as anyone around there got to being paid—he still didn't want to let anything go to waste. So he worked from dawn to dark, picking and preserving everything he could. Meredith had come around twice, once with a pie and the second time just for a visit—without the kids.

But he hardly spared her a moment, saying he had to get the garden in before everything went to seed. He could tell she was disappointed, but then wasn't he as well? Disappointed with himself mostly.

He was threading shucky beans on twine to make leather britches one afternoon when Able stopped by. "Got a good producing garden spot there," he said, collapsing into a chair like a collection of disjointed sticks.

Jeremiah smiled at his neighbor. Able was all arms, legs, and rawhide, but he had a heart of spun sugar. "I'm guessing it's got more to do with you than the location."

Able grinned and hooked his thumbs in his galluses. "Guess garden stuff does alright for me." He watched in silence for a few moments. Jeremiah didn't say anything. Able always got around to what was on his mind eventually. "You gonna marry that gal?"

Jeremiah froze, then reached for another bean and stuck his darning needle through it. "Meredith?"

"You courtin' another 'un?"

"No, can't say as I am." Able was Meredith's great-uncle, which, Jeremiah guessed, gave him the right to stick his nose in.

Able leaned forward and braced his forearms on his legs. "Ain't much been courtin' this one, either."

"A lot to do after being away."

Able nodded. "Reckon so. 'Course, when I was courting, seems like I had enough fire in me to get my work done and sit on the porch with a pretty girl of an evenin'."

Jeremiah sighed and tied off the end of his string of beans. "I'm too old for her. Don't know why she'd want me anyhow."

"Oh, I don't guess she's thinking it's a love match, but she sure enough needs somebody to help her look out for those young'uns." Able pulled out a pocketknife and began cleaning his fingernails. "And she knows a good man when she sees one." He squinted at Jeremiah. "Question is, are you a good man?"

"Hey now, what do you mean by that?" Jeremiah felt like a dog that had been kicked off the porch.

"I mean, a good man wouldn't string her along. A good man would marry her or cut her loose." He laughed softly. "Might be you ain't the only fish in the pond."

"Meredith's seeing somebody else?" He felt a mixture of surprise and relief—which told him a great deal about what he should do next.

"No, but she could be. Fella come through selling embalming fluid, of all things, while you was gone, and he's come 'round again, which means he's either a poor businessman or he's besot."

"Is he . . . would he be a good husband for Meri?"

Able shrugged. "I can judge horses pretty good, men not so much. But he seems alright, and the way he looks at that girl . . . well, she could do a lot worse." He snapped his knife shut and dropped it in his pocket. "I asked around. He was a farmer before he took to traveling. I don't doubt he could settle down to it again, given the right encouragement."

Jeremiah blew out a breath that felt like it had been in him too long. "I'll talk to her this evening."

Able nodded. "Been alone a long time now myself, but it wasn't always that way." He tilted his head back as though taking in the way the sun lit the clouds along the horizon. "In my experience, it's better to be lonesome than to live with somebody who makes you wish you was."

Jeremiah let his thoughts turn, as they so often had since he got home, to a kindhearted woman with soft brown hair and a spine of steel. "Guess some of us are just meant to be alone."

Able snorted. "Don't know about that. More like some of us are determined to be alone." He unfolded himself until he was standing again and hopped down off the porch like a man half his age. "I reckon there's a plan for everybody. Don't go putting words into God's mouth—they're bound to be the wrong ones."

This time, Gainey packed a proper bag. She was going to Hawks Nest and she was going to be a help to those poor men and their families. No more being cowed by men in power. She was going to do what was right. She started to fasten the bag, then paused and added the Bible from her son's grave.

Gainey stopped by the store to collect her pay before beginning the trip to Hawks Nest. Susan was not pleased with Gainey's decision. "Perhaps I've been leaning on you too much in the store and post office. But really, this is nonsense, this running off to, what, play Clara Barton to colored men?"

Gainey gripped the handle of her satchel more tightly. "They need someone to care. Everyone needs someone to care."

"I need someone to help run the store." Susan softened her tone. "You're an institution in Mount Lookout. Respected, admired."

"Perhaps more than I deserve." The words were like biting into a lemon. "I'm not altogether proud of my past, but I hope to be proud of my future."

Susan bit a fingernail. "Arbutus did say something that took me by surprise. Guess I thought she'd misheard." She flicked a look up from her nails, then down again. "It's probably not even true."

Arbutus. So she had heard. "If you're referring to the fact that

I had a child out of wedlock and gave him up when I was little more than a girl, then she got the right of it."

Now Susan lifted openly shocked eyes to Gainey's face. "You had a baby?" The words came out hushed, like the secret might still be kept. Gainey didn't answer, just looked at Susan with defiance in her eyes. "Oh, Gainey. Everyone makes mistakes. And it must have been a long time ago. I certainly won't be talking about it, and even if other folks know, they'll forget all about it as soon as something worse comes along." Susan flushed a deep scarlet. "Not that you having a child is bad. I mean, babies are wonderful—"

"No need to explain yourself," Gainey cut in. "And even if others move on from this morsel of gossip, I will never forget that I had a son whom I was never blessed to know." She felt tears rise and blinked them away. "He may very well have died alone, without a mother's comfort. If I can ease even one man's suffering . . . well. It will have been worth whatever I must sacrifice to do it."

Susan frowned. "It seems to me you're willing to sacrifice far too much for . . ."

Gainey held up a hand. "I failed to make the sacrifice when it would have meant raising my son. I only hope this will, in some small way, make up for that." She turned to go, then stopped and spoke without turning around. "The only person whose forgiveness I long for is dead. I owe the people of Mount Lookout nothing."

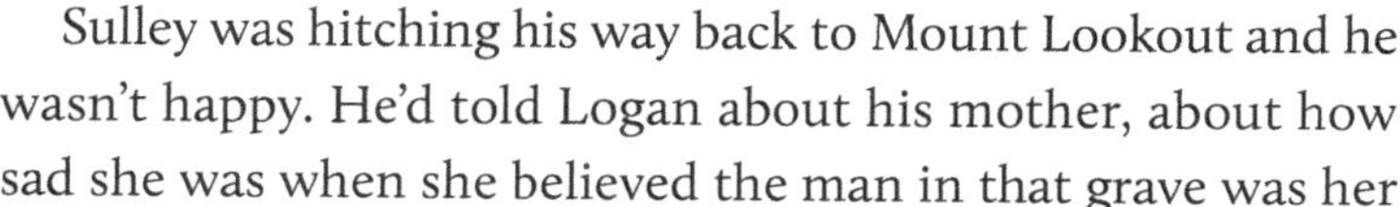

Sulley was hitching his way back to Mount Lookout and he wasn't happy. He'd told Logan about his mother, about how sad she was when she believed the man in that grave was her son. Now that he knew the truth, he could see that Logan had her eyes and his hair was the same color. As he talked about Gainey, he found his own disappointment fading. By golly, if he couldn't find his own mother, putting Gainey and her boy together felt almost as good.

"Reckon we can travel together back to Mount Lookout," he finally said. "Can't wait to see Gainey's face when she lays eyes on you!"

Logan gave him a puzzled look. "I wasn't planning on going to see her."

"What? Why in the world not?"

"I was raised by good people who gave me a good life. I've got responsibilities here with my family." He shrugged. "I made peace with being adopted a long time ago. I guess I might look her up one of these days, but I'll have to think about it—pray about it, too."

"But you . . . she's your mother."

Logan smiled. "My mother is Ethel Williams and a finer woman never lived. Now I've got to tell her what happened to Henry, and she'll likely think it's her fault he got mixed up in something bad." He shook his head. "I'm not gonna break her heart even more by running off to see the woman who gave me up all those years ago. Like I said, maybe one day, but I'm in no hurry."

Sulley was so stunned he couldn't think what else to say. And he could almost always think of something to say. He'd turned down Logan's offer of a meal and a place to spend the night, instead going off to sleep on the ground where he had room to think.

And now he was on his way back to tell Gainey her son was alive. Logan might be reluctant, but Sulley knew Gainey would want to meet her son. And he was equally sure that once Logan met her, he'd be glad. Sometimes, when people didn't make sense, you had to up and make sense for them.

He couldn't do it. Jeremiah balanced another length of wood on his chopping block, hefted his ax into the air, and let it fall until it bit into the wood with a satisfying *thunk*. He picked up the thicker of the two pieces, rebalanced it, and repeated the process. He might be a fool, but at least he'd be a warm fool come January.

And he just might be a married fool. Able's words almost gave him the courage to break things off with Meredith once and for all, but he just couldn't do it. She and those kids were counting on him. And even if he really did have a mind to go courting Gainey Floyd, it was a ridiculous idea. She lived in Mount Lookout and he lived in Kline. Sorting out that piece would be much too hard.

He set down the ax and began stacking the cut wood. Shoot. He was lucky a woman like Meredith wanted him. He chuckled. He was lucky any woman wanted him. No, he'd make the best of what, in all honesty, was a pretty good situation. He was too old to be dreaming anyway.

Lost in thought, he didn't hear anyone approaching. "Jeremiah?" He jumped and dropped a piece of wood on his foot.

"Oh, my goodness—I'm so sorry!" Meri was suddenly there, peering into his face as if to see if he might burst into tears like one of her young'uns. "Are you alright?"

He straightened and wiggled his toes inside his boot. "Fine, fine—you just gave me a start." He pushed his lips into a smile. "As a matter of fact, I was just thinking about you."

She frowned. "Were you indeed?" She laughed, but then again it didn't sound quite right. "Guess you must've known I was coming."

Jeremiah decided there was no time like the present. Now that he'd made up his mind, he might as well jump in and ask Meredith to set a date. "Say, Meri, I've been thinking—"

Even as he spoke she was speaking, too. "Jeremiah, there's something I've gotta tell you—"

They stared at each other.

"Ladies first," he said.

She bit her lip. "Can we sit down over yonder?"

He led the way to the porch and let her have the rocking chair he favored. He sighed. If she and the kids moved in, he guessed that would likely become her chair. Well, he'd just have to get a second one. Maybe he'd make a short bench for the little ones—

"Jeremiah." The look on her face told him he'd missed hearing what she said. He raised his eyebrows and waited. "With you coming and going this summer and never having spoken really, I figured you wouldn't mind."

"Wouldn't mind what?"

She looked annoyed. "Jay and I are getting hitched. Ain't you listening?"

Jeremiah wanted to tug on his ear to make sure he was hearing right, but he restrained himself. "Jay? Is he the salesman Able was talking about?"

She huffed. "Leave it to Able. He's worse than an old woman for meddling. What'd he tell you?"

"Not much. Just said he thought there might be something between the two of you and that you could do worse."

She narrowed her eyes. "And how'd you feel about that?"

Jeremiah pursed his lips and tried to think. He was not handling this right. Nothing new there. "Guess I didn't much believe him." He tried a smile. "Like you say, Able's bad to gossip."

She bit her lip. "Jeremiah, I didn't want to hurt you. I figured if you hadn't asked by now, maybe you weren't going to." A smile spread across her face that she obviously couldn't help. "And Jay's awful nice. He treats the kids good, and although he ain't rich he can take care of us alright." She stood all at once. "Anyhow, I wanted to be the one to tell you. Wanted to let you know we appreciate all you've done for us and to wish you well." She darted forward and down the steps before he could respond. "Don't take it too hard, Jeremiah. Maybe you'll find somebody else." She hurried away while the rocking chair she'd been sitting in still swayed forward and back. Jeremiah reached out a hand to stop it out of habit—it was bad luck to set an empty chair to rocking.

He smiled. Which was funny since today it felt kind of like his luck had finally turned for the better. He whistled his way into the house and pulled down his rucksack.

thirty-one

"Will you read me the one about the boy what killed a giant with a rock?" The man with the sunken cheeks sat propped up on his bed in a room with five other men. Gainey was grateful for the cool of the evening and the fact that she could sit on the doorstep with the Bible that had been buried with her son open across her knees. Otherwise, she wasn't certain she could stand the smell of unwashed men. And the last thing she wanted to do was add to the insults they were already suffering.

She read from the seventeenth chapter of the book of Samuel about the shepherd boy who dared to take on the Philistines' champion when everyone else was afraid. Although coughs were inevitable here, the men worked hard to stay quiet, listening with an intensity that had made Gainey uncomfortable at first. Now she admired it. These men were hungry for any comfort they could find, and what could be better than God's Word? Of course, they'd rather she read about David and Goliath or Moses parting the Red Sea than, say, the Ten Commandments, but she supposed it was all good for them.

When she finished the story, the men sat quiet a moment. Then one said in a hushed voice, "'The Lord saveth not with sword and spear: for the battle is the Lord's.'" He swayed from side to side. "Mmm-hmm. I like the sound of that. It'd sure be good to have God fighting my battles for me."

Gainey opened her mouth to tell him that's exactly what God would do, but then she snapped her mouth shut again. Was it? Men had died. Were dying. And for what? She supposed the electrical power the tunnel would provide once it was completed was important, but at what cost? Each and every day was a battle for these men, and she wasn't at all certain that God was helping them fight it.

Goodness—what about her own fight for a quiet, respectable life? She'd had to trade her own child for that, and now it was gone. Where was God in that fight?

"I'd best head on back to Ansted," she said, "before it gets dark."

"You comin' again tomorrow?" The man who requested the story stood and walked with her to the edge of the camp. He shuffled along, breathing heavily as though they were climbing a mountain instead of a slight incline.

"Yes, is there anything special you need? Anything I can bring you?"

He turned his head to cough, then spit. She'd gotten used to this sort of thing—the men didn't mean any disrespect by it. "Miss Gainey, just you bring yourself on back safe and sound. You being willing to come here is more than enough."

They reached the road, and Gainey saw one of the supply trucks approaching. The drivers were good to give her rides each morning and evening. She'd been uneasy about it at first but soon realized the men had become protective of her. Well, most of the men. There were a handful who thought she was either up to no good or about to bring the wrath of the boss man down on them. And in all honesty, she feared those in charge wouldn't appreciate her meddling, but thus far she'd been left alone.

When she reached the Tyree Tavern, she clambered down trying not to think about how carefully Jeremiah had handed her down when they returned from Gauley Bridge not so long ago. She supposed he was back in his own home, returned to his life—his real life. She firmed her chin and pursued that line of thinking no further.

Inside, Ruth, the proprietress, stuck her head out from the kitchen. "That you, Gainey? Come eat a bite with me."

Gainey was only too glad to oblige. "Be right there," she said before going to her room to wash her face and hands.

The back door of the kitchen was propped open to let in the cool of the late July evening. Gainey sat at the table with a sigh and breathed in the aroma of the stew Ruth ladled into her bowl. "That smells delicious," she said, reaching for a biscuit and buttering it. "Who knew reading aloud could work up such an appetite?"

"It's good, what you're doing for those poor men," Ruth said as she tucked into her own bowl. She shook her head. "The condition so many of them are in. They've taken to calling Gauley Bridge 'the town of the living dead,' there are that many of 'em walking around sick."

"It's little enough I do." Gainey crumbled bread into her bowl. "I wish there were something more."

"I heard the Jones family outside Gauley Bridge is in a real bad way—half the family dying of whatever illness they catch down in that tunnel. I've been wanting to take them some necessities, but I can't ever get away from this place."

"Where's their home? Could I take some things for you?"

"Just north of town. My boy Andy's making a run over that

way tomorrow. He could take you if you can stand to ride in that rattletrap heap of his."

"Alright then, I'll do it."

Ruth beamed at her. "I'll pack some food and some castoff clothes that got left behind by somebody passing through." She laughed. "How a person forgets to take their britches with them when they travel I'll never understand."

Gainey laughed, too. She was tired but it was a good feeling—the sort of tired that came from doing for others. She hoped she might be even more tired tomorrow. She had not slept well since the truth about her son became common knowledge. But honest weariness turned out to be the best sleeping draught she could ask for.

"Mr. Sulley, you come back!" Arbutus whooped and jumped off the porch of the store to greet him. "People keep leaving. It's about time somebody came back!"

Sulley grinned. "It's not often I visit a place twice. But you're makin' me glad I've come again." She bounced around him like an eager puppy. "Mr. Jeremiah, he left more'n a week ago and ain't nothing interesting happen since." She looked at him wide-eyed. "Why'd you come back?"

"I've got news for Gainey. She inside?" He started for the store, but Arbutus didn't follow him. He turned back to find her looking very serious.

"She's gone, too." She looked all around and lowered her voice. "Miss Gainey had a baby way back when and she didn't have no—any—husband." She looked at the ground. "Guess maybe word got out." The guilty look on her face suggested to Sulley how it might've gotten out.

Sulley felt the wind leave his sails. "Where'd she go?"

Arbutus shrugged. "Didn't hear that part. She kept worryin' over those men working in that tunnel, though."

"I think I know where to look for her."

The girl perked up. "You gonna go fetch her?"

Sulley huffed a laugh. "I don't think anybody's ever persuaded Gainey to do anything she wasn't already of a mind to do, but maybe." He cocked his head. "Or I just might persuade her to come on over to Fayetteville with me. There's somebody there I think she might like to meet."

Jeremiah traveled faster this time. He was no longer tracking a scoundrel, although he was heading for a showdown of sorts. And with a woman this time. He would grovel if necessary, but he was determined to plead his case to Gainey. And what he wanted was a whole lot more than her forgiveness.

He'd spent a lot of years trying to make other people happy. This time, although Gainey's happiness was high on his list, he knew it was his own he was finally after.

"I'm here to call on Miss Eugenia Floyd." Sulley stood with his hat in his hand on the front porch of the tavern. The woman eyeing him clearly wasn't impressed by his good manners.

"She's traveling today. If you'll give me your name, I can let her know you stopped by when she returns."

Sulley bit down on his frustration. This was more trouble than he'd ever gone to for anyone other than himself. He was half a mind to give it up. But then he pictured how Gainey's face would look when he told her that her son was alive, and he figured he'd keep going. "Will she be back soon?"

The woman lifted her nose a notch. "I couldn't say."

Wouldn't was more like it. "Do you expect her back today? Tomorrow? Next week?" He knew he sounded testy. So much for being a charmer.

"Sir, I don't know what business you have with Miss Floyd, but she's a respectable woman and I take the privacy of my boarders seriously." She pressed her lips together for a moment. "Now, if you'll excuse me."

Sulley swore under his breath. Perhaps not softly enough, since the woman's back stiffened even as she marched away. He thumped down on the edge of the porch and tried to think what to do next. He could just wait until Gainey turned back up, but he was itchy to share his news. He could also head down to the workers' camps to see if anyone there knew where she'd gone. But he was weary. Do-gooding was a whole lot more work than he'd anticipated.

"What you want with Miss Gainey?" Sulley jerked his head up to see a waif of a girl with lank red hair standing at the end of the porch.

"I have news for her about her . . . family."

The girl glanced through the window of the tavern. "Miss Ruth don't trust nobody." She came a few steps closer. "I sure would like it if'n somebody come to tell me 'bout my family." She stubbed a bare toe in the dirt. "Don't got none to speak of."

"Me neither," said Sulley.

"She's gone to see the Joneses in Gammoca." The girl smiled. "She's do-goodin' and 'bout time somebody did. You can hitch a ride far as Gauley Bridge, then it ain't much to walk. Folks'll tell you the way once you get close."

"I thank you," Sulley said, wishing he had something to thank her with.

She shrugged one shoulder. "You ever find any folks by name of Jenkins, maybe come back and tell me. 'Specially if they's missing a girl 'bout my age."

Sulley hesitated, then plunged in. "How did you come to go missing?"

"I ain't certain, but seems like they might not have been able to keep me with times as hard as they are. Least that's what Miss Ruth say. She took me in and give me work to do." She worried a frayed cuff with her fingers. "Guess maybe most folks would be glad to be shut of kin who'd do such a thing, but maybe . . . well, maybe they're sorry now." She smoothed the cuff into place. "Anyhow, I'd like to find out."

Sulley stood and extended a hand. The girl glanced all around before sidling closer and taking it. Her small palm was rough and cool against his as his fingers engulfed hers. "I'll keep an eye out." She nodded solemnly, then scurried away.

thirty-two

The walk from Gauley Bridge to the Jones home was lovely, following the Gauley River all the way. A soft breeze stirred the hair at the back of Gainey's neck, and she was glad not to be offered a ride, preferring the exercise and the opportunity to do some thinking. She'd spent so much of her life with a firm plan for what she would do and how she would live her life. Now she was surprised to find that she enjoyed simply waiting to see what assignment God would give her next.

She asked directions from a farmer harvesting corn in his field and soon found herself standing on the Joneses' front porch with a hand raised to knock. Before her knuckles met the edge of the screen door, a child appeared with wide eyes. Gainey leaned down. "Could I speak to your mother or father?" The child turned and scurried away. A few moments later, a woman with unkempt hair and tired eyes came to the door.

"Do I know you?" she asked, squinting through the screen.

"Ruth from over at the Tyree Tavern sent me with some items for your comfort." Gainey held up the basket she'd switched from hand to hand for two and a half miles.

"That's good of her," the woman said and pushed the door open with a screech of the hinges. "Come on in and sit a spell. I'm Emma."

"My name is Eugenia Floyd, but friends call me Gainey. I'd be pleased if you did so."

The woman dug out a careworn smile as she led Gainey to the kitchen. "It's not often I get to sit and visit with a lady. Mostly menfolk around here."

Gainey unpacked Ruth's gifts—food, a packet of needles and thread, and some feed-sack fabric.

This time Emma's smile went deeper. "That Ruth, she knows I like to sew of an evening. She saves me the prettiest sacks from her supplies. I oughta make her a quilt, if I can ever get ahead enough to do it." She fingered the colorful cloth. "I've got some coffee on the back of the stove—it's mostly chicory, but you're welcome to a cup."

"That would be nice," Gainey said. She'd tasted coffee made from the dried roots of the blue flowers and didn't think much of it but knew it would be insulting to turn down this woman's hospitality.

Once they were settled at the table with their thick cups of bitter liquid, Gainey came to the point. "I understand some of your family works at the tunnel."

Emma gathered her sorrow tighter around her shoulders. "Too many of 'em. Three of my boys, my husband, Charley, my brother, and a boy we took in when his mother died. It's a real bad place to work, but we need the money." Her eyes were red and filling with tears. "Shirley died in June, and I'm afraid Cecil's not doing good, either."

"Oh—I'm so sorry. I didn't realize you'd lost a son."

"Just eighteen and such a good boy. He died hard, too. Asked me to let the doctors cut him open after he was gone, so they could prove it was working in the tunnel that killed him."

"Was it?"

"I think so, and the doctor thinks so, but I'm not sure it matters. Cecil's got him an attorney what filed in court for him." A look of wonder crossed her face. "Suing for five thousand dollars. Now, wouldn't that be something?"

"Do you think he'll get it?" Gainey asked, sipping from her cup.

The woman shrugged her burdened shoulders. "If the rest of my boys die like Shirley did . . ." The tears fell then. "No mother should have to see a child she birthed and washed and loved go through something like that. No amount of money will atone for that."

Gainey felt tears press her own eyes. "No," she whispered. "I don't think there's anything worse."

"You have children?"

"I had a son, but he's dead now." Emma reached out and clasped Gainey's hand. They didn't say much more after that, just sat with sorrow flowing in and through and around them. Gainey would have expected their combined grief to double, but when she finally left to begin the walk back to Gauley Bridge, she was surprised to find that her basket wasn't the only thing feeling lighter.

This was harder than he'd expected. Jeremiah trudged into Ansted and made his way to the inn where he'd found Gainey once before. If he'd thought he would sail back into her life and sweep her off her feet, he clearly had another think coming. When he turned up at the store, Susan Legg railed about how

Gainey abandoned her to manage the store and post office on her own—which he suspected hurt Arbutus's feelings. Then he'd run into Luisa Johnson, who seemed embarrassed to see him, perhaps because both of them knew Gainey's secret. He began to feel like he'd personally run her out of town.

And now he was turning up at her boardinghouse, hat in hand, ready to humble himself in hopes she'd let him court her. He was less optimistic than he had been when he left Kline. He knocked at the door with the business about the Gray Dragoons carved above it.

"Are you in need of lodging?" It was the woman he'd met briefly before. Ruth, if he recalled.

"Not at the moment. I'm looking for Miss Floyd. Heard she was staying with you again."

The woman frowned deeply. "Do I know you?"

"We met last time Miss Floyd was lodging with you."

If anything, the frown deepened. "I'm starting to wonder about that woman. All sorts of men turning up here looking for her."

Jeremiah panicked. Was he about to ruin her reputation here as well? "Who else is looking for her?"

"Not for me to say. I turned that one away just like I'm turning you away. If she wants to associate with male acquaintances, she'll need to do it elsewhere." She made a scornful sound and slammed the door. Jeremiah turned, took two steps, and met Gainey coming down the walk.

"Jeremiah." She said his name with a kind of wonder that made him forget how much trouble he might be in. "What in the world are you doing here?"

Her eyes were bright, her cheeks taking on a pinkish flush. Why, she looked like a mere girl in that moment, and Jeremiah found himself grinning like a fool. "I'm here looking for you."

"Why?"

"I didn't get a chance to tell you goodbye before I left." He could have kicked himself. Surely he could do better than that.

She huffed a little laugh. "And you traveled all the way back from Kline to tell me goodbye properly? I'm finding that a bit hard to grasp."

"No, no, you're right." He glanced around and spotted a circular bench built around the trunk of a tree. "Mind if we sit?"

She glanced at a watch pinned to her blouse and nodded. "For a moment."

He dropped his rucksack on the ground and waited for her to sit before he did. Then he wished he could pick the bag up again so he'd have something to do with his hands. "I . . . thing is, I owe you an apology."

She stiffened. "Indeed. For what exactly?"

"For blabbing your business." She didn't respond, and he guessed he'd have to dig deeper. "I figured somebody you knew as well as Luisa would already know about . . . your son. I never would have said anything otherwise."

"It's interesting that you say I know Luisa well. I have come to realize I don't know anyone well and I suspect it's because I haven't allowed anyone to know me. My son, Harmon"—she softened when she said his name—"I have so longed to talk about him, to dare to wonder what became of him. But the few who knew my secret—my parents, one or two others—were deeply ashamed. I suppose when I spoke to you and Mr. Harris, it was because I thought the risk of exposure was worth the opportunity to finally learn what happened to my child." She sighed and looked up into the oak above them, watching a squirrel scamper among the green leaves. "And men sometimes judge less harshly than women when it comes to such things."

"It was a long time ago," Jeremiah offered. "I wouldn't have thought anyone would still hold it against you."

She snorted. "You are rather naïve for a man your age."

Jeremiah flushed. He needed to get this conversation back on track. "Anyhow, I was hoping I could make amends—let you know how sorry I am and maybe . . . be friends?" He wanted to be much more than that but figured it was a good place to start.

Her shoulders drooped and she leaned back against the tree. "I am a bit short on friends at the moment." She smiled. "Although I think I'm making some new ones in the camps. Of course, they would be unacceptable back in Mount Lookout, but since I have become less acceptable, perhaps it's for the best."

Jeremiah tugged at his beard. He really had mucked her life up. "What if you were wed, wouldn't that make you respectable?" Oh dear God in heaven, what had he just said?

She laughed, full-throated and merry. "And trade my freedom for respectability? I've only just begun to realize how my fear of discovery has kept me chained all these years. I don't intend to exchange one sort of captivity for another."

"But, the right man—"

She stood and took two steps away. "Jeremiah, thank you for coming all this way to make your apologies, but it really wasn't necessary. And now if you'll excuse me, I really am quite tired and would like to get my rest before I continue offering what solace I can to those poor workers again tomorrow."

Jeremiah staggered to his feet. "I'll walk you in."

"Really, Jeremiah, you need not be so solicitous. It would seem that I am perfectly capable of managing on my own." She turned to leave, but he heard her final words, spoken under her breath. "It would seem I must."

Jeremiah was still sitting on the bench, trying to think what to do next, when a girl came out to dump dishwater on some flowers growing nearby. He nodded a greeting.

"Miss Gainey, she shore is popular with the menfolk," the girl said. "You kin to her?"

Jeremiah shook his head. "No, just a friend." He tilted his head. "What do you mean about her being popular with men?"

"Some other fella come 'round to tell her about her family. I thought maybe you was the family."

Jeremiah frowned. Who would know anything about . . . ? "Would this other fella have wavy hair and blue eyes? Wearing overalls?"

"Yes sir. You know him?"

"I believe I do, and I can't think what he'd have to tell Gainey about her family that she didn't already know."

The girl shrugged and glanced back to the tavern. "He seemed real eager to talk to her. I think he was going looking for her over in Gauley Bridge, but she's back now." She propped her dishpan on her hip. "I ain't supposed to talk to the guests or I'd ask her did he find her."

Just then a woman's voice called, "Francis, are you dawdling?" The girl rolled her eyes and scurried for the house.

Jeremiah watched her go, trying to think why in the world Sulley would turn back up here and what new information he could have to share with Gainey.

thirty-three

Everywhere he turned up, he'd just missed Gainey. Sulley groaned. For a woman who apparently hadn't left Mount Lookout in decades, she sure was on the move now. He'd done some chores for the storekeeper at Chimney Corner in exchange for a hot meal and a chance to bed down in an outbuilding. He was grateful that the deal apparently included some hoecakes for breakfast after which he had the distinct impression he was expected to move on. Now he was headed back to Ansted. He didn't believe he'd be welcome at the inn, but he could position himself to watch for Gainey.

Once in town he picked a spot along the road leading to the Tyree Tavern where he could make himself comfortable among the rhododendrons and wait. He pulled out his worn book of Frost's poems. He liked to imagine his mother—maybe pregnant with him—reading each poem and underlining a word here or there. He'd long thought it was as close as he would ever get to knowing anything about her.

"Like a bad penny." Sulley jerked his head up from where his chin had fallen to his chest and saw Jeremiah Weber peering at him through the leaves. Jeremiah wedged his large body under the rhododendron and dropped to the leafy ground beside Sulley. "Heard you were back."

"Heard you were long gone."

"Guess folks are surprised to see both of us around here."

Sulley stretched his legs, which had gotten stiff from sitting too long. "You still after hauling me back to Kline? I thought you might've given up on that by now."

Jeremiah laced his hands across his belly. "I have. Been to Kline and back. I wouldn't say you're forgiven, but folks are sure trying to forget you."

Sulley grinned. "I'm pretty memorable."

"That you are. So, what's this news about Gainey's family?"

Sulley felt his smile slip. "You're worse than an old woman to meddle in other people's business." He shifted to where he had a better view of the tavern. "Where is Gainey anyhow?"

"Tracking down anyone sick with that tunnel disease and trying to help them."

"Why? Does she think she has to make up for folks knowing about her having a child? If she does, she needs to learn to ignore what folks think. Most of 'em aren't worth bothering about." He glanced at Jeremiah, who he thought had a guilty air about him. "Say, you wouldn't have anything to do with people finding out about her, would you?"

"You answer my question and I'll answer yours."

Sulley stood and brushed leaves from the seat of his pants as he moved out into the open. "I forgot the question."

Jeremiah crawled out from under the shrub as well and stood next to Sulley. Had he realized how big the man was before this? "I heard you brought her news about her family. Can't think what that would be or why you'd bother to come back here to tell it."

A truck pulled up in front of the tavern, and Gainey climbed down. Sulley glared at Jeremiah and then trotted across the road. This was none of Jeremiah's business, but he guessed it would be up to Gainey to run him off if she wanted to.

"Gainey!" he called. She turned and was clearly surprised to see him. He drew closer. "I've got news." He felt his earlier excitement rise. This was going to be big.

"Mr. Harris. This is unexpected."

Were they back to mistering again? "Yeah, well, like I said, I've got something important to tell you."

"Honestly, I can't imagine what it would be. I put faith and trust in you, Mr. Harris, and now I understand you're little more than a swindler and a confidence man. We were only fortunate in Mount Lookout that you managed to do what you claimed you were able." She saw Jeremiah approaching and frowned. "I understand others did not fare so well." She looked Sulley in the eye. "I'm disappointed in you. I had hoped for better."

Sulley was caught flat-footed. To be taken to task when he'd brought such news. Of course, she didn't know yet. Didn't realize he'd been trying to help her all this time. He whirled on Jeremiah. "Good grief, man, can you not keep from telling tales wherever you go? Pouring poison about me into Gainey's ear. Blabbing about her son to folks in town." That arrow found its mark as Jeremiah paled. "You need to learn to tame your tongue."

He turned back to Gainey and saw that she didn't look any happier than Jeremiah. "Mr. Harris, I will thank you to leave me alone. My life is quite unsettled enough without your adding to it." She spun around and stalked into the tavern.

He watched her go, thinking of Frost's lines from "Fire and Ice" that had been underlined heavily in ink:

. . . But if it had to perish twice,
I think I know enough of hate
To say that for destruction ice
Is also great
And would suffice.

Indeed it would.

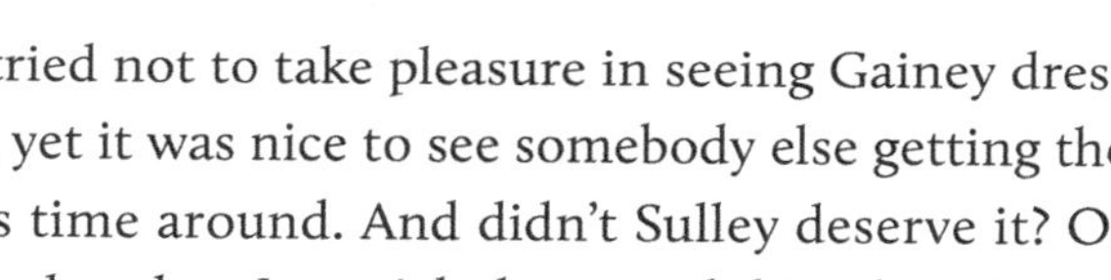

Jeremiah tried not to take pleasure in seeing Gainey dress Sulley down, yet it was nice to see somebody else getting the what-for this time around. And didn't Sulley deserve it? Of course, he tried to drag Jeremiah down with him, but Gainey must've considered him already sunk. She hadn't even glanced his way before marching into the tavern, leaving the two men staring after her.

"Doggone. She didn't even let me tell her the news." Sulley looked like a pup left behind from a hunting trip. Jeremiah almost felt bad for him.

"Well, what did you expect?"

Something hardened in Sulley's face, and Jeremiah took a step back without meaning to. "I expected her to be different."

"I . . . well, she's had a tough time here lately. And you are a scoundrel."

Sulley moved his shoulders and stretched his neck like he was shrugging something off. "Yeah. That's me. Don't need nothing or nobody." He gave Jeremiah an appraising look. "That said, if you had some victuals in your pack there, I'd be willing to make camp and share 'em with you."

Jeremiah laughed. Doggone if he didn't like this fellow in spite of himself. Plus, he still wanted to know what Sulley had tried to tell Gainey. He wasn't quite ready to give up on her yet. "It's not much, but I'm glad to share."

Jeremiah cracked an eye open to see that the sun was sending its first rays through the trees, making the birds sing so loud no one could sleep. He stretched and sat up, stiff from sleeping on the hard ground. He was getting too old for this kind of thing.

Glancing around, he saw that the fire ring was cold—not that he had a pot or coffee to put into it, but a fire cheered a man of a morning. Sulley wasn't in his spot, and Jeremiah wondered if he'd absconded once again. He stumbled down to a stream and washed his face in the icy flow, drinking water that was cold enough to wake him almost as well as coffee would.

Wide-eyed and refreshed, he made his way back to their makeshift camp. Today he intended to find Gainey and offer his assistance as she went around helping people. He figured it was the only hope he had of trying to woo her.

He began gathering his few things back into his rucksack when Sulley crashed through the trees, clearly out of breath. "What in tarnation are you doing?" Jeremiah asked.

Sulley panted, "Thought that tavern keeper was gonna catch me. I'm pretty sure that girl saw me, but I think she'll keep quiet."

"What have you done?" Jeremiah guessed he should have known better than to trust this hooligan even for one night. Sulley held up a thick black book. "Is that—?" Jeremiah moved closer. "Where did you get that?"

Sulley grinned and it was the easy, playful grin Jeremiah had first seen when he arrived in Kline prepared to sell them all a pig in a poke. "This belongs to Gainey's son."

"It belongs to Gainey! How'd you get it?"

Sulley began stuffing his own pack, wrapping the Bible in his spare shirt before tucking it inside. "Stole it." Jeremiah just stared with his mouth hanging open. Sulley scoffed at him. "You gonna go tattle on me?"

Jeremiah snapped his mouth shut. "I just might."

"If you do, tell Gainey I'm taking it to Fayetteville. To the Williams farm."

"What are you talking about?"

Sulley slung his pack over his shoulder and moved to stand in front of Jeremiah. He looked him hard in the face. "I know why you came back. You like her. And I'm betting she shut you down. Well, here's your chance. Bring her to Fayetteville and look up Logan Williams. He'll have her Good Book."

"You're talking crazy. None of this makes sense." Jeremiah wanted to believe Sulley had lost what few marbles he possessed, but the man looked as though he knew exactly what he was doing.

"Oh, it'll make sense." He smacked Jeremiah's shoulder with the back of his hand. "And I'm doing you a mighty big favor." He tipped his hat and trotted off through the trees, turning once to call back, "You're welcome!" before disappearing.

Jeremiah figured he had two choices—go back to Kline and live out his days as a lonely old bachelor or see what Sulley was up to. He laughed and shook his head. What did he have to lose?

thirty-four

Gainey finished her breakfast and went back to her room for her Bible. While the way in which it had been returned to her was heartbreaking, she was glad it was seeing some good use now. God certainly worked in amazing ways.

Fifteen minutes later, Gainey hurried back down the outside staircase, having turned her room upside down searching for the Bible. Could she have carried it with her to breakfast? Might she have left it in the common room? When she came to the landing, she saw Jeremiah standing in the yard, seemingly waiting for her. She slowed and made her way down the remaining steps. "I had thought you'd have returned to Kline by now."

"Doesn't feel like there's much there for me anymore." His words made something buzz inside her, but she pushed it aside. "Any chance you're missing something this morning?"

"Why, yes. I can't find my Bible. How did you—?"

"Sulley took it."

"He—what? What do you mean?"

Jeremiah shrugged. "He said to bring you to see somebody down in Fayetteville if you want it back. You know a Logan Williams?"

"I do not. Are you telling me Sulley stole my Bible in order to lure me to call upon some strange man in another town?"

"That's about the shape of it."

"And this sounds like a good idea to you?"

Jeremiah laughed. It was rich and deep with a sort of hopeful joy ringing through it. "No, ma'am. Sounds like nonsense, but then I've come to expect that of Sulley." He looked thoughtful. "I don't think he's a bad man so much as he's a lost one who doesn't quite know how to get along with people for more than a day or two."

"Could it be some sort of trap? Is he out to hoodwink us?"

"Maybe. But if it is a trap, I don't think it'll be too terrible, and I plan to keep you close."

This time she was unable to stifle the thrill of pleasure his words sent through her. "What if I say it doesn't matter and I won't come?" Did she sound coy? She hadn't meant to sound coy. Had she?

"Then I'll go without you and bring you back your Bible even if I have to fight him for it." Jeremiah was grinning now in a way that made her stomach feel tight. "But I'd sure like it better if you came, too." Mercy. How old was she to be feeling like this? "Anyhow, aren't you curious what he's up to?"

Gainey released the smile she'd been suppressing for too long. "As it happens, Mr. Weber, I am." There. That time she'd meant to sound coy.

Jeremiah thought he had an inkling of what Sulley was up to. He wouldn't have tried to talk Gainey into this trip if he hadn't. He glanced at her riding beside him on this fine summer day, a cool breeze making the brim of her hat dance. Who was he kidding? He would've risked more than this for a chance to spend the day in her company.

"Could Sulley be less of a scoundrel than we think?" Gainey asked, then laughed. "Or more of one?"

Jeremiah chuckled. "It could go either way. Or maybe the rest of us are more scoundrels than we realize. Lately I think the worst one to try to fool me is me."

"How so?" She placed a hand on her hat as she peered at him from beneath the brim.

Jeremiah figured now was as good a time as any. "Guess I've spent a lot of time trying to be a help to other people. Like that would make me a better person, score some extra points when I get to the judgment seat." He steeled his nerve. "Shoot, I was gonna get married just because other folks thought I should. Just because the lady in question needed a husband."

Gainey stared straight ahead, but there was something in the timbre of her voice. "You *were* getting married? You're not now?"

"Not to Meredith. Guess neither one of us saw it as what you'd call a love match." He grinned. "Somebody else came along while I was off gallivanting after Sulley, and I guess she likes him better."

"Do you mind?"

"Mind? Well, I thought about letting my pride get in the way, but mostly I'm relieved."

"Marriage isn't for you, then."

"Oh, I didn't say that." He tried to look at her without turning his head. "I might get hitched yet." He cleared his thick throat. "If I find the right lady."

"It's yours, take it." Sulley thrust the Bible at Logan. He'd been skulking in the woods across the road most of the day. Finally, he'd seen Logan walk into the barn and barged in without waiting for an invitation. Logan acted like strangers popping in on him wasn't all that uncommon.

"Where'd you turn this up?" Logan took the Bible as if it might fall apart if he was too rough.

"I told you. Your mother had it."

Logan flipped the book open and thumbed through the pages. "And she sent it to me? Which means you must have told her about me. I'm not sure how I feel about that."

"Aren't you supposed to honor your mother? Isn't there something in that book about that?" Sulley was mad, although he couldn't say why exactly. He just felt frustration and disappointment and anger rolling around inside him, looking for a way to come out.

Logan laughed. "Well, you're right about that—it's one of the Ten Commandments. But I like this part." He flipped pages until he was pretty far back in the book. "Here you go, Ephesians six. 'Children, obey your parents in the Lord: for this is right. Honor thy father and mother; which is the first commandment with promise; That it may be well with thee, and thou mayest live long on the earth.'"

"There you go," Sulley said, crossing his arms across his chest. "You're supposed to do right by your mother."

Logan nodded. "That's so. I sure want things to be well and to have a good, long life." He smoothed the page and gave Sulley a thoughtful look. "But what if I'm supposed to honor the woman who *acted* like my mother? The one who raised me and is the only mother I know. What if getting in touch with the woman who gave birth to me would dishonor that mother?"

"You're talking in circles. Your mother is your mother. If you're mad at her and don't want anything to do with her, that's something you'll just have to get over." He smiled like he'd won the argument. "That is, if you want to obey this God you seem so all-fired sure of."

"You say that like you're not so sure."

"What?" Sulley wasn't prepared for the change in conversation.

"Of God. Not so sure of God." Logan squinted at him. "You a churchgoing man?"

"Not if I can help it." The words came out before Sulley had time to think about them. He sure as shooting didn't want this fella throwing Jesus at him.

"You might try it sometime. Of course, the wrong church is worse than no church at all. You're welcome to come go with us sometime." He held the Bible up. "Good place to put one of these to use."

"I didn't come here to be preached at. I just thought you oughta have that, and since you weren't going to go get it, I figured I'd bring it to you."

Logan chuckled. "Butting in pretty deep into other people's business, aren't you? Makes me wonder why."

Now Sulley was really mad. Who did this man think he was? Throwing a good deed like this back in Sulley's face. He didn't deserve a mother like Gainey. Didn't even want to know what he was missing out on by refusing to have anything to do with her. "Because I'm not such a fool that I'd throw away a chance to at least meet the woman who brought me into the world, especially when somebody's standing right in front of you telling you what a good woman she is."

"Your mama must be extra special." Logan set the Bible down and picked up a pitchfork and began cleaning out a cattle stall.

"What? What's that got to do with anything?"

"Well, the way you're fired up about me meeting my mother, I'd have to guess yours must be a humdinger." He slanted a look at Sulley. "You being such a proponent of mothers and sons getting together."

Sulley felt heat suffuse his face. He balled his hands into fists. "Why, you—"

"Halloo the house." A man's voice sounded outside, and Logan calmly set down his pitchfork to amble over and see who it was. Sulley took a deep breath and tried to get ahold of himself.

"I suspect you're about to get your wish," Logan said. "I've got a funny feeling about that woman standing in the yard."

thirty-five

She twisted and untwisted the handkerchief around her fingers. Jeremiah had taken the lead in approaching the house where Logan Williams was supposed to live. Gainey couldn't say for certain why she was so nervous. She just had the strangest feeling . . .

"Howdy." The voice came from their left as a man approached from a barn. That mouth. That chin. He looked like . . . Archie. She gasped and pressed the handkerchief to her lips. But—that didn't make sense. The man stuck out his hand, and Jeremiah took it. Gainey saw a flicker of movement in the barn doorway but couldn't tear her eyes away from the man standing in front of them. Could he—? But no. Her son was dead.

"Are you Logan Williams?" Jeremiah asked.

"Sure am. How can I help you?"

Gainey felt Jeremiah's eyes move to her. Logan followed his gaze and frowned.

"We, uh, we're looking for a fella called Sulley. Had a notion he might have come here."

"Quite the character, isn't he?" Logan looked back to the barn. "We were just talking in the barn there. You friends of his?"

"We are."

Logan looked harder at Gainey and took a step closer. "Say, you wouldn't be . . . ?" He stopped and shook his head. "Did I say he's a character? I meant meddlesome. He's just plain meddlesome." Logan sighed. "Well, since you're here, you might as well come and sit down. Can't unring a bell, can you?"

Gainey realized she was clutching her blouse at her throat. Her mouth was dry, and she couldn't remember how to form words. Couldn't think what she was meant to do next. Jeremiah took her by the elbow and nudged her forward. She moved toward the house like she'd forgotten how to bend her knees and allowed Jeremiah to settle her in a rocking chair on the front porch. Logan sat in a swing while Jeremiah pulled up a straight-back chair. She took this all in as though noting where each person sat would somehow give her the information she needed right now.

Logan set the swing into motion. "You're my mother, aren't you?"

Gainey burst into tears.

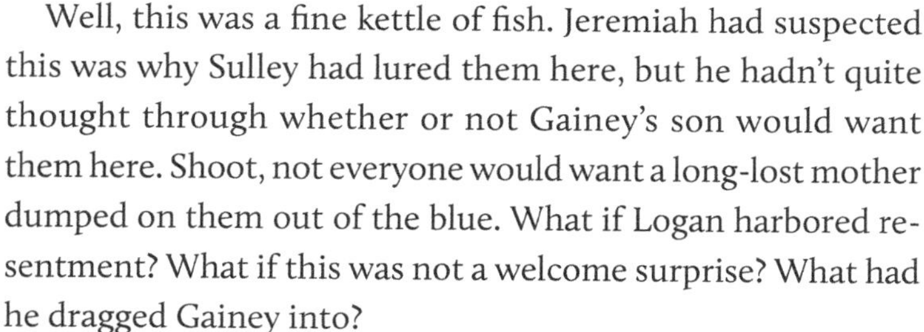

Well, this was a fine kettle of fish. Jeremiah had suspected this was why Sulley had lured them here, but he hadn't quite thought through whether or not Gainey's son would want them here. Shoot, not everyone would want a long-lost mother dumped on them out of the blue. What if Logan harbored resentment? What if this was not a welcome surprise? What had he dragged Gainey into?

He exchanged a look with Logan, who appeared just as uncertain as he was about what to do next. "Where's Sulley?" he asked for lack of anything else to say.

"While I don't know him well enough to say for certain, I have the feeling he's hiding in the barn watching us right now."

Jeremiah laughed and then choked it off. This was no time for high spirits. "I've gotten to know him fairly well and that sounds about right to me."

A woman came out on the porch and took in the scene. "What in the world?" she said, moving to Gainey's side and patting her shoulder. Gainey's outburst seemed to be subsiding. She blotted her face with her soggy handkerchief. Jeremiah fished out his bandanna and handed it over.

"Logan, what's going on?"

"Annie, my dear, it would seem this lady is my mother."

"Well then, why are you all sitting out here?" She clicked her tongue at them and began herding everyone inside. "Come sit in the parlor and let's sort this out."

As they went inside, Jeremiah saw Sulley ghost out the back of the barn and drift toward the house. He didn't know what the man was up to, but he didn't have time to worry about him right now.

Inside, there was rustling and shifting as everyone settled in the small but immaculately tidy room with its cold fireplace and antimacassars over the backs of the chairs. Jeremiah sat gingerly, afraid he might break something. The room seemed to give Gainey some of her equilibrium back. She sat on a velvet settee with her ankles crossed and her hands folded in her lap over his bandanna. He had to say, even after a burst of tears, she remained a handsome woman.

Once they were all seated, an awkward silence fell. Annie, who sat near her husband, nudged his foot with hers and nodded toward the group. He shifted and cleared his throat, but before he could say anything, Gainey spoke. "This must be terribly strange for you."

"I get the feeling it's not necessarily what you were expecting today, either."

Gainey frowned. "I thought—oh, my Bible." She noticed that Logan had carried it in with him and placed it on a low table. "Or, I suppose, it's your Bible now. At least I always meant for you to have it. How did . . . ?"

"How did it find its way back to me?"

Logan leaned forward and scooped the book up. "Sulley brought it." He shook his head. "It was always a point of contention between Henry and me."

Jeremiah saw his own confusion mirrored on Gainey's face. Who was Henry?

"Oh, that's right," Logan said. "You know him as Harmon." Gainey grew even paler, yet she didn't make a sound. "Harmon—his real name is Henry—was my stepbrother. We weren't but a year apart. It seems my parents hadn't been able to have children, so they adopted me." He smiled and laughed softly. "And then Henry came along right after that. Ma called him her 'little miracle.' She'd tell you she spoiled him. Thinks it's her fault he was a rapscallion." He leafed through the pages of the Bible in his hand. "Here you go, Proverbs thirteen: 'He that spareth his rod hateth his son: but he that loveth him chasteneth him betimes.' She used to quote that after Henry left. Said she and Dad ruined him by doting on him." He closed the book. "They're good parents—good people. I think Henry just had a wild streak no one could change."

"So then you—" Gainey pressed Jeremiah's bandanna to her mouth. "You've had a good life?"

Logan set the Bible back on the table. "The best. Guess that's why I'm not sure how to take meeting you. Oh, I've been curious over the years—took a fit when I was twenty or so of trying to figure out where I came from. But when I saw how it worried Ma, I let it go." He reached out and took his wife's hand. "I've got everything I need. A good wife and kids. A farm that'll keep us even if the country keeps struggling. A house that's paid for—God has blessed me more than I deserve." He blew out a breath. "I don't want to upset you, but I guess maybe you did a good thing giving me up." He flicked a look at Jeremiah. "I'm guessing you weren't, ahem, married?"

Gainey flushed but maintained her composure. "That's correct. I was . . . engaged to a man who died unexpectedly." She lifted her chin. "Which, of course, does not make it right. I wanted you very much, but given the situation, I couldn't think how to keep you with me."

Annie came over and sat beside Gainey, laying a gentle hand on her shoulder and giving it a pat. "That must have been hard," she said.

A tear escaped and ran down Gainey's cheek but no more than that. "It was." She took a deep breath and looked all around the room, then clasped Annie's hand. "But I can see that I did the right thing. I fear Logan would not have had the advantages—the good name—he's had with a mother and a father." She smiled at Logan and Jeremiah, who could see that she was drawing on strength she hadn't expected to find. "I think, now that I've seen you, I can go on without any regrets."

She stood and looked toward Jeremiah, who lurched to his feet. Were they leaving already?

"But wait," Annie said. "Don't you want to meet your grandchildren? They're at their grandmother's house across the way."

A sort of whimper escaped Gainey, and she pressed the bandanna to her mouth again. Once composed she lowered it. "No. Thank you for asking." She looked directly at Logan. "They have a grandmother, and I don't want to confuse them or upset Logan's . . . mother." The word *mother* came out hoarse, as though it scraped her throat on the way out.

Logan nodded and stood. "I think that's best. Thank you for understanding."

Gainey bit her lip. "I'm so very grateful to know that you are well. That I did not ruin your life." She twisted the bandanna in her hands. "I'm sorry for the loss of your brother."

Logan sighed. "So am I. Although I'm glad to know what became of him. We might have gone on wondering, if not for your Bible." He smiled. "Life's mysterious enough without adding to it."

Gainey turned to Annie, who didn't look altogether happy. "Thank you for your hospitality. I won't be troubling you any further." She moved toward the door, and Jeremiah trotted after her. He saw Annie shoot a look at her husband.

"If you wanted to," Logan began, "it'd be alright if you, uh, wanted to write now and again. It might be that, once we get used to the idea—and break it to Ma and the kids—well, I'm not promising anything, but we might get together again sometime."

"I'd like that," Gainey said. And based on the light in her eyes, Jeremiah guessed she'd like it a whole lot.

Once outside, they took their leave with an odd formality. Jeremiah and Logan shook hands. Gainey and Annie hugged briefly, and then they started for the Model T.

"What's going on here?" Sulley was suddenly in front of them, appearing from the side of the house where he must have been eavesdropping through an open window. "You two are kin. Mother and son. And that's it? That's all you have to say to each other? And maybe you'll *write*?" He said the last word like it was utterly foreign to him. "This is a miracle you've been waiting on for forty years and you're done with it in twenty minutes?"

Jeremiah had never seen Sulley like this. He always played his cards so close to his chest, but at this moment his emotions were spilling over faster than any of them could keep up with.

"What business is it of yours?" Jeremiah thought he needed to step in at last. He'd stayed quiet, hoping his presence was a comfort to Gainey. But now he felt the need to defend her.

"I found him," Sulley said. "I keep finding people. I never mean to, but there they are. And if I'm meant to find them, there must be a reason. So 'hey howdy, write me a letter' isn't good enough!"

Jeremiah fisted his hands and stepped toward Sulley, but Gainey moved in front of him. "Thank you for finding my son, Sulley. But the truth is, he didn't especially want to be found. And when it comes right down to it, I'm not his mother." She glanced back toward Logan. "His mother is the woman who reared him. The woman who was there to soothe him when he woke from a nightmare and to nurse him when he was ill." She smiled and it reminded Jeremiah of a picture he'd once seen in a church of Mary holding the baby Jesus. "Being able to correspond with Logan is more than I deserve, and it is, most certainly, good enough."

Sulley cursed, grabbed a bucket sitting on the edge of the porch, and flung it with all his might. It crashed into a tree with a great rattle and bang. "I've been wondering who my mother is my whole life. All I've got of hers is a beat-up book of poetry, and I'd let you cut off my right hand if it meant I could spend a day with her." His chest was heaving like he'd been running.

"You people talk about miracles and God, and then when He hands you something like this, you just throw it away. Every last one of you is a fool and a hypocrite."

Sulley turned and fled. Back into the woods. Back on his own, the way Jeremiah suspected he preferred to be.

thirty-six

"Mind if I pull over here a minute to, uh, refresh myself?" Jeremiah asked. Gainey looked up as though she'd forgotten he was driving.

"Oh, certainly. Take your time." She turned her head pointedly as he pulled over and disappeared into the underbrush, making sure he was well away before relieving himself. When he returned to the Model T, she had climbed out and was stretching her back. "It's a lovely spot," she said. "I thought I'd stretch my legs a minute."

Jeremiah sat on a fallen log, and Gainey soon joined him. The cool of the shade and the whisper of the breeze made it an ideal place to linger, and Gainey seemed in no hurry—once again lost in her thoughts. "Will you go back to Mount Lookout?" Jeremiah finally broke the silence.

"I was going back to the tunnel camps to help there, but now . . . well, I think I may go home." She wound a stem of grass between her fingers as she spoke.

"So Logan will know where to write to you."

She gave Jeremiah a grateful look. "Yes. Being the postmistress will finally have its own reward, won't it?"

He chuckled. "I think everything you do is rewarding."

"Jeremiah, I—thank you for taking me to meet my son. Did you know that's what Sulley had up his sleeve?"

"No, but if I'm honest, I suspected as much."

"I'm troubled that he was so upset. I continue to like Sulley in spite of my better judgment, but I surely don't understand him."

Jeremiah cocked his head to the side. "He mentioned his mother to me once before. Guess he's been missing her all his life." He cleared his throat. "Might be he thought you could have been his mother."

"Oh." Astonishment creased her face. "Well, that would explain a great deal, wouldn't it?"

Jeremiah slanted a look at her. "What about you? Notion ever cross your mind?"

"Of course not," she said quickly, then slanted a look of her own back his way. "Well, perhaps for a moment, in the beginning, but I quickly decided it was not possible." She gave a sigh and added, "For most of my life I've considered whether nearly every young man I've met might be my own." She smiled. "And now that I know where he is, it's a great relief."

"Even though Logan didn't much want to get to know you better?"

"That's to be expected." She gripped Jeremiah's arm, and he welcomed her touch. "He's a good man. A husband and a father." Jeremiah could see tears rising and longed to stop them. "I don't have to wonder anymore whether or not I ruined him."

And with that, he stopped fighting it and simply wrapped his arms around her. It felt like the most natural thing in the world. It wasn't what Jeremiah had planned at all. Gainey wasn't the sort of woman he expected to welcome the public embrace of a man. Which left him surprised and delighted when she softened in his arms and pillowed her head against his chest.

"Gainey?" She didn't raise her head, but he could tell she was smiling.

"Yes?" He drew back just enough to look into her face. She was flushed, her lips parted slightly. He could see her pulse throbbing at the base of her throat.

He brushed his lips across her forehead. "I'd like to court you."

She shivered even though the day was anything but cold. "I'd like that, too."

Then he pressed his lips to hers right there on the side of the road. When he released her, they were both breathless in the best way possible. He grinned at her and she ducked her head. "We should continue our journey."

He nodded and released her reluctantly. "Speaking of journeys, what would you think of coming to Kline with me?" He gave her his best boyish grin. "Mostly for a visit to see my farm, maybe meet a few folks." The grin grew wider. "See if you like it there."

He saw some of the joy drain from her. "I . . . are you supposing that if we . . . that is to say, you mean to continue living in Kline?"

"Well, yes. I've got a house, a little bit of land. I'm the teacher there, and school will be starting back soon." He smiled, but he could feel a dimming. "I know you want to stay in Mount Lookout right now, but it's not so very far. You can come for a visit. I'll come back here at Christmas." He injected some wattage back into the smile. "And by next spring maybe you'll be ready for a change of address."

Gainey bit her lip. "Jeremiah, I have no notion of changing

addresses. I, too, have a house and a bit of land. And as . . . fond as I am of you, I want to be near my son." She cleared her throat and swallowed. "I have high hopes that I will get to meet my grandchildren, and Christmas or even Thanksgiving would not be a moment too soon for that to happen."

Jeremiah silently cursed his brashness. Of course. She was no girl ready to give up everything for a man. "I see," he said at last. "I should have given this more thought."

Though she didn't say so, he could see that she agreed. "I regret—" she started.

He held up a hand, then reached out to touch her cheek. "No, that's fine. You've got the right of it. I guess you made me feel like the young man I once was—full of dreams and willing to chase them without too much thought." He stood and led the way back to the automobile. "I will write to you, though, if you'll let me."

"I'd like that," Gainey said. And there wasn't much else left to say after that.

Jeremiah didn't see Sulley again before he left for Kline, and he was glad of it. That man had caused him too much grief already. Even if it had been indirectly. He had half a mind to give everything up and stay put, yet the families back home were counting on him. And Gainey, while pleased to see him, was clearly more interested in the incoming mail than anything he might offer.

So, in early August, he headed home—again. He only hoped Meredith had firmed up her plans with that salesman. The last thing he wanted was to resurrect any interest on her part.

He'd teach the children, write a letter once a week or so to

Gainey, and consider himself a summer poorer but at least one friend richer. It would be enough, he told himself.

Sulley sat under the tree staring at Harmon Wilkins's grave. Or was it Henry Williams? Did it even matter? Would Gainey spare this poor soul a thought now that she knew he wasn't her son? From what he'd heard about this fellow, Logan was probably satisfied with simply knowing what had happened to him. Sulley guessed that was how it would be when he was gone. One or two people might wonder but no one would miss him—not really.

He'd been camping near the cemetery field since he left the Williams farm. He'd watched trucks come and go, adding to the unmarked graves littering the field. He felt an affinity for them—whoever they were. The lost. The forgotten. He kept vigil with them as though they might know he was there keeping a tally no matter how inadequate or incomplete. He'd walked through the field with his dowsing rod, feeling it twitch in his hand over and over again. He didn't doubt it anymore. There was much to find here, only no one was looking.

He saw a flicker of movement near the road and faded back into the trees. He was careful to make sure no one saw him. But this time it wasn't a truck with bodies stacked in the back like cordwood. This time it was a lone figure threading its way through the pocked field. A woman, he thought.

As she drew nearer, Sulley felt a jolt of recognition. Yes—he knew this one. Gainey carried a large basket over her arm. Her expression was serious, dark eyebrows slashes across her pale face. She walked slowly but directly to the tree where Henry's body lay. Sulley had stacked stones at the head of the grave, a precarious tower he expected to topple one day, but for now it stood.

Gainey stopped and considered the pile of stones. Then she knelt as though it were hard on her knees and pulled a trowel from her basket. She dug several small holes and began placing something in them—bulbs, Sulley thought. Daffodils maybe? Or crocuses. She patted each one in place like a mother tucking in a child at night. Finally, she pulled out a jarful of flowers—cardinal flowers, Queen Anne's lace, black-eyed Susans—and made a hollow for the container. She sat back on her heels to examine the results of her labor.

Seemingly pleased, she struggled to her feet. Sulley resisted the impulse to go and help her up. She glanced again at the grave, then looked all around. Her high, white forehead shone in the sunlight, and she brushed some wayward strands of hair from her face. Then she clasped her hands, and Sulley could see her lips moving, could hear a murmur but could not make out any words other than a final "amen." And perhaps even that word was only something echoing in his own mind.

She picked up the trowel, dropped it in her basket, and made her way slowly back through the field, pausing now and again. Sulley didn't believe in such things, but if he did he would have thought she was blessing the forgotten souls tucked beneath their meadow blanket. He kept watching until she disappeared.

Finally, he crept back to his camp and lay down, closing his eyes. All too often, when he thought the worst of people, he was proven right. For once, it was good to be wrong.

thirty-seven

Mount Lookout, West Virginia
August 1933

Noah stepped up to Gainey's mail counter with a smile. "Ma wants you to come for Sunday dinner." Gainey smiled back—such invitations had become more and more common. In those first months, after the truth about her son came out, her relationship with Luisa had been freighted with unspoken words. Then one day Luisa broke down in tears right here in the store. She'd begged Gainey's forgiveness for judging her. "You helped return my son to me. How could I want any less for you and your son? No matter how he came to you."

After that, Gainey found her friendship with Luisa—and Verna, for that matter—deepened and strengthened. Now, even though their differences might seem obvious, the fact was that they were all mothers mourning their children in different ways. Verna's son was dead. Gainey's, while found, was still a stranger. And Luisa's son had been marked by his time in the tunnel. The once hale-and-hearty boy was a shadow of his former self. Even so, he had a quiet peace about him that overshadowed the illness, which was clearly shortening his days.

"What can I bring?" Gainey asked.

"Ma said you'd ask that." Noah grinned, stretching the sparse flesh across his cheekbones. "She said if you did, to hint that if you've got any more of those watermelon rind pickles you brought to the Fourth of July picnic, they wouldn't go amiss." He smiled even more broadly. "Maryanne seems to be craving pickled stuff these days."

Gainey looked at him more closely. He was positively beaming. "Do you mean to say . . . ?"

He chortled. "I'm expecting to be a daddy come the first of the year. Of course, Jackie's like my own, but even he's excited." He shook his head. "And Ma acts like Maryanne hung the moon."

Gainey felt her own smile widen—an expression that came more easily these days. She'd found smiles harder to come by after Sulley disappeared and Jeremiah returned to Kline. There had also been a great deal of sadness in her return visits to Emma Jones, who was losing her family to the tunnel one by one. Shirley died first, then her son Cecil—the one who brought a lawsuit against the company that built the tunnel—died back in September. And now a third son, along with her husband, were walking the same path they all knew would likely end in death. For a time, Gainey had made weekly visits to the camp at Gauley Bridge to write letters for the men there, but the camp rouster eventually made it clear just how unwelcome she was, and she gave in to fear. Now that the tunnel was finished, Gainey tried to visit Emma monthly, if only to serve as witness to her sorrow.

But even with all the grief Hawks Nest brought, each letter from her son—arriving with increasing frequency—helped her rediscover her joy. The letters from Jeremiah hadn't hurt, either.

Life did go on after a disappointment. Sometimes it took

forty years to gain momentum, but still. She was grateful for each moment.

"Tell Luisa I'll bring the pickles along with a cucumber salad."

Noah looked pleased. "Now that does sound fine." He coughed into a handkerchief. "We'll be seeing you at church come Sunday."

Gainey watched him leave. He moved slowly, like a man three times his age. She supposed the dust he'd breathed would eventually be the death of him, but she knew his family was thankful for every day and she prayed that healing would yet come to the young man. Especially now that his responsibilities were growing.

She was grateful for the distraction of Sunday dinner with the Johnson family. It kept her from thinking overmuch about her plans for Saturday. Logan had finally asked if she'd like to come meet her grandchildren. And of course she'd said yes, although now she was having doubts. What if they didn't like her? What if they blamed her for abandoning their father? What would they call her—did she even want to be Grandma Gainey?

She heard the bell over the door ring again but was too intent on her thoughts and the mail she was sorting to pay it much mind.

"I don't suppose I could get a stamp?"

Gainey jerked her head up to find Jeremiah standing at her counter, his cheeks ruddy above his neatly trimmed beard. He was smiling but there was uncertainty in his eyes.

"Jeremiah?" She snapped her mouth shut.

"Have I changed so much you don't know me?" he asked.

"No—it's just I didn't expect you." Gainey felt heat spread all through her body and hoped no one was watching. After giving up all hope of this man being anything more than a pen friend, seeing him standing in front of her was more than she could process.

"When you wrote that you'd be meeting Logan's kids this weekend, I figured you could use some moral support. So I thought I'd surprise you."

She tried to laugh but it didn't sound right. "You've succeeded." Oh dear. Did she sound like she didn't want to see him? Like she wasn't glad he was here? Why hadn't he written first so she could prepare herself? Their correspondence had been such a bittersweet delight to her this past year.

It was as if he could hear her thoughts. "Figured if I told you I was coming, you might try and change my mind." He brushed what she suspected was imaginary dust from his sleeve. "And I had a hankering to see you." He raised his eyes, and their warmth seeped into all the cold places inside her. "I've missed you."

The simple words made Gainey's heart go soft. She'd convinced herself she was over any notion of romance this late in life, but he was making her wonder how strong her convictions were. "I . . . you've been missed." That wasn't what she'd meant to say. She couldn't seem to get her thoughts in order.

"So you don't mind that I've come?"

She leaned into the counter wishing it weren't there between them. "I'm glad," she said. "It's good to have a friend to count on right now."

He leaned against the counter on his side. Now they weren't far apart at all. "I was thinking—"

But she didn't get to hear what he was thinking. Arbutus came in just then. "Mr. Jeremiah, you've come back!" She was at his side in an instant, tugging on his arm. "Why'd you stay away so long? How come you're back now? You coming to stay with us?"

Jeremiah chuckled. "That's a bunch of questions. Might take me a minute to sort 'em out. Although now you mention it, I'd sure be glad of a place to stay."

"Come on, then. Mama will be so glad to see you. She's not as sad as she was, but she'll lose some more sadness when she sees you." She turned pleading eyes on Gainey. "It's just about the end of the day. I can go take Mr. Jeremiah to the house, can't I?"

Gainey sighed and took a step back, smoothing her dress over her hips as she did so. If she wasn't mistaken, Jeremiah was watching her every move and it made her feel . . . goodness, incredibly alive. She didn't want him to go and yet at the same time thought he'd better. "Yes, child, go on with you both."

Jeremiah laid his hand palm up on the counter, and without thinking she placed her hand in his. "I'll see you soon," he said. "We can talk more then." He squeezed her fingers, then released them, winked, and followed a chattering Arbutus out the door.

It wasn't until they were out of sight that Gainey realized she was cradling her hand against her heart.

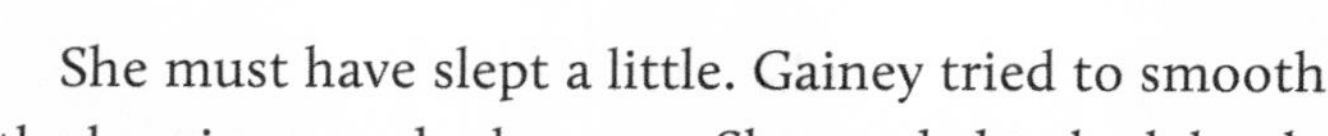

She must have slept a little. Gainey tried to smooth away the bagginess under her eyes. She needed to look her best for Logan, Annie, and their children.

Her grandchildren.

Her family.

This was going to take some getting used to. She sipped her coffee, hoping it wouldn't turn her stomach. She never missed breakfast, but on this morning the thought of anything—even a piece of toast—left her stomach roiling. She hadn't felt this unsteady since she'd been pregnant and trying to convince herself she wasn't.

The difference this time was that she was glad to have a son. Not to mention a daughter-in-law and four beautiful grandchildren. The letters between Fayetteville and Mount Lookout had been cautious at first but had grown in frequency and intimacy. Not that she could claim to know her son well, but she did feel as though he was less a stranger than he had been. And she'd cautiously shared a few of her own thoughts and dreams.

If she was honest, she'd hoped this day would have come sooner. When no invitation arrived for Thanksgiving or Christmas, she'd begun to harbor a dream that she would be asked for Mother's Day in May. The disappointment when no invitation arrived had been sharp. She might have shared more of that with Jeremiah than she should have. And now he was here. Which both unsettled and comforted her.

But she'd think about him later. Right now she needed to get over to the Leggs' to borrow their mule cart for her drive that day. She had no time to waste mooning over what might have been. She snuck a smile. Or might yet be, for that matter.

She finished dressing her hair and was cleaning her teeth when she heard a knock on the door. Rinsing her mouth quickly, she hurried to see who it might be. Susan knew she wouldn't be at the store today, but she hadn't mentioned anything to Arbutus. It would be just like the girl to come chasing after her. She opened the door and pressed a hand to her bosom before she could catch herself.

"Jeremiah. What are you doing here at this hour?"

"Thought I'd drive you down to Fayetteville." He motioned toward a wagon and mule in the road.

"Is that Tobias?" The mule swung his head around at the sound of his name.

"That's him. Susan might have mentioned your mode of

transportation to me. And Tobias, well, I think he remembers us fondly."

The mule snorted and turned away. Gainey laughed. "Maybe he does at that. Just a moment while I get my things."

She bustled back into the house, where she tucked a handkerchief into her pocket and added another jar of preserves to her basket of gifts for the children. As a final afterthought, she tucked her Bible inside.

She was thankful that it wasn't too terribly hot—at least not for August. Recent rain had left the trees lush and green, and today's sky was a clear blue with high white clouds. She fought to quell the butterflies in her stomach, but Jeremiah's smile and his gentle conversation soon made her forget her uneasiness about meeting the children of the son she'd abandoned all those years ago.

It seemed mere moments before they arrived at the Williams farm even though it was a good fifteen miles. Two boys came tumbling out of the barn, jockeying to be the first one to reach the new arrivals. They fell to a halt and elbowed each other until Jeremiah pulled Tobias to a stop.

"Hello there," he said. "You fellows look like just the ones to help me with my mule."

Both boys stood taller and stuck out their chests. Gainey could see that they were twins, nearly alike but not quite. One was a little taller, while the other had more freckles. They both were sandy-haired, and she could see shades of her own father in their narrow upper lips.

"Twins ran in my mother's family." She spoke as a natural extension of her thoughts, then wished she'd held her tongue. The boys' eagerness to help Jeremiah instantly changed to a look of suspicion.

The taller boy cocked his head at her. "Are you supposed to be our grandmother?"

She flushed, but before she could answer, she saw Logan step out onto the porch. "You boys help get that mule put up, then come on in the house." He nodded at Gainey. "Good trip?"

"Yes, thank you," she said as Jeremiah helped her down from the wagon. "Mr. Weber was kind enough to drive me. I hope you don't mind that he's come along."

Annie appeared behind Logan's shoulder. "The more the merrier," she said. "We enjoy company around here. Now come inside out of the sun."

Gainey was grateful for the woman's—her daughter-in-law's—persistent cheer. She was afraid her own emotions were too muddled for her to even say what they were at the moment.

Inside, a lovely girl in her teens took Gainey's straw hat—the same one she'd been wearing the last time she'd visited here. It made her think of how Sulley had been present then, which was the last time she'd laid eyes on him. She supposed it was because of him that she found herself welcomed into her son's home today. Rapscallion or not, if she could thank him for that, she surely would.

Jeremiah and the two boys came tromping in along with a third, older boy—young man really. The house was breezy with the windows open wide and smelled of fresh baked bread and roasting meat. Now that the initial meeting was over, the children were laughing and jostling and Annie was calling out to set another place and for the boys to wash up and for heaven's sake to leave their shoes outside. Logan stood taking it all in with a look of deep satisfaction on his face, and for a moment Gainey thought she might burst into tears. The joy and the sorrow washed over her in alternate waves, and both made her want to cry.

"Looks like a fine bunch." Jeremiah's words were soft beside her ear. She nodded wordlessly. "I know giving that babe up must have been awful hard, but it's sure turned out well. Guess the Lord meant it for good."

Gainey turned grateful eyes on Jeremiah. Her friend. Come all this way to drive her and comfort her. She'd never been more grateful for another person in all her life. Not even for Archie. Not even for Logan. "Thank you for being here." She took his hand and squeezed it tight before releasing it, turning, and wading into the fray that was so unexpectedly her family.

Jeremiah whistled as he hitched Tobias to the wagon and drove it around to pick up Gainey at the door. They'd had a wonderful meal and afterward sat and told tales over coffee. The young'uns had talked Gainey into playing cards with them, and he didn't think he'd ever seen a human being look happier. Now everyone was standing out on the porch, the kids cutting up, Annie pressing something into Gainey's hands, and Logan standing back a little, watching. Finally, he stepped forward and took Gainey's hand. He spoke a few words and Gainey nodded. Then Jeremiah was there, and Logan handed Gainey—his mother, Jeremiah thought with a start—up into the wagon, and they were off. Neither of them spoke at first; Jeremiah just kept whistling softly.

"He wouldn't keep the Bible," she said at last.

"What's that?"

"I wanted Logan to have the Bible I left with him when I

. . . gave him away. But he said it had always been a reminder that his mother had given him up." She tried to continue but choked on tears. Jeremiah handed her his handkerchief and waited, listening to the steady clop of the mule's hooves. She cleared her throat and tried again. "He said he didn't need it anymore." She swallowed and placed her fingers against her lips briefly as though pulling the words out. "Now that his mother has re-claimed him." She began to sob, and Jeremiah drew the wagon to a halt on the side of the road. He turned to Gainey and took her in his arms. She came willingly, clinging to him as she wet his shirt with her tears.

After a few minutes she drew back slightly, blew her nose, and looked up at him. "Why did you come back?"

He pushed back a piece of hair stuck to her damp cheek. "I missed you. Wanted to see you. And I thought—hoped—you might need me."

"Oh, Jeremiah, I have missed you. You've been such a comfort to me today, but I'm afraid . . ." She ducked her chin and rested her forehead against his shoulder. "I'm afraid to get too used to having you here."

He reached down and lifted her face to his. "What if I were to stay?"

Hope lit her eyes and ignited his heart. "Would you?"

"Sold my house, so I may as well."

This time her eyes widened in surprise. "You sold your house? Why would you do that?"

"There's this woman I'm partial to, and she doesn't live in Kline. Got me asking myself why I'd want a house in a place she wasn't."

She drew back again and got a solemn look. "Don't toy with me. I'm too old for such nonsense."

He tightened his arms a notch and felt her come close again. "So am I. How about this? I've come to court you and, if you'll have me, to make you mine."

Her lips parted in an o of wonder, and he took that as invitation enough to dip his head and kiss her right there on the side of the road. She tensed, then softened in his arms. And just when he was thinking he could get used to this, Tobias gave a jerk and brayed.

Gainey gasped and drew back, although she remained in the circle of his arms. "I think Tobias is ready to get home to his oats."

Jeremiah grinned. "Saw they've added a jenny to the herd. Guess I can't blame old Tobias for wanting to get back to his lady love." At that, he was gratified to see Gainey's eyes sparkle and her cheeks glow rosy pink. "Why, Miss Floyd, you look the picture of a girl who's been kissed."

She swatted at him and turned to the front of the wagon, smoothing her hair. "And you, Mr. Weber, look the picture of a boy who's been sneaking cookies out of the jar."

He threw his head back and laughed as he set the eager mule back into motion. "I trust I might get another cookie before the day's done?" he teased. The look on her face convinced him he would.

thirty-eight

Gainey hummed as she walked out to the Johnson farm. Not only had her fears over meeting Logan's children come to naught but she now had a beau. It had been so long since she'd allowed a romantic thought to even enter her mind. And now she couldn't stop thinking about a burly, bearded fellow who had given up his past to come and woo her. She wanted to hug herself and laugh to the sky but settled for a secret smile. One never knew who might be watching.

She was so consumed by thoughts of Jeremiah that when he appeared before her, she imagined for a moment that she had conjured him up.

"May I escort you?" he asked.

She flushed and waved him away. "You needn't go out of your way for me."

He offered her the crook of his arm. "As it happens, the Johnsons have included me in today's invitation."

Gainey chuckled. "Have they indeed? My, word does travel quickly." He winked at her and they walked on arm in arm.

Over supper it was obvious that Luisa meant to hurry their romance along. Gainey wondered if she thought to make an honest woman of her after all these years. Normally, this notion would have chafed, but Jeremiah's solid presence soothed her in a way she hadn't allowed in far too many years.

"Jeremiah, do I understand you've come to Mount Lookout to stay?" Freeman asked the question in a way that made Gainey suspect Luisa had put him up to it. The way Noah smirked at Maryanne reinforced the notion.

"Hoping to," Jeremiah said with a twinkle that told Gainey he was aware of the game being played.

Then Freeman must have gone off script based on the look his wife gave him. "Must've been hard to sell your place, what with no good water. Didn't I hear Sulley couldn't find you a well?"

Jeremiah swallowed his bite of smoked sausage and patted his lips with one of Luisa's hemstitched napkins. "Well now, that's the funny thing." He leaned back with a Cheshire cat grin. "That last well we dug behind the church? It's brimming with good water."

"What?" Gainey set down her fork. "I thought it was dry."

"It was." Jeremiah nodded. "When I got back to Kline last summer, it was bone-dry. Then this past spring the kids were back there playing, and we figured we'd better fill it in before somebody fell." He added more rösti to his plate. "But when we uncovered it, we realized it was full up with the best water in the whole county."

"How can that be?" Gainey asked.

Jeremiah shrugged. "Maybe there was a spring that finally found its way through. Maybe we just didn't wait long enough for it to fill."

Noah pushed some green beans around his plate. "Maybe it's a miracle."

"Could be," Jeremiah agreed. "Stranger things have happened."

"I like to think God's still in the business of miracles," Noah said, muffling a cough with his napkin.

"That he is." Luisa patted her son's arm. "He returned you to us, didn't He?"

After a few moments of heavy silence, Jeremiah changed the subject. "I was sorry to hear that trial over tunnel workers getting sick didn't amount to anything. Ended in a hung jury, didn't it?"

Noah sighed and tented his napkin over his plate as if to hide his lack of appetite. Maryanne and Luisa exchanged a look but neither spoke. "Seven jurors for the workers and five for the company. Not near good enough. Still, word is there's going to be an out-of-court settlement." He leaned sharp elbows on the table. "Most likely I'll get a piece of that. Along with quite a few other fellows." He shrugged. "Guess it's better than nothing."

"I know Emma Jones," Gainey said. "It was her daughter-in-law who pursued the case on behalf of her husband, Cecil, Emma's son. That poor woman has lost two boys now." Gainey felt her own appetite waning. "I can't begin to imagine . . ." She remembered the sorrow in Emma's eyes over the loss of her youngest son, not to mention the sorrow of losing Cecil and watching another son and her husband waste away. And now a jury had failed even to agree that anyone was responsible. "Doesn't seem like there'd be enough money to make up for something like that."

Noah laughed—choking when it turned into a cough. "There isn't. But money doesn't hurt."

Later, when Gainey was helping Luisa wash up—they'd insisted Maryanne rest—her friend was unable to hide her tears. "He's dying," Luisa choked out as the steam from the dishpan mingled with the moisture on her cheeks. "We don't want money; we want him to be well." She scrubbed a pot as though it were to blame for her grief. "I'd give a thousand dollars for him to take a deep breath again. To help his father in the orchard."

Gainey wrapped an arm around Luisa's shoulders. "Don't stop hoping. God has done more astonishing things in my experience."

Luisa turned sad eyes on her. "Has He? You lost your son even though he was still alive. For so many years."

"Yes," Gainey agreed, "and now he's been restored to me. Not fully. And not as if I'd reared him. But it's enough. And I'm beginning to think that with God's help, whatever He grants us turns out to be enough if we're patient. If we give Him a chance to finish the work He's doing in us."

Luisa laid her head on Gainey's shoulder, and they held each other with hands still wet from the dishwater soaking their blouses. And, for at least that moment, it was enough.

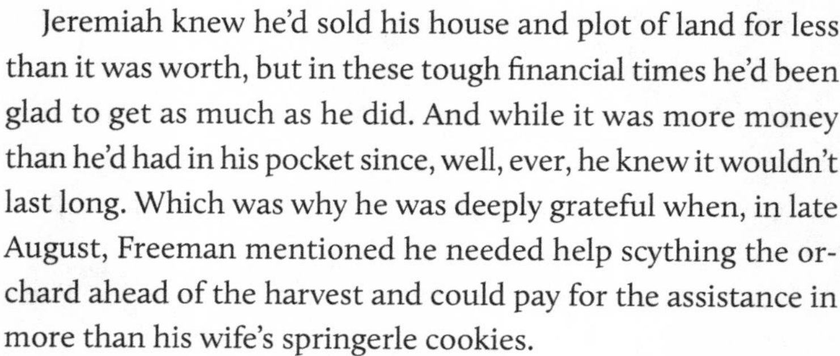

Jeremiah knew he'd sold his house and plot of land for less than it was worth, but in these tough financial times he'd been glad to get as much as he did. And while it was more money than he'd had in his pocket since, well, ever, he knew it wouldn't last long. Which was why he was deeply grateful when, in late August, Freeman mentioned he needed help scything the orchard ahead of the harvest and could pay for the assistance in more than his wife's springerle cookies.

Jeremiah and Reggie arrived in the cool of the morning as fog clung to the bottomland and drifted across the face of the mountains as though reluctant to rise into the sky and relinquish the beauty of summer.

Freeman was busy pruning water sprouts from the apple trees loaded with ripening fruit. Jackie shadowed him like a pup, handing him tools and carrying cut branches to the burn pile. Freeman pointed the men toward sharpened scythes, and it didn't take much instruction to understand that they should start at one end of the orchard and work their way to the other.

"You done this before?" Jeremiah asked Reggie.

"Sure enough. Mr. Johnson's good to work for. Don't push too hard and keeps his workers in those spicy cookies his wife makes." Reggie grinned. "Plus, Verna comes out to help Mrs. Johnson with the summer harvest, and them women usually get us up a mighty fine dinner about the time the sun hits the middle of the sky."

"That does sound fine," Jeremiah agreed. "Do we rake the grass once we cut it?"

"Nope—Freeman leaves it lay for mulch and fertilizer."

The two men set to work, and Jeremiah was soon lost in the rhythm of the swinging scythe laying down swathes of orchard grass. He ceased thinking and simply soaked in the peace and pleasure of seeing the difference he was making. It came as a surprise when he heard a loud whistle and looked up from the far end of the orchard to see Freeman waving him in. He'd only paused once to sharpen his blade with a whetstone and now stood a moment, stretching his back and taking in the work they'd accomplished. It was a far cry from a classroom full of unruly children, and at that moment the change suited him right down to the ground.

He trotted toward the house along with Reggie. The two men met at the back porch, where Luisa had set out a basin of cool water, a bar of soap, and some white toweling. It looked too fine to use. Freeman whistled again and beckoned them over to one of the wells Sulley had found for them. He pulled up a bucket of water, stripped to his waist, and sluiced handfuls over his face and neck. Jeremiah and Reggie did the same, then put their shirts back on and finished with the fussier setup on the porch.

"If we don't use it, Luisa will carry on," Freeman said, winking as he dabbed his cheeks with the pristine towel.

A table and chairs had been arranged under a leafy maple in the side yard. The women were carrying out dishes that made a man glad he'd worked all morning and had a good appetite. Jeremiah felt a jolt of pleasure when Gainey gave him a sidelong glance, then looked away with a blush.

By golly, he just might have a future here.

Noah joined them as they all sat and prayed over the summer bounty on the table. There was stewed okra with tomatoes, corn on the cob, cucumbers, biscuits, salted pork, and green beans with new potatoes swimming in butter. "Try Gainey's biscuits," Luisa said in her lilting accent. "They are as light as a cloud."

Jeremiah helped himself and was gratified to see the woman he'd come to love blush once again. "There is also peach cobbler for dessert," Luisa said. "So do not founder on what is before you now."

Jeremiah dug in and was so focused on his food he didn't realize for a time that Noah looked . . . what, upset? Angry? He eyed the younger man more closely and it occurred to him that it must be hard for him to be left out of the labor being done on the farm.

"Noah, I hear you're a fine hand with a whetstone," he said.

The younger man looked surprised and stopped nibbling at half a biscuit. "Well, I guess I am pretty good with a blade."

"I tried to sharpen that scythe your pa gave me to use, but it's not much better than before I started. Think you could give it a go when we're done here?"

Light dawned in Noah's eyes. "I could do that." He turned to Reggie. "Your blade need sharpening?"

"I reckon it do," Reggie said.

Noah relaxed and took a proper bite of bread. He chewed with a satisfied look on his face that was mirrored by his parents.

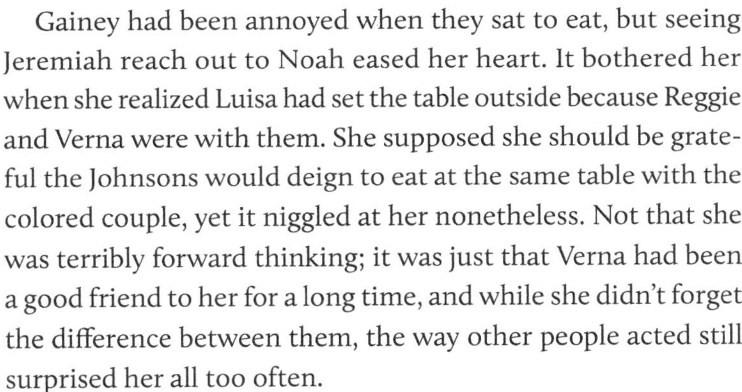

Gainey had been annoyed when they sat to eat, but seeing Jeremiah reach out to Noah eased her heart. It bothered her when she realized Luisa had set the table outside because Reggie and Verna were with them. She supposed she should be grateful the Johnsons would deign to eat at the same table with the colored couple, yet it niggled at her nonetheless. Not that she was terribly forward thinking; it was just that Verna had been a good friend to her for a long time, and while she didn't forget the difference between them, the way other people acted still surprised her all too often.

But Jeremiah made her heart glad, and now she could think of little else beyond his muscular forearms exposed to the sun, his broad shoulders straining against his damp work shirt, and the way the water he'd used to wash still sparkled in his beard. Which was nonsensical thinking for a woman her age, and yet . . .

As the men returned to their work, she tried to shake such yearnings from her mind while she helped clear the table and wash the dishes. Of course, Luisa didn't mind Verna coming in the house to help with the work. Especially since it meant she could send Maryanne—who was battling morning sickness all day—to take a nap.

Once the kitchen was set to rights, they went out to the shade of the porch and began thinly slicing a bushel of early apples Freeman had brought in with him at dinnertime. They placed the slices on screens in the sun and covered them over with cheesecloth to dry. Luisa's apple stack cake had won a ribbon at the county fair more than once and would be a wonderful treat in the long winter days ahead.

At first, the women focused on their work, speaking little. Then, after a silence, Luisa huffed a sigh. "They have made what they call a settlement for the men who are sick or even dying from working in the tunnel," she began. "Would you believe they are giving our Noah only eight hundred dollars? I know it is a good deal of money, but"—she lowered her voice and made sure her son was out of earshot—"he will never work again. And I fear for his future."

"I heard there was four million dollars in lawsuits," Gainey said. "How could he get so little?"

"These lawyers, they do not care. These judges, they do not care. And the company?" She made a sound of disgust. "They only care for their money and will part with as little of it as they can."

Gainey saw a tear drip from Verna's chin and realized the settlement would likely include James. She laid a hand on her friend's arm. "I assume the settlement will compensate families who have lost someone in the tunnel as well."

"We got a check," Verna said.

"I know it can't make up for losing James, but at least there's been something," Gainey said. "Eight hundred dollars could help in a lot of ways."

"We got sixty dollars," Verna said, raising her chin as though bracing for a blow.

Luisa and Gainey both stopped their work and stared. "Is that an installment?" Gainey asked.

"They said he owed for house rent and coal and I don't know what all. Said sixty dollars was all that was left." Verna kept on working while the other two women continued to stare.

"That's not right," Gainey said.

"There's a lot *not right* this side of heaven," Verna said, leaving them all in silence.

thirty-nine

"I bet Sulley would get a kick out of hearing the well he told us to dig got water." Jeremiah and Gainey were out for a stroll in the cool of the evening. It had become their habit most days as September arrived with the first signs of autumn.

Gainey breathed in the sweet aroma of the maiden's bower spilling over fence posts and lining the roadways. She'd always loved the way the little white flowers cascaded like a veil, and this year they were giving her ideas she didn't dare dwell on too long. "I wonder what became of him?" she asked.

"I thought he might turn back up eventually, but I guess it's been too long now. Probably moved on south last winter ahead of the snow." He plucked a wand of goldenrod and tucked it in his shirt pocket. "He was pretty upset the last time we saw him."

Gainey picked a stem of deep purple ironweed and tucked it in beside the goldenrod. Jeremiah took advantage of the motion to wrap his arms around her and tug her closer. She resisted for a moment, then decided life was too short for games and relaxed against his broad chest. "It was hard for him to see a mother and son reunited the way Logan and I were." She sighed. "It would be fair to say neither one of us quite knew how to take it. Sulley was a rascal, but I think he was hurting."

Jeremiah laced his hands at the small of her back and looked down at her. She felt snug and safe and like she was exactly where she ought to be. "Sulley didn't get what he wanted." She could feel the rumble of his voice and the beating of his heart. "I've spent most of my life trying to make sure people around me got what they wanted. Seems like I left my own wants out over the years."

She looked up at him and felt her breath catch. "What do you want these days?" She kept her tone light, but even she could hear the hope behind the words.

"A kiss," he said, and then he bent to take what he wanted. And closing her eyes, Gainey let him.

Jeremiah had a surprise in mind. Gainey's birthday was September thirteenth, and he was going to make it the best one she'd ever had. Or, if everything went wrong, the worst. But there would be no middle of the road. He'd cleaned up his Model T as best he could. Now he and Gainey were bouncing along the mountain roads and she was smiling like a girl off to a Sunday picnic.

"Where are we going?" she asked for the third time.

"You sure have gotten demanding. I thought you were the quiet, submissive type."

She swatted his arm. "You did not. My only hope is that you don't care for that type."

Jeremiah let his laugh roll out the open window. Yes indeed, things were looking more and more promising.

He pulled up at the Tyree Tavern and hurried around to

open the door for Gainey. He helped her down, and by golly she was grinning. "Now, why would you bring me here? And on my birthday no less?"

"Come and see," Jeremiah said. He took her arm and escorted her up the walk and into the dining room. Business had slowed for the tavern considerably since the drilling of the tunnel finished up the previous December. There was still plenty to do before hydroelectric power would be produced, but the job no longer required hundreds of men working at the same time. As a result, Ruth had been only too glad to make the preparations he requested.

A table set for two took center stage. Jeremiah escorted Gainey to her seat and then sat himself. His nerves jangled and he fumbled his napkin, bending to retrieve it and coming up red in the face. Which made him flush even deeper.

Ruth sashayed into the room with two plates loaded with fried chicken, creamed potatoes, and green beans. She set one in front of each of them while Francis—the girl he remembered from the year before—followed with a basket of biscuits and a pitcher of iced tea. Once everything was situated, Ruth stepped back as though admiring an especially nice picture on the wall. Jeremiah cleared his throat and waited. Nothing happened. Finally, he gave Ruth a pointed look.

"Well," she said, "if that's all you'll be needing . . ."

"Yes, thank you," Jeremiah answered. "I'll holler if there's anything else."

Ruth nodded and left the room, pausing in the doorway for one last, long look. When she disappeared at last, Jeremiah released a pent-up breath and turned to face Gainey, who was . . . laughing.

"Tickle your funny bone, does it?"

Gainey dabbed at her eyes with her napkin. "You are the dearest, sweetest man. I think it makes you something of an oddity in these parts."

At that, Jeremiah found his sense of humor creeping back. He chuckled, then guffawed, and they spent the next few moments simply laughing together. Once their merriment died down, Jeremiah reached across the table to take Gainey's hand, which she placed in his most willingly.

"Woman, I'd meant for this to be fancy, but turns out I'm just not fancy. Now, before this fried chicken goes stone cold, will you marry me?" Gainey froze, then tears began to streak her cheeks, which worried Jeremiah although she still looked happy. "My taters are getting cold," Jeremiah said, rubbing his thumb across the back of her hand.

"I'm not a very good cook," Gainey said.

"I am. Plus I've had your biscuits and I think you might be underselling yourself. Now what's that got to do with my question?"

"I . . . I don't want to disappoint you."

Jeremiah stood and drew Gainey to her feet. "Since the day I first laid eyes on you behind that postal counter, I've felt just about everything except disappointment. And right now, what I feel is love filling me up like one of those wells that's been dry too long." He reached up to thumb away a tear. "And I'm feeling a little bit afraid. You're making me right worried that I've overstepped and made a mess of things."

Then Gainey was in his arms, pressing her lips to his and murmuring, "Yes, you wonderful man. Yes, yes, yes," until finally Jeremiah managed to silence her and in doing so forgot all about his chicken getting cold.

Gainey now understood what people meant when they said they were "walking on air." It was as though she couldn't maintain contact with anything around her. She ate her meal but couldn't say if it was good. She carried on a lively conversation with her . . . *betrothed*, she thought, smiling at the word, yet she couldn't have said what they talked about. She walked with him arm in arm around the tavern, still talking and talking and still not knowing what she said.

It was only when they returned to the porch with its exterior stairs that she finally felt like she was settling back into herself a little. Jeremiah kissed her ever so gently and sweetly and told her to wait while he brought the Model T around. She sighed—for the hundredth time most likely—and sat in a rocking chair to wait.

Francis came outside. "Is there anything else we can get you'uns?"

"Not a thing," Gainey said, and her voice sounded gay and happy.

"You and that man gettin' hitched?"

"That we are."

The girl smiled. "I'm glad for ya. He seems like a good 'un, and you can't beat having family around."

"I agree completely." Gainey patted the chair beside her. "Sit with me a minute while I wait. You were such a good worker when I was here last summer. Do I remember correctly that you were in search of your own family?"

The girl's eyes lit up. "Yes, ma'am, and we done found each other. Well, my grandma anyway. Guess my ma's dead and my pa drowned in the river. But I'm grateful to have anybody. We live together now, and I take care of her."

Gainey smiled, feeling expansive and glad to celebrate with

anyone about anything. "That's wonderful to hear about your grandmother. How did you find her?" She saw Jeremiah pull the auto up and get out to collect her.

Now the girl practically bounced in her seat with excitement. "That's just it. I didn't find her, Mr. Sulley did."

Gainey felt her eyebrows rise. "Mr. Sulley?"

"Yes, ma'am. I told him how if he ever run up on my family, he should let me know. And not a month later, he come 'round to tell me he found my grandma. Don't guess we would've ever come up on each other 'cept for him." She stood at Jeremiah's approach. "I best let you'uns get on your way, but if you ever see Mr. Sulley, you tell him me and Grandma are real happy together." She smiled wide and bright. "Happiest I ever been."

Gainey stood and watched the girl scamper off. Jeremiah took her hand. "Did she say Sulley found her grandmother?"

"She surely did. Guess he wasn't done finding things after all."

"Do you suppose that means he's still around?"

Gainey furrowed her brow. "That must have been nearly a year ago. Surely not." Jeremiah nodded and held the door open for her. But even in her haze of happiness, she couldn't help but wonder about Sulley and how what he'd found for that child was so much more than water to drink.

Sulley finished stacking wood next to the lean-to he'd built. It wasn't much, just cut branches laid against a crosspiece between two saplings. He'd made it good and thick, though, with plenty of evergreen branches to keep the weather off him. And it wasn't so noticeable that anyone would find it unless they were looking. Of course, these days, quite a few folks knew he was here. But it was mostly just the Negroes, and they weren't about to talk. There were several places he knew he'd be taken in if the weather got real bad. He'd stayed in those homes now and again last winter.

He squinted at the setting sun to gauge the time, then checked the squirrel he was stewing in a pot on the cook fire. Folks left him food too, but he liked to add to it with some fresh game now and again. And he was partial to squirrel. It wasn't a bad life. And he'd done as much good as he knew how but figured his time here was winding down. Fewer folks came 'round now that the dirty work of digging the tunnel was over.

He tried to think where he should go next. Then again maybe he should just wait for whatever came next to find him. Seemed to be how his life worked nowadays. Dipping some stew onto his plate, he blew it cool and fell to eating. No siree Bob, not a bad life at all.

forty

"Logan wants to come pay his respects to Henry." Gainey had mixed feelings about the latest letter from her son. "He'd like to see where he's buried and suggested he might even want to move him to the family plot." She and Jeremiah were walking hand in hand along a creek. The leaves were changing now, and she felt nostalgic for her girlhood when her grandmother had taught her to make corn-husk dolls with yellow and red leaves for dresses in place of precious fabric. "I planted jonquil bulbs there late last summer," she added.

"Did you now? Well, that was nice."

"I wonder if they bloomed? I thought to go back and see a time or two but never did it."

Without even discussing it, they sat together on a fallen tree trunk. Gainey loved how often they seemed to know what the other was thinking before either spoke. "I guess Logan's been thinking about doing this for quite a while. He did some asking around and learned that Henry—posing as the Reverend Harmon Wilkins—was responsible for encouraging men to continue working in the tunnel even when they were sick. He was likely paid to do so, and Logan supposed his nefarious ways finally caught up with him." She watched fallen leaves swirl by in the burbling water. "I don't suppose we'll ever know how he came to be buried in the edge of that field."

"Might be some things are better left a mystery," Jeremiah said. "It's good Logan's coming to grips with the loss of his brother—no matter how it happened. When's he want to come?"

"Before the wedding." She felt her cheeks flush at the thought. They planned to be married the first week of October. Jeremiah would come to stay in her little house and would continue working for Freeman in the orchard. He'd proven himself to be a patient and careful worker, and while Freeman couldn't pay much, they didn't need much. She'd never been happier in her life and wasn't particularly enthusiastic about revisiting the somber field in Summersville. There were likely even more graves there by now. Rumor was the local undertaker had been paid fifty-five dollars for each corpse he handled—much more than was customary for a pauper's burial. The whole affair cast a shadow she preferred to leave behind her.

But if her son wanted to come to see where his stepbrother was buried, well, she'd do it for him. And hope that the joy she and Jeremiah carried with them wherever they went would somehow compensate for the poor forgotten souls in that field.

"We'll all go together," Jeremiah said. "It'll be good to, well, truly put this behind us once and for all."

"Yes," she agreed and gave him a peck on the cheek. But Jeremiah wasn't satisfied with that, and it was quite some time before, slightly rumpled and flushed now, they made their way back to town.

A group was approaching on foot. Sulley eased behind the massive chestnut tree. It offered an excellent vantage point for observing people as they neared. He didn't always make his presence known, especially when visitors were white. It was the families of the Negroes he most often interacted with.

As he waited he thought it looked like the threesome was headed directly for him. He started to drift back into the denser forest, then paused. There was something familiar . . . He waited until they were within earshot.

". . . makeshift marker, although I don't know who." The woman was speaking. "And of course there's the cross high on the trunk there." Sulley sucked in a breath. It was Gainey, and she had Logan and Jeremiah with her. What were they doing here?

Sulley flattened his body against the tree and listened with every fiber of his being. If he moved to where he might get a better look at them, they would surely see him. And somehow he wasn't ready for that.

"It's a pretty spot." That must be Logan speaking. "Although this place has a strange, uncomfortable feeling, too."

A deeper voice this time—Jeremiah's. "That'd be all the unmarked graves in the field there. Men working on that tunnel project died and were sometimes buried before their kin even knew. It's a shame, but then what can anyone do about it? Even the lawyers can't make the company pay up or even admit to anything. Not really."

"What's this?" Gainey was speaking again, and she sounded farther away. "Some of them are marked. It's not much, but there are wooden markers here and there." Sulley could hear a rustling movement. "It's hard to make out, but I think this one says Eugene Abraham."

A man's distant voice said, "This one says Thomas Hunt, and here's one with Dewey Flack on it."

"They're not all marked, though," Gainey said. "Who do you suppose put these here? They weren't here when I came last year."

Sulley eased around the tree and squatted at the foot of Henry's grave. He watched Gainey, Jeremiah, and Logan wind through the field, discovering markers and calling out names. "Got an Enoch Thompson. And here's Willis Stokes." Then another name and then another were called across the field as the afternoon sun turned dying grasses to gold. Sulley watched and waited. They'd notice him soon enough.

Logan was the one who drifted back to the tree and froze when he spotted Sulley. "Lordy man, I thought you were a ghost."

"Some days I think that myself," Sulley said.

Gainey and Jeremiah heard their voices and hurried over. They stood and stared for a moment as Sulley rose and crossed his arms over his chest, still watching and waiting.

Gainey was the first to find her voice. "Why, Sulley, where have you been all this time?"

"Here."

She looked around, confused. "Here? Do you mean in Summersville? We thought you must have moved on south."

"No, here, in this field."

Logan laughed. "Well, not here surely. It's not as though anyone lives here."

"No, this place is reserved for the forgotten dead, but I live right back yonder in the woods a ways." Sulley tilted his head in the direction of his camp.

"Since we last saw you?" Gainey sounded incredulous.

Sulley let a smile quirk his lips. "I've built it up some in all that time. It's right snug, unless the wind blows too fierce, but there are folks who'll give me a pallet for the night if I need it."

A look of frustration crept over Gainey's features, which Sulley had been thinking—until that moment—were softer and prettier than he remembered. "Do you mean to tell us you've been living alongside a cemetery for more than a year now?"

"I wouldn't call it 'living'—more like existing."

Gainey had fire in her eyes now, and Sulley was getting a kick out of goading her. He'd given up on charm a while back. But before she could speak again, Jeremiah stepped forward. "You been doing much dowsing lately?"

"You could say that." Sulley gave him a sharp look. "Not for money, though."

Jeremiah nodded. "No, I guess not."

Sulley turned to Logan. "Guess you decided to claim Gainey as your mother, then."

"We've been writing. Seeing each other now and again." Logan sounded like a man who was afraid to say too much. Or not enough.

Gainey took a step closer. "Now, look here, Sulley . . . what are you about? Living in such a desolate place. Slipping up on people like a wraith. I simply don't understand." She looked like she wanted to stomp a foot but was holding herself back. "I've seen how you can charm people, befriend them—why would you choose to live this way?"

Sulley snorted. "Befriend. Folks'll be your friend right up until they decide they don't like the way you wear your hair or talk or eat. They'll be friendly right up until they don't have a use for you anymore." He squinted at the sky and the sun slanting toward the horizon. "Best to move on before that happens."

"But you haven't moved on, have you?" Jeremiah was looking at him in a way that made Sulley uneasy. Like he'd been caught with his britches down.

"I'm moving on now," he said, then turned and pushed his way into the trees and brush that would hide him from view.

"What was that about?" Gainey sounded testy, even to herself.

"That man may know how to find an easy mark, but he's got a long way to go yet to find what's been gnawing at him most of his life." Jeremiah wrapped an arm around Gainey's shoulders. "There's almost as much hurt buried in his heart as there is in this field."

Gainey wanted to shrug his arm away. She'd forgiven Sulley. Had written him off as a scamp and a scallywag who was no longer part of her life. And now he'd resurfaced to trouble the peace she'd worked so hard to find with Jeremiah and Logan. "Well, he needs to learn to deal with it and move on like the rest of us," she said. The words were too sharp, but she wanted to lash out with them. At what, she wasn't entirely certain.

"I think that's just what he's doing." Jeremiah gave her a squeeze and moved closer to Logan, who was looking at the words carved into the tree over his brother's head.

"I'll have to look that verse up when I get home. Wonder why whoever buried him picked it." Logan hadn't been paying much attention to the two of them, and for that, Gainey was grateful.

Jeremiah recited the verse from Luke. "'Are not five sparrows sold for two pennies? Yet not one of them is forgotten by God. Indeed, the very hairs of your head are all numbered. Don't be afraid; you are worth more than many sparrows.'" He rested a big hand on Logan's shoulder. "I wonder if it's here for Henry or for all those men in the graves behind us."

Gainey jerked her head up and looked all around. The sun had dropped lower still, edging ever closer to the horizon, and its rays bathed the field, shadows from the wooden markers stretching long. "All those men," she whispered, "lost to their families with no one to say their names."

"Except someone did," Jeremiah said. "For some of them at least."

She looked at Logan. "Did you ever feel abandoned or forgotten? Because I thought about you every day of my life."

Logan rubbed his chin where the first shadow of a beard was appearing. Gainey remembered with a start that Archie's beard had grown fast. "I don't think I ever did. Not really. My parents taught me pretty early on that I only had one true Father—God—and I've always been satisfied with that." He chuckled. "Don't get me wrong. I've wondered over the years, felt some curiosity. But I don't guess I've lost much sleep over it."

"That's what Sulley couldn't understand," Gainey said. "I think he feels abandoned and he couldn't understand why you didn't. I suppose he feels awfully alone."

Jeremiah stared into the trees where Sulley had disappeared. "Most likely because he is."

Sulley lay down on the fresh branches he'd layered under his lean-to just that morning. And a good thing too, since he didn't feel like doing anything right now. Those three back there in the field. Taking for granted that they belonged to each other. Mother and son. And he'd seen the way Jeremiah looked at and even touched Gainey. If they weren't married, they were headed that direction. Everyone had someone except him.

Yup. It was time to move on. He'd done what he could for the ones he could. No need to drag this out any longer.

forty-one

Jeremiah rose before the day had dawned. Whippoorwills called to each other from the tree line, slowly at first, then faster and faster. An old wives' tale said hearing the birds call near the house was a bad omen, but he'd heard it often enough with no bad results to ignore such tittle-tattle. As he drove the ten miles to Summersville, mist hung in the valleys and clung to the mountaintops. He made it to the burial field by late morning. It was a perfect day—the sky that deep, rich blue that only happens in autumn when God needs just the right backdrop for the glory of red and gold and orange leaves.

He walked to the chestnut and then began making a methodical search of the woods beyond. It was on past noon by the time he found the camp. Sulley had a neat setup with water nearby, a sturdy lean-to, and a fire ring with the ground well-worn around it. Jeremiah supposed Sulley had prepared and eaten many a meal here. Or maybe he just sat by the warmth of a fire waiting for sleep to overtake him.

There were worse ways to live.

Unfortunately, it was clear Sulley was no longer living here. The ashes in the fire ring had been washed by the last rain, and there was nothing in the camp to suggest someone was coming back. No spare clothing or rucksack. No cooking tools or personal items. This camp had been vacated. Jeremiah crouched down and worked his fingers through the ashes just in case there was any remnant of heat. Nothing.

Whatever had kept the man here for so long had released him.

Jeremiah told himself it didn't matter. He'd tried to find Sulley and help him. He could go on back to Mount Lookout and marry Gainey and never give Sulley another thought.

He made his way back to the cemetery and saw that there was at least one new marker in the field—Calvin Harvey. He sighed deeply and climbed in the Model T for the return trip. In spite of his best efforts, he suspected he'd be thinking of Sulley—and all those graves yet unmarked—for a long time to come.

Gainey hadn't been this nervous since—well, since she'd had to tell her mother she was in the family way. Of course, that had been a different sort of nervousness. No, a woman recently turned fifty-six and marrying for the first time had an entirely different set of reasons for being nervous.

Verna had made her wedding suit. It was a beautiful dove gray with a nipped-in waist, peplum, and wide collar with contrasting white trim that revealed a few inches of collarbone. Which, Gainey thought, lifting her chin and looking in the glass, was still quite nice. Her neck might not be as firm as it once was, but she'd certainly seen worse on women her age. She allowed herself a smile of vanity. Or younger, for that matter.

Susan walked with her to the church manse, where Reverend Stokes would marry them in a simple ceremony in the parlor.

Gainey knew this was a disappointment to many in the community. As postmistress she was known to almost everyone, and they would have been delighted to view the spectacle of a woman her age marrying a man who had been willing to sell out his own place to move to hers. But she preferred not to be a spectacle and she knew her neighbors wouldn't have the nerve to show up at the manse uninvited. Even so, she felt many an eye on her as they walked the short distance.

Susan pressed a coin into her hand just before they entered the house. "It's the sixpence my grandmother from England gave me when I married. I thought you might be hard-pressed to find one otherwise."

Gainey smiled as she recited the wedding poem: "'Something old, something new, something borrowed, something blue, and a silver sixpence in her shoe.'" She laughed. "I have the rest taken care of, but you're right—I hadn't even considered that there might be a genuine sixpence in all of Mount Lookout."

They entered the parlor, where Jeremiah already stood waiting. He wore a charcoal double-breasted suit with a fine stripe in it that Gainey thought made him look taller. Although there was no disguising how broad-chested he was. She felt a thrill that seemed inappropriate until she reminded herself that they would soon be man and wife, which caused a flush to wash over her cheeks. Well, her whole body for that matter.

Jeremiah wore a besotted grin that Gainey would once have scorned. Now she simply couldn't believe that such a blessing was to be hers. And there was Logan at Jeremiah's elbow, acting as best man to Susan's matron of honor.

Logan's whole family had come, and along with the Johnsons, George Legg, and the pastor's wife, they filled the room to overflowing. Gainey told herself that was why she was feeling so warm on this cool October afternoon.

Without undue ceremony, she took her place beside Jeremiah in front of the pastor, who smiled at them in a way that seemed like he was genuinely delighted to be rendering them this service. And why not? Surely their chances of success were better than those who married too young and without a great deal of thought. Gainey snuck a sidelong glance at her betrothed and caught him doing the same. She bit back a smile and gave her full attention to Reverend Stokes as he began reciting the words that would bind them for the rest of their lives.

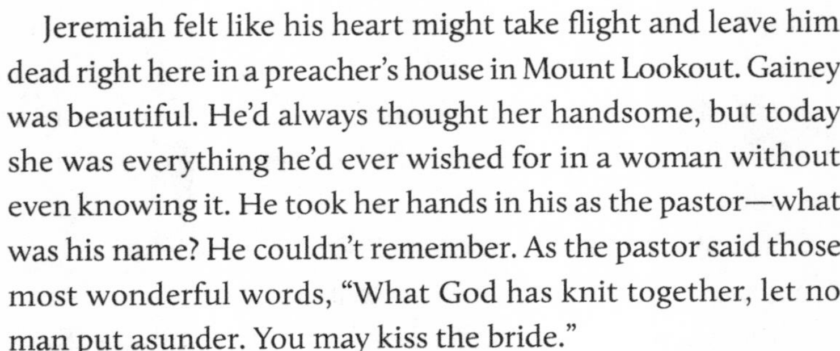

Jeremiah felt like his heart might take flight and leave him dead right here in a preacher's house in Mount Lookout. Gainey was beautiful. He'd always thought her handsome, but today she was everything he'd ever wished for in a woman without even knowing it. He took her hands in his as the pastor—what was his name? He couldn't remember. As the pastor said those most wonderful words, "What God has knit together, let no man put asunder. You may kiss the bride."

He pulled her snug against his chest and kissed her like he meant to from this day forward. Logan let out a low whistle that was cut short like someone might have jabbed an elbow in his ribs. But Jeremiah quickly lost track of anything other than his wife pressed to him—the length and breadth and smell and taste of her were better than striking water in a dry place. And he wished there was no wedding supper. No celebration with friends and family. He didn't need anyone or anything else.

They pulled apart, and Jeremiah realized the room was silent around them. Gainey stood in the circle of his arms, flushed, with her eyes still closed and her face still lifted to his. He wanted to trail kisses along her collarbone, yet even as that thought formed, the pastor cleared his throat.

"Ahem. And now I believe we can all retire to the dining room, where Mrs. Stokes, Mrs. Johnson, and Mrs. Legg have prepared a fine wedding feast."

Gainey's eyes flew open, and her already-flushed cheeks glowed even brighter, but she didn't take her eyes from Jeremiah's. "I love you," she whispered, and there was a promise in those words he could hardly wait to claim.

They sat side by side at the table with their friends and family—his left knee touching her right. He couldn't have said what they ate, only that he wasn't hungry. At least not for the food before them. Finally, Luisa carried an apple stack cake in—a traditional mountain wedding treat.

"It's got sixteen layers," she crowed, setting it before them. "I used the apples Gainey helped me dry in August and it has been mellowing for three days now." She handed Gainey a knife. "You will cut the first slice for your husband, yes?"

Gainey cut a generous slice, then handed the knife to Susan. "Jeremiah and I will share," she said and picked up her fork.

He grinned at her. "That we will. Everything."

Dusk had fallen by the time Sulley finally saw Jeremiah and Gainey come out into the road holding hands. Other people had left earlier, but it was the happy couple he'd been waiting for. He stepped out of the shadows so they would see him.

"Why, Sulley, is that you?" Gainey's face glowed, and she looked . . . beautiful.

"Came to see the two of you and heard you were getting hitched. Didn't want to interrupt the festivities."

Gainey stepped forward, a girlish bounce in her step. "But you should have joined us. There was food and cake—more than enough for everyone." She glanced back toward the house, where a few guests still lingered, visible through the bright windowpanes. "There still is. Come inside."

"Appreciate the offer, but I'd rather not."

Jeremiah looped his arm around Gainey's waist and drew her near. "Add any more names to the field?" he asked.

Sulley jerked his head around and narrowed his eyes. "What do you mean by that?"

Jeremiah shrugged. "I figure folks were coming around looking for their kin and you were dowsing for them. Showing people where to put the names of the men they'd lost to the tunnel."

"Somebody tell you about that?"

Jeremiah released Gainey and motioned for Sulley to follow him to the church where they could sit on the steps. "I'm supposing you developed a knack for finding more than water. You found Noah for his family. You found Henry and then Logan. And you even found that girl Francis's grandma. Guess you have a way of running missing folks to ground." He drew Gainey down beside him as if loath to let her too far from his side. "Somebody was marking those graves. And there you were, camped out next door. I put two and two together."

Sulley slumped on the lowest step below them. He couldn't think what to say. Couldn't remember why he'd thought it was so important to come here before he lit out for who knew where. For nowhere, truth be told.

"Did you dowse for them?" Jeremiah asked.

Sulley blew out a breath and let his hands go slack. "I did." He shook his head. "Don't know that it worked, though." He felt pressure behind his eyes and was grateful for the waning light. He swallowed hard. "That stick would twitch in my hands, sure enough, but I didn't know anymore if it was real or just me wishing."

"Does it matter?" Gainey asked. He slanted a look at her. Gainey was the last person he expected to tolerate anything less than the strict truth. "What I mean is, if you were able to give people closure, to give them an answer to a question burning a hole in their hearts that they could never answer otherwise, to remember the ones they love, well, that seems like a wonderful gift."

"Might've been nothing more than lies and wishful thinking," Sulley said. Why was he confessing his doubts like this? "I can't tell you how many times I pretended when I was dowsing for wells. How many times I just guessed and got it right." He hung his head. "Jeremiah knows how I left those folks in Kline high and dry. Wasn't the first time, either."

"There's water in that last well you told us to dig."

Sulley jerked his head up. "What?"

Jeremiah chuckled low and soft in the gathering darkness. "When we went to fill in the hole, it was full of water. Good water. Your well made it so I could sell my house and little plot of land and move here to claim this woman." He drew her arm through his as though stitching the two of them together.

"Well I'll be." Sulley shook his head. Truth be told, he hadn't ever thought there'd be water there. It was just where folks wanted water to show up and so he'd gone along with it.

"Maybe," Gainey said, "it's not about you and whether or not you can find water, or people, or gold, or anything else. Maybe

God's been using you all along to find the things He didn't want to be forgotten."

Sulley sniffed against whatever was rising in his chest, condensing in his eyes, and pushing toward the surface like water bubbling up in a well. He'd been dry for so long. So very long. He buried his face in his hands, desperate to hide whatever this was. "But who will remember me?" he moaned.

forty-two

Summersville, West Virginia
March 1936

Sulley whistled his way down the back stairs of the general store where he was met by Gilead, a collie mix sitting at attention. He rubbed the dog behind the ears and smiled. If you'd asked him five years ago if he'd ever have a place to call his own, he would have sworn he didn't want one. But, much to his own surprise, he liked living above the store and post office. Although he still spent a night in the woods now and again—just for the pleasure of the wind sighing in the trees and the smell of leaves turning back to dirt beneath his head. Not to mention the whiffling snore of a dog at his feet.

He stuck his head through the back door and called out to Susan, "You sure you can spare me today?"

"Go on with you. You're not as indispensable as you think." She smiled and made a shooing motion.

Sulley grinned back and started for the little house shared by Jeremiah and Gainey. He had a pretty good path worn between his door and theirs. While the Leggs traded him room and board for helping out around the store, he took his meals with the Webers many an evening.

He hadn't intended to become gainfully employed, but he'd lingered in town after that night on the church steps with the newlyweds. And it quickly became apparent to Susan that he was as good at selling dry goods as he was at selling pipe dreams. He refused to take pay, preferring to putter around the store and chat up customers as it suited him. George hit on giving him the room upstairs and feeding him regular. He guessed he was one step up from a stray they'd decided to keep around, but that was all right with him. He smiled at the dog keeping him company—taking in strays worked out now and again.

Myrtle Hampstead was walking toward the store and caught sight of him. "Oh, Sulley," she called, waving pudgy fingers. "Mittens has gone missing. Won't you find her for me?"

Sulley grunted. He hadn't been able to shake his reputation for finding things or people or cats, for that matter. "You know I don't go in for finding things anymore," he said.

"But Mittens might be cold and alone somewhere. I can't stand not having her with me by the fire of an evening." She fluttered her eyelashes, which didn't do a thing for Sulley. She was old enough to be his mother. He grinned at the notion. He'd likely never know what happened to his mother, and if she were Myrtle, he'd just as soon not know.

"Isn't that cat pregnant?" he asked. "She's probably gone off to have her kittens."

Myrtle flushed deeply. "I wouldn't know about such things."

Sulley shook his head. "I'll keep an eye out." She smiled her gratitude and hurried on her way.

Jeremiah was in the yard, getting ready to start the Model T, when Sulley walked up. He nodded at Gilead. "You know that dog's going to follow us all the way to Summersville."

"So let him ride in the back with me. His paws are clean and he won't talk your ear off."

Jeremiah chuckled. "You could talk a fox out of its den."

Sulley shrugged. "Only if he really wanted to leave it in the first place. The trick to getting people to do things is to figure out what it is they've been wanting to do all along and then give them permission."

Jeremiah gave him an appraising look, but before he could say anything else, Sulley heard a mewling sound. He held up a hand and peered into the back seat. A cat blinked green eyes at him. He noticed a wriggling mass and realized she was suckling three kittens.

He sighed. "Guess I just found Myrtle's Mittens."

Jeremiah frowned and stuck his head in beside Sulley. He guffawed. "Were you looking for her?"

"Not on purpose," Sulley said, shaking his head.

Gainey bustled out of the house with a basket of garden tools, took stock of the situation, and quickly got the new family settled in a crate with some soft rags. "We'll drop them off to Myrtle along the way," she said. She didn't even look twice when Gilead joined Sulley in the back seat, clearly intent on guarding their interesting cargo.

After returning the cat and kittens to Myrtle, Sulley slumped in the back seat, one hand tangled in the dog's fur. He tilted his hat low over his eyes for the ride to Summersville, a smile playing about his lips.

The threesome made their way into the field without speaking. It was the first warm day that wasn't quite spring but was close enough for the jonquils Gainey had planted several years earlier to push their sunny petals up through the remnants of snow. Gilead frisked back and forth between them, but they all knew he loved Sulley best and would return to his heels at the least bit of encouragement.

"Looks like the weather's been rough on these markers," Jeremiah said, reaching down to lift one that had fallen.

"Time doesn't favor any of us," Gainey said. She set down her basket and began working her way along each row, righting the wooden crosses Sulley had fashioned. He'd gotten good enough at making the carved crosses that the locals now paid him to make markers for their loved ones. Gainey supposed it was his only real source of income now that he'd given up dowsing for money. Although he was known to find a well if someone was in need.

The two men gathered any branches or debris until the field was, if not quite tidy, at least more so than it had been. By unspoken agreement they met at Henry Williams's grave. Logan had not moved his brother's remains after all, but he had placed a small stone marker under the tree, along with one of Sulley's simple crosses. Oddly, in Gainey's opinion, the marker didn't have the usual dates or sentiments on it. It simply said, HENRY WILLIAMS—GONE BUT NOT FORGOTTEN. Jeremiah told her it was poetic, which pleased her. In all truth, he was more romantic than she was, and she reveled in plumbing the depths of her husband's heart each and every day.

"Don't guess we'll ever know all the names," Sulley said, staring at the carved trunk of the chestnut tree. The markings there were already less sharp than they had been, and Gainey supposed they would fade into illegibility one day. "Shame what they did here." He let his gaze travel over the field, and Gainey shivered at the look in his eye. As if he could see beneath the soil to the poor souls hidden there.

"And the government's sure not going to do anything about all this," Jeremiah added. "Not after that fiasco of a hearing."

Gainey sighed. This was a frequent topic of conversation at their dinner table—especially when Sulley joined them. Which was often. The Committee on Labor in Washington, D.C., had held a hearing that ran from January sixteenth to February fourth. They'd heard all sorts of damning testimony from surviving laborers, family members of those who died, a social worker from up north who'd tried to help, doctors, and others. And the result had been a letter of finding that ran less than twenty paragraphs.

They found that the tunnel had been built with an utter disregard for the health and lives of the workers. That many of them had died and were still dying of silicosis due to willful, or at least inexcusable, negligence. She had memorized some of the lines—not intentionally but because, having spent time with those men and their families, the words were seared on her heart.

The record presents a story of a condition that is hardly conceivable in a democratic government in the present century. It would be more representative of the Middle Ages. It is the story of a tragedy worthy of the pen of a Victor Hugo—the story of men in the darkest days of the Depression, with work hard to secure, driven by despair and the stark fear of hunger to work for a mere existence wage under almost intolerable conditions.

And that was that. She hoped something more would come of it. That something would change, that those whose very breath had been stolen would be redeemed one day.

Sulley broke into her thoughts. He let his eyes rest on the shallow indentations pocking the field as he spoke. "I've been meaning to say something to the two of you." He didn't meet their eyes, exhibiting a shyness unusual for him. "I've been feeling lonesome all my life. Forgotten like those poor men lying under the grass out there." A smile curved his lips. It wasn't the smile of the charmer that had first made her regard him with caution. Instead, it was a soft, sweet smile that soothed her mind, unsettled by this unhappy place. "I don't guess I'll ever know who my ma was or is, much less who sired me." He cleared his throat, and when he spoke again, there was a hoarseness to his voice. "But knowing I can count the two of you as family . . . well, I guess that might be what I've been hunting all along."

Jeremiah stepped closer and slipped his big, warm hand into Gainey's. Sulley glanced at them, then turned and threw a stick for Gilead. He watched the dog run, the embodiment of joy in the sunshine. "Some things oughtn't to be forgotten." Gilead dropped the stick at Sulley's feet, and he reached down to rub those soft ears. "I don't guess we'll ever know who all is buried in this field. But as long as I'm around to come back every spring and set it to rights, there'll be at least one person who hasn't forgotten them." He bowed his head, and Gainey suspected it was to hide the tear that streaked his cheek. "And from what I've read in that Bible of yours, Gainey, I'm starting to think that maybe there's somebody who doesn't forget anybody. Not even a scoundrel like me."

Author's Note

How do you write a satisfying story about a real event that simply does NOT have a happy ending? I've long been haunted by the Hawks Nest Tunnel disaster and wanted to build a novel around it. But it's such a tragic story. Without a satisfactory ending. And I've promised my readers (and myself) to always write happy (or at least satisfying) endings.

Since there's no comeuppance of the corporation, no underdog winning the day, and no return to health of the men who were so blatantly robbed of it, I had to look elsewhere for satisfaction. Much as we often do in real life. And I considered, what if the satisfying ending is to be found in simply remembering who those men were and what they suffered?

Several times now I've visited the little cemetery at the end of Whippoorwill Road off Route 19 as I travel between North Carolina and West Virginia. It's a lovely spot, even though the highway thunders close by. This is the final resting place of what little is left of those men buried in an anonymous cornfield outside of Summersville, WV. They were forgotten there until a highway came through. Then they were relocated to Whippoorwill Road in 1971, where they were once again forgotten.

It's thanks in large part to local newspaper publisher Charlotte Yeager that the cemetery was restored and, in 2012, consecrated and dedicated. The site is now maintained, and an impressive monument has been erected to ensure the dead are not forgotten again.

In the novel, when Gainey, Jeremiah, and Logan discover markers in the original cemetery, each name they read is the name of someone who worked in the Hawks Nest Tunnel and was buried in that original field. You can find a list of all the known names at www.hawksnestnames.org/names. The ones who were buried in the cornfield are listed with "White Farm, Summersville, West Virginia."

On that list you'll also see the names of the Jones family, which I included in my story. Yes, all three sons and their father died, as well as an uncle. The very least I can do for Emma Jones is to send Gainey to comfort her and to include her name in my story. She should not be forgotten, either.

The death toll from the Hawks Nest Tunnel is estimated at 764 men. It's estimated because so many of them died after leaving West Virginia. They may have returned home or moved on in the never-ending search for work during the Great Depression. It's very likely that the silicosis those men contracted resulted in many more deaths over the years. Regardless, it was the worst industrial accident in U.S. history.

And yes, the final "reckoning" was no more than the letter of finding described in the last chapter. While there was some financial compensation, the bulk of it went to the attorneys, and what did reach the workers is accurately depicted in the disparity between what the Johnsons and the Fridleys received, none of which is very satisfying at all.

And so I gave Sulley, Gainey, and Jeremiah their happy ending against the backdrop of a tragic event that was all too real. And while I hope you'll join me in celebrating the resilience of the human spirit, in finding romance at all stages of life, and in the joy to be found in families of all kinds, I also hope you'll join me in making sure the men who died at Hawks Nest in the 1930s are never, ever forgotten.

For Further Reading

Hawk's Nest by Hubert Skidmore. A moving novel in the vein of John Steinbeck's *The Grapes of Wrath*.

The Hawks Nest Tunnel: An Unabridged History by Patricia Spangler. A journalistic overview of the tragedy, including newspaper articles, congressional testimony, and other documentation.

The Hawk's Nest Incident: America's Worst Industrial Disaster by Martin Cherniack, MD/MPH. A scholarly, investigative look at the tragedy in impressive detail.

Acknowledgments

While the act of sitting down to write is a solitary endeavor, there are SO many others who support that act. Thanks have to go to my agent, Wendy Lawton, my editor, Dave Long, and to the entire team at Bethany House, who not only work their tails off to get the best stories possible out into the world but are also really, really nice people!

I simply couldn't do this without the support of my husband of more than twenty-five years! Thanks for reading my books, and for getting a little choked up by them now and again. And thanks for letting Thistle out (and back in . . . and back out) when I'm lost in the pages of a new story. While all authors should write with a dog at their feet, it helps to have a second pair of hands to help cater to the dog.

To attorney Steve Williamson, thanks for the train story!

But the thanks can't stop there. I'm so grateful to the podcasters, bloggers, contest directors, reviewers, and authors who read my stories and say something to the effect of, "Hey, this is pretty good—check it out!" Because, ultimately, readers are the whole reason books exist. I can tell stories all day long, but if there's no one listening (reading), then what's the point? So *thank you*, readers. And yes, I'm including you, one-star reader/ reviewer. I'm sorry you didn't like the story, but I'm glad you took the time to read it. Tell me what you didn't like and maybe I can do better next time.

Soli Deo gloria.

Sarah Loudin Thomas is a fund-raiser for a children's ministry who has time to write because she doesn't have children of her own. She holds a bachelor's degree in English from Coastal Carolina University and is the author of the acclaimed novels *The Right Kind of Fool*, winner of the Selah Book of the Year Award, and *Miracle in a Dry Season*, winner of the INSPY Award. Sarah has also been a finalist for the Christy Award, the ACFW Carol Award, and the Christian Book of the Year Award. She and her husband live near Asheville, North Carolina. Learn more at www.sarahloudinthomas.com.

Sign Up for Sarah's Newsletter

Keep up to date with Sarah's latest news on book releases and events by signing up for her email list at sarahloudinthomas.com.

More from Sarah Loudin Thomas

When deaf teen Loyal Raines stumbles upon a dead body in the nearby river, his absentee father, Creed, is shocked the boy runs to him first. Pulled into the investigation, Creed discovers that it is the boy's courage, not his inability to hear, that sets him apart, and he will have to do more than solve a murder if he wants to win his family's hearts again.

The Right Kind of Fool

You May Also Like . . .

After the rival McLean clan guns down his cousin, Colman Harpe chooses peace over seeking revenge with his family. But when he hears God tell him to preach to the McLeans, he attempts to run away—and fails—leaving him sick and suffering in their territory. He soon learns that appearances can be deceiving, and the face of evil doesn't look like he expected.

When Silence Sings by Sarah Loudin Thomas
sarahloudinthomas.com

After a terrible mine accident in 1954, Judd Markley abandons his poor Appalachian town for Myrtle Beach. There he meets the beautiful and privileged Larkin Heyward, who dreams of helping people like those he left behind. Drawn together amid a hurricane, they wonder what tomorrow will bring—and realize that it may take a miracle for them to be together.

The Sound of Rain by Sarah Loudin Thomas
sarahloudinthomas.com

After Pearl Harbor, sweethearts Gordon Hooper and Dorie Armitage were broken up by their convictions. As a conscientious objector, he went west to fight fires as a smokejumper, while she joined the Army Corps. When a tragic accident raises suspicions, they're forced to work together, but the truth they uncover may lead to an impossible—and dangerous—choice.

The Lines Between Us by Amy Lynn Green
amygreenbooks.com

BETHANYHOUSE

More from Bethany Hous

After an abusive relationship derailed her plans, Adri Rivera struggles to regain her independence and achieve her dream of becoming an MMA fighter. She gets a second chance, but the man who offers it to her is Max Lyons, her former training partner, whom she left heartbroken years before. As she fights for he future, will she be able to confront her past?

After She Falls by Carmen Schober
carmenschober.com

Widower Mitch Jensen is at a loss with how to handle his mother's odd, forgetful behaviors, as well as his daughter's sudden return home and unexpected life choices. Little does he know Grandma June has long been keeping a secret about her past—but if she doesn't tell the truth about it, someone she loves will suffer, and the lives of three generations will never be the same.

A Flicker of Light by Katie Powner
katiepowner.com

When a renowned profiler is found dead in his hotel room and it becomes clear the killer is targeting agent in Alex Donovan's unit, she is called to work on the strangest case she's ever faced. Things get personal when the brilliant killer strikes close to home, and Ale will do anything to find the killer—even at the risk of her own life.

Dead Fall by Nancy Mehl
The Quantico Files #2
nancymehl.com

CPSIA information can be obtained
at www.ICGtesting.com
Printed in the USA
LVHW092028300122
709771LV00002B/66

9 780764 239434